Praise f

'Fast-paced, enthralling a... ...t it down'
                                    C. L. Taylor

'A s...ong, edgy debut that deserves to do well'
                                    Clare Mackintosh

'Fa... ...urious, fantastic…One killer thriller!'
                                    Mark Edwards

What the reviewers said:

...ly exciting new arrival in the world of Euro Crime!'

...my nails all the way to the end!'

...thtakingly brilliant'

...inds me of the best Scandinavian crime writers like
Jo Nesbo and Stieg Larsson'

'Truly outstanding'

'An intricate, fast-paced and utterly compelling thriller'

'Without a doubt a true 5 star read!'

'Work of art'

'Intelligent, moving, filled with tension and entertaining'

Marnie Riches grew up on a rough estate in Manchester, aptly within sight of the dreaming spires of Strangeways prison. Able to speak five different languages, she gained a Masters degree in Modern & Medieval Dutch and German from Cambridge University. She has been a punk, a trainee rock star, a pretend artist, a property developer and professional fundraiser. In her spare time, she likes to run, mainly to offset the wine and fine food she consumes with great enthusiasm.

Having authored the first six books of HarperCollins Children's Time-Hunters series, she now writes crime thrillers for adults.

By the same author:

George McKenzie eBook series
The Girl Who Wouldn't Die
The Girl Who Broke the Rules
The Girl Who Walked in the Shadows
The Girl Who Had No Fear

Born Bad

MARNIE RICHES

avon

This novel is entirely a work of fiction.
The names, characters and incidents portrayed in it are
the work of the author's imagination. Any resemblance to
actual persons, living or dead, events or localities is
entirely coincidental.

Avon
A division of HarperCollins*Publishers*
1 London Bridge Street
London SE1 9GF
www.harpercollins.co.uk

A Paperback Original 2017
1
Copyright © Marnie Riches 2017

Marnie Riches asserts the moral right to
be identified as the author of this work.

A catalogue record for this book is
available from the British Library

ISBN 978-0-00-820393-1

Typeset in Minion by Palimpsest Book Production Ltd, Falkirk, Stirlingshire
Printed and bound in Great Britain by Clays Ltd, St Ives plc

MIX
Paper from
responsible sources
FSC **FSC™ C007454**
www.fsc.org

FSC™ is a non-profit international organisation established to promote
the responsible management of the world's forests. Products carrying the
FSC label are independently certified to assure consumers that they come
from forests that are managed to meet the social, economic and
ecological needs of present and future generations,
and other controlled sources.

Find out more about HarperCollins and the environment at
www.harpercollins.co.uk/green

For Caspian

If my name is on the spine, and the story comes from my heart, then you are surely the lungs of this book, since you have breathed life into all of my words. In a world full of bollocks, you're the dog's, Mr Dennis. Never forget it.

Chapter 1

Sheila

The leather case containing the guns was cumbersome and heavy, making her shoulder muscles scream with the effort of pulling it towards her. Looking around to check that she wasn't being watched, she tried to drag it out of the boot of her Porsche Panamera. Dead weight. Looked around again towards the garaging. The doors were closed. No sign of *his* car, thankfully.

'Come on, Sheila,' she counselled herself. 'Grit your teeth, girl.'

With a grunt, she heaved the case out. Dropped it heavily onto the gravel, narrowly missing the peep toes of her purple suede Louboutins. Slammed the boot shut, chipping a nail in the process.

'Bastard thing,' she said, lugging the guns awkwardly across the courtyard and up the steps to the front door. She would definitely have a couple of bruises on her shins by tomorrow. Shit. But at least the determined Mancunian rain wasn't falling on her freshly blow-dried hair.

Inside, her house was silent and pristine. The wooden floors shone. The smell of furniture wax was pungent in the air. The cleaners had gone for the day and the gardener wasn't due until Friday.

'Anybody home?' she called out. Her voice bounced off the hard surfaces of the glazed banister and naked oak of the staircase. No response, though she hadn't expected one.

Flinging her keys onto the sideboard, Sheila kicked off her heels, carrying the guns to the lower level of the house. She bypassed the spa area and pool to enter the cinema room. It smelled of stale cigar smoke and the dregs at the bottom of Paddy's empty single malt bottle and dirty tumbler. She made a mental note to chastise the cleaners for having missed it. Wrinkled her nose at the manly stink that reminded her too much of the Green Room in her brother-in-law's club.

'Hide it with the other guns and surprise him with it after tea, or leave it out for him to find?' Sheila contemplated aloud, setting the leather case on the coffee table and clicking open the antique silver locks. She appraised the delicate metalwork of the shotguns, studded with semi-precious stones. Both guns were safely ensconced in their own blue velvet bed. Not her cup of tea, but she knew Paddy would appreciate these Ottoman flintlock rifles. Seventeenth century, the dealer had said. They'd go with his collection of swords, pistols and other shit, he had assured her. It was a perfect apology. She'd forked over a pile of her own cash for them, hoping they would be the ultimate oil to pour on troubled waters after Paddy had 'discovered' the email she had sent to Mam and Dad.

All those years she'd fantasised about reforging the bond with her parents that Paddy had insisted she jettison. Decades of being desperate to tell her folks about the girls; about her life; about how much she missed them every single day. Bloody typical that Paddy had gone snooping

2

through her email account when she'd finally had the balls to contact them on the quiet. She made a mental note to change her email password. Couldn't hide anything from that nosey old bastard. Still, he had her best interests at heart, didn't he?

'Paddy, Paddy O'Brien,' she intoned, looking over at the oil painting of her imperious husband that made him look a good deal less hatchet-faced and more sanguine than he really was. 'You difficult, moody sod.' She snapped the gun case shut. 'I hope to God these cheer you up.'

The sound of a door slamming against a wall and a trill of what she was sure was a woman's laughter made her freeze. Sheila stood tall. Breathing in shallow gasps, she strained to work out where the sound had come from. The spa, perhaps? There was certainly somebody in the house with her. Snatching one of the antique long-barrelled flintlocks, she held the gun out ahead of her and stalked towards the spa. Heart thudding. Forcing herself to be brave. No way of creeping back upstairs to see from the alarm keypad if there had been an intrusion via another zone in the sprawling Bramshott mansion.

To speak, or not to speak. That was the question.

'Who's there?' she said quietly. Unconvincingly.

The thick grey carpet swallowed the sound of her shoeless footfalls. Just ahead loomed the glazed door that separated the cinema room from the spa area and pool. A glimpse of the turquoise glittering pool, its spot-lit ripples dancing white and silver on the vaulted brick ceiling. There was the laughter again.

'Oh, Paddy!' shouted a woman's voice.

Paddy's low voice, rumbling. Saying something indistinct. More laughter.

Sheila edged open the spa door, shaking with adrenalin,

poised for fight or flight. Her sharp eyes darted to the left. To the right. Scanning the tranquil scene. Clean, pale grey tiles. Perfect azure water, still but for the gush of the filtration jets set into the sides of the pool. Teak loungers, arranged at an artful angle. There was nothing to see. And yet, she had not imagined the voices.

Her heartbeat bounced her forwards, almost audible in a lofty space where only the air-conditioning unit buzzed quietly in the background.

'Come here, you dirty girl. Come to Paddy.'

And there it was. No doubt in her mind. Paddy's voice, thick with the lustful intent that she recognised immediately. Blatant, inconsiderate bastard. Shitting on his own doorstep. This was a new low.

Though she knew the flintlock was not loaded, she kept the heavy gun hoisted high on her shoulder. Deciding how to tackle this situation. Her options were: walk away and pretend she had not happened upon what was almost certainly a clandestine coupling; shout, 'Hello!' announcing her presence, giving them time to make themselves respectable and fashion some bullshit excuse; or creep up on the bastards and give them the fright of their lives.

Padding towards the sound of heavy breathing and the rustle of fabric, Sheila realised the sauna held her husband and his extra-marital mate. The door was standing open. The sound of giggling and Paddy's lascivious groaning slid out on the steamy, seamy air.

Following the gun's line of sight, Sheila held her breath. Anger grabbing her natural reticence by the throat and squeezing the apologetic life out of it. She took a noiseless step into the cedar-clad cabana and hefted the gun up to Paddy's head. His eyes were shut. A beatified smile was plastered across his lying, scheming face. At his feet, a naked young blonde was crouched, gobbling his cock with some enthusiasm. The soles of her feet were dirty, the heels crusty with dried skin.

'Surprise!' Sheila said, savouring the sight of her sexually incontinent husband grabbing at his heart and almost leaping clear of the cabana bench.

With a yelp, the young woman – no more than a girl – jumped to her feet, covering her silicone breasts with splayed fingers. Bitten fingernails. Not a mark on her belly, though. This one had certainly not borne children. But then, Paddy always liked them young.

'Who are you?' the girl shouted.

'I'm his damned wife,' Sheila said, intoxicated by the heady bloodlust. She swung the barrel of the flintlock towards the girl and dug it into her right breast. 'That's who I am. Mrs Bleeding O'Brien. And you're trespassing in my house and on my husband.'

The girl's face wrinkled up into an expression that threatened tears or a bout of hysteria. But there was something familiar about her.

'Sheila. You're out of fucking line!' Paddy said. 'It's not what you think. You're frightening her, you bullying bitch. She's only a kid.'

Only a kid. Only a kid. *That's* where she knew the girl from. She scrutinised the line of the girl's eyebrows beneath the heavy, dark eyebrow pencil. Noticed the shape of her lips beneath the now-smudged Ronald McDonald red lipstick.

'Didn't you go to school with my Dahlia?' she asked, pushing the barrel hard into the girl's breast bone. 'Stacey Wheelan.'

'Tracy Wheelan,' the girl said. A meek, almost infantile voice, as her false lashes flickered shamefully down towards her vajazzle and back up towards Paddy. Pleading eyes, clearly wishing her sugar daddy would sweeten this bitter confrontation and make Sheila somehow dissolve clean away.

'Get out,' Sheila simply said. 'Go on. Sling your hook, you little slag.'

'Go on, love,' Paddy told the girl. His voice was soft, but Sheila could see from the hard set of his mouth that he was seething. And his livid gaze was trained directly on Sheila, scorching its way through her skin.

The storm was coming. Sheila felt suddenly far less brave. Knew instinctively that the unloaded flintlock would be her undoing.

'I'm sorry,' Tracy Wheelan said to neither of them in particular. She grabbed her cheap clothes and scuffed stilettos and shuffled over to the subterranean spa exit. Clattered up the stone steps to ground level. Was gone.

Paddy grabbed the barrel of the gun and wrenched it out of Sheila's hands.

'You bitch,' he said. On his feet now, his nakedness in that enclosed space felt suddenly oppressive. The roundness of his belly pinned her up against the sweaty wall. His erect penis stuck into her navel like an angry thorn. She could smell beer and cigarettes on his breath. He had spent lunchtime in the pub, clearly. Probably some shithole in Parson's Croft, where he and Conky had swung by to collect protection subs.

'I was only doing her a favour. Giving her a bit of a shoulder to cry on. Her mam's just died, for Christ's sake. She was cut up. I was tense. I've been working all the hours God sends and getting no comfort off you. I was giving you space, She.' Paddy's eyebrows knitted together. His nostrils flared as he breathed rapidly. In, out, in, out, like a panther waiting to pounce. 'There was no harm in it. But you've just scarred a young girl for life, you jealous, snooping cow.'

Realising she could not easily make a bolt for freedom now that she was pinned against the wall, Sheila whispered, 'Sorry, Pad.' Defensively, she raised her hands to her face.

Paddy rammed the butt of the flintlock into her ribs. The air escaped her lungs in a hiss. The pain was intense.

'Nasty, bullying bitch.' Spittle flew from Paddy's mouth as he brought the flat of the stock down onto her cheekbone.

'Stop, Paddy!' Sheila cried, clasping at the side of her face. 'That's going to bruise, for Christ's sake! I bought you the guns to say sorry. I'm sorry, Pad!' Tears streamed from her eyes, though she struggled hard to hold them inside. Didn't want to show him how much she was hurting or how frightened and vulnerable she suddenly felt.

He stopped abruptly. Stared down at the gun, as if only noticing it then for the first time. Turned the weapon over in his hands, running stubby fingers over the filigree metalwork.

'Ottoman?' he said, raising an eyebrow. He raised the flintlock to his shoulder and stared down the barrel at Sheila. Pulled the trigger. 'Bang.'

Sheila winced.

Paddy winked.

'Nice gun,' he said. Then, he hit her over the head hard with the barrel.

Chapter 2

Conky

'I'll be down in a tick,' Paddy shouted to Conky McFadden, poking his head out from one of the doors on the galleried landing. Fastening the cuffs of his shirt. On his bottom half, he wore only his pants. Hairy, freckled red legs on show. 'I'm just going for a shit.'

'You take your time, boss . . .' Conky said, peering down at the shine on his new shoes. '. . . While I hang around like a fart in a trance,' he added, lowering his voice to a half-whisper. 'Sure, I've got nothing better to do at eleven pm on a Friday night.'

Conky stood at the bottom of the stairs, hands folded behind him, sighing. Remembering how Paddy had stunk their cell out when they'd done time together, all those years ago. He had always laughed that it was the evil coming out. Bloody hell. Nothing changed, did it?

Glancing into the oversized mirror by the cloakroom, he double-checked that his trusty hair-piece was still reliably fixed into place, with his own dwindling hair successfully combed over the artful construction. He poked at it gently. It was robust, with no visible bald bits. Excellent. He must pay that bean-counting eejit, David Goodman, a little intelligence-sourcing visit soon, while his hair was looking quite so regal as to be almost intimidating. Maureen Kaplan's son-in-law always blabbed a little louder with proper use of The Eyes, the power of The Hair and, of course, a pistol in his flapping mouth.

Conky tried to lessen his frustration by focusing on his thoughts about *A Brief History of Seven Killings* – the Man Booker Prize winner he was meant to finish in time for his book club. Which he had missed tonight because of Paddy. He checked his watch. There was a Dutchman waiting at the club to discuss the supply of mephedrone in the north-west. A big meeting, called at short notice at Paddy's behest. But Paddy loved to keep people waiting. Conky, however, liked to be on time. Trapped in the punctuality paradox of being Paddy O'Brien's muscle, Conky scratched at the nervous rash that started to itch up his neck beneath his best shirt.

'Alright, Conks?' Sheila said, emerging from the kitchen.

He turned around to greet the boss' wife with a warm smile. Pushed his Ray-Bans up his nose to kiss her on the cheek. She smelled of exotic home cooking and perfume. He drank her aroma in and tried to commit it to memory. Her small, soft hand felt like a child's inside his. He prayed his palms were dry. And that she wouldn't see his irritable rash morphing into a blush.

'Sheila,' he said. Not knowing what to say next.

'Want something to eat? I made a lovely paella. I'm just putting aside the leftovers. There's plenty.' She started to untie the apron from her tiny waist.

'Aye. I could eat the arse of a baby through the cot bars, so I could,' he said. Normally, she trilled with laughter when he used those old Norn Iron turns of phrase from his Belfast boyhood. Tonight, there was not even the glimmer of a smile. 'I was only going to grab a burger at the club. Paddy's due there in ten. So, I might have to eat it on the hoof, if you don't mind, Sheila. The boss—'

'Paddy can wait,' Sheila said in a low voice. The lines either side of her mouth seemed etched deeper than usual.

She turned away from him. He followed her diminutive gym-honed form over to the range cooker, never taking his eyes from her. Savouring the opportunity to look without being seen or judged. But there was something unusual about her gait. She was walking gingerly.

'Are you okay, She?' he asked.

Turning to face him, Sheila's gaze only reached as far as his chin. 'Fine. I overdid it at the gym.'

He took several strides towards her and raised his glasses to his forehead, putting aside any self-conscious discomfort in knowing she would be able to see his protruding eyes. Stooping, he scrutinised the delicate bone structure of her face in the bright sparkling light of the chandeliers. Could see the ghost of a livid green bruise on her forehead, lurking just beneath a layer of heavy makeup.

'What happened?' He stroked her cheek gently.

She didn't retreat from his touch but nevertheless refused to meet his gaze. She was blinking rapidly. 'I tripped over my step in aerobics. Landed on one of my five-k barbell weights, face first, didn't I?'

She looked furtively over at the kitchen door, as though she expected Paddy to be standing there, eavesdropping. Started to dish paella clumsily onto a plate, treating Conky to more uncomfortable silence, as though she resented him for drawing attention to the obvious.

'If there's anything you need to talk about, Sheila,' he said, feeling the pressure of so many unspoken words, accumulated over years, pushing behind his thyroid eyes.

10

Her body stiffened suddenly. She turned back to the cooker. Busy with her frying pan.

Conky realised Paddy had appeared, and was now standing behind them.

'Leave the grub, mate,' the boss said, eyeing him carefully. 'She'll probably poison you with all that foreign shit anyway, won't you, She? I nearly dropped my guts down that carsey.' Paddy strode over and slapped his wife's behind. Treated her to an aggressive kiss on the neck that she pulled away from.

Glad to leave the awkward atmosphere behind, Conky bid Sheila farewell and drove the boss beneath the fool's gold of the streetlights down the A56, away from the leafy Cheshire suburbs, through Stretford and towards Manchester's trading-estate wastelands. They ringed the centre like a shit city wall – identikit, corrugated iron super-sheds, punctuated only by the terraces of Old Trafford, the space-station-like construction of the Emirates cricket stadium and the gaudy blue dome of the Trafford Centre in the distance. All of that invisible as night fell in earnest, leaving only anonymous, hulking grey boxes behind high iron fencing that rusted in the Mancunian drizzle.

M1 House looked like any other premises, but for lasers that seeped skywards from the Perspex lights in the roof and the thump-thump of dance music that emanated from within.

'Alright, our Pad,' Frank said, greeting his older brother at the door deferentially. He thrust a full whisky tumbler towards him. 'Come on. Come on, man. That Dutch bloke's been waiting hours and he's boring as fuck.'

Conky eyed the gaunt, twitchy figure of Frank O'Brien, wincing as Paddy grabbed the drink from him with one hand and administered a brotherly blow to his kidney with the other. Frank was already waxy-faced from whatever cocktail of drugs the daft wee fecker had managed to lay his hands on that evening, dressed like a 1990s throwback in a baggy long-sleeved top and cargo jeans. Shuffling through his giant temple to dance music in grotty old sneakers. A reluctant Pontius Pilate, Conky mused, serving beneath Paddy who was always channelling Tiberius on a good day; Caligula on a bad.

The bass-heavy music enveloped him, pulsating through the hot, damp air – it was almost tangible. Deafening shite. It was certainly no Dvořák or Mozart – it made Conky's teeth sensitive and aggravated the pains in his legs whenever his thyroid was out of whack. Strobe lights flick-flickering all around, dimmed only slightly by the tinted prescription prisms in his Ray-Ban lenses that mitigated some of the thyroid eye disease that plagued him. Lasers flashing green and red in precise fans, pointing upwards, moving downwards to slice through the fog of the dry ice. Everybody caught in nanosecond freeze-frames. Hands in the air. Shaking that thang. Fecking eejits. Staccato dancing like possessed puppetry where the DJ was the puppet master.

'Make some noise, M1 House!' the DJ shouted as he blended the groove of one track into another, perfectly maintaining 128 beats per minute.

Jack O'Brien. Son of Frank O'Brien and number one nephew to Paddy. An accidental Adonis thanks to his dead mother's Balearic colouring. The crowd worshipped this man, turning towards him in unison. Screaming and cheering up to the distant warehouse ceiling – above the lighting rigs, through the corrugated Perspex to the night sky beyond; out into the universe where their love would mingle with the stars.

Frank cheered. Pointed towards him.

'Spin those records, son!'

The heaving sea of firm, slender young bodies parted to let them through. As they did so, Conky spotted the enemy: a mixed-race lad with a lightning flash shaved into the dark stubble of his scalp. Bell something, if memory served. A biblical name. Deuteronomy or something of that ilk. Paddy elbowed Conky in the ribs and nodded, giving the order. Dutifully, he grabbed Frank by his baggy top and yanked him at speed through the cavorting crowd to the backstage area.

At his side, Paddy had thunder behind his eyes.

'Twat!' He cuffed Frank on the side of his head.

Frank was ashen-faced. 'What's up, Pad? How comes Roy Orbison here has got a grip of me? I babysat your supplier, didn't I? I wanna go and vibe with me adoring public, now. Know what I mean?' Frank toyed with the sleeves of his top.

'Who've you got dealing tonight?' his older brother asked, gesticulating towards the dancefloor, visible beyond Jack in his booth.

Frank shrugged, still twitching as though he had withdrawals from the dancefloor. 'Business as usual, man. You know? The Parson's Croft kids. Degsy and his girls. Nicky, Maggie. They're flogging Hong Kong Colin's latest batch of E and meth, like you told them. Dealing some super-fine super skunk. Few baggies of coke. Making the happiness and contentment go round, man.' He drew a heart in the air, ending with both hands making the peace sign.

But Paddy looked anything but peaceful and content. He smashed his whisky tumbler on the floor. Grabbed his younger brother by the back of the neck like a mother cat taking its wayward kitten in its maw. Pushed his face towards the crowd. 'It's crawling with Boddlingtons, you dozy wanker.' Slapped him on the back of his sweaty head with a freckled, hairy hand.

Narrowing his eyes, Conky refocused on the sea of faces. The boy with the lightning flash was palming tabs in a baggie onto some girl and pocketing cash. That much, he could see. Very shoddy procedure.

Frank opened and closed his mouth. Rolling his head, as though panning for an explanation in his empty druggy head like a prospector hoping to find an elusive gold nugget in the mud.

'I don't know how he got past the fellers on the door, Pad. Honest. Maybe someone let him in the back. Maybe he just slipped through with a group of people. There's two thousand kids in here. I can't keep tabs on them. Know what I mean?'

Turning to Conky, Paddy's thin lips arced downwards into a scowl.

'Find Degsy. And get that little Boddlington shit back here. I'm not having stray dogs pissing on my territory.' Hunched shoulders beneath the suit said he was bristling with anger.

'Well, strictly speaking, Pad, it's *my* territory,' Frank said, wide-eyed. 'As long as people are having a good time, I'm not bothered, me.'

'Fucking dickhead.'

The slap that Paddy gave him across his face clearly had some weight behind it. Frank rubbed his cheek, suddenly looking like a small boy. Conky knew better than to intervene.

'Get that Boddlington arsehole and Degsy back here,' Paddy said.

Amidst a flurry of disingenuous apologies, Conky returned with Degsy and the Boddlington interloper, kicking them at the heels to make them move forwards with his gun trained on their backs. Taking pride in the fear he instilled in Degsy, at least. He was the O'Brien firm's Loss Adjuster. He had a reputation to uphold. All who came before him in the Conky McFadden court of justice quaked in their boots.

'This is Leviticus Bell,' he announced, pushing the Boddlington low-level dealer to his knees. Not Deuteronomy, but still a biblical-standard cheeky arsehole. 'And our very own lovely Derek.' He poked Degsy in the back with the barrel of his gun.

Paddy cracked his knuckles. Took something shining from his breast pocket and slid it onto his hand. A knuckle duster. Degsy, a tall bundle of oversized G-Star Raw and Diesel with spots around his mouth that said he smoked just as much meth as he sold, paled instantly.

'On your knees, you lanky twat!' Paddy said, breathing heavily through his nostrils.

Degsy's Adam's apple bounced up and down in his scrawny neck.

'Sorry, Mr O'Brien. I don't know why I'm here, like, but whatever it is, I'm sorry. I told Mr McFadden.'

The left hook that Paddy delivered to Degsy's temple sent the dealer's head spinning to the right with a crack. Blood spatters clinging in a jaunty red to the black nightclub walls.

'Christ, Pad. There's no need for that,' Frank said, wincing.

'Shut your trap, Frank. I don't give a stuff if Queen Elizabeth's name's on the liquor licence above the door. I'm the boss here. Me.' He dug into his chest with a stubby thumb.

Paddy dragged Degsy to his feet. Though he towered

above even Conky, Degsy seemed small next to the King. 'You want to work for me and stay alive, Derek, you keep Boddlington scum out of my venues, right?'

Degsy nodded contritely. Seemed a little dazed. Touched the blood on the side of his head that now seeped onto his clothing.

'Yes, Mr O'Brien. Sorry. It won't happen again.'

Struggling against Conky's grip, the young mixed-race Boddlington interloper spat at Degsy.

'Parson's Croft piece of shit!' he shouted at him. Turned to Paddy and Frank. 'I'm not bleeding scared of yous, man.'

Conky cuffed his ear with his pistol. 'You'd better be, you wee shite. I'm gonna enjoy putting a bullet in you.' His practised words came out automatically as he dwelled all the while on his missed book club and the strangeness of Sheila's behaviour. Decades of doing the same job could do that to a man.

The boy turned to Conky, frowning. 'Oh yeah? You want the Fish Man to come and fillet you, old man? 'Cause that's who you're dealing with if you lay a frigging finger on me.'

'What's your name again, son?' Paddy stepped closer and grabbed him by his chin. Pushed his face upwards, examining his delicate bone structure to see if nobility was hidden in his genes.

The boy spat a second time on the floor at Paddy's side. 'Leviticus Bell.'

'Plucky little bastard, aren't you?'

The boy somehow wriggled free of Conky's grip. Lunged at Paddy. A flash of something metallic, under the dim backstage lights. Red, spreading quickly through the suit-fabric covering Paddy's forearm. The boy, running away; sprinting like a hunted gazelle through the emergency exit.

'Boss!' Conky shouted. He pushed his glasses onto his

forehead to get a better look at the wound. His breath coming ragged with an accelerated heartbeat as he stared down at the gash.

'It's just a scratch!' Paddy said, pressing his fingers into the wound.

But then, something more sinister, as Paddy's look of surprise and anger turned into a wide-eyed hundred-yard stare. Clutching at his chest, he began sinking to his knees.

'Jesus. I feel—' he said. Grimacing, then, his eyes clamped shut.

'Call an ambulance!' Conky barked at Frank.

As Frank punched 999 into his phone, he seemed to be watching with part-glee, part-dread as his brother slumped to the floor, unconscious.

Chapter 3

Paddy

The heart monitor beeped in syncopation with the bing of the oxygen saturation gauge. Constant noise, in those bloody places. Bright lights that made Paddy squint. And that smell. He hated that smell.

'What is that stink?' he asked Katrina. 'Do you reckon it's . . . ? I dunno. Floor cleaner like Mam used to use and . . . human shit, maybe?' He sniffed the air. Wrinkled his nose. Felt tired. 'I can't stand it. I want to go home, Kat. Tell our Sheila she's to come and get me.' He shuffled uncomfortably on the hard, rubber mattress. 'My arse has gone dead.'

At his side, Katrina sighed and patted his hand. Her freckled Celtic skin looking so pale next to his. Her nails had been bitten down into utilitarian submission. Requirements of the job.

'Ah, Patrick. You always were a terrible patient,' she said, smiling wistfully as she watched his jagged heart rate peak and trough and peak and trough in a thin blue-green line. 'Remember that time when you were doubled up in pain in the middle of the night and Mam called the doctor on you? You couldn't have been more than ten.'

18

Paddy smiled weakly. 'Eleven. I told him I was just constipated.'

'It was peritonitis.' Katrina smoothed her navy habit. Her hand travelled down to the large, silver crucifix hanging over her heart. She tapped it thoughtfully. 'You've always played the hard man, Paddy O'Brien. Trying to impress Dad.'

A mental image of their father foisted itself on Paddy's memory. A stocky little hard-nut of a man, who robbed the local bookies and did two years in Strangeways. Smelled of Marlboro cigarettes and stale ale, with breath like a dog's fart. His hands and the pores on his face had always been ingrained with motor oil, when he could get work as a mechanic. Chasing him and Frank down the street with a tyre-iron for a laugh. Taking a swing to test their reflexes. They had been thirteen and seven.

'Dad was a pure bastard,' Paddy said. 'At least he laid off you, though. You were his favourite because you were clever.'

Katrina smiled wryly. 'Well, you can pretend all you like. I know you tried to live up to his expectations. But now this ridiculous life you lead is catching up with you. Time you made some changes.'

He rolled his eyes. Remembered how much he hated his sister's well-meaning sermons. Yanked at the wires connected to his chest in irritation, scratching at the itch from the gel adhesive pads. 'Save it for your flock, Sister Benedicta. I just need to get out of this dump. I'm fine.'

Brandishing his notes, Katrina looked down her nose through her thick-framed, plain glasses, as though about to give a schoolboy a ticking-off. She tutted loudly. 'A heart attack, Patrick. And a stab wound. You are absolutely not fine. Too much of the high life, too much of the low life and too much stress.' She hooked the clipboard of notes indignantly back onto the end of the hospital bed. Sniffed pointedly as Paddy's heart rate picked up, ragged and hasty, as though it were somehow trying to flee the scene of a crime. 'You carry on like this and you'll not make sixty.'

'I *am* sixty.'

'Smart Alec. You can't die on me, Patrick. I've got the Lord's work to do. I'm not babysitting our Francis. That's your responsibility.'

Paddy tried to shuffle himself up the bed. Didn't have the energy. Hated himself for being weak. 'I'm a businessman. I do business.'

His older sister leaned in close until he could smell the convent's nursing home on her. A permanent whiff of institutional dinners, industrial laundry and maybe talc.

'Dirty business,' she said, frowning. 'The heavenly Father is watching, Patrick.'

Paddy started to cough violently. Beep, beep, beep, complained the heart monitor. Bing, bing, as his oxygen levels took a dive. Too many cigarettes and fry-ups, he knew. He could feel his sister's well-meaning eroding his conviction.

'It's taken its toll, hasn't it? Admit it. It's time to get out.' Her well-scrubbed face – perhaps handsome in her youth, but never beautiful – was etched only with fine lines, far fewer than could be expected for a woman of her age. The face of a woman who had never seen drunken debauchery at 3am in Ibiza or a sunbed or a surfeit of gin. The face of a woman who slept nights with a clear conscience.

What did she know about real life?

'It's alright for you,' he said. 'The church takes care of you. I've got a family and the firm, all looking to me for money, support, leadership. I'm the heavenly fucking Father in this town, Kat. I've got the O'Brien name to uphold.'

Abruptly, Katrina stood up, shaking her head and glowering at him, as though she was channelling the displeasure of the Father, the Son *and* the Holy Spirit. She scraped the visitor's chair noisily along the lino. Smoothing down her drab navy skirt, her feet perfectly together in those ugly flat shoes they all wore. Prim and righteous – no different from when she was a kid, Paddy mused.

'I've not got time for any more of your nonsense, Patrick,' she said, dabbing at her nose with a white cloth handkerchief. 'You should be thinking about your future. Carry on like you have been doing and you face an early death, and worst of all, the eternal fires of damnation.' Her voice was quiet. Considered. Deadly. 'Sheila and the girls will be left to fend for themselves. Francis will end up in jail, overdosed or killed. But that's fine, because you'll be gone, you selfish, thoughtless man. Think about how you could be spending your ill-gotten millions in a more meaningful way. Do it, Paddy! Make the changes before Death comes for you early, like it did for Mam and Dad.'

Alone in that side room in the hospital, Paddy wept openly, perhaps for the first time since he was a small boy. Let the fear of losing everything flood through him. *I don't want to die*, he thought. Wiping his eyes on his crisp bedsheet, he rifled among the scores of Get Well Soon cards from neighbours, friends, family, lackeys and sycophants on his bedside cabinet. Drew out the framed photograph of Sheila and the girls. Taken at Christmas time last year, when he had paid for them all to spend a fortnight at the Rayavadee Resort in Krabi. They had been snapped by their waitress, dining as a family around a table situated on the beach, their togetherness framed by the limestone cliffs that rose sheer out of the turquoise Andaman Sea and the lush jungle green that fringed the shoreline. Amy and Dahlia, fully grown now, with lives of their own. One at university and one working a proper job in the City of London. But they had still found time to be with their old dad, hadn't they? It had been the most perfect time in his life. Turning sixty, surrounded by his girls. After six decades of struggling to get as far away from the grime and stink of his childhood home and those foetid, rotten roots, that trip had epitomised his success.

He clutched the photograph to his chest. Tried to conjure the smell of the sea and the sound of the palms, rustling in the warm Thai breeze. At his side, the beeps of the heart monitor spread further apart. Slowing, slowing until they settled into a gentle rhythm.

Paddy knew what to do.

'What do you mean, you want to sell up?' Sheila asked, her baby-doll beautiful face freezing mid-smile. Paddy was relieved to see she had covered up the bruising to her forehead. No need to remind him of that.

She dropped her oversized handbag onto the hospital lino. Flung her slender frame onto the seat that Katrina had occupied earlier. Michael Kors or Armani or whatever it was she wore, clinging to her curves. Fur. Leather. Silk. Louboutin stilettos that cost him a small fortune. The antithesis of his sister. When she dared to get angry, it made him want to conquer her.

Paddy forked baked potato into his mouth enthusiastically. Chewed the fluffy mush with relish, as though this was the first time he had ever really tasted food. Sheila would come round. She always did as she was told with a little persuasion.

'I've thought it all through, She. I'm selling the business.' He set his fork down authoritatively on the tray. Grinned.

But Sheila's scepticism was etched across her face. Those fine eyebrows raised archly.

'It's not a sodding barber's or a chain of corner shops, Paddy.' She lowered her voice. Looked over her shoulder, though they were alone, with the hustle and bustle of the ward on the other side of a heavy fire door. 'It's a Criminal. Fucking. Empire.' She leaned in further with each word. Tapped every syllable out on his dinner tray with almost perfectly manicured electric blue nails – one shorter than all the rest.

Undeterred, he ushered more potato into his mouth. Pictured the tropical paradise of Krabi, so very far from Manchester's never-ending rain and Frank's idiot schemes and the daily grind of having to look over his shoulder continually. Spoke with his mouth full.

'Tariq and Jonny. They'll have it. I bet you. I reckon ten mill, and me and you can just get on a plane and swan off to Thailand. Open a bar.'

Sheila shook her shining blonde mane.

'You're tapped,' she said. 'You think the Boddlington gang are gonna shove you ten million quid for something they've spent the last twenty years trying to nick for free?'

Paddy nodded, beaming at his own brilliance. He felt happiness register itself in his groin, overpowering the agitation that she had dared to call him tapped.

'Suck us off, She.' He pointed at Little Paddy, making his presence felt beneath the honeycomb blanket.

Eyes narrowed, Sheila was folding her arms. Paddy mused that the blow-job was looking unlikely. He didn't have the energy to insist otherwise.

'Tariq Khan and Jonny Margulies are a pair of thieving bastards, Pad. *You're* a thieving bastard, too, or had you forgotten?'

'They'll snatch me bleeding hand off, She! Especially if they think there's a chance I might sell to some hip-hop, drive-by snot-rag from London with his arse hanging out his trousers. Or some Scouser. It's what they've always wanted, Tariq and Jonny. They've got north Manchester and now I'll sell them the south. Fair and square. The gambling dens, the pharmaceutical side, the guns . . .' He started to count his interests on his fingers, as though this would somehow curry her favour. '. . . The endangered species shit that the Chinese love, the nail bars, the moody art, the lot! Bollocks to it. If they pay up, they can have our kid's club and your cleaning business too.'

Out of her chair like a jack-in-the-box.

'My frigging company?' She shook her head. Waggled her finger. 'Oh, no, no, no, no you don't, Patrick O'Brien.'

Her pixie chin stuck out defiantly. Reminded him of the time he had asked her out on that first date, after a Wednesday night at the Haçienda's *Zumbar*. He'd spotted her during the intermission – before the cheesy cabaret act had come on. Parading down the catwalk, modelling clothes from some local fashion school wannabe. Legs that went on forever and tits that had a buoyancy all of their own. She had been seventeen. He, thirty-seven – old enough to have his minions selling drugs in clubs, but too old to enjoy them himself, as a rule. But it had been Frank's birthday that particular Wednesday, with his band playing downstairs in the Gay Traitor bar, so Paddy had relented. His cash hadn't impressed young Sheila, but he had worn her down with sheer romantic persistence and, later, rightful dominance. She'd relented in the end, just as she would relent now, he felt certain.

'You can get a new hobby in Thailand, babe. I'll buy a big fuck-off villa. You can get it done out like a five-star spa hotel. That'll keep you busy.'

24

'Nine years, Paddy,' she shouted. 'Me and Gloria have built that sodding cleaning company up over nine years! I'm just about to get a healthcare contract, cleaning a big private hospital. I've done quotes this week for two law firms in town and a bank! It's not a hobby, you cheeky bastard.'

'Hey! Wind your fucking neck in, woman, or I'll wind it in for you!'

'I've got women relying on me.' Her generous, pink lips had thinned and were now arcing downwards.

'They're bloody trafficked skivvies from Um Bongo, aren't they?'

'The Democratic Republic of Congo, Patrick. Not bloody Um Bongo. And some of them are from Nigeria and Ghana and are legal, *actually*! Gloria knows them from church, the Ghanaians and Nigerians. They're glad of a job. I am a responsible employer.'

Paddy snorted. 'What? You don't reckon you'd be leaving your nice African ladies in good hands? You think Tariq Khan and Jonny Margulies are incapable of screwing over slave labour and refugees as good as you? Do me a favour!'

Sheila glared at him. She clearly thought she could gain the upper hand, while he was laid up and at the mercy of a medical team. Cocky bitch.

'I care about my staff.'

'You're full of shit, is what you are, Sheila O'Brien.' Paddy picked up the framed photograph taken in Thailand. Thrust it towards her. Pointed at the girls. His heart rate picked up pace, as it occurred to him that – for perhaps the first time ever – without his being able to squeeze the defiance out of her physically, Sheila might put her foot down and refuse to bend to his will. 'This isn't about money, She. We've got enough to last us ten lifetimes. This isn't about some scrubbers you don't even know, or that nagging, sanctimonious bitch, Gloria. This is about me, staying alive for our daughters. For us. Family.'

Sheila's face had a pinched look to it as she chewed her bottom lip. Her gaze flicked from the photo to Paddy and back. She was refusing to make eye contact with him and staring intently only at his chin or his forehead. Nostrils flaring gently, as though she were processing some internal argument.

'You've made your mind up, haven't you?' she asked in a quiet voice.

'Yes.' He held the photo to his chest. 'For better or for worse, She. How bad could twenty years of tropical sunshine be?' He grinned triumphantly. 'I'll buy you an elephant.'

'Piss off, you daft bastard.'

'You'd save a bomb on the sunbed.'

She dropped her gaze to her eternity and engagement rings, running her index finger over the large, solitaire diamond. Closed her mournful eyes.

'If I agree, does this mean you're getting out for good? No controlling the business from the end of a phone or a laptop? A clean break?'

He nodded. Felt his neck muscles start to relax.

'It'd better be a damned big elephant, Paddy O'Brien.'

Chapter 4

Jonny

Biting into his bagel, Jonny Margulies mused that it was a fine morning. From the vantage point of his desk, positioned by the office window, he could see the sun hitting the dreaming spires of Strangeways prison. The red brick was on fire today, giving an impression of baking warmth in a city that never thawed or properly dried out. The steep slate roofs shone – slick from the overnight rain, now reflecting sunshine like the solar panels on some distant satellite. Negative energy inside those walls, though. He imagined the poor bastards in the central building, walking round and around Her Majesty's Victorian hotel, wondering what on earth had gone wrong with their lives. At least he was safe. And the warmth that spread from his groin to the rest of his body was genuine.

'Not so hard, sugar,' he said to the girl on her knees beneath the desk. 'Flick your tongue around it while you suck. Okay?'

The blonde paused and looked up at him quizzically. Smudged eyeliner ringing her eyes looked like it had been applied days ago and never washed off or replenished. Oh well. She had a nice mouth and a sweet face and he had a hard-on the size of Texas. All was well.

'You not like?' she asked. Said something in Polish or Estonian or whatever the hell language she spoke. She smiled uncertainly. Cupped her small breasts. 'You want I play?'

Jonny shook his head, batting the uninvited mental images of Sandra that encroached on the fantasy. *Get out of my head, for God's sake.* Sandra, with her orange face and prune mouth. The half-starved and gorgeous Mrs Margulies – mother of his legitimate children but not sexy like this tasty little Eastern European tart.

'No love. You're fine.' He set down his bagel and cupped her face in buttery hands so that she looked up at him. He mimed the technique he wanted her to adopt.

'You want more lick. Yes?'

He nodded. 'That's right, love.'

The girl smiled. Her teeth were clean. He liked that. The dentist looked after all the girls' dental hygiene well. He reached down and stroked her breasts. Felt his erection grow harder still. Wanted to put it inside her tight little pussy. He pulled her up towards him, not caring if anyone from the upper floors of the prison could see him. He just wanted to screw this girl right now.

'Sixteen?'

'I?' She nodded enthusiastically. 'Sixteen. Yes.' She rubbed her breasts on his face. Soft pink nipples brushing his stubble. Not a single blemish on her young, pale flesh. She was far younger than his daughter – but she wasn't his daughter.

Reaching in her thong, he could feel her, soft and wet. Hot, where his finger slid inside. Two ties at the side came loose easily. She climbed onto him and started to ride him – inexpertly, but what the hell?! This was a glorious start to the day. Until . . .

The knock at the door was insistent.

'Jonny!' came a man's voice on the other side. 'The tax inspector is back.' Strongly accented, pronouncing inspector as *inspecter*, betraying his Jerusalem origins.

Pushing the girl off his lap, Jonny's desire cooled immediately.

'Come in, Asaf, for Christ's sake!' he shouted, zipping his deflating penis into his chinos. He waved a hand at the girl. 'Get dressed! Anyone asks, you were asking directions to TK Maxx.'

The girl looked at him blankly until he threw her clothes at her in a bundle.

'Ah, dress. Yes.' Scrambling to cover herself, she had at least picked up on the urgency in his voice.

The office felt smaller with the tall figure of Asaf Smolensky standing in it. Clad in his usual black double-breasted suit with its old-fashioned overdone padding to the shoulders. The thin, white strands of his ritual tassels – tzitzits – hanging outside his trousers. Scuffed shoes and a stained waistcoat juxtaposed against the immaculate cropped hair and ringletted sidelocks of the Hassids. He smelled of chopped and fried fish. He looked like he meant business.

'Is it that tax bird again?' Jonny asked him, feeling the blood drain from his face faster than it had from his dick. His pulse was racing. Suddenly, the half-eaten bagel in his stomach felt like lead. His brain whirred into overdrive, checking through the list of changes he and Tariq had instigated last time the stupid bitch had come calling, demanding to snoop around. They had fobbed her off, but only temporarily.

Smolensky nodded. Perched on the edge of the oversized desk, wearing a grim expression.

'Yes. Ruth Darley. She's come with two assistants today and some official-looking paperwork. HMRC wants your blood, Jonny.' He toyed with his unruly beard, a thick eyebrow raised archly.

'Tariq know?'

'He's at Sefton Street.'

'I'll call him.' Pulling his mobile from his trouser pocket, Jonny inclined his head towards the young prostitute.

'Do us a favour. Get Lev to get her away from here without anyone seeing. And make yourself scarce.'

Asaf stood tall and grabbed the girl by her upper arm. Said something to her in an Eastern European language that Jonny didn't understand. The girl looked afraid, clutching her shoulder bag close as Asaf steered her through a second door in the office which led to the stone stairwell at the back of the building.

Locking both doors shut, Jonny dialled Tariq's number. Sweat breaking out on his top lip. Tariq answered on the fourth ring.

'What's up, bro?' Tariq asked. The chatter of workers was audible in the background, along with the whirring and clanking of a production line.

'Darley's back.'

Tense silence hung between them for too many moments.

'I see,' Tariq said. 'Do you want me to come over?'

Jonny peered out of the window to the car park immediately below, avoiding looking at Strangeways, now, for fear that he might somehow jinx his precarious freedom. There were two cars he didn't recognise parked out front, next to his own Maserati. A silver Toyota and a black Mondeo. Tax man's cars. He willed his hand to stop shaking. Gripped the phone harder.

'No, you're alright. I've got it covered. If they've got eyes on the street and spot you coming out of there, we're totally buggered. Stay put. I'll call when they're gone.'

His secretary's instantly recognisable rat-a-tat-tat on the door said it was time to put on the grand performance.

Clad in a frumpy blue suit with her banana legs and fat ankles stuffed into cheap shoes, Darley was already strutting through the warehouse, examining the stock. Jonny willed himself to smile before she had even turned around to face him, lest he make it too obvious that he'd like Asaf to bone her like a haddock with his sharpest knife. In his peripheral vision, he clocked her minions – two men: one who looked about ready to retire and the other who didn't look more than twenty. They were speaking to the workers, who were bundling the cheap jewellery into even cheaper packaging.

'Ms Darley,' Jonny said, adopting his magnanimous and friendly voice that he used for PTA meetings. 'What a pleasure to see you again.'

Darley turned on her heel, a grim expression on her face that implied the pleasure was not mutual. 'Mr Margulies.' She held out her right hand and treated him to the iron handshake of a woman who broke balls for a living. In her left hand, she clutched an oversized accountant's briefcase. 'I'm here to search your premises. Please make all your accounts and employee records available.'

Jonny felt like his bowels were somehow ingesting themselves. The tell-tale sensation of needing the toilet, fast. But he wouldn't show this bitch any fear. The authorities were like dogs; the moment they caught a whiff of guilt, they knew they had you. Tariq was relying on him. Both of their families depended on his giving a convincing performance. He put one foot in front of another and showed her to an office that looked onto the main factory floor through a large plate-glass internal window.

'You can work in here,' he said politely, switching on the flick-flickering strip lighting and pulling out an uncomfortable-looking brown plastic chair. It was cold in there. The thin carpet tiles were peeling upwards, revealing perished rubber underneath. Let the tax bastards suffer.

'Where is Mr Khan?' she asked, touching her no-nonsense brown bob. It appeared rigid and moved only slightly.

'Family emergency. He's been called away.'

Darley looked over her purple plastic-framed glasses, fixing him with hard hazel eyes. 'Convenient.'

Shrugging, he held his palms aloft in a gesture of honesty. 'Am I my business partner's keeper?'

Jonny wished he could run away. Give it all up. Hide on a beach in Israel or South America or even crappy Marbella would do right now. Silently, he cursed Tariq for having chosen that morning, of all mornings, to visit their other place, leaving him to sort out this gargantuan shit-storm on his own.

As the day wore on, Jonny felt his spirit ebbing away, answering intrusive questions and observing his book-keeper, old Mohammed, delivering box after box of files to the temporary hub of HMRC investigation.

Knocking timorously on the door, he popped his head in to see Ruth Darley busily going through a sheaf of invoices with a determined look on her face. Her underlings flanked her, like Padawans studying beneath some great Jedi. Jonny looked at his watch pointedly.

'It's getting late,' he said. 'Would you like my secretary to bring you and your colleagues a coffee?'

Darley looked at him and slid her glasses further up her nose. Glanced at Jonny's wrist. 'I don't need a Breitling watch to tell me what time it is, Mr Margulies.' She offered him a grimace that was an approximation of a smile. 'We'll be leaving in ten minutes, but we'll be back tomorrow.'

Jonny folded his arms. Imagined for a second that he could hear the inmates inside Strangeways jeering at him from behind their barred windows.

'Back? Oh. You haven't seen everything you need today? I thought Janice had given you access to the full monty. We've got nothing to hide here, you know.'

Ruth Darley stood and held a separate sheaf of invoices aloft. Invoices written in Chinese, by the looks of it. At that moment, a sweat broke out on Jonny's top lip and he wished, however improbably, that he knew the difference between Mandarin and Cantonese. Had the invoices somehow got mixed up? Maureen would surely never allow that to happen.

'I have found anomalies, Mr Margulies.' Her smile was genuine that time.

Shit. Those were the last words he had wanted to hear.

Chapter 5

Irina

Irina didn't like the tall man who smelled of fish. She looked up at him and wrinkled her nose. She had heard tell of Jews back home, but had never seen a real one until coming to Manchester. Asaf, the beast was called. He looked like something out of the old stories she had been told as a child by her dear old Babička. He even had the curly sidelocks she had described, though not the horns, it would seem.

Instinctively, she held her bag close to her body, thinking of the photo of Mama and Babička that she had hidden in a special zipped compartment. Bad enough that these bastards had taken her Slovakian passport away from her. She would never let them have that photo. It was all she had left of her old life. How she missed her Mama. How disappointed Mama would be if she knew that her lover Dominik had betrayed them both by getting her pregnant and then – as if knocking up his girlfriend's teenaged daughter weren't bad enough – arranging her transport to England with the promise of a hairdressing career that had turned out to be nothing more than unpaid prostitution.

She patted her stomach. The baby wasn't showing yet.

She didn't want a baby. This was not a world she wanted to bring a child into.

Spitting on the floor, she tried to get the taste of the boss-man's dick out of her mouth.

Asaf looked down at her. 'Hurry up,' he said in her native tongue, grabbing her upper arm. 'You've got an appointment.'

'An appointment?' Her heart fell. Another punter, no doubt. Perhaps some sweaty builder with dirt beneath his fingernails. Perhaps a businessman in one of the local offices. Clean hands, but the same stench of lust and lies evaporating from their pores, as they all cheated on their wives with some firm, forbidden flesh.

The Fish Man pulled her towards a battered purple people carrier, parked outside a run-down warehouse, marked out from all the other run-down warehouses by a sign in the window – written in English in poorly cut-out dayglo letters, the meaning of which she didn't understand. An 'F' hung askew at the start of two words – 'ANCY GOODS'. Beneath it was scrawled in black on a giant, fluorescent green poster, 'WHOLESALE ONLY'. A dark-skinned man was sitting behind the wheel of the vehicle. Into his scalp was shaven a lightning bolt. He glanced at her, looked her up and down, and looked away. Perhaps derision or disgust or furtive lust. It was hard to tell.

'Are you taking me back to the house?' Irina asked the Fish Man. Suddenly, she was buoyed by the hope of a hot drink, a shower and a chat with her own kind. The house was full of other teens on the game for these sons of bitches – all from Eastern Europe, give or take the odd African. The black ones mainly kept themselves to themselves.

He opened the rear door to the people carrier and pushed her into the seat.

'No. Not back to the house. Something else. Lev here will

take us.' He rummaged in a deep pocket sewn into his coat and frowned. 'Stay put. I've got to go back and get something.'

He engaged the child locks and slammed the rear door, leaving her trapped in a vacuum of awkwardness with the stranger in the driver's seat.

Clasping her hoody around her tightly, Irina stared at the back of the driver's head. She recognised him as the man who came round to the house to collect money from those spotty-faced pimps that kept her and the other girls under lock and key, Tommo and Kai.

'You doing alright?' the driver asked.

Irina jumped at the sound of his voice, struggling to understand his words spoken with a strong Mancunian accent. She inadvertently locked eyes with him via the rear view mirror and immediately looked down to her lap, heat burning in her cheeks. It was best not to engage with these animals. You never knew when they were going to pounce on you, expecting sex.

'Okay?' he said.

Irina nodded, surprised by the softness to his voice. He never sounded like that when he was guffawing with laughter at something the two pimps said.

'You're pretty new, aren't you? What's your name?'

She understood that much. 'Irina.'

'Mine's Lev.'

In the rear view mirror, lightning bolt blinked hard and opened his mouth several times without saying anything, as though he were trying and failing to expel a thought.

'I'm sorry . . .' he finally said, eyes flickering down towards the scratched car stereo. Furrows appeared in his forehead. He stretched out the fingers on his smooth-skinned hand. Bitten fingernails said all was far from perfect in his world, too. She realised then that he couldn't have been a great deal older than her. '. . . Sorry for all this shit. It's not right. I wish I could—'

But Lev fell silent as the Fish Man opened the passenger door and slumped down into the seat, bringing with him the pungent scent of fish and menace.

They drove several blocks down the wide road that bisected the main Strangeways business district, the car bouncing and jerking as it hit pothole after pothole, making Irina's jaw clack. Rubbish, whipped up by the wind, adhered itself to the car's sloping bonnet.

They pulled up outside a large red-brick building that looked as though it had once been a giant factory, now with its large, multi-paned windows cracked and broken. The grime of a century's existence clung to the façade like a mourner's veil. No jaunty sign outside this one. But the noise of industry and voices coming from within. The Fish Man opened the doors and pulled Irina out, leaving Lev behind in the people carrier.

'Be friendly,' the Fish Man told her, ushering her through a heavy steel door that was opened by means of a buzzer entry system. 'Smile.'

What Irina saw brought morning sickness on, bloating her like a quickly inflated balloon, stretched to popping point with bad gas. She held her hand over her mouth, willing herself not to vomit.

There were people everywhere, beavering over production lines. Mainly men. Predominantly Asian, she could tell. Small and thin, as though they weren't properly nourished. Chattering animatedly as they stuffed white pills into baggies at this workstation, put CDs into CD cases at that, packaged branded trainers into boxes. Just do it. The air was thick with pungent smells. Sweat. Bad breath. Dust. Hot machinery, where conveyor belts chugged ropey-looking dolls in various stages of assembly from one end of the factory to another. Everywhere, there was life. Everywhere, she smelled the clashing scents of desperation and hope. Were these workers all slaves like her? Perhaps just illegals. Lucky bastards.

'Go to the back,' the Fish Man said, prodding her between her shoulder blades. 'The office, there.'

Irina's heartbeat, already ragged, sped up further. Adrenalin doing battle with nausea. At the rear of the factory there was a door – battered khaki paint that revealed grey beneath and red beneath that. The Fish Man opened the door and pushed her inside a cold room that was furnished with a cheap old melamine desk and an ugly brown metal filing cabinet. Behind the desk sat a man dressed in beige tunic and baggy trousers. On his feet, which she could see poking beneath the desk, he wore blue flip-flops. His greying, shorn hair was covered in the main by a flat round hat that reminded her of the loaves of rye bread that her mother used to bake.

The man's brown eyes darted in her direction, furtively taking a snapshot of her face. He looked back up to the Fish Man.

'Tariq,' he said simply.

'Sit!' The Fish Man pushed Irina into a torn grey twill typing chair, opposite the strange man.

Would she have to sleep with him? She looked at his fingernails. He was clean enough, at least. Oddly, he seemed more nervous than she felt, if that were possible, fidgeting as he was with his beard. Those darting eyes were dogged by dark shadows that said this man wasn't someone who slept.

Presently, Tariq entered the dingy office. Irina recognised him. The other boss-man. The one who hadn't tried to screw her. A well-dressed Asian man who smelled like heaven and would have been good-looking were it not for his beak-like nose that put her in mind of a hawk.

'Hello, love,' he said, smiling at her like a benign father she didn't want. 'How you doing?' He rubbed the ends of her blonde hair between his fingertips, as though he were appraising the quality of a wheat stalk, saying something in a language she did not recognise to the man in the hat.

A conversation ensued during which Tariq never sat down, though he spoke calmly. He released her hair to jangle his gold watch and then turned to the Fish Man.

'Get the fee from our client, here,' he told him. 'Fifteen K as agreed.'

'Don't you want to count it, boss?' the Fish Man asked.

Tariq held up his hands and closed his eyes. 'I've got a five-a-side team to manage at my son's school. You take the money and give him details of the registry office.' With a fleeting glance at Irina, he muttered, 'Congratulations,' and started to scroll absently through the texts on his phone.

The nervous man's watery smile suddenly had something predatory about it. Sensing that something was afoot, Irina stood. Turned to the door. The Fish Man pushed her back into her seat.

'What's going on?' she asked in her own tongue.

'You're getting married to Mohammed here so that he can stay in the country. You can't get kicked out because you're a pregnant EU citizen. He's an Afghan national who's been threatened with deportation.'

'No!' Irina yelled, tears welling in her eyes. She tried to force herself up and out of the chair but the Fish Man's grip was too strong. 'You can't make me.' Turning to Tariq, she cried in English, 'Help, please!'

But Tariq's phone was ringing. He turned away, speaking into the device.

'Jonny. Slow down. What's the matter?'

Irina struggled and tried to scream but, as if he had anticipated her protest, the Fish Man's large hand pressed firmly over her mouth. She could smell stale herring on his fingers. The man in the round hat squirmed in his chair, counting out £20 notes as though his every move were being observed by some hidden camera. He looked almost apologetic.

'HMRC have found *what*?' Tariq shouted, opening the door to the hallway. Suddenly, he seemed to think better of it and shut himself back inside the small office. He shot an agitated glance towards the Fish Man, gesturing impatiently that he should lessen his grip on Irina. Held his finger to his mouth, motioning to her that she should resist the urge to scream.

For some reason – perhaps the sharp boning knife that the Fish Man had just taken out of his coat pocket and pressed to Irina's throat – she felt obliged to obey.

'This is bad. Very bad,' Tariq said, pressing his fingers to his temples. 'Oh hang on, I've got another call coming through . . . It's Maureen. She'll deal with this. Yeah, I'll get back to you.'

Irina watched, pinioned to her seat by the Fish Man and a mixture of intrigue and fear. She didn't fully understand Tariq's words or whether they had any bearing on her fate or not. He greeted the caller named Maureen, whoever that was. His eyes grew wide. A smile, then – an unexpected sunburst brightening the stormy expression on his face.

'You kidding me, Mo? The O'Briens are saying *what*?'

He whooped with apparent joy just as the Fish Man drew a bead of blood from Irina's neck.

Chapter 6

Lev

'What do you mean they can't do surgery?' Lev asked Tiffany, grabbing her by her thin, scarred arm. Adrenalin coursed around his body, making him feel breathless, light-headed, nauseous. This was the last thing he had hoped to hear. In fact, he hadn't even contemplated the option.

She shook him loose. Glared at him, as though this was somehow all his fault. As though he had wished this fate on his son or brought some terrible curse on little Jay by walking out and not coming back. Her voice was husky with cigarettes and too many late nights smoking weed. Harder highs, when she succumbed to the pull of the brown, leaving those ugly red pinpricks tracking up her limbs.

She was avoiding eye contact. Covering her ears as Jay started to wail again in the back bedroom. 'Fucking hell. He does my head in when he goes off on one like this.' She stumbled away from the boy's noise, towards the top of the uncarpeted stairs.

'Hey!' Lev shouted, half-wishing he were the sort of man who could just hit a woman and feel more in control. 'I asked you a question. What do you mean, it's inoperable?'

'The tumour's in a funny place.' She started to descend,

41

turning her ankle sideways in those heeled mules she always wore. White thong visible through her too tight yellow miniskirt. 'If you'd come to the scan, Le-viti-*carse*, you'd know that, wouldn't you? Dick.'

'Spare me the lecture, yeah?' He glanced back towards the source of the woe – the door to his son's bedroom was ajar. Confront her or comfort the boy? She was already in the hall, dragging those skanky, ramshackle heels into the skanky, ramshackle lounge.

Lev marched into Jay's room, the sharp tang of damp in his nostrils as he lifted his son gently out of a cot he had long outgrown.

'Jesus. She's still not bought you a big boy bed,' he whispered. 'I don't know why I bloody bother.'

He had been put to bed in his jeans and a jumper. Sweating like a pig, the poor little bastard.

'Come on, big man. Shhh, Daddy's here. Daddy's here.' He held Jay's small, hot body close, hoping that his voice and physical presence would be soothing. But the boy was beside himself, screaming now, tearing at his tight blond curls, clamping his chubby palms to his temples. Snot was plastered over his honey-brown skin in a shining, viscous film. With some struggle, Lev managed to remove his jumper. Changed his nappy. Cleaned his face with a cool wet-wipe and brought his son downstairs, holding him over the excruciating ache in his own heart. Rocking him gently, though the child arched his back, testing his father's strength to the limit.

'I couldn't get to the scan, Tiff. I've had to lie low,' he said, sitting among the crumbs and empty wrappers on the sofa. Jay's screams reverted to crying, slowed to a hiccough and intermittent whinge. 'I had a run-in with the O'Briens in M1 House. Had to keep a low profile. You know the sort of people I'm involved with. If I piss the wrong man off and I don't watch my back, I'm dead. And I pissed the wrong man *right* off, good style.'

'Oh, shut the fuck up, will you?' Tiffany said, flicking the television on, absently. She lit a cigarette. 'I don't wanna hear your excuses. You should have been there. He's your son too.'

'Do you think I don't know that?' Lev asked, keeping his voice deliberately low, though his instinct was to bawl her out. With his free hand, he switched off the television. Grabbed the cigarette from her and stubbed it out in the overflowing chipped glass ashtray. 'You shouldn't smoke in the house. Is it any wonder he's ill?'

'Stuff it up your arse, you tosser.' Tiffany defiantly lit another cigarette, filling the room with acrid yellow-blue smoke that only barely masked the smells of cooking grease and the stale wine that stood at the bottom of three bottles on the laminate coffee table. More empties on the telly table. She clearly still fancied herself as the molten core of every party that erupted from the pub after closing.

'Where's the money I give you for his big boy bed? Why's he still in the frigging cot? He's got a brain tumour, Tiff! And you're letting him bang his head on the bars every five fucking minutes. You're not on. Where's the money?'

Tiffany narrowed her eyes and blew smoke in his and Jay's faces. Chewed on her bottom lip.

'You blew it on gear, didn't you?' Lev said, shaking his head in disgust. 'I sell my soul to the devil to look after yous, and you just burn through it on shit. Selfish cow.'

Jay had fallen asleep in Lev's arms. Passed out through sheer exhaustion, or maybe it was the tumour that caused him to swing from apoplectic one minute to comatose the next. Perhaps Lev just had the magic touch, whereas his babymother merely had the conviction that she somehow deserved better than to be a single mother to a dying child in a shitty damp terrace on the Sweeney Hall estate.

Silence between them put a temporary sticking plaster over the acrimony.

'So, what are we gonna do?' Lev asked, trying to be calm. He stroked his son's hair, wishing he could somehow draw the tumour out through his hand and take it on himself. 'We can go private. Get a second opinion. I'll ask my bosses for some money.'

Resignation in Tiffany's voice. She turned to him, treating him to a dead-eyed stare. 'All they can do is try to shrink it. Radiothingy. They said it's grown into his nose and around the optic nerves. He's going blind. Doc said there's not a surgeon in England has got the savvy to get it out. He's shafted . . .'

Lev looked down at Jay and felt tears leak onto his cheeks. Imagining the tumour within his son, wrapping itself around the boy's beautiful green eyes, suffocating the healthy tissue, eating into space that his brain should by rights fill, replacing thoughts of *Postman Pat* and *Chuggington* and whatever other shit the kid watched on CBeebies with pain. Somehow, he had failed the boy. Somehow, it was his fault. There had to be a way to make it better. His mother had always told him the Lord was merciful.

'. . . Unless we can get him to the States.' Tiffany inhaled her cigarette deeply and blew the smoke over Lev's closely shorn hair.

A glimmer of hope. 'You what?'

She nodded slowly. Flicked her fingernails with her thumb. 'There's this brain surgeon in Baltimore. The place is called John Hopkins Brain Centre or summat.'

'Right,' Lev said, wiping the tears from his cheeks determinedly. 'He's going. We'll take him.'

'It's a hundred and fifty grand. Maybe more. Where you gonna find that kind of cash, smart arse? Flogging baggies of coke in town on a Saturday night? Get a grip!'

Lev's heart, buoyed instantly by the thought of a cure that glittered with promise on the other side of the Atlantic, took a slow trip back down to the soles of his Nike Air-Max trainers. He mentally rifled through the hiding places he had for cash in the Sweeney Hall high-rise he called home. The toilet cistern contained £2,500 and a gun that was worth a few quid, wrapped up in plastic bags. There was another £1,900 at the back of the gas meter in an old Brillo box. £5,000 in a carrier bag, gaffer-taped to the underside of his wardrobe. He couldn't even make ten grand.

'We'll find it,' he said. 'I'll ask Tariq and Jonny for more work. Maybe I can help out as muscle. The Fish Man gets paid a mint.'

Tiffany snorted. 'You? Muscle? Where, in your pants? That's the only place you ever had muscle, Le-viti-*carse*.'

His hours spent at the gym every week were clearly lost on that cheeky, head-wiggling cow. Or maybe she was bitching because she wasn't getting it any more. Yes, that was it. The jibe stung less when he looked at it that way. But this was no time for hurt sensibilities over the quality of his six-pack.

'I'll have it saved, borrowed or stolen inside six months. I promise. The full whack.' The words came out as a half-whisper, bound for his sleeping son's ears.

'Six months? You *are* joking,' Tiffany said, picking her cigarette dimp out of the ashtray. She put it back inside her cigarette packet, stood and grabbed the empties from the table. No trace of emotion in her indifferent face. 'The doctor reckons he'll be dead in three, even with radio-whatsit. We need a miracle. How about you talk to that shithouse, your mother. She's pretty fucking friendly with God, isn't she?'

But the words *he'll be dead in three* were ringing in Lev's ears like bad tinnitus. He looked down at Jay, frowning in his sleep. Golden downy hairs on those honeyed, rubicund cheeks. The only beautiful thing in this godforsaken hole. The only beautiful thing in Lev's entire beleaguered existence. Lev imagined his son lifeless and stiff, his eyes, staring blankly into the abyss, the childish shine all gone. His small body, interred in the autumn-hardening ground of Agecroft Cemetery, a fancy white coffin the only cold comfort remaining at the end of a life left unlived and mourned bitterly by wailing female relatives who should have looked after the poor little bastard better. Then, he pictured himself by his son's graveside. Wearing his only suit, normally worn for court appearances, weddings and the odd stag night. Here is the homecoming for the son of Leviticus Bell – a pure soul begat by a sinner, snatched back to heaven by an unforgiving God that expects more from his flock than petty drug-dealing, cheap sex and knife crime.

Lev allowed the darkness to engulf him. Chastised himself for being useless at a time of need. Reminded himself that he was one of life's fighters. Remembered that Jay still had a chance while Dr Whateverhisorhernamewas at Johns Hopkins in Baltimore existed. 'Jesus Christ, Tiff. Our Jay can't die. I won't let him. I'm gonna sort this.'

Chapter 7

Gloria

Gloria Bell was finding it hard to praise Jesus that Sunday in the Good Life Baptist Church. Her bunions were stinging for a start. She looked down at her feet, grimacing at the protrusions through the brown patent leather. Perhaps the Lord was punishing her for vanity. There had been no real need to wear heels, if she was being honest. Flats would have been a more sensible choice, even though she was wearing her new best summer dress and matching shrug. But in her heart of hearts, Gloria admitted that she quite liked the way the pastor looked at her legs when she was wearing these heels. And maybe Jesus would appreciate her suffering and self-sacrifice to brighten His servant's Sunday morning spiritual travails with a nicely turned ankle. The pastor did put an awful lot of passion into his sermon and singing, after all. That had to be tiring.

'He's got great stamina,' her friend Winnie whispered in her ear, almost taking Gloria's eye out with the sharp petrol-coloured feathers that protruded from her best hat.

Gloria nodded, never taking her eyes off the pastor's shapely, muscular bottom in those too tight suit trousers he wore. Whipping the choir into a frenzy was hot work.

Ordinarily, Gloria liked it when he took his jacket off and turned his back to the congregation. But today, she was distracted by her infernal bunions and by the conversation she had had only yesterday with Sheila O'Brien.

They had been sitting at Sheila's breakfast bar: she, drinking a simple mug of boiled water, Sheila, guzzling a vodka tonic. The call that had precipitated the visit had felt like a summons, judging by the frost in Sheila's normally warm voice. Small wonder, then, that her one-time boss turned business partner had delivered a body-blow she could never have anticipated.

'It's over, Gloria,' Sheila had said. 'Our business. I've got to jack it in. Me and Pad are moving to Thailand. I'm so sorry.'

Gloria had set her mug carefully back on its coaster and studied Sheila's serious expression. Her eyes were clear, despite the early V&T. She'd looked at her hands to see if she had the shakes. But the myriad of platinum charms on her ostentatious bracelet always rattled; it was hard to tell. 'Are you drunk?'

Sheila had sighed. Her white skin, normally warmed with spray tan and cosmetics, had looked wan that morning, giving her a flat, defeated look. A developing bruise beneath the skin on her forehead had been evident. 'I wish I was. We're selling up. It's all decided. 'Cos of his heart attack.'

Pressing her hands to her mouth, Gloria had shaken her head. Visualising the Nigerian women from the church whose families back home were all dependent on their cleaning business for income. What would she tell them? How could she look any of them in the eye? And the girls in the flat . . . The illegals.

'We're responsible for over a hundred women, Sheila,' Gloria had said, folding her arms and feeling the Lord's righteous indignation puff a little wind back into her sails. 'I'm a respected figure in my community.' She poked herself in the chest with an honest, unpolished, work-worn finger.

'I know. Look, I said I was sorry. What can I do?' Sheila had held her hands up, as though this somehow absolved her of any guilt for dismantling Gloria's hopes and dreams – carefully built into something edifying and impressive over many years – in under twenty minutes.

'Can't you sell me my share of the business?' she had asked, mentally calculating how much she would get if she remortgaged her modest Chorlton semi and sold her beloved Mazda MX-5. 'We were just on the cusp of doing really well, Sheila. You know we were.'

'No.' Sheila had shaken her head. 'Paddy wants a clean break. I don't want any trouble following me to Thailand. It's not like selling a proper business. We run a bent cleaning agency, Gloria. I can't let you take the reins for something I set up. If it goes tits up and you get your collar felt, it will come back to me.'

In an ungodly way, Gloria had found herself balling her fist and wanting to make contact with Sheila's Botoxed forehead. *What would Jesus do, Gloria? The meek inherit the earth. Take a deep breath like the pastor advised. Be better than your animal impulses.* She had hidden her fist beneath the worktop. Had barely been able to get the words out, her mouth had been so tight. 'We've got girls in their teens from Benin City that we rescued from those heathens in Birmingham. Remember? They'd shaved off the poor mites' intimate hair and told them they'd cast spells so they'd die painful deaths if they didn't cavort with dirty old men. Those girls had been beaten and burnt and thrown out of moving cars. But we made them safe! We gave them jobs! How can you turn round now and tell them they've got to go back to the hell they were living before?'

'Look. I don't like this any more than you do.' Sheila had stood and trotted to the large Maytag fridge–freezer. Poured herself another vodka and dropped three ice cubes into the glass with a merry plink. Fizzing tonic making that kitchen sound like a cheerful place, with its super-modern chandeliers and its shining surfaces.

'Then, name me a price!' Gloria's fist had had a life of its own, thumping the granite worktop. She had gazed at it, alarmed at the pain that had ricocheted up her arm. Refocused on her business partner. 'I bet Paddy's selling his blasted enterprises. I bet he's not giving his life's work up, as though the O'Brien empire had never existed. Eh? Am I right?'

Sheila had blushed. Colour finally creeping into those pasty, duplicitous cheeks.

'Oh, so I *am* right. *He* gets to sell. But let me guess. He ordered you to just walk away from the lot, because anything we've done as women counts for nothing. Is that it? Have I hit the nail on the head?'

Sitting on that hard pew in the church next to old Winnie, Gloria remembered with dyspeptic discomfort how she had left the O'Briens' Bramshott mansion, feeling like a member of the domestic staff who had been summarily dismissed after being caught stealing the silverware. Exacerbated by the knowledge that she had, in fact, started out as Sheila's cleaner, all those years ago.

'Just a white woman's rubbing rag,' she muttered under her breath as the pastor was otherwise engaged in speaking in tongues. Mindful that the pride and wrath and envy she was currently entertaining would not be doing her any favours in her journey along the path to righteousness.

As the service ended, Gloria braced herself to pass the woeful news on to her employees. The Nigerian women, colourful in their traditional batik print wrapper dresses and head scarves, came towards her, smiling. Greeting her with warmth, clasping her hand and sharing embraces as though she had always been some revered elder in their inner circle. And there were the young girls from Benin City. Dressed in their modest best. Waving to their beloved Auntie Gloria. In a way, these were her children, whom she had led from the heart of darkness into the arms of a loving and forgiving Lord. Only right, then, that one day, she and the pastor should be together, instead of that ugly, fat wife of his, Kitty.

Gloria knew that her strong point was her faith. She had faith that Kitty, who smelled of three-day-old chicken and who looked like a side of beef in Primark knitwear, would one day be history. She had faith that she would be able to break the bad news to her employees and safely lay the blame at Sheila's pedicured, lazy, white-woman's feet.

'Sisters,' she said, ushering her flock towards the vestibule of the Good Life Baptist Church, making sure the pastor got a good look at her legs and her shining, relaxed hair beneath her best fascinator, bought in the John Lewis sale. 'Let's go for coffee. We need to talk.'

Being brave, like she had always been brave, winking surreptitiously at the pastor while Kitty Fried Chicken was shaking hands with an elder, Gloria led the group towards the harsh daylight streaming in through the ecclesiastical arched door. They piled out into the bustle of Parson's Croft high street, thronging with satisfied church-goers, shoppers on a mission for bargains and gaggles of over-excited Muslim girls wearing hijabs and pretty sequinned salwar kameez, squealing with laughter into each other's mobile phones.

At first, she did not notice the tall, dark figure standing outside Clyde's Caribbean Takeout. A figure, wearing a burnt orange padded gilet, a long-sleeved T-shirt and those jeans that they all wore with zips and too many pockets and silly logos. Trainers on his feet. No. There was no reason why she would have paid any attention whatsoever to this man, who looked like every other self-styled gangsta fool under the age of maybe thirty in Parson's Croft. On his head, he wore a branded baseball cap. Stylish, sporty sunglasses with mirrored lenses hid his eyes. But ambling along towards the café, surrounded by her beloved Nigerian sisters whom she would let down gently, it barely registered with her that this was a familiar man, overly dressed as though to conceal his identity. There was something about the line of his nose and the almost delicate point of his chin. His build. His body language. The way he stepped off the stoop of Clyde's with hands in pockets – hands that were empty of the delicious Caribbean offerings sold inside. The way he started to keep pace with her, though the wide pavement was four or five people deep. Kept shooting her glances from behind those creepy sunglasses. Now, Gloria had started to take note of this man, though he lurked in her peripheral vision.

She sped up. 'Come on, ladies. Cake beckons! My treat.'

Protected by the laughter and the sheer number of bodies that surrounded her; there must have been twenty of her cleaners, bustling along that road. Maybe it was a coincidence and she was just on edge.

But no. The man was still there. He took his hands out of his pockets. Extended a hand towards her. Opened his mouth to say something.

Gloria stopped short. Held her handbag to her chest defensively, ready to clobber the scumbag with it if needs be before he had a chance to snatch it.

'Get away from me!' she yelled.

Before her companions realised that an attack was afoot, the man pulled the sunglasses from his face to reveal soulless, sinner's eyes she would recognise anywhere. Her own eyes.

'It's me, Mum,' he said, reaching for her. Brushing her fingers with his.

She snatched her hand away as though it had been burned and took a step back. Trod heavily on somebody's foot, though she could not tear her gaze from her son's anguished face to see who she had injured and offer apology. She was filled with a mixture of dread and fear and that old, familiar poison – hope.

'Leviticus Bell. You treacherous, criminal toe-rag. What in the Lord's name do you want?'

Chapter 8

Paddy

'Don't open your mouth,' Paddy told Frank. 'Let me do all the talking.'

On the back seat of the XJ, in semi-darkness that was lit only by the street-lamps flashing by, Paddy saw his brother nod. Cock his head to the side, as if letting the simple words soak in.

'Alright, Pad. No worries, man.'

Paddy patted Frank's knee, though even that felt like over-exertion since the heart attack. Frustrated, he was still very much King of the Alphas in his head, but now, his body had finally betrayed him. Katrina had been right. He was pushing his luck. Age and a hard, fast lifestyle had finally caught up with him, and boy, was he feeling mortal now. Vulnerable too, since he had been sent home from the hospital with nothing more than some poxy meds and a flea in his ear regarding his abysmal diet. Left to his own devices, the care of the medical staff now felt too far beyond easy reach.

As Conky steered the gliding car from the opulent, leafy suburbs of Bramshott down the M56 towards Manchester, tension started to mount inside him, stiffening his limbs and the set of his jaw with ice. The pressure of the impending meet bore down on his shoulders; he felt he might simply disappear down the back of the leather seat.

'I haven't seen those bastards, Tariq and Jonny since 2005,' he said to the back of Conky's head. Met his gaze through the rear view mirror – a rare occurrence, since Conky only took those ridiculous Roy Orbison glasses off to drive, revealing his bulging eyes in all their frightening amphibian glory. The arsehole's hair-piece was showing through the comb-over. He resolved to say nothing. 'Do you remember?'

'Aye,' Conky said, slowing for a speed camera on Princess Parkway. 'There were a lot of sawn-off shotguns, pointing at a lot of hard men in that tower. Troubled times.'

Had he felt this vulnerable over a decade ago, standing in that half-built shell of the Hilton Hotel's tenth floor, with the wind and the rain biting into his younger man's skin? Calling a cease fire, after the turf war between the O'Briens and the Boddlington gang had escalated to the point where there were fresh bodies stacking up in the morgue every single day for more than a month. It had been madness, then. It was still madness now.

'Are you tooled up?' he asked Conky. He looked behind him through the rear window at the large black Mercedes four-wheel drive hugging their tail. It carried their small army of foot soldiers. 'Your lads packing?'

'You just leave all that to me, boss,' Conky said, leaning over and patting the closed glove compartment. 'I've taken care of everything. And Maureen's arbitrating. Sure it'll be fine.'

The Jag slowed at the lights. An eerie tangle of shadows that was Southern Cemetery on the left, reminding Paddy of where he could so easily end up if tonight went badly. He tried to visualise swaying palms on a Thai beach to slow his heartbeat but could only think of that little Boddlington shit with the lightning flash shaved into his head, lunging at him with the knife in M1 House. Wondered if the lad would be there tonight and if he might have the opportunity to exact revenge on him in some way; Paddy's forearm was not the only thing that had been punctured.

Moss Side flashed by in vapour trails of neon light and bong smoke. Parson's Croft beyond it. The streets would be filled with O'Brien girls and boys, he knew, doling candy out to the starving, unwashed masses. On the other side of the Mancunian Way, the Hilton Hotel's Beetham Tower, long-since finished, punctuated the Manchester night sky like an exclamation mark without a point. A brightly lit, uncompromising phallus, reminding Paddy that in this tough place, men ruled. Men like him. Once he had grown old enough to realise he could shed the rough skin of the dirt poor that had been the crappy legacy of that snake, his father, this fine, hard city, and all that lay south of the dividing line, had become his very own playground. He was Manchester's number one son. He knew all of her secrets. The thought calmed him.

'Am shitting myself, me,' Frank said, breaking the silence. 'And why are we meeting in a gallery of all places? I haven't been to one of them since we was at school.'

Wired, as usual. Paddy listened to three further minutes of Frank's musings on the lunacy of having the meet on neutral turf, rather than in his club, before slamming his hand over his brother's mouth.

'See, this is why you keep your gob shut when we get in there. Understand?'

Frank looked him in the eye. An appropriate amount of fear and respect, there. He nodded. Fell silent once more as Conky navigated the bright lights and double parking of Chinatown, pulling up at the back of Manchester City Art Gallery.

Inside, Maureen Kaplan stood at the top of the grand, stone staircase with her arms outstretched. She was wearing a sharp navy trouser suit, though now that she had piled on a good couple of stone in her middle years and her hair was short and expensively dyed blonde instead of those gorgeous, brassy blue-black curls she'd once sported, Paddy wondered that he had ever fucked her with such enthusiasm.

'Patrick,' she said, smiling the lethal, self-assured smile of a woman who held sensitive information about every crook in town. 'Punctual as ever.'

'Maureen. My favourite number cruncher. Rachel Riley's got nowt on you, cocker.' He winked.

'Schmoozer! Come on up.'

Flanked by Frank to his left and Conky to his right, with five of Conky's bravest taking up the rear, Paddy climbed the stairs slower than he would have liked. Tried to conceal the fact that, only half way up, he was practically asphyxiating with the effort. Praying that his dicky ticker wouldn't burst. *One step at a time. Appear statesmanlike. Don't show weakness or grimace.* He pretended to admire the pre-Raphaelite masters on the walls and the chandelier above him, though in fact, he was praying to Jesus, Mary, Joseph and whoever else would listen that he wouldn't cark it there and then.

Blithely unaware of his brother's suffering, Frank trotted ahead, treating Maureen to a smackeroo on the cheek and offering her the too-warm embrace of a man who had spent his youth eating mainly E. Only Conky stood by Paddy, discreetly taking him by the elbow. Nodding at the artwork and playing along with this façade that his King was merely moving at a leisurely pace through his own choosing.

'Where are they?' he asked Maureen, finally reaching the summit. Even more lined around her eyes than she had been last time they had met.

'In there.'

Allowing Conky to frisk her, she gesticulated towards the large gallery up more stairs, to her right. She wore the flowery scent of a girl but gave off pure essence of fully grown praying mantis.

'Jesus. Couldn't you have got a venue with a sodding lift?' Paddy whispered in her ear.

'I always did like to hear you pant,' Maureen said, winking.

The gallery was stately in its proportions, lit fully as though the place was still open to the public and this wasn't 10pm at night. Giant, priceless oil paintings hung on the wall, reminding Paddy that the O'Brien empire was but a small footnote in local history compared to Manchester's stake in a grand Victorian past. The parquet floor shone. The air was scented with beeswax polish. It could have been an evening to enjoy, had it been a private viewing or a charity function. But it wasn't. And there were his nemeses at the far end of the space. All turning towards him, now. Jonny Margulies. A bald wide-boy, wearing a pink shirt that accentuated his pregnant paunch over pin-striped suit trousers. Grinning hungrily, with arms folded. He looked like he had spent the day prosecuting criminals in court, as opposed to trafficking drugs and people through north Manchester from every major hub in the world. And there was Tariq Khan. All boyish-looking, despite his forty-odd years. Silver-grey streaked through his thick thatch of otherwise black hair. Decked out in designer versions of the young man's clothing that his underlings wore, as though his supremacy within the Boddlington organisation was beyond question or doubt. Sitting on the edge of a display cabinet, giving the impression that this was his living room and Paddy was just a visitor. But there, lurking at the back, was that little dick who had stabbed him. The one with the lightning flash.

Paddy grimaced at him. Drove himself forward, stifling the urge to seize a painting from the wall and smash it down onto the lad's delinquent, disrespectful head.

Maureen abandoned the safety of her sons – Zac, Steven and Louis – and her son-in-law, David Goodman to quickly seize control of the posturing men.

'Boys! Boys. Welcome.' She beckoned them to her, encouraging them to close the gap until they were within killing distance. Turning to Paddy, she smiled confidently. 'Paddy here has requested this meet, as you all know.' She turned to the Boddlingtons. 'Tariq and Jonny have agreed to parlay.'

Paddy watched with admiration as Maureen faced down the various muscle on the warring sides: Asaf Smolensky, standing like a faux-Hassidic approximation of Death in his long, black coat. Holding a shining machete in his right hand as a warning, though this was Friday night, and Paddy was sure religious Jews weren't supposed to be hanging around like long streaks of threatening piss in galleries on a Friday night. Damned fraudster. And there, like a distorted reflection, was his very own Conky McFadden, holding a sawn-off shotgun which he'd had concealed about his person until now. Equally as demented-looking, Paddy mused, with that Just For Men clip-on quiff of his and the specs. What was it with muscle?

'Now, I don't need to tell you, do I,' Maureen said. '. . . That there'll be no bullshit while I'm arbitrating. No violence. No heated words. No sudden moves.' She seemed taller than every man in that room. She too had her support in her sons and son-in-law, suited and booted on the sidelines. Everyone in the room knew they had something far more deadly than knives or guns at their disposal. They had receipts and invoices for nefarious dealings that would never be declared on a VAT or tax return. Cold, hard evidence. Enough to put everyone in the room away at Her Majesty's leisure indefinitely.

'Don't worry, Mo,' Jonny said, unfolding his arms and clasping them before him like an overweight choirboy. 'We're on our best behaviour. Promise. Aren't we Tariq?'

Tariq nodded. Looked deferentially down at his stupid sneakers when Maureen scanned his face for bullshit. Smolensky and Conky stared straight ahead like robots who had had their batteries temporarily removed. The lesser players hung back out of earshot at Maureen's behest.

'Right, lads. Paddy and Frank are here to sell. Jonny and Tariq are here to buy.' She turned to Paddy. 'The floor's yours.'

Taking a deep breath, Paddy ran through the speech he had prepared in his head at double-speed. It came out somewhat disappointingly as, 'Ten million in cash for the south side. All drugs, all girls, all gambling, all imports and exports. All subsidiary enterprises. The whole south side. Ten mill.'

'Apart from my club, like,' Frank blurted. Beaming winningly. Sticking his hands in the pockets of his tracksuit, as though he were willing himself not to go disco, despite the sobriety of the situation. 'That's not for sale, man. Soz.'

'Why would you think we'd pay you all that money when we've got successful business interests of our own?' Tariq asked.

'Not that it's not a very interesting offer,' Jonny clarified, cocking his head as though he were listening intently for what came next.

Paddy could see they were playing good cop, bad cop or some such nonsense. He had no time for it. 'I want to retire. I don't want my business going to some cocky dipshit from London or those Scouse twats. I've worked my arse off for what I've got. Like yous.'

'Listen,' Tariq said, running his hand through that hair. Stroking his short, chinstrap beard. 'We've been at war for how long? Fifteen years? More? Why should we trust you?' Perched on the edge of the display cabinet, he crossed and uncrossed his legs nonchalantly. A slight whiff of whatever shit he spoke at home coming through in his otherwise pure Oxford-educated accent. Certainly no trace of the Lower Boddlington origins in him. 'I mean, why would we want to do business with a man who's put thirty-two of our men in the ground since we took control of the north side?'

'We respect you as our competition, Paddy,' Jonny said, placing a conspiratorial hand on Tariq's shoulder. 'But we've got obligations to service the business we've already got. We've got HMRC breathing down our necks, as I'm sure you have. We've got that donkey from CID, Ellis James, on our case constantly. Ten million quid for twice the aggro maybe isn't worth our while.'

Paddy could feel haggling on the horizon and he wasn't in the mood to negotiate.

'I don't give a stuff about the tax man or the coppers,' he said. 'That comes with the territory. Men like us have to be ready for anything. And as for the bodies . . . well, it takes two to tango, boys, and I seem to recall you were dancing on *my* soldiers' graves and all.'

61

Jonny shook his head. '*Two* million in cash. The cost of retraining your people to operate like ours will be massive. Crippling. The cost of the added risk—'

'*Ten* mill.' Paddy felt queasy. Blood draining away from his stomach to his brain. *Stand your ground, Pad.*

Suddenly, a voice behind him shattered the illusion that they were somehow speaking intimately in a sound-proof room.

Degsy: 'He's taking the piss, Pad. I'll put a bullet in him if you want.'

Paddy swung around and grabbed Conky's gun hand. Pistol-whipped Degsy so hard and so unexpectedly that he fell backwards into a painting of a big red-head with nice white tits and frizzy long hair. Degsy's blood spattered onto the woman's painted green dress. Paddy placed his foot on the dealer's scrawny neck.

'You speak when I say you can speak. Dickhead.'

Wiping his bloody nose with the sleeve of his hoody, Degsy didn't dare answer. He merely looked up at Paddy with fearful, resentful eyes. Nodded.

'Ten million pounds,' Paddy said, rounding on Tariq and Jonny once again. 'This isn't a fucking medina, boys. This isn't the mosque or some two-bit Jew diamond dealer's. This is half of Manchester. I'm selling to you. Or I'm selling to out-of-towners. But the price is still ten million nicker, whoever the hell you are and whatever overheads you think you've got. No more murders. No more turf wars. A going concern that will more than double the riches in your wildest dreams.'

He stepped towards Jonny Margulies. Invading his space. Gut to gut. Poking him in that fleshy overhang so that Smolensky raised his machete.

'Take it or leave it, Jonny. But if you leave it . . .'

Behind him, Conky put two cartridges into the shotgun.

'. . . you might find yourself leaving this life for the next one sooner than you think.'

Guns pulled from every holster and breast pocket in the room. The gallery's still air was a-whirr with the metallic sound of safeties coming off.

Paddy held his breath.

Closed his eyes.

Waited for what came next.

Chapter 9

Sheila

Sinking beneath the deep layer of foam and the silken surface of the water, Sheila mused on how comforting it was to shut the world out. Holding her breath. Counting, counting, until all she could feel was the crushing sensation in her chest and the beat of her pulse, thumping in her ears. Reminding her that she was yet living, though she felt dead inside.

The girls were grown and gone.

The flower of her youth had withered.

She was Paddy's Queen, imprisoned in a tower of her own design, awaiting execution or a slow death. Not even Thailand would change that.

Pushing against the tall sides of the freestanding bath, she surfaced, gasping for air. Racking sobs suddenly pushing their way out of her body like skeletons tumbling from a closet she had been keeping under lock and key for decades.

'Why?' she shouted to the TV screen set into the unforgiving stacked-stone slate wall. It showed some plastic fantastic American actress, jabbering at her fat friend, occasioning unearned canned laughter at the end of every sentence. The TV was as good a confessor as any. 'How has it come to this?' She splashed her hands down violently into the foamy water, sending it scudding around her naked body. 'Washed up just as I was about to ride the crest of my own wave. All 'cos of Paddy. That domineering, bad-breathed, dicky-tickered wanker, with his shitty flaky scalp and his skidmarks in his undies and his hairy back and his psycho bullying bullshit and his bitch mistresses with their fake tits.' Years of solemn therapy sessions at the Priory, in which she had talked around the problem to a sympathetic man in a Spartan room, were now proved redundant. For her ears only, in that empty bathroom, the truth she had been holding inside about the root of all her unhappiness was finally outside. 'Paddy, you bastard! I hate you. I fucking hate you.' She slammed her palms down onto her knees with a splash. 'But I love you and I'm scared and I don't know how to be alone. Please don't let him die tonight, God.'

Visualising her husband, standing in the gallery, clinching the deal of a lifetime with the Boddlington bosses . . . Perhaps the Boddlingtons would bring a suitcase full of cash like you saw on the films. She didn't know how deals that size worked – her cleaning deals were all dodgy invoices and almost bona fide transactions to slightly shady offshore accounts or cash, no questions asked. But she knew that if the sell-out went ahead, they would be rich enough never to have to think about money again. Off to Thailand, flying first class. Trapped forever, hidden away from what few friends and family Paddy allowed her to have.

And what if the deal failed and he was killed tonight? What then? Patrick O'Brien was all she had known from being a girl, becoming her father figure long before her own father had disowned her. She visualised his gravestone.

Here lies Patrick O'Brien, survived by his ungrateful wife and doting daughters.

Freedom at last.

She shook the thought away. What a prize cow she was!

Sobbing in the bath until the bubbles had all burst, her fingertips and toes had become wrinkled and the water had grown cold. Shivering. Teeth-clacking. She turned on the hot tap, shoving her purple toes under the gushing warm water, wondering how it was she could feel so many conflicting emotions at once.

'I've made my bed,' she finally told the television, feeling guilt start to pull her under again. The water level was rising fast . . . 'Loyalty keeps this family together. I need to keep us together.'

She slid down the bath until even her buoyant breasts were covered. Her hair swished around her like weed on the bottom of a pond. Water seeped up to her chin and into her ears. Over her nose. Under. Contemplating if she should stay there forever, choosing a watery way out of this life and these wifely obligations.

But then, in amongst the thunder of the hot water, now so dangerously near the rim of the bath, she heard another insistent sound. A chime from far away. Was she drowning? Was this destiny calling from the other side?

The bell.

She emerged abruptly from the bath, spilling water all over the floor. The chime was insistent – somebody was at the gates, pressing and pressing on that button. Who the hell was it at this time of night?

Conky had a fob for the gates. Paddy had a key for the door. They weren't due back until 11pm at the earliest, unless it had all gone very badly wrong, of course . . .

Ignoring the mess, she skidded across the bathroom,

grabbing her robe from the heated towel rail. Hastened down the oak staircase, stepping gingerly with wet feet on the bare, polished treads. The intercom and CCTV screen were close to the front door in the glazed, double-height vestibule. She was vulnerable here, at night with the chandeliers blazing. Anyone lurking in the dark out there would be able to see her. Her heart was pounding, all thoughts of a watery end gone now. Visualising instead where Paddy had the shotguns and live ammo stashed, in case the Boddlington gang had turned up thinking they could claim O'Brien Towers as spoils of war.

A woman was on the screen. Or was it a girl? A small figure with a pinched, frightened-looking face. Difficult to see as the night-time footage wasn't helped by being black and white. She looked familiar to Sheila. Was this a trap? Was she a dealer, pushed up to the camera by some gun-toting monster because she looked less threatening at a glance?

Chiming, chiming – the visitor was insistent. Sheila could have just walked away. Turned off the lights and retreated to the bedroom. But her battered conscience said she should answer this girl's plea.

'What do you want?' she barked down the intercom.

'Mrs Sheila, it's Efe!' The girl had a heavy Nigerian accent. 'I work for you. Please. I need to speak to you.'

Sheila scrutinised the girl's face, mentally running through the staff records that Gloria had meticulously put together. Comparing the haunted girl on the CCTV screen to the photographs stapled to fact sheets. Click. She found a match with one of those trafficked girls from Benin City. She wasn't lying. Exhaling heavily, she was only now aware she had been holding her breath.

'What do you want, Efe?' Sheila asked. 'It's late. I was going to bed.'

'Can I come in?'

'No. Call Gloria in the morning if you've got a problem.'

'Please! You must hear what I have to say.'

'You shouldn't have come here. Hasn't Gloria told you we're closing the business?'

The girl started to weep, clinging to the gatepost for support.

Against her better judgement, Sheila buzzed her in.

'You cannot let us go, Mrs Sheila,' Efe said, hiccoughing. She dabbed at her puffy wet cheeks with some kitchen roll that Sheila gave to her. Sipping at a glass of milk. Doleful eyes not even taking in her surrounds. Just focusing on Sheila, then her work-worn hands. On Sheila, then the hands. 'There are five of us living in that flat Gloria found. We are so grateful for you getting us away from those bad men in Birmingham. You saved us. You are both like aunties to us.'

Sheila poured herself a vodka and orange. She sighed heavily. 'I didn't save you. I'm no angel, Efe, and I'm not your auntie. It's business. You're just numbers on a spreadsheet, love.'

'Mrs Sheila! If we don't work for you, what will we do? We don't want to go home. We can't get benefits.'

'Look, it's not my problem, is it? You're a free woman, now. Apply for a visa,' Sheila said, swigging the drink rather more quickly than she should. Wet hair, dripping down the back of her robe, as she willed herself not to pity this shabby, tired-looking girl in a duffle coat and old-fashioned jeans who couldn't have been more than seventeen.

Efe's mouth turned down at the corners. She tugged at her hair, styled in a loose Afro, and pulled it off in one piece – a wig, much to Sheila's surprise. Pointed to a patch of unsightly scarring on her scalp where the hair no longer grew.

'You see this? This is where one of those bad men threw petrol at me and set fire to me. Then, he pushed me out of a car because I didn't want to go with the disgusting pigs he brought to the house where we were being held prisoner.'

Sheila winced, trying to picture the scene. Felt the long shadow of guilt dim the brightly lit kitchen and fall across her. 'What's that got to do with my cleaning company?'

'I need that job. I need my flat. I don't want to have to work for bad men again, giving my body to strangers just so I can eat.'

'Go back to Nigeria.' Sheila examined her nails, unable to look the girl in the eye. Wishing she'd put the wig back on.

'I can't! I can never go home. I'm ashamed. We all are. We'd be untouchable back home after the things we've done. We want to stay here. We want to be safe, working for you. Gloria is like family to us.'

'Then I suggest you give her earache instead. Not me.' She drained her glass and stood, making it clear that it was time the girl left.

'But she is your friend.'

'Gloria is a business associate. Nothing more. And that business is finished. Numbers on a spreadsheet, Efe. I'm sorry.'

Efe pulled her wig on forcefully, glaring at Sheila. Pushing the milk away, undrunk. She wiped her eyes with a balled fist, her defiance not quite concealing the deep, deep hurt. 'Then you must not have a beating heart inside your body, Mrs Sheila.'

She stood and snatched up her cheap plastic handbag.

Fastened the toggles on her threadbare duffle coat. 'I will pray for you. You are a woman who only sees other human beings as commodities. That is no way to live and certainly isn't the will of God. I feel sorry for you.'

Guilt, anger, embarrassment reacted together inside Sheila. An explosion was inevitable. 'Get out of my house!' she yelled, hurling the glass from her vodka and orange against the wall. It smashed, scattering gleaming fragments of crystal over the kitchen floor.

By the time Sheila had located the dustpan and brush in the utility room, Efe was long gone, having slammed the front door with enough force to make the glass in the vestibule reverberate. The confrontation left Sheila only with the feeling that she was nothing more than a gangster's moll. No, worse than that. She was a materialistic, unfeeling lump of shit with no true friends, a family that kept its distance either through embarrassment or fear, no sense of community, no conscience. She was nothing. In fact, she was less than Efe. Efe, once a slave and a whore and a prisoner, was now none of those things. She was free. Whereas Sheila was all of those things but with a better manicure and more expensive clothes.

Rhythmic crunching of gravel on the driveway snapped her out of her reverie. The thrum of an engine. She was not alone.

Chapter 10

Lev

Loose stones kicked up against the discreet, anonymous-looking people carrier. It bounced along the potholed road, past the girls on the street corners, who ducked and dipped like erotic waterfowl to make eye contact with the driver every time they saw a car slow down. Thigh-length boots and miniskirts. Cut-off tops, whatever the weather and whatever time of night it may be. Preening to attract a fast mate who would pay hard cash.

'Look at these poor cows,' Tariq said, gunning the vehicle towards T&J Trading. 'Risking life and limb to make the rent. Not like our girls.'

'Our girls don't make bloody rent,' Jonny said. 'They pay off my colossal mortgage and fund Gorgeous Sandra's Botox habit, thank you very much!' Guffaws of laughter and elbows in the ribs. Obviously on top form after what had taken place at the gallery. 'What would they do without Uncle Jonny and Auntie Tariq, keeping them off the streets?' More laughter.

'Cheeky sod.' Tariq playfully punched his business partner. 'Last time I looked, you were the one with well-trimmed testicles, my friend. Snip, snip.' Miming Gorgeous Sandra, no doubt.

But Lev was only partly paying attention to the banter. He sat on the back seat, uncomfortably sandwiched between Asaf Smolensky and a giant of a man called Nasim he had never met before until that evening – apparently Asaf's apprentice and a second cousin of Tariq.

He felt his pulse. It was still racing after that loon Paddy O'Brien had lunged for him, trying to squeeze the breath out of him as some sort of retribution for M1 House. The arsehole had fingers of steel. How any of them had walked out with their lives intact with all of those guns and knives drawn was nothing short of a miracle. No, he mused. Actually, it wasn't a miracle. It was down to that accountant woman. She was the scariest bastard he had ever met. Holding a briefcase that some loser in a suit had handed to her. Reminding them that it contained damning documents and that if they didn't put their dicks away and stop the pissing competition immediately, she would have her man, who knew a man, place a few strategic phone calls to a few strategic people in Greater Manchester Police and HMRC. That had shut the lot of them up.

Now, Lev was trying to work out how to tap up his bosses for £150K, while they were still feeling triumphant as the new Kings of the Wild Frontier. Their coronation was all but certain, as soon as this down payment was made. Provisional supremacy to the tune of a mill in cash. Maureen Kaplan had decreed it, witnessed by her sons, Dopey, Grumpy, Bashful and her son-in-law, Doc, so it had to be so. The King would be dead. Long live the Kings.

Nearing safety, they passed the hulking silhouette of Strangeways tower to their left.

'Am I going mental with post-traumatic whatsit, or did I just clock that little schmuck, Ellis James, in a Mondeo?'

Jonny asked, craning his head to see the bonnet of the black saloon that was now just out of sight.

'The cop? Where?' Asaf asked.

'Parked on the corner.'

'Maybe he's cruising for a lady of the night,' Tariq said, steering the people carrier into the loading bay and pulling up in front of the metal shutters. He applied the handbrake. 'A gnome with a face like a smacked arse like him would have to pay for it.'

'It'd better bloody not be Ellis,' Jonny said, suddenly seeming decidedly less cocksure. 'Not tonight. Not with what we've got to do.' He turned to Tommo, who normally manned one of the brothels, and Tariq's second cousin, Nasim. 'You both stay here. Keep an eye out for that snooping bastard. Call me if he gets out of his car.' Turned to the rest of them, wearing an expression that said he had more than just Gorgeous Sandra snipping away at his balls. 'Come on. Let's get inside.'

Lev followed the others into the factory, trailing behind the tall figure of Asaf. With the machinery off and only one or two lights on, the space seemed eerie – not a place he was yet wholly familiar with as a lowly Sweeney Hall street dealer. He tried to block the mental image that flickered in his mind's eye like an epilepsy-inducing strobe: his former colleague, Suspicious Sid, lying dead at the top of a multi-storey car park in Bury. Filleted like a side of salmon, complete with cucumber laid like scales over his flank in the way that only Asaf Smolensky, the infamous Fish Man, left his kills. Had Suspicious Sid's count not been short several times of late, Lev would never have been promoted to a rank he wasn't entirely comfortable with.

'Tariq,' he said, patting his boss on the shoulder blade.

Tariq swung around and treated him to a smile and a wink. 'How's the neck, son? Gave Pissy Pants Paddy a run for his money, didn't you? You'll go far.' Normally a controlled man who seemed to consider every word before he spoke it, tonight, Tariq's exuberance was almost tangible.

Maybe now was the time to get him onside. 'Can I ask—?'

'Not now. We've got to get this cash out and over to Conky McFadden by midnight.' He took the pistol out of the inside pocket of his reefer jacket and shoved it into the waistband of his jeans. Took his jacket off. 'You and Asaf wait here. Some things only me and Jonny can do. Know what I mean?' Wink.

The bosses disappeared off upstairs, presumably to where the offices were situated. Lev was left alone with the Fish Man – a situation he was far from happy with. What on earth should someone like him say to someone like Asaf Smolensky? Should he talk to him about Jay? Did Smolensky have a family? Lev couldn't see it somehow. No wedding ring. No warmth. Very little in the way of any discernible humanity. He doubted the stresses of being a provider and fatherhood in general were the Fish Man's chosen topics of small-talk.

Asaf took a sandwich out of the pocket of his coat. Started to eat hungrily. It smelled meaty. Lev's stomach growled. Since the business with Jay and the money and confronting his lost cause of a mother, he hadn't really been eating.

'What you got there?' he asked, gazing wistfully at the snack.

'Ham.' Asaf wiped butter from his beard. Chewed noisily.

'But you're an Orthodox Jew.'

'I'm Israeli,' he said, spitting as he spoke. 'Ex-Mossad. Know what that is?'

Lev shook his head, still staring at the doorstep of a sandwich.

'The hardest military men in the world. Like the US Marines but with bigger bollocks. I'm a highly trained operative. Don't be fooled by the hat and the peyes.' He flicked his ringletted sidelocks. 'This Hassidic bullshit is just a cover. I'm hiding in plain sight. Nobody suspects a part-time fishmonger to be an executioner.'

Suddenly, Lev didn't find the sandwich appetising in the slightest. He kept visualising Suspicious Sid, with his insides leaking all over the concrete floor in that car park. He hadn't seen the body personally, but he'd heard tell how gruesome the scene had been from a few of the lads dealing over in Bury and Radcliffe. How the hell had he ended up rubbing shoulders with the likes of a psychotic murderer on a daily basis? Somehow he doubted Smolensky sat as he did during a rare evening off, wondering how he could get the hell out of this life of class A crime with its high stakes of category A prison or violent death.

'I'm a damned good fishmonger though.' Asaf raised an eyebrow, chewing away contemplatively.

When Tariq and Jonny started to bring boxes downstairs, Lev was relieved. There weren't as many as he had anticipated.

'Is that it?' he asked, wishing he could pocket some of those plastic money bags full of twenties.

Jonny gesticulated towards Tariq's box. 'There's a money counter in there. Get it out and start stacking the twenties.'

'Where was all this?' Lev asked, tugging the cash out of the stubborn plastic envelopes.

'Mind your own business, son,' Tariq said.

Sweat beaded on Lev's forehead as he fed sheaf after sheaf of notes into the machine. The cloying, greasy smell of cash in his nostrils. The sense that he was being tested and that every pair of eyes in the room were on him. He felt dizzy. Overwhelmed. The words were on the tip of his tongue – *Can I have a loan of £150,000 for my dying son, please?* – but he knew this was neither the right time nor the place to ask. Especially with the Fish Man breathing down his neck.

Finally, Asaf belched. 'I'm going for a slash,' he said, tipping his homburg hat back like a confused cowboy.

With the others on sentry duty in the loading bay, there were just Lev, Jonny and Tariq left. Now was his moment.

'I know this is a bad time to ask, right,' Lev began. 'But I've got this personal . . . issue. I hope you don't mind me bringing it up, like.'

Tariq looked quizzically at him. Jonny did not tear his gaze from the whirr of the money in the machine.

'Go on,' Tariq said. 'Spit it out.'

Relief of sorts flooded him with warmth. Lev opened his mouth, poised to issue forth about all that had gone on with his boy; outlining how British surgeons couldn't operate; delivering a heart-rending appeal for a sum of money that was surely a piss in the ocean for men like Tariq and Jonny.

'Well, you see, it's proper bullshit, right? My son's been diagnosed with this—'

A deafening clang, followed by multiple footsteps, stemmed the confessional tide. Damn it! It was Tweedle Dumb and Tweedle Dumber from the loading bay. Panting. Clearly agitated.

'It's the copper!' Nasim half shouted, half whispered.

'You sure?' Asaf asked.

'Dumpy white bloke with glasses and a buzz cut?'

'That's him,' Tariq said. His Adam's apple was pinging in his throat like a bagatelle ball.

'Well, he's in the loading bay, shining a torch in the car.'

Jonny's eyebrows knitted together. He flashed a desperate look at Tariq, who was suddenly glassy-eyed and silent. Stalked prey in the night-time.

'Get the money out of here!' Tariq finally said, tearing a black bin liner from a fresh roll and opening it up. He started to pile the cash into the sack. Motioned that Lev should follow suit. 'Quickly.'

Knocking on the shutters sounded impossibly loud inside the empty factory. Insistent rapping with knuckles that denoted the impatience of a confident man. Possibly with a warrant.

'What we gonna do?' Lev asked, sweeping uncounted twenties and fifties into the bin liner, seeing Jay's operation and life disappearing along with the money.

Jonny snatched the bulging sack from him. Stuffed another pile into a Home Bargains carrier bag until only the counting machine remained.

'We'll have to let him in. What choice do we have?' He thrust the money into Asaf's arms. 'Take the gelt up to the ladies on the second floor. Lock yourself in a cubicle. Don't come out until I say. Okay?'

'Act natural,' Tariq told Lev. 'We were just stopping by to check everything was okay because I had a call from someone, saying the alarm had gone off. Right?'

For a man of sub-ordinary stature, Ellis James walked with a degree of swagger. He reminded Lev of a psychopathic PE teacher who had given him a hard time at school. Had the manic look of a man who was on the hunt for something that was always just out of reach.

'Evening, gents,' Ellis said. Hands thrust into his raincoat pockets.

'Detective,' Jonny said, sitting legs akimbo on a worker's high stool. Arms folded. Owning the place, as was his right. All of the jubilation after the gallery meet had gone now. His tone was prickly, almost combative, though a wry smile remained on his face along with a sheen of sweat. 'Funny time to come shopping for fancy goods. Can I interest you in a nice handbag for the wife? Bit of jewellery, perhaps?'

Ellis James approached Lev and stood closer than he was comfortable with. The copper only reached collarbone height on him. But Lev could smell his breath. Sickly sweet, with a lingering hint of farts, as though he had been eating doughnuts and drinking coffee in the Mondeo. The classic stereotype of a cop on a stakeout. Lev took a step backwards.

'Leviticus Bell,' he said, staring up at the zig-zag bolt of lightning shaved into Lev's scalp. 'I've had you in my station. I remember your mugshot.'

Play it cool, Lev. Don't get on his wrong side. Think of Jay. If you get your collar felt by this tosser, you're gonna be sod all use to your son. Defiant words were desperately trying to push their way out, but he held it together.

'I think you must be getting me mixed up from some-where else, mate. I sometimes do charity work for me mam's church.'

The cop turned to the bosses, finally, thankfully.

'Bit late for a lads' get-together, isn't it?'

'You got a warrant?' Tariq asked.

'I don't need a warrant to make friendly enquiries.' There was no mirth in the detective's smile. 'A friend of mine – Ruth Darley from HMRC – says she found some interesting paperwork in here the other day. Showing some transac-tions between T&J Trading and a couple of Chinese shell companies. Seems you've been importing fresh air from ghosts. What would you say that sounds like?'

Tariq rounded on the uninvited guest, toying with the cuffs of his shirt. 'This is a legitimate business, Detective James. Right? And my associates here and I came out to check on the premises because the alarm apparently was going off. If we've been swizzed by some dodgy company in China, that's not our problem. We export and import goods from all over the world. Sometimes we get lumbered with a dodgy business contact. It happens.'

Jonny finally abandoned his stool. Pulled the belt of his trousers up. Positioned himself next to Tariq, standing shoulder to shoulder. Presenting a united front that made Lev wish for the solidarity and support of a reliable friend, relative, woman . . . anybody at all!

'I don't see what our accounts have got to do with you, detective.' For a man with a high-pitched voice who normally came across as affable, Jonny sounded like the dangerous gangster he was. 'And I don't see the point in you being here at nearly midnight unless you've got a legitimate reason to be here and a warrant. Now, we've got homes to go to and we've got to be up very early in the morning. And I think you'll find, if you check our company's records, that we pay enough tax to keep you and all your little harassing friends back at the station in your jobs.'

'Where's Smolensky?' the detective asked. Beady eyes through the lenses of those glasses had clearly clocked all of them on their approach in the people carrier.

'Don't know what you're talking about,' Jonny said.

'Asaf Smolensky. The lunatic fishmonger. Where is he?' Ellis James took those steel-rimmed glasses from his nose and started to polish them on the edge of his coat, as though he had time to kill.

'I don't know Asaf Smolensky personally, detective, but my wife tells me he gives excellent weight and his smoked salmon's the best in Cheetham Hill. You fancy some herring or a nice piece of hake, detective, I suggest you go to see Mr Smolensky yourself at his splendid fishmonger's on Monday. Because it's Friday night right now, and I'm sure even an ignoramus like you knows that religious Jewish people are tucked up at home on the Sabbath. So, as for him being here . . .' Jonny cast an arm around the empty, dimly lit factory. 'I really don't know what the hell you're talking about, I'm afraid.' Glanced at his watch. 'Now, if you don't mind, my associate here will show you to the door.'

'Well, wish Mr Smolensky a happy Sabbath from me, won't you?' Ellis said with a maniacal smile that barely belied the pure acid in his voice. 'I'll see you again very soon, boys. Very soon.'

Nasim ushered the persistent interrogator out. Finally.

'Shit,' Tariq said, tapping at the face of his watch. 'We've got to get this cash down payment across town to McFadden in fifteen minutes or the O'Brien deal's off.'

Chapter 11

Conky

'Have a drink, Conks,' Frank shouted over the thud, thud, thud of the garage music. Thrusting a bottle of Cristal in his general direction, so that the foaming liquid sploshed onto his suit trousers.

Conky pushed the bottle away. Stood abruptly, sick of being penned into that damned VIP area, surrounded by a wall of gyrating young girls dressed like cheap strippers, though the club had only just started to fill up in earnest. Early birds, catching the worm. All of them, on the lookout for a man with a fat wallet, a small dick and lack of moral fibre. He hated it. This was nothing more than a prison made from fat silken rope instead of bars.

'No. Thanks all the same.'

Frank looked momentarily crestfallen. 'But we're celebrating.'

'The boss is celebrating,' Conky said, looking over at Paddy, who was in the process of pouring champagne onto the cleavage of a blonde girl, sitting on his lap. Licking it off, as though that was merely hors d'oeuvres for the main course, which would inevitably be enjoyed in the back room of the club later. Poor bloody Sheila. 'I don't see why you're so happy, Francis.'

But Frank wasn't listening. He shrugged. Smiled. Swigged from the bottle himself and started to dance along to the deafening music as though he hadn't a care in the world. A harmless prick, but a prick nonetheless.

Checking his watch, Conky assessed with some relief that it was time to escape the childish, hedonistic bullshit of M1 House. He didn't bother excusing himself. Paddy would not thank him for the interruption.

Pushing his way through the phalanx of sweaty bodies, careful to avoid having his hair arrangement knocked by the dancing, prancing kids' flailing arms, he wondered how life would be once he was no longer in the employ of the O'Briens. Frank had offered to keep him on, but he sure as hell had no intention of working for that gurning buffoon.

Outside, the air was fresh and smelled only a little of diesel from the passing buses and taxis. The night reverberated with the beat of the music, as though the club contained within it a giant throbbing heart, trying to burst its confines. Conky lit a cigarette and exhaled heavily.

'Three months,' he told the pink haze of the city's sky. 'After twenty long years.'

In three months Paddy would be up, up and away, Thailand-bound – Sheila on his arm, which would be more than enough for any man under normal circumstances – hell, he'd be happy to spend his life in Glasgow's Gorbals or Runcorn if Sheila was his – and without a care in the world. Until then, Conky had agreed to work out his notice for severance pay that was more than generous. No doubt he would be paid his six-figure sum out of the first mill he was about to take receipt of from those arseholes, Jonny

Margulies and Tariq Khan. Conky McFadden – an independently wealthy man. What a thought! He would somehow launder it to pay off his mortgage, raised ten years ago on a lacklustre end terrace in Didsbury, using fake payslips from O'Brien Construction Ltd.

Paddy was a generous benefactor. Too generous. And that was the problem.

On the drive to meet the Boddlington bosses, Conky took a detour, slowing the Jag as he traversed the city's invisible borders into Parson's Croft. Peering down street after anonymous street of Victorian terraced housing, where Degsy and his girls dealt drugs. From here to the outskirts of Wythenshawe, every shitty pub operated as a hub where locals would go to receive Maundy Money even on a Thursday from their monarch. Those were places where disputes were solved, work was asked for, respects and dues were paid. The shopkeepers whom Conky collected protection money from paid up on time. The disloyal and disobedient were punished by him at Paddy's behest. There was a pecking order. There was structure and routine. People liked that sort of thing.

'This place is going to be bedlam,' he said aloud over the top of the Dvořák cello concerto that resounded from the car's stereo. Sped up, not stopping until he pulled into the builders' yard.

Checking his watch, he saw that it was already gone midnight. Where the hell were the Boddlingtons? Under normal circumstances, being late to an O'Brien meet at the yard attracted a physical penalty. Usually trapping the miscreants' hands in the jamb of the door. He was good at releasing the pressure before the fingers actually broke. A skill he would soon have no need of.

In the kitchenette at the back of the neat little office, he made himself a cup of redbush tea, using bags that he carried with him everywhere. Sat out front in the shop with the fluorescent lights blazing. Surrounded by builders' merchandise. Tape measures. Brickies' protective gloves. Overalls for asbestos workers. A broad-shouldered manne-quin wearing very useful cargo trousers with in-built knee pads and an excellent quality tool belt. Conky eyed the utilitarian garb, thinking how, if he had chosen another path, he too, like so many of his brethren from across the Irish Sea, would be spending his back-breaking pre-retire-ment days on wet English building sites, toiling over fine brickwork or perhaps taking pride in a handsome slate roof. He might have a wife and children. Live in an over-de-veloped bungalow in Saddleworth. Drive a white van during the week but a nearly new Range Rover at the weekend. Go on holiday to Torremolinos during the winter to ease the rheumatoid arthritis that would almost certainly be settling in by now. Too late to go back, however. He had chosen the path of the Loss Adjuster.

Waiting. The clock showed 00.13. He took out his copy of Conn Iggulden's *Lords of the Bow*. It was the third time he had read the novelised series describing Genghis Khan's life, but Conky liked to channel a little Genghis when a confrontation was afoot: marvelling at a chapter where the disciplined training regime of the Mongolian army was laid out in detail, he waited for that vicarious rush of adrenalin and pseudo-military pride to wash over him; expecting the sheer bloody-minded determination of Genghis himself, in the face of all adversity when his horsemen were woefully outnumbered by the enemy, to strengthen his own spine. Though the Mongolian Emperor would have little chance to inspire him tonight. Headlights at the builders' yard gates, shining onto stacks of timber.

Abandoning his book, he stood and watched a dark people carrier advance to the Portakabin shop. It parked out front. But there was only one man in the vehicle that he could see. The tall figure of Asaf Smolensky emerged, carrying a black sack.

'Oh, shite. Not that nutter,' Conky said under his breath. 'He's the kind of eejit keeps a shovel of shit on the table to keep the flies off the butter.'

A merry tinkle as the door to the shop opened. There he was – his opposite number, dressed in all his eccentric religious regalia, with those unhygienic ritual tassels hanging down his trousers and that ridiculous black satin coat. Conky had read enough about Judaism to know that the imitation Hassid who stood before him constituted nothing short of blasphemy.

'Smolensky,' he said, proffering his hand.

The Fish Man cocked his head to the side and peered at Conky's hand quizzically. Ignored the gesture, thrusting the black bin liner towards him.

'It's all there,' he said.

'I'll count it if you don't mind. In the back, there. Sit out here or follow me and watch. Suit yourself. But don't try anything stupid.'

'Please don't insult my intelligence and professionalism.' The Fish Man's mouth settled into an uncompromising straight fissure in an otherwise impermeable flint-face. His thick, dark eyebrows knitted together over too-shiny mad man's eyes.

Many a time had Conky met this man's type in prison. Bat-shit crazy. Probably.

Smolensky trudged through to the office, bringing with him a pernicious trail of eau de fishmonger. Conky coughed. Wondered if he should bother trying to make conversation with this odd character whom he usually saw only from a distance, on the opposite side of the battle lines.

'The money counter's banjaxed,' he explained, omitting the information that Paddy had broken it during one of his episodes, hurling it towards Degsy's head. 'You'll have to be patient.' With practised fingers, he started to count the money manually. 'Would you like a tea?' he asked, thumbing through the twenties. 'Help yourself.' Nodded to the kitchenette. 'There's all the facilities. Milk in the fridge.'

Smolensky sat in a typing chair. Took a green packet out of his inside pocket – the word *Noblesse* emblazoned across the front, followed by something written in Hebrew. He removed a cigarette and tapped it on the packet.

'Not in here,' Conky said, pointing to the no-smoking sign. 'Rules are rules.'

'This is not O'Brien's place any more,' the Fish Man said.

The sentence sounded hostile, spoken in a clipped Israeli accent with an upwards inflection that irritated the shit out of Conky. *Exercise Genghis-like control, Conk. You are a disciplined warrior. Do not stove the eejit's head in.*

'It is until your bosses have paid in full, my friend.'

'I am not your friend. We have merely been two soldiers with the same rank, fighting for warring armies. But maybe now it is almost like we are brothers-in-arms.' He flashed Conky an unexpected smile.

Pausing to sip his redbush brew, Conky studied Smolensky's somewhat younger face. Hard to judge a man's expression under a big, messy beard like that. But there was a certain earnestness behind the fervour in those eyes.

'Do you really think this deal is going to be a success, Fish Man?' he asked. 'Do you think your bosses are going to sweep aside all that my boss has built over decades and replace it with their own structure, culture and processes?'

'Of course. I am a man of faith. I believe that some things are *beshert* – that means—'

'Meant to be. Fated.'

'Precisely. It's fate that the Boddlingtons should rule Manchester.'

Conky sipped his tea. Fell silent. Visualised those tired, dog-turd-studded streets, those beer-sticky pubs, those mildewed houses where desperation was mixed into the very mortar and where the O'Briens were worshipped like Jesus Christ's own emissaries on earth. 'Communism.'

'Pardon?'

'The Bolsheviks thought they could sweep Russia's glorious regal history and religious commitment aside and replace it with a new order. The Nazis thought so too. And the British thought they could take Northern Ireland and remould it in their own image. See how that's all worked out for them over time.'

'I don't understand what you're getting at. Can you count the money please? I get low blood sugar. I need to eat regularly.'

Crossing his legs and sitting back in his chair, the truth of the situation became clearer to Conky with each lesson from history that occurred to him.

'You want to know what I think?' he said to the Fish Man. 'I don't think Manchester is going to let Paddy O'Brien go.' He interlaced his fingers behind his head. Full of philosophy in the early hours of Saturday morning. 'Too many people have a vested interest in my boss staying the King. Changing the order of things from the top down is not as simple as people think.'

Smolensky sighed. Tugged at his beard. 'Just count the cash, McFadden. Business is business and you're talking too much for my liking.'

'I'm a man of words and a man of my word.' Conky nodded slowly. 'People will continue to fight for their King long after the throne's been given up or taken. You usurp a leader and try to crush an established culture and you're gonna get an uprising on your hands at the very least.'

His phone rang, just as he was about to explain the finer points of revolution to Smolensky. It was Sheila, sounding harassed on the other end.

'Calm down, She,' he said, ignoring the Fish Man's obvious irritation. 'What's wrong?' A pause. 'Who's come to the house? I'll be over as soon as I can.' He hung up. Irritated at this transaction having been interrupted. But flattered. Torn. Sheila needed him urgently to help with an unwanted visitor. A woman in a big house like that on her own. It was Conky she had called. Not Paddy. But by rights, this was Paddy's jurisdiction. He should be there to defend his own wife in his home in the middle of the bloody night. But he wasn't. The boss was in M1 House, celebrating like a twenty-year-old with his idiot brother, no doubt pausing in his champagne consumption only to go in the back and hump that blonde teenager he'd pulled.

'Let's pick up the pace,' he told Smolensky. 'I've got somewhere I need to be.'

'Woman trouble?' The Fish Man treated him to a knowing wry smile.

'I'm not likely to discuss my personal business with you, Fish Man. Now shut your bake and let me concentrate.'

Thinking of Sheila in need, Conky leafed through the money as quickly as his stiff fingers would allow him. Agitated that he couldn't just down tools and go to her aid immediately. Counting a million pounds wasn't a five-minute job. Irritated that Smolensky was sitting too close to him, sharpening a gutting knife with a whetstone and breathing noisily through his mouth. When he took out a bagel wrapped in cling-film that stank of egg and onions, he tutted loudly.

'Do you have to do that in here?' he asked. 'It fucking stinks.'

Smolensky took a large bite from the bagel and spoke with his mouth full. 'I told you. Low blood sugar.'

He proceeded to chew with his mouth open, making an angry clacking sound as his molars ground the food down. Conky grimaced, reasoning that his retirement pay-out was probably peanuts if he took some of the shit he had had to put up with over the years into consideration.

Two cups of tea later, feeling the burn of lactic acid in his overworked hands, Conky was done.

'Consider the Boddlingtons' down payment met, Fish Man. We'll be in touch about paying the balance.'

'Sign the receipt,' the Fish Man said.

With a flourish of his pen on a piece of paper that Maureen Kaplan would later file in her safe room, no doubt, and a reluctant shake of the hand, the first stage of the sale was concluded. Conky's thoughts turned to Sheila . . .

When he reached the O'Brien mansion, he recognised Gloria's Mazda parked out front immediately. Using his key, he let himself in. Drew his gun, more as a reflex action than anything. Surely the situation couldn't be that desperate if it was just Gloria. And time had passed since the call. Surely they had calmed down and made up.

The yelling took him by surprise. Super-heat in women's sharp-edged, steely words, conducted all the way from the TV room in the back of the house to the entrance hall. And there Sheila and Gloria were, entangled in something that looked like two cats fighting in a pro-wrestling match. All hair and nails and, 'You bitch!'

'Ladies! Ladies! Break it up!'

Conky pulled Sheila from Gloria as gently as possible, though the two women fought against him with balled fists and venomous slaps.

'About time too! Get her out of here!' Sheila said.

'You're making a big mistake!' Gloria shouted. Normally so primly dressed, Conky was surprised by the defined, almost manly musculature of her arms. She was grabbing at Sheila again. Shaking her like a wayward child. 'I need this final deal to go through. I need money. It's all right for you.'

But the diminutive Sheila was no pushover. She pummelled Gloria towards the door like a mini-Sumo pushing her opponent to the chalk line. 'All these years, we worked as business partners and you're still thinking it's all right for me? You cheeky, chippy cow! You were my cleaner and I made you rich.'

Gloria halted in her offensive. Stepped back suddenly, her hands in the air, her neck at an awkward, sassy angle. Blinking hard like the *Ricki Lake* show had never been taken off air. 'You made me rich? I'm sorry. I cleaned your mess up for the first ten years of your marriage and have all but run your business single handedly. But you. Made me. Rich. You. In your frigging mansion.' She gasped. 'Look at that. You made me swear, you terrible woman.'

Sheila poked the taller woman in her chest with a manicured fingernail. 'You were nothing until we started the agency together. Nowt. An old washed-up scrubber from Sweeney Hall with a Boddlington scumbag for a son.'

Conky sucked the air in between his teeth. Ready to step between the women yet again but privately relishing seeing the feisty side to Sheila come out.

'Now, come on girls. Don't be saying anything you're going to regret tomorrow.'

'Too late for that,' Gloria said. 'There's no coming back from this. All the things I could say about you, you over-indulged, anorexic white cow.'

'Oh, I'm really losing sleep,' Sheila said, hand on hip in her satin bathrobe. Sarcasm dripping thickly from every syllable.

'My future's ruined, thanks to you!' Gloria shouted. 'All because you couldn't be bothered to do one more lousy job, you heartless hussy. *A false witness will not go unpunished.* Proverbs 19:5!'

'Gloria!' Conky snapped, grabbing her by the upper arm. 'Time you went home.' He had only got the gist of the conversation but could see from the tears standing in Gloria's eyes that things weren't good for her. He felt a pang of unexpected sympathy.

'And you think my life's easy, do you?' Sheila opened her mouth, as though there was much more to say. But the question simply hung in the air between them – rhetorical and loaded with insinuation. Sheila put her hand over her own mouth. Gathered her robe about her and hugged herself. Spoke in a quiet voice. 'I'm sorry you feel this way, Gloria, but a promise is a promise. Me and Paddy are packing up and going to Thailand. You want to start your own cleaning company, go ahead. But you can't have mine. I have the majority share, and Pad says it's over. All of it.'

Gloria snatched up her handbag. Glared at Conky as though this contretemps were somehow his fault. 'Fine,' she said, throwing her coat over her arm. 'Leave all those women in the lurch. Forget about the likes of little Efe. Forget about me. Forget about your own hopes and dreams. I'll see you around.'

As the front door slammed shut, Sheila burst into tears. A small woman who suddenly looked like a vulnerable scrap of a girl. Conky put his arm around her tentatively. Stroked her hair, wondering if it would be appropriate to plant a gentle kiss on her head. He decided against it.

'She's so tight,' Sheila said. 'Calling *me* a heartless bitch!' She hiccoughed the words out, beside herself, now. 'I never thought it would be so hard just to down tools and step away from all this.'

Feeling that she was holding onto him with a little too much vigour and not sure if he could trust himself, Conky ushered her to a bar stool and bade her sit down.

'I'll make some tea,' he said. Started to rifle through the convenience food in the kitchen cupboard; rummaging behind the packets of Smash, the tins of beef stew and Patak's jars to find what he sought. A packet of chamomile tea he had bought Sheila at a time when she had complained that she wasn't sleeping. He prepared the infusion in silence, allowing Sheila to process her hurt. She blew her nose heavily on some kitchen roll and took the vodka bottle out of the cupboard.

'No need for that,' he said, taking it from her and stowing it away again. 'It'll keep you awake all night. Have this hot drink I've made you instead.'

He watched with some satisfaction as Sheila sipped from the cup. Her hiccoughs slowed before stopping altogether.

'What do you want to do?' he asked her finally.

Sheila shook her head. Looked as if she were about to share her innermost thoughts. Placed her hand on top of his, then thought better of it. 'I do whatever my Paddy wants me to do. And you need to go home, Conks.'

Chapter 12

Lev

'Patrick O'Brien cannot step down.'

Those words were ringing in his ears still. Unequivocal. And there was a price tag attached.

'A hundred and fifty K, Lev,' his would be benefactor had said. 'That's what you need? That money's yours if you can stop this crap.'

Lev stared at the ceiling, watching a small spider make its way from one side of the room to another, circumnavigating the elaborate white Perspex light fitting that hung above Mia Margulies' bed. All night long at the club, he'd been mulling the offer over. During sex, he'd been replaying the conversation. As Mia tried to engage him in pillow talk, wanking on and on and on about that ponce Jack O'Brien and how he was a bastard and how he'd ruined her life and blah blah blah . . . There hadn't been a single waking moment when he hadn't been contemplating this indecent proposal. And there had been no sleep whatsoever.

He rose from the bed. Took a lengthy piss in the toilet of her en suite bathroom. Looked in the mirror and saw a young man in his prime staring back at him, though he felt old beyond his years with the weight of the world on his shoulders. If he took the money, little Jay might make it to adulthood. If he didn't take the money, Jay would be dead inside a month or two. His son. His baby boy – with honey-coloured skin, green eyes and a head of golden curls that were too good for an angel – would be dead. But if he took the money and got found out, he would be joining his son either in heaven or in hell. *You live by the sword. You die by the sword.*

Swallowing a desperate sob, Lev walked back into the bedroom. Beneath the duvet, Mia was stirring. He prayed she would drift back off into a deeper sleep, giving him time to think. Climbed carefully into bed and propped himself up on fat pillows that smelled of fresh washing and Mia's perfume. Switching on his phone, he brought up the gallery and thumbed through the photos of Jay. Jay in the park on the swings. Jay in a high-chair, eating and wearing his dinner simultaneously. Jay on Tiffany's lap. He thumbed past that one quickly. If he could turn back time, the one thing he would do differently would be to choose a better woman to bear his child. His innocent son deserved so much better than that selfish, junkie cow for a mam. If only he had a normal job and could apply for custody. If only . . .

He scrolled through more photos. None of Jay with his grandmother, of course. Heartless old bag had kept her distance from both of them, thinking she was so much better than a cheap, backstreet drug-dealer. She refused to acknowledge the part she had played in making Lev what he was. Bible-bashing bitch.

Feeling agitated, he switched the phone back off.

'Morning, gorgeous,' Mia said, planting a stale-breathed kiss on his lips.

Lev could barely arrange his face into a smile. How he

wished he'd gone home last night or that at least, she'd slept beyond 6am. But no. There she was, sitting up in bed in an ugly, baggy grey vest, wearing a big smile on her face and panda eyes from where her eyeliner and black eyeshadow had smudged. Her complexion, so alabaster smooth last night, looked florid this morning with orange peel open pores. That dark hair, so luxuriously thick and tamed last night, was now ragged and thin. Unclipped hair extensions lay on her dressing table, accompanied by spidery eyelashes. Women. This morning, he didn't need any of the artifice, unwanted affection or attention-seeking bullshit. He had a conundrum on his hands and it needed solving fast.

'How's my gorgeous hunk? Did you sleep?' She wrapped herself around his body, kissing his chest.

'No. I'm gonna have to go, babe. My head's been swimming all night and besides, I don't wanna get copped.' The tighter she clung to him the more claustrophobic he felt. Time was tick, tick, ticking away and the longer he left the proposition unanswered, the closer Jay was getting to the end. 'If your old man finds one of his lackeys in his princess' bed, he'll string me up by the balls. I'm not chancing a run-in with that psycho dick, the Fish Man, either. Do you get me?'

Pushing her off gently, he picked up his pants from the floor. Briefly savoured the thick carpet between his toes. Under different circumstances, it might have been nice to linger in his boss' mansion instead of hurrying home to his mildewed flat with its condensation and lifts that always stank of second-hand bodily fluids. But this was no time for self-indulgence.

'Fine,' Mia said. It had an unexpected edge to it. Ushering in an outburst that was nothing short of a tantrum. 'Bugger off back to your crappy high-rise. Leave me here on my own, why don't you? Mia Margulies – good for a lay but not worth hanging around long enough to wake up and smell some freshly ground coffee. Am I right?' She gathered the duvet to her, kneeling up. Yelling. Starting to cry, so that her chin dimpled and her makeup, already smudged, ran ghoulishly down her face. 'You're no different from that bastard, Jack O'Brien.'

Lev pulled his pants up and leaned in to placate his lover. Realised that if he pissed her off too seriously, things would not go well for him. 'Hey! Hey! Chill out, babe. I'm nothing like that big ponce. Anyway, why you bringing him up again?'

Mia sniffed hard and wiped the back of her hand aggressively across her eyes. 'He blanked me last night. Didn't you spot him when we were in Belgrano's? With that slaggy blonde on his arm, doing shots. He looked right through me.' She glanced uncertainly, apologetically up at Lev, as though she'd only just remembered it was her new lover in whom she was confiding about her ex. She shook her head and blinked nervously. Back-tracking. 'I mean, he's been putting stuff on Facebook for the last couple of weeks. Bitchy, piss-taking comments about some girl he'd been seeing. Talking about her chunky legs and . . . well, basically describing me. Snide pot-shots at my dad.' The pitch of her voice rose an octave and tears flowed freely anew. 'He's disrespecting me, Lev! And now, you're using me up and spitting me out, too!'

Frustrated at how his hopes for a fast getaway were being dashed, Lev said the first placatory words that came to him. 'Baby, you've gotta understand. It's not you, it's me.'

'Seriously? Like I haven't heard that corny line before? Do you really think I'm that stupid?' Mia yelled. She dismounted the bed and stormed into the en suite, slamming the door and shrieking from the other side. 'I'm sick of men like you. Get out of my house! Go on. Sling your hook! I don't need Jack O'Brien telling me how dumpy and unattractive I am. And I don't need you, Leviticus Bell.'

Head in hands, hands thrown in the air, Lev couldn't believe the turn the morning was taking. 'Come on, Mia. I didn't mean it like that. I've just got a lot on my plate.'

Something thumped against the door. A foot, perhaps. *Hell hath no fury like a woman scorned.* Lev remembered his mother saying those words when he had been a child and his father had left. Upped sticks and left them in order to shack up with some loose-moraled hussy in Salford, his mother had said. *No fury like a woman scorned.* She had kept saying those very words the other day too, during the conversation that had paved tentative steps towards a fledgling reunion, of sorts, pivoting on Jay's illness. Now, they resonated deep within Lev, stoking up a strange sensation of being excited and anxious, all at once. His head started to buzz, as an idea formed and grew solid out of the primordial soup of stress and sleep deprivation.

Using the sugared words of a lover, he coaxed Mia out of the bathroom and held her until she finally relaxed her taut, tense body and stopped crying. Stroked her shoulders and back. Started to kiss her neck. Lifted her onto the bed, tracing a line down her middle from her breasts to her groin with his treacherous lover's tongue. He pleasured her until she came to a shuddering climax.

'See?' he said, wishing he could rinse the taste of her from his mouth with a nice hot cup of tea. 'I'm on your side, baby. I'm nothing like that shag-sack, Jack O'Brien.'

Mia lay spread-eagled with a contented smile on her face, fixated by that spider on the ceiling. 'Ugh. Don't ruin the moment.'

'But he dissed you in public, babe,' Lev said, noticing how Mia's body started to stiffen at the very mention of the DJ's name. 'And you can't let bastards like him get away with that shit. Not when you're Jonny Margulies' daughter. Know what I mean?'

Curling into a foetal position, now, Mia peered up at him with childish, sheepish wonder in those panda eyes. Poor little rich girl just needed a man to pay her some attention when Daddy was out all day running a criminal empire and Mummy was shagging her gym instructor. 'He broke my heart.'

'It's a piss-take, babe. It's the O'Brien crew laughing up their sleeves at the Boddlingtons. And your dad's letting that happen. Did you tell him about the Facebook shit?'

'Yes.'

'Well, he's done sweet FA about it.'

Mia closed her eyes and breathed out heavily. 'Dad never takes anything I say seriously. He thinks I'm just a joke.'

Lev shrugged. 'If it was me, I'd have to get back at both of them somehow. Put them in their place. You know?' He frowned, as if giving her situation some thought, though he had already decided exactly how this conversation would pan out. 'You can't have men taking the piss out of you, Mia. You just can't. It's not feminist.'

'Oh, Lev.' She leaped at him and smothered him in unwanted kisses, last night's champagne rancid on her breath. 'You're my hero.'

He pushed her gently away. 'Let me finish. What I was gonna say, right, is that if I wanted to dump Jack O'Shiny Bollocks proper in the shit and take your dad down a peg or two into the bargain, I'd shout rape, me. Belt it out like Beyoncé from the rooftops.'

'Rape?' She narrowed her eyes. There was a glimmer of a grin turning the corners of her mouth upwards.

'Yeah. Think about it,' he said. 'Your dad will go mental when he finds out. Jack O'Brien will get his head kicked in. Frank and Paddy O'Brien are bound to come back at your dad, meaning you'll stoke up a nice little pile of shit for him to sort out. Everyone sees their arse and you get a bit of well-deserved revenge and maybe even an apology.'

Mia grabbed his face and kissed him on the nose. 'Lev, you're a bloody genius! I'm so sorry for being negative and I'm sorry for not trusting you. I shouldn't always look on the black side of everything. I'm young and beautiful. I've got a hot secret fuck-buddy.' She clapped her hands together like a seal. 'From now on, I'm just going to count my blessings.'

Nodding and smiling, Lev started to mentally count that £150,000, pound by life-saving pound.

Chapter 13

Jonny

'Jack O'Brien did *what*?' Jonny was up and out of his seat, clutching his phone to his ear. On the other end, every racking sob that Mia heaved sliced into his heart. 'When did this happen?' he asked, shooing his secretary Barbara and Mohammed, the book-keeper out of the office. Slamming the door. The rooftops of Strangeways felt as if they were encroaching through the window on an office that felt suddenly claustrophobic as any cell. His baby. His daughter. This couldn't be happening.

Mia's response was garbled. In amongst the hysteria, he recognised the words, 'April' and, 'date rape'.

'April? You've kept shtum about this for that long? Did you report it? Did you go to the police? They need to take statements and swabs and that, Mia!'

The skin around his mouth prickled with icy dread, seeping from his pores in the form of cold sweat. Why hadn't he noticed there was something wrong with his princess? How could he be such a shitty father? All this time, when he'd been so absorbed in the tax inspection and cutting the deal of his life with that arsehole, Paddy O'Brien, his little girl had been harbouring a dreadful, painful secret.

It didn't matter what answers she was giving. He was no longer listening. The fury built and built inside him, blocking out all sound and salient thought beyond the urge for revenge. Jack O'Brien. Big, overly pumped-up poser, with his face plastered across those glossy music magazines that Mia brought home. Some two-bit semi-celebrity who was nothing more than a spoiled brat playing records, spawned by that has-been halfwit, Frank O'Brien. Defiling his baby girl and then publicly humiliating her.

'I'll deal with this, Mia,' he said calmly. His voice was deadly. 'You call your mother and tell her what you've told me. She'll sort out the woman's stuff. I'll put the wheels in motion my end, and then I'll be home, princess. Daddy's going to make it right.'

Jonny dialled Asaf Smolensky. The Israeli picked up on the ninth ring. There was the bustling sound of a fishmonger's in the background – knives being sharpened with a metallic scrape; women's chattering voices, excitable with gossip and orders for fish mix. Friday late morning rush.

'Get over here immediately,' he said. 'I've got a job.'

Sitting by the window, peering out at the prison, Jonny knew he ought to be mulling over his options. He drummed his fingers impatiently on the desk, calculating that if Asaf dropped everything he had been doing immediately, he should make it over to T&J Trading within ten minutes. Even in that clapped-out rust bucket of an old Previa. Fifteen at most.

A knock on the office door. Smolensky, so soon? Jonny's spirits rose fleetingly as he felt resolution and absolution from a father's guilt draw a step closer. The door opened abruptly but it was Tariq who walked in, dressed in the tunic and loose trousers he always wore on a Friday morning.

'Everything alright?' he asked, cocking his head to one

side. He perched on the edge of the desk. 'Mo said you'd called time in the middle of a meeting. Said you seemed a bit flustered.'

At the back of Jonny's mind somewhere, the notion that he ought to discuss what had happened with Tariq nagged dimly at his conscience. But the storm clouds had descended, heavy and blackened by bloodlust. There was no place in his head or his heart for the kind of reasoned debate Tariq would demand. The fewer people knew what he was planning, the better.

'It's fine, mate. Just some stuff at home. You know how it is.' He waved his hand and shrugged. Embarked on his henpecked Jewish husband routine, which he knew Tariq loved. 'Sandra's got some people coming for dinner. The caterer hasn't delivered. You know. A big disaster, and it's all, "Jonny, my life is in ruins" this and "Jonny, I blame you for the dry chicken" that.' He grinned as convincingly as he could, gripping the arm rests of his typing chair, willing his business partner to get out and go stick his nose in someone else's business before the Fish Man got there.

Tariq chuckled. 'My Anjum's dragging us to some auntie's house in Bradford, God help me, for her second cousin's mehndi thing this weekend. I'm just going to eat myself into a meat stupor and sit in the front room, praying I get forgotten about. Bloody women, am I right?' Fist bumps, to show brotherly solidarity. 'Well, listen. I'm taking my dad to the mosque, now. You need me, give me a shout, okay?' He pulled on a white crocheted mosque hat and left.

Breathing a heavy sigh of relief, Jonny watched the two men climb into Tariq's Mercedes CLS. The younger man an upright version of the almost bent-double elder. The older man an upstanding version of the crooked younger. He watched them pull away to seek solace and forgiveness from their God. Good.

Only three minutes later, a battered, dented people carrier pulled onto the forecourt. A tall man wearing no coat but otherwise dressed in the garb of a Hassidic Jew got out of the car, long legs and big homburg hat emerging simultaneously, reminiscent of some strange creature hatching from a steel egg. Jonny counted the seconds.

The knock at the door finally came. Asaf Smolensky entered without waiting to be asked, looking dishevelled in his waistcoat and shirtsleeves. He brought in with him his usual pungent aroma.

'Close the door and sit down,' Jonny said.

The Fish Man raised an eyebrow and did as he was asked. Sitting bolt upright in the chair on the opposite side of Jonny's desk. 'This is an unscheduled meeting, Jonny. You know Friday morning is a busy time for me in the shop.'

'It's an emergency.'

'Oh?'

'And I want you to keep it under your hat,' Jonny said, staring at the wide brim of the black felt homburg. 'In fact, bugger that. I want you to keep it under your yarmulke. Understand? This is between me and you.'

The Fish Man frowned. Tugged at a sidelock and studied Jonny's face. 'What's so bad that you need to keep it to yourself? You know I work on contract for you and Tariq on equal terms. By rights, I should tell him—'

'You can't. It's personal, Asaf. This is my honour at stake.'

By the time remorse and doubt had started to eat away at Jonny's resolve, Smolensky was no longer answering his phone. Too late to refine his instructions. He realised his impulsive actions might have deadly consequences that would go far beyond the fate that awaited Jack O'Brien.

Chapter 14

Jack

'You get off, Suze,' Jack said to the manageress of the bar. He looked at his Breitling watch. Gone lunchtime. Looked back at the middle-aged woman, clutching a pile of towels with arthritic, gnarled red hands.

'I don't mind, cocker,' Suze said, smiling. Nicotine-stained teeth matched her nightclub tan – a fetching shade of pale primrose. 'I've got a stock take to be getting on with. It's no bother.'

Never seeing the light of day was hard on an ageing woman who had a family to feed and couldn't afford choice, Jack mused. Poor old cow. He looked swiftly away from her swollen ankles, lest she feel self-conscious.

'Go home. See your kids, for Christ's sake. You need some rest. God knows, I bloody do! I'll catch you tonight.' He winked and was rewarded with a one-armed hug. Suze smelled of strong washing powder, cheap perfume and Murray Mints to mask a whiff of stale cigarettes. It was a maternal smell. A pang of emptiness reminded him that he missed his own mother, perished many years ago in a Harpurhey squat because she had never been able to resist the pull of the brown. Jesus. What a legacy.

Jack liked it when the club was empty and he could sort through the playlist for that coming evening. He was sober. He was clean. No girls. No ego. No sycophants. No distractions. No Conky McFadden and Uncle Paddy swanning in when they felt like it, reminding him and Dad that M1 House was an O'Brien crew stomping ground and drugs market first and foremost, rather than a temple to music and dance.

Sifting through the vinyl he had selected and placed into his DJ's storage box, he started to make notes. Momentarily distracted by the memory of the call he had taken only that morning, asking him to headline at the new, hot nightspot, Fuentes in Ibiza. A massive fee for a few hours' work, beating several top name London DJs to the gig. He was on the map with a big pin, now. Dad would be proud when he heard that bit of good news.

Lost in optimistic thoughts, humming a new deep house tune he had just discovered, Jack didn't even register the sound of the main door squeaking as it opened. Clanging shut. The noise must have reverberated through that enormous, lofty space, but he was neither aware of that nor the footsteps, click-clacking on the polished concrete floor towards him.

When Jack looked up and saw the tall figure of Asaf Smolensky, dressed from top to toe in black like an impersonator of Death himself, he only had time to frown through lack of comprehension. Then, as if someone had violently removed the stylus from the vinyl soundtrack to his life, there was the sharpest and deepest of scratches, followed by silence and the eternally spinning blackness of God's own celestial turntable.

Chapter 15

Paddy

'Did you see that bastard's face? Did you?' Paddy screamed at Conky. He could feel the fire in his cheeks. Venom coursing through his clogged arteries at a BPM that would make the house music in Frank's club seem like one turgid ballad. Only vaguely aware of what the doctor had said about keeping calm. *Sod the doctor!*

'He was smirking.' The memory of Ellis James . . . that gnome-like detective who had a hard-on for the O'Brien empire. A sly smile in those squinty copper's eyes that saw everything. Paddy had registered the naked glee at the sight of his dead nephew, lying in a pool of his own blood, and the sound of bereft wailing from his poor bastard of a kid brother. 'Smirking, Conks!'

Conky stood with his head bowed in the empty back office of the builders' merchants. Hands held behind him like the Duke of Edinburgh. Already dressed in a black overcoat and suit, as though the funeral was imminent. *That* was respect. That was how someone should behave when royalty was assassinated.

'I know, boss,' Conky said. 'Let me count the ways in which I hate the fecking peelers. Especially that moronic little shite.'

'He was enjoying every minute!'

Paddy, already aware of a pink-orange haze of agitation surrounding him, felt the red mist descend in earnest. Flickering images in his mind's eye like bad footage from an old home movie: Jack, the victim of what the forensics wankers had described as a 'frenzied attack', punctured like a pin cushion and all bled out. Coppers everywhere. Frank's thin face, contorted in horror. Screaming like a woman. Dropping to his knees. Having to be carried out to an ambulance. Cameras flashing. The hiss of police walkie-talkies. His own phone nagging to be answered. But that fat little bastard, Ellis James, savouring every tormented minute.

As though it was a sentient entity separate from him entirely, Paddy's Rage spotted the pickaxe leaning up against the wall in the corner of the office. The Rage picked it up, hardly registering the weight of the thing. The Rage flung it through the window. A deafening bang, as it made contact with the glass. An explosion of crystalline shards, and the damp Mancunian wind was suddenly whipping the Venetian blinds in and out of the jagged aperture.

'Boss!' Conky's voice was calm but seemed to come from another time and place. 'Boss. Take a deep breath. Count to ten.'

But the Rage hadn't finished. It picked up the typing chair with the strength of Goliath and swung it into the air as though it were an Olympian tossing a hammer. The chair sailed across the office, where it found its mark in the dead centre of a shelf full of files. A strange rain of paperwork fell to the ground, covering the grey carpet in legitimate business records. The chair lay on its side, broken and split open like Jack. Dislocated shelving hung at an awkward angle, still clinging to one lever arch file, which slid slowly down to meet its erstwhile companions. A dent in the plaster that the Rage could fit its fist into, which it did. Repeatedly.

'Patrick O'Brien! Stop! You're going to give yourself another heart attack, man.'

The Rage acknowledged Conky's voice but connected hearing Paddy's full name spoken in a castigatory tone with Paddy's mother. *Jesus, Mary and Joseph, Patrick O'Brien! What have you done this time? You just wait till your daddy gets home! I can't protect you, son. He's going to give you the beating of your life.* Mam in a starched white pinny, carrying him under her meaty arm like a bed-roll, up the stairs to his and Frank's room. Anger and fear and regret in her eyes. She would cop it too, once Dad had finished with him.

Paddy stood in the middle of the office. Red mist subsiding now, taking the Rage with it. Heart still racing, panting, he was at least himself again. He peered round at the devastation, frowning with confusion at the sight as though some other person had caused it. Conky was setting the typing chair back in its rightful spot. Gathering the paperwork from the floor. Paddy felt his heartbeat begin to slow a little. Salient thought was once again within his grasp.

'We need an internal investigation into this, Conks,' he told his enforcer. Some satisfaction in watching the big man clear up at his feet. 'Jack is family. Was family. I want you to find the bastard that did this and end him.'

Conky straightened up, with an audible click somewhere in his lower back. 'Of course. It's a downright disgrace, so it is. I feel like I've lost a nephew myself.' Was that a tear that Paddy observed rolling from beneath one of Conky's black lenses? 'All of his life, I knew that poor wee boy. Cut down in his prime. Poor bloody Frank. A father should never bury his son. It's not the way of nature.'

'Who do you think did this?' Paddy asked, wondering why he couldn't cry over the death of his own flesh and blood. Or maybe he was just a harder, better man than Conky McFadden. He suddenly felt disgust towards his henchman. 'I'm supposed to be out of the game. What arsehole would come after me and start something, just as I'm about to disappear off into the sunset?'

Wiping the tear away on the tips of his fingers, Conky sniffed. Looked towards Paddy, though with those glasses it was hard to see if he was staring directly at him or just in his general direction. 'Maybe this isn't about you. Jack's a prominent public figure and a big boy. Maybe he had enemies of his own.'

Paddy wasn't sure about that. Everything always led to him because he was the head of the family. It was all he could do to stop himself snorting in derision at Conky's theory. 'Yeah. Right.'

'Leave it to me, boss,' Conky said, pushing his Roy Orbisons up his nose. Prodding his stupid fucking pretend hair. 'I'm all over this like a rash. And I've already got a few theories.'

Chapter 16

Lev

'Shit. It's Mum. She's home,' Mia said, backing away from the window of the TV room in a near-crouch, wearing only her knickers.

'Get your stuff and get out of here before she sees you,' she whispered. Hastily switching off her father's vintage porn DVD, which she'd liberated from his 'secret' home-office collection, she snatched the disc out of the machine. The skin on her face was still blotched red from crying, but a glint in her eye said that Lev wasn't the only one feeling a whole lot better for her having made the call to Daddy Dearest.

'My clobber's upstairs,' Lev said.

'Come on, then!'

The two scrambled up the staircase to Mia's room, all thoughts of sex long gone. Downstairs, the bing-bong of the contact alarm on the front door heralded her mother's entry. Metallic rattling, just about audible as she presumably tossed her door or car keys onto the table in the hall. Humming a happy tune. Lev didn't want to be around when Mia broke the 'news' to her mother that Jack had raped her. Lev didn't want to be around, period.

'I'm gonna shoot, babe,' he said, backing into the en suite,

110

blowing her kisses. 'I'll be in touch.' Closing the door, he pulled on his clothes hastily, already thinking through his fast getaway. Through the door he could hear the voice of another woman. Marginally deeper. Full of enthusiasm. Then, Mia's. Would the mother spot the bed, still dishevelled from their morning session and come looking for him? Raised voices, suddenly.

'What? He did *what*?'

The sound of weeping and hysterical babble. Mia, getting herself worked up all over again.

Get the hell out, Lev.

His heart was thumping. Adrenalin flushed through his body. He could hear the mother's voice getting louder.

'Have you had a man in here?'

Easily audible through the door, now. Pulling on his shoe. But where was the other shoe?

'Whose is this shoe? Mia! You *have* had a man in here! Are you hiding him? Is he in the bathroom?'

As the handle was depressed on the other side, Lev opened the window. Knocking some shitty nick-nack or other into the garden as he clambered through. Perching on the sill, his taut, tense body flooded with relief when he spied the wrought iron fire escape that descended from the loft conversion above past the en suite window. It was more or less within leaping distance.

More or less.

He looked down at the substantial drop into the side garden. Only wheelie bins to break his fall. But through the obscure glazing, he saw the dark figure of Mia's mother emerge through the door. Gripping an overflow pipe that protruded from the brickwork above, his feet barely accommodated on the thin ledge – one shoe on, one shoe off – he had a split second to decide.

'Hey!'

She'd spotted him.

He leaped across the breach, praying in that split second between life and probable death to a God that didn't give a shit. Caught hold of the banister . . . just. Fingers slippery with sweat. *Little Jay needs you, man.* Clinging on for his son's dear life. Legs flailing, he flung himself onto the steps and scrambled downwards to safety. Sprinting away. Willing her not to follow.

'I saw you, you cheeky little toe-rag!' The angry words of an over-protective mother still rang in Lev's ears as he reached the bus stop.

As Lev boarded the bus to Sweeney Hall with one wet foot, he didn't notice the dented old Toyota Previa pulling away from the kerb on the other side of the road. When he alighted at the mouth of his estate, his head was too full of plans to collect his six-figure bounty and book a flight to the US for him and Jay to notice the Previa sliding out of sight behind the ramshackle one-time Scout Hut that was now a needle-exchange.

Limping to the door to his block of flats, he pressed his fob against the automatic lock. Peered over his shoulder, feeling that he was being watched, but saw nobody apart from a giant of a woman moving very slowly along the pitted, rubbish-strewn pavement on a mobility scooter.

Ten floors up, closing the door behind him, Lev considered his options. He pulled off his clothes. Stood under a hot shower in the mildewed bathroom. Tracked the blackened grout with his thumbnail, wishing his shitty flat smelled less of damp and more of clean and new, like Jonny Margulies' mansion. His stomach churned at the iniquity of one man having so much and one man having so little.

Spoiled Mia. A pampered princess. Why did she deserve such good fortune when his own son had been cursed at birth with a bad mother and a short, brutish childhood spent walking the thin blue poverty line?

Lev shook his head. Turned off the shower. Counselled himself not to compare his sad lot with the fortunes of others. He was young. He would make his own way. Somehow, he would save Jay. Bitterness and envy were acidic, rotting people from the inside out. It had fuelled his mother to be the prize bitch that she was, but he didn't have to be that guy. He plugged his discontent with a slice of Warburtons toast. Ravenously hungry, now the adrenalin had subsided.

Booting up his tablet, he checked the *Manchester Evening News* for signs of an almost certain aggravated assault on Jack O'Brien. Had he correctly anticipated the incendiary links in the chain of events that lighting a fire under Mia would spark? He knew Jonny. Not such a cuddly teddy bear. Should he go straight to his new benefactor and claim the money or wait until it was a sure thing? Poking, clicking on the screen. He could see nothing in the web-pages . . . yet. But then even if Jonny had ordered the Fish Man to pay the DJ a visit immediately, it was unlikely the press would have got wind of anything only six hours after Mia had made the call. Or perhaps his plan had backfired.

'Stop this negative shit, man!' he chided himself, turning the tablet off.

His heart swelled at the thought of being a hero to his infant son. Seeing the boy grow into adulthood, looking up to a caring, strong father figure. Unlike that twat, bio-Dad. *Block the bastard out.* But suddenly, Lev's heart was pounding at the thought of jetting off to the hospital in Baltimore. Realised that he might not be able to handle a terminally ill boy and a pile of luggage on his own.

There was only one person who could realistically help him.

He had better tell the witch.

As Lev peered through the steamed-up hairdresser's window on the corner of a Moss Side red-brick backstreet, he was unaware of the Previa pulling up to the kerb. Even if he had clocked the car, the reflection of the thick grey-white cloud that bounced from the windscreen would certainly have obscured the distinctive appearance of the driver.

'Mam!' He tapped on the window with his knuckles. 'Mam!'

And there was the inglorious Gloria, wearing a red cape around her shoulders, having her hair braided by some young sister who looked like a black Marge Simpson. Gazing at her youthful reflection as though it were a portrait to rival Dorian Gray's.

He entered the salon – little more than somebody's front room turned into a few chipped backwashes and those big round dryer helmets that the old ladies used. It smelled of cheap coconut shampoo and chemicals. She still hadn't spotted him though. Until Marge Simpson stood back and eyed him suspiciously.

'You!' *Now*, she had spotted him. Gloria's reflection collapsed into a portrait of almost grey-faced disappointment. 'What do you want with me, boy? Can't you see I'm getting my hair done?' She sucked her teeth.

Lev balled his fists and thumped them against his thighs, trying to bat away memories of him standing like this as a kid, wanting her to come home instead of spending all

Saturday getting some elaborate up-do ready for church the following day.

'I've got the money. At least, I think I've got the money for our Jay,' he said.

Gloria leaped out of her seat, red fabric billowing behind her like the caped crusader that she was; fighting a Holy War against her son with that old gold cross hanging over her ample bosom – a talisman to ward off his ungodliness. She grabbed him by the wrist and dragged him close to the backwashes, out of earshot of the hairdresser.

'Don't come in here, spouting your gangster nonsense, Leviticus Bell. I'm an upstanding member of this community. I don't need your bad reputation rubbing off on me any more.' Her voice was low and thick with disdain. 'Those days were over when you chose those two-bit hoodlums over me.'

Biting back the urge to call her a hypocrite, Lev breathed deeply. Tried to concentrate on the smells in that place. Hairspray. Old magazines. But there it was. His mother's heavy floral perfume. Suffocating him. Usurping his own scent.

'I thought you'd wanna know. I'm hoping to book a flight. I wondered if you'd come to Baltimore with us. To the hospital.'

Gloria released her grip on his wrist. 'What about that whore, Tiffany?'

Lev looked down at his mother's feet. Perched above dainty, prissy court shoes were swollen ankles attesting to the onset of rheumatoid arthritis, though Gloria had always been convinced she had the best legs in town. Like her gnarled hands, jazzed up with nice nails. They were cleaner's hands, at odds with the smooth face and shapely figure of a much younger woman. Nothing was quite as it first appeared with Gloria Bell.

'Tiff is next to useless. I'm not taking her. I wanna file for custody when Jay's better. I wanna make things right for the kid. He's everything to me and he deserves much, much better. I need your help, Mam. Please.'

The words left a sour taste behind, which he tried and failed to swallow down.

His mother merely looked over at the nonchalant hair-dresser who stood, comb in hand. Blinked hard. Turned back to him and tutted. 'Don't come looking for me again, Leviticus.'

'Old bastard,' Lev muttered under his breath. Hands stuffed into his jogging bottom pockets, he kicked at a cola can that dared to roll across his path. Wished it was Gloria's swollen shitty ankles.

It took him over an hour to get back over his side of town to Tiffany's dump. He needed to tell her what the score was. Break it to her as gently as possible that he was going to take over care of the boy. He was banking on her being relieved to hand over such an enormous responsibility that she had shouldered unwillingly, but he knew she would go fucking mental when she realised she would be losing a raft of benefits as a result.

The bruised, brooding clouds that had threatened to burst all day crackled white with electricity. Rumbling with discontent. One drop. Then another drop. Unexpected and icy on Lev's shorn scalp. More droplets, fat with ill intent, pocking the mid-grey asphalt with dark spreading circles like a malignant wet rash. Gathering momentum. The rain started to fall in earnest, now. Dampening Lev's spirits, as it soaked through his thin jacket.

He trudged through the narrow, potholed streets of the Sweeney Hall estate, past pocket wilderness gardens that grew broken cars and Staffordshire bull terriers, tied to ramshackle fencing, apoplectic that the heavens had dared to open. Past boarded-up windows; broken windows; dirty windows, behind which people led furtive, little lives, barely hidden by dirty nets.

Thumbing through the news on his phone. Searching under Jack O'Brien, M1 House, assault, gangland. Anything he could think of. There was nothing. He didn't realise until he was standing on the step that the door to Tiffany and Jay's house was slightly ajar.

'Tiff?'

Shitty, smudgy fingermarks on the edge of the faded yellow undercoat that covered a well-used door. Lev pushed it open. Peered inside into the murk. The lounge curtains were shut. No sound of Jay, crying or otherwise. Lev's heart hammered against his ribcage, all senses on fire. A strange top note above the usual smell of damp, old frying and stale alcohol. He tried to place it but failed.

Advancing down the hall past a broken plastic trike, he peered into the kitchen on his left. The remnants of lunch were strewn across the small kitchen table like spoils of war. Empty otherwise. But he was drawn to the lounge. Why were the curtains shut? What were they concealing?

'Tiff!'

Tiffany lay sprawled across the sofa, an angry-looking hypodermic syringe hanging from the vein in the crook of her right arm. The colour in her face had all but gone. Lev slapped her cheek.

'Tiff! Wake up!'

Coughing, then, as his babymother stirred from her OD slumber. The cough sounded lumpy. Lev knew what was coming next. He turned her on her side. Vomit sprayed the back of the sofa.

'Shit!' he said, pulling the phone from his pocket.

But there was no time to dial 999. Upstairs, a child's shriek pierced the rancid air. Jay.

Lev thundered up the stairs. Realised what that top note was, too slow, too late. Fish.

He entered his son's bedroom and there was Asaf Smolensky. Holding a writhing, screaming Jay in his left arm. Brandishing a boning knife in his slender right hand too close for comfort to Jay's slender neck.

'Hello, Leviticus,' the Fish Man said. 'I've had my eye on you. I think we need to have a little chat.'

Chapter 17

Conky

'I want him to have the best,' Frank said, wiping tears from already puffy eyes as he stared blankly at a pearlescent white coffin. 'Gold for royalty, right?' Forlornly, he pointed to the gilded handles and gold satin interior. Sniffed hard and dropped his head towards the tiled floor of the showroom. Tears, plopping onto his sneakers. 'He was my best, best boy.'

Conky put his arm stiffly around Frank's heaving shoulders, wishing he could offer some measure of real comfort to the poor, wee, raggedy bastard.

'I think gold's grand. The boy would love it, so he would. Flashy little bastard always did love his bling.' Issuing a hollow chuckle, he tried to jolly Frank along. But how in God's name could you jolly along a man who had lost everything to the game? First his wife. Now, his only child. Frank had nothing. Nobody. Ten days in, and Paddy was still at the bottom of a beer glass somewhere, proclaiming war, feeling his nephew's murder as some kind of personal affront. And here Conky was, as usual, tasked with picking up the pieces.

'A good choice,' the sombre salesman said, nodding sagely.

A half-smile on his crooked face. Clasping his hands like some ecclesiastical charlatan in front of his priestly black suit.

You could see the pound signs in the bastard's eyes. Coffins. Cars. Cocaine. Greasy with snake-oil, whatever the actual product he might be selling, Conky assessed.

'My friend here needs a little time out,' he said, wanting to slap the disrespectful smile off the salesman's face. He removed his sunglasses. Gestured with a sharp flick of the chunky arms that this wanker should disappear, pronto.

He and Frank were alone, sitting on the edge of a graphite-coloured coffin with a pink interior. People were trudging by outside, glancing in before looking swiftly away, as if that showroom reminded them all too uncomfortably of their own mortality.

'I'll find who did it,' Conky said softly. 'I swear to God, Frank. Jack's death won't go unavenged.'

Frank blew his nose on a piece of royal blue satin that Conky had torn from a sample book. Nodded. Shrugged. Hiccoughed when he spoke haltingly.

'It was the Scousers, wasn't it? That's what Pad reckons. Copper told the papers it was gangland shit, and all.'

'I'm not sure of anything just yet,' Conky said. 'Maybe it was someone from out of town. This was a frenzied stabbing. Not like anyone we know. Not a professional. It looked like the work of a kid with anger management issues. But the boss employs me for my variety of skills, and doing a bit of digging is in my job description, as you know. When I come down on a man like the vengeful God almighty, I want to make sure I'm taking out the *right* man.'

Finally, Frank's hiccoughing subsided. Just contemplative silence between them. Conky pictured the muscular shape of young Jack O'Brien, framed with ruffles of gold satin and makeup on his face to ensure he kept up appearances while lying in state. What a tragic waste. He suddenly felt old.

'Good-looking lad, Jack,' he said to Frank. 'Successful too.'

'Damn straight.' Frank started to weep silently anew. 'He was the best thing that ever happened to us. I feel robbed, man. Totally robbed. Everything I ever had that was worth owt has gone. And for what? Our Paddy reckons that someone was using my Jack to square up for a fight with him. To wind him up, like. A warning. All he ever sees is a dick-swinging competition with him in the middle. Paddy O'Brien. Mr Big Dick.'

Standing abruptly, Frank began to march up and down the showroom, his skinny arms flailing. 'I wish I'd never got involved in all this bullshit, Conky. I wish I'd stuck to my music and told our Pad to go fuck himself.' He poked himself hard in the chest. 'I killed our Jack. Me!' Tears beaded in the corners of his eyes, though his face was twisted in apparent rage. 'Because I got sucked into all this gangster crap of Paddy's. And our Jack got sucked in too. *My* club being used to deal drugs out of. All them beatings in the back. Brothels full of little slags being trooped through *my* club to service Paddy's "business associates".'

He framed the term with inverted commas – four fingers aloft and derision thick in his voice. 'Shit sticks, Conk. I let Paddy's shit stick to me like it sticks to everything, and now . . .' His voice broke up like a phone with bad reception. His chin dimpled; lower lip trembling. He inhaled deeply, clearly struggling to gain some composure, but Frank's breath came in ragged dry heaves, as though it were his lungs that had been punctured repeatedly, not Jack's. His shrunken face, aged by another decade overnight, glistened with tears. 'Now, I'll never see my son again. Never.'

Conky bade him sit. Made him a vending machine coffee. Sat beside him and patted his hand while he wept. Remembered the adoring crowds at M1 House, worshipping their bronzed musical demi-god. Mused that Frank was wiser than he knew.

'Francis. You have a good understanding of shit's adhesive qualities, alright. But did Jack have any enemies of his own? Had there been some altercation before the murder?'

Frank blew the steam from his coffee. 'Come again?'

'Arguments? Did Jack get into a set-to with anyone that you can remember?'

The salesman burst through the door from the back office to the showroom. Conky took off his glasses. Gave him The Eyes. The salesman withdrew sharpish.

Nodding, Frank's brow furrowed.

'Yeah. As a matter of fact, he did. It wasn't a row, as such. Silly bastard had been slagging some bird off on Facebook. He was like a dog with a bone. Had his statuses set to public and everything. It went viral.'

'Viral *what*? You understand all that kids' computer nonsense, do you?! A man of your age?'

'Run a club, don't I?' Frank dug his hand into his jacket pocket and brought out his smartphone. Swiped through to show Conky a myriad of brightly coloured graphics. 'I've got all the social media apps.'

'I don't even want to know what a fecking app is,' Conky said, closing his eyes. 'It's an aberration. The unravelling of polite society, is what it is. And I remember your Jack taking one of those selfies practically every time he went for a shite, boasting about putting it on Twatter or whatever the fuck it's called. But I digress. Tell me about the girl.'

'Well, this was the last bird he should have been starting aggro with.'

'How so?'

'Mia fucking Margulies, wasn't it? Jonny's daughter.' Frank rubbed his eyes with his free hand. His sagging lids were bright red, closing over bloodshot sclera. His nose, glowing and bulbous. A thin, elastic man who looked like he had been stretched to his outer limits. 'Our Jack had been knocking about with her. You know. I've seen her in the club before and I warned him that he was shitting on his own doorstep.'

'Sleeping with the enemy,' Conky said, nodding sagely.

'Yeah. But you know our Jack. Any hole's a goal.' He chuckled but it was a hollow sound.

'And Jack rejected her?' Conky asked.

Frank exhaled hard through pursed lips. 'He humiliated her. I told him. "For Christ's sake, man. Your Uncle Pad has just got into bed with her dad for ten mill. Give it a fucking rest." But our Jack wasn't having any. He says to us. He says . . . I don't know. Summat about her texting him all the time and showing up to parties where she knew he'd be. He reckoned he had to be cruel to be kind because she just wasn't getting the message.' He raised his eyebrows in contemplation. 'And then he apparently seen Mia the night before he was killed, when he had some new bird on the arm. Blanked her in a bar.'

Conky visualised Mia Margulies in his mind's eye, dressed up like a cheap whore. He had caught sight of the girl in the club during the winter, all over young Jack like a rash. Evidently her father Jonny hadn't known his daughter was fraternising with an O'Brien, else they'd all have woken up with salmon's heads in their beds. But come the spring, Jack – the nearest thing to a son of Paddy O'Brien – had systematically ridiculed this daughter of a rival crime boss until she was a laughing stock. Surely no coincidence, then, that the golden boy had been found dead the day after he had flaunted a new squeeze in front of her. Conky was pleased with this deduction.

'What other qualities does shit have apart from its excellent adhesion, Francis?' Conky asked Frank.

'You what?' Frank was open-mouthed. Eyes narrowed, trying to fathom what adhesion meant, in all likelihood.

'What might a person do with shit when they've had the rise taken out of them in public by an ex-lover? The representative of a rival crime family, no less! But that person found themselves unable to wreak retribution directly . . .'

'What?'

'What would you do, if someone made life difficult for you, Frank, but the only recourse you had was to make life difficult for them in turn?'

'I'd twat them one.'

'No, Frank.'

'I'd get you to twat them one.'

'Possibly. But would you ask me directly or go complaining to my boss?'

'Eh?'

'Oh, Christ on a bike, Frank! You'd take a big spoon and you'd stir the shit up, for God's sake.' Conky slapped himself over the forehead. 'Metaphors are lost on you!'

Though Conky was fairly certain that Mia was somehow implicated in the murder, in his professional opinion, Jonny Margulies' daughter was too slight in build to have done the deed herself.

'I've got a theory about shit-stirring,' he said to David Goodman, whilst cocking the safety on his handgun.

The accountant was unable to speak with the barrel inserted all the way in his mouth like that. In fact, he was gagging. Conky pulled it out a way, amused by Goodman's flaring nostrils.

'I think if I was a wee girl with a grudge, I'd go to Daddy. That's my theory. I'd light a fire under Daddy Dearest, so that he did my dirty work for me.'

David Goodman, normally so smartly turned out in his nice King Street accountant's suit, pissed his pants. Conky looked disapprovingly at the dark stain that spread across the man's crotch, leaking onto the wooden kitchen chair and forming a splish-splash puddle at his feet. He tutted.

'Sure, you're nothing like your mother-in-law,' he said. 'Maureen's tough like a warrior. She'd never have let me get past the front door, let alone shove a gun in her big mouth. I respect strength in a woman.'

The accountant tried to nod. Eyes clamped shut.

'You're going to tell me what you know,' Conky said.

More nodding. Small movements, given the physical limitations. But Conky could tell Goodman was malleable. Willing, in fact. He withdrew the weapon slowly.

Goodman moaned. His voice was hoarse. He clutched at his neck.

'I would have told you what I knew without the bloody gun down my throat, McFadden! For God's sake! My wife will be home from school with the kids in ten minutes!'

'You'd better make it snappy then.'

He savoured the fear that evaporated from Goodman's pores. He'd been able to smell it on him the moment he had started working for his mother-in-law. This was a limp dick, and the kind of men who lacked the requisite testicles to make it in a life of cut-throat crime were loose cannons. Good for exploiting for insider information but a grassing risk. Still, Conky found these regular visits kept Goodman in line, and it was a grand way of knowing what Margulies and Khan were up to.

The young, spineless pen-pusher gulped and pressed slender fingers that hadn't seen a day's manual graft to his temples. 'I overheard Maureen talking to Jonny.'

'Oh? Do go on.'

'In fact, I was listening in on the line. I rigged it up like you told me.'

'And?'

He took the glass of water from the kitchen table, raised it to his mouth with a shaking hand and drank deeply. 'Well, Maureen had seen the report in the *Manchester Evening News* about Jack O'Brien's murder. She was straight on the phone to Paddy, offering her condolences. Then, she was on the phone to Jonny, asking him if he was behind it.'

Conky removed his sunglasses and watched the pupils in Goodman's eyes dilate. The Eyes worked every time. He didn't even need to say anything.

'Jonny denied it for most of the call. But in the end, Maureen pressed him. You know.' Goodman looked down at his crotch. Sighed. 'She can be very persuasive.'

'And?'

'After a while he just caved. Said Jack had raped Mia, apparently, and he'd told Smolensky to off him, but to make it look like someone else had done it. Hush, hush, like.' Goodman glanced at the kitchen clock and looked up at Conky with desperation in those naïve brown eyes. 'I've told you what I know. Will you go? Please?'

Patting the boy's hand, Conky put his gun away. 'Don't tell your mother-in-law that we've spoken, will you? No need for her to know about our regular little chats.'

Goodman shook his head. Sweating freely on his top lip. 'I never do. I never have! Honest. But what does this mean for the deal?'

Conky raised himself to his full height and buttoned his coat shut, inwardly contemplating Paddy's reaction to this news.

'Oh, there'll be no more deal, David. There'll be war.'

Chapter 18

Lev

'I'm here for collection,' Lev told the new girl, edging his way down the narrow hall of the rambling Victorian house, following the progress of her pert bottom as it swung to and fro beneath her cheap yellow polyester robe. She responded to him only with the flap, flap of her bare feet on the bare wooden boards. The dirt had created quirky black question marks on her soles.

In silence, she beckoned him deeper in without turning round.

He clocked the bowl of condoms on the radiator cover. Tasteless erotic posters on the walls in cheap frames. The smell of latex and sex was so thick in the air, Lev was surprised it wasn't visible as some kind of decadent fog. It clung to the very fabric of the house – on the ancient flock wallpaper that covered the walls, in the dated soft furnishings – in the same way that acrid damp and mildew clung to his. He wrinkled his nose, trying not to breathe in deeply. 'Where's Kai and Tommo? They should be expecting me.'

The girl padded through the erstwhile dining room that acted as a kind of waiting-cum-selection-area for punters, as well as a thoroughfare that led to the kitchen. Today, the space contained only a coffee table full of old porn mags, creased and curled up at the edges, and two white men, seated on threadbare old armchairs. One young, with the worst acne Lev had ever seen. One in his sixties, who looked like he'd not had a bath or a haircut in a good twelve months. A pungent whiff of unwashed arse confirmed Lev's assessment. Both punters immediately looked at their shoes as he bypassed them, following the girl to the kitchen.

'Where are they?'

'I tell you,' the girl said in a heavy Eastern European accent. She stopped short by the filthy worktop, covered in used, unwashed crockery. Reached for a pack of cigarettes and a box of matches. Her robe parted to reveal round tits with large, pale pink nipples that were perfect but for almost luminous blue veins running over them. Naked white flesh that bore testament to her rarely leaving the house. She re-tied the gown. Her eyes were unfocused. Dead like a shark's through drugs or depression or both. She took a cigarette out of the pack. 'Basement. They play cards.'

'What happened to your neck?' Lev narrowed his eyes at the livid scar that ran part-way across her throat.

The girl replied in a string of unintelligible vowels and syllables. Something Eastern European, no doubt. But when she drew a line across the skin with her index finger and said, 'Fish Man,' he understood, alright. A sudden flash of recognition came over Lev as he stared at the girl's face.

'You're Irina, aren't you?' he said. 'I've driven you before. We spoke. Remember?'

She locked onto the lightning flash on his head with a glum stare. Scratched her armpit with bitten-down fingernails. Blank-eyed, the girl lit her cigarette and blew smoke towards him. 'Irina. Yes. My name.'

He flushed with embarrassment and shame that he hadn't

been able to help her that day, beyond the empty gesture of asking if she had been okay. This girl was supposed to have been sold in a sham marriage. One of many. He'd heard about how Smolensky had turned on her during the trans-action. The buyer had chickened out and made a snappy exit. If only he'd done something to stop that chain of events. If only he'd been the brave, chivalrous man he aspired to be instead of a corruptible streak of piss that couldn't even get his shit together to file for custody of his own kid.

Lev reached out and touched her stomach. Felt the slight bulge. She grabbed his hand and pulled it down onto her warm crotch. 'No,' he said, staring at those firm veined breasts and feeling himself harden, despite his best intentions. 'You shouldn't be doing this in your condition,' he said. He snatched his hand back, as though he had been burned.

The girl gasped. She retreated to the glazed patio doors at the end of the kitchen, shooting him a wounded glance. Hurling a string of abuse at him, which he probably deserved for being part of this. She started to sob, pausing only to exhale clouds of blue smoke.

The urge to grab that cigarette off her and throw it down the sink was almost unbearable. Hadn't he watched Tiff smoke her way through her pregnancy with Jay? Selfish cow! Relieved at least that his hard-on had receded as quickly as it had appeared, he sighed and closed his eyes. It was going to be one of those days.

'Do you think I want to do this for a living?' he asked the girl. 'You think I woke up at the age of ten and thought, "I know. I wanna push drugs on a shitty council estate and collect brothel money for a living"?' Deep inside him, he could feel the anger and disappointment ferment and swell. He was sure the girl couldn't understand any of what he said, but the words forced their way out nevertheless. 'You think I don't wish every day that I'd made something of myself? Listened at school, instead of playing silly-buggers and wagging off? But what's a thick wanker like me gonna do when he grows up? Spend my life claiming Jobseeker's Allowance or stacking shelves for peanuts, when I can make hundreds a week selling weed? And then our Jay comes along and it's money for this and money for that? What would you do, you judgemental bitch?' He thumped the worktop. Remembered Asaf Smolensky standing in Jay's little bedroom, holding a knife to the boy's neck, just as he had to this prostitute's . . .

'Tell me what you're up to,' Smolensky had said in Israeli-English that had a sing-song quality to it. 'Tell me why you've made contact with your mother, or I'll stick the boy.' His dark eyes had seemed to have only unfathomable depth to them, like a sinister well that led all the way to the scorching core of the earth. There was something wrong about him – beyond the fake Hassidic get-up and the tough-man ex-Mossad bullshit that he sometimes spouted. Lev had seen it in Jay's bedroom. Lev knew hard-cases. But they were generally just flawed, tortured meat-heads. Smolensky was different. It was as if he was broken or missing a key component that you needed to make a human. Smolensky had had no compunction about pressing the knife into his screaming son's vulnerable, baby-soft skin.

'I haven't seen my mother in donkey's years,' Lev had lied. 'Give me my son, you loon.'

'I've been watching you,' Smolensky had said, his husky voice booming above Jay's hysteria. 'You're up to something. You're in bed with the O'Briens and you're a liar. I saw you with her.'

Lev's heart had pounded so hard, he wondered if it had been visible, pulsating beneath his T-shirt. No point bluffing. 'My son's ill. I only made contact with my mam because I needed her to know. It's just family shit, man.'

'It's always family shit,' Smolensky had said. 'And you are balls-deep in Mr Margulies' family, aren't you?' He had winked. Gripped the knife between his teeth and set the boy down deftly, allowing Lev to breathe again. Removing the knife from his mouth. 'I'm keeping my eye on you, Leviticus.' He had pointed the tip of the blade towards Lev. Even with the cot between them, Smolensky's arms were long enough to have enabled a fatal lunge. 'You're up to something. I know it. I can't prove it and I'm not yet sure what it is, but I want you to know I'm watching every move you make.'

Lev had snatched a bewildered-looking Jay out of the cot. The child had been wide-eyed and suddenly silent, as if realising that whatever his father chose to say next could either sustain life or bring death. Lev's inclination was to tell Smolensky to go fuck himself, but he was brighter than that. 'Well, you keep all the tabs on me you want, Fish Man. I've got nothing to hide, mate. Just a sick son. And an OD'd ex – thanks to you, I assume.'

Smolensky had laughed. Stepped out from behind the cot, sheathing his knife and straightening his hat. 'If I have reason to come back here, Leviticus, next time both of them will be dead. You understand?'

Both of them will be dead. Jesus. Standing in the squalid kitchen of the brothel, Lev shook his head, trying to dispel the memory of Asaf Smolensky's threat and the pungent, lingering smell of fish, followed by the pointless, panicked locking of all doors and windows once the uninvited visitor had departed. Waiting for the ambulance to come for that irresponsible twat, Tiffany.

Now, Irina padded away, blowing smoke in his face defiantly. Lev was left alone, standing his ground uselessly in

132

a kitchen, empty but for filthy pots, stinking wine bottles and a floor scattered with lentils.

'Basement,' he said, remembering why he was in a whore house.

Downstairs, navigating his way through the dank warren of subterranean rooms, he found Tariq's brothel-keepers, Kai and Tommo, playing poker at an old, battered card table positioned beneath a bare bulb in the largest chamber towards the front of the house. They were both swigging from bottles of Czech beer. Both wearing the informal Boddlington uniform of puffa jacket, G-Star jeans, Nike Airs. Kai, a brother with the beginnings of an Afro who had been two years above him at school. Tommo, a fat white boy from Cheetham Hill, hiding his prematurely receding hairline under a baseball cap. Lev did a double take at the golden 'M'.

'You wearing a McDonald's cap, Tommo?' Lev asked. 'Serious?'

Tommo looked up from his cards. Flipped Lev the bird with a chubby, stubby digit. 'Shove it up your arse, man. Our kid trod dog shit into me Yankees one, so I nicked his, didn't I?' He pointed to the embroidered initial. 'M stands for fucking Babe Magnet, right?'

'Babe Magnet begins with B, you knob end,' Lev said, amid guffaws of laughter from Kai.

'M for Massive Arse,' Kai suggested, punching himself in his pillowy chest with his cards.

Tommo scowled, as tears of mirth ran from Kai's eyes. But then Lev reflected that he had been promoted above these two chumps. He was on the periphery of Tariq and Jonny's inner circle, working his way further towards the centre, where the pot of gold was stashed.

'Money. Come on lads. You wanna drink and piss about

playing poker? Do it on your own time. Remember how acting the twat worked out for Suspicious Sid. There are two customers upstairs, waiting for girls, and one skinny blonde piece wandering around with a face like a smacked arse. Get it together!'

He folded his arms. Legs akimbo. Showing them he meant business.

'Who stuck a wasp up your arse?' Kai asked.

'Pay day!' Lev said.

Scraping his chair rebelliously along the rough-rendered concrete floor, Kai sucked his teeth and walked to the safe, set into the distempered brick wall. Click, click, clicking the dial round, he opened the hefty door and pulled out bound sheaf after sheaf of tens, twenties and fifties.

'It's all there,' he said, piling the wads into an anony-mous-looking black rucksack. Into the sack he also placed a black and red ledger and a spike containing vouchers.

Tommo looked wistfully at the money and fingered the M on his cap. 'There's them two, sitting on a mountain of the Queen's face. And here's me, sitting in a shitty cellar, doing their dirty work – earning a bit of cash-in-hand on top of my dole to keep my mam in whisky and our kid in chip butties. I must be some kind of mug. We all must be.'

'Some of us is to the manor born. Some of us is to the council house born. Stop moaning, get upstairs, and sort them two punters out, you lazy fat bastard.' Lev hauled the bag onto his shoulder and climbed the stairs to where the air was fresher, but only marginally so.

Squinting in the sudden shaft of daylight that came from the back door, his senses were suddenly on fire as he heard the squeal of tyres on the road, directly outside the house. Car doors, slamming. He froze. Gripped the bag tightly. Turned around just in time to hear a deafening bang. At the end of the long hall, the front door burst open and a tall, scrawny man marched in, holding a sawn-off shotgun. Behind him came a butch girl with a high ponytail.

Lev recognised them immediately. Degsy. Maggie. The dealers. Shit.

'On the floor! On the floor!' Degsy shouted, shooting at the ceiling so that fragments of lathe and plaster rained down.

But Lev just stood there, waiting for his instincts to decide whether it was time for fight or flight.

Tommo emerged, holding a handgun from the basement. His bulk, blocking Degsy from view. Kai followed, brandishing a baseball bat. Girls screaming upstairs. Punters yelling, as Maggie poked a pistol into the dining room.

Then, several things happened:

The house shook with a boom. A cartridge exploding from the end of the sawn-off shotgun, sending Degsy reeling backwards, erupted inside Tommo. A giant of a man, becoming a firecracker of blood, bone and soft tissue. A hazy cloud of red obscuring Lev's vision. Kai ran forward, yelling hoarsely. Too late to bring his baseball bat crashing down on Degsy's rat-like head. Another bang, ringing in Lev's ears as Maggie let off a shot from her pistol. Bullseye. It hit Kai cleanly between the eyes. He collapsed to the ground.

Man down. Man down, was all Lev could think. Silly lines from shoot-em-up and cop movies.

And still, he stood there, clutching his rucksack full of immoral earnings. They were coming for him. He held his breath. Watching girls run forward, towards the door, only to be gunned down by Maggie and Degsy. Two psychopaths, shooting at everything that moved, as though they had been set loose inside an arcade game.

Lev's ears were ringing. He was going to die, he realised. Unless . . .

Turning back, he saw Irina, scrabbling to unlock the back door using a knife.

'Forget it!' he cried.

He picked up the large, steel kitchen bin and used it to smash the glass in the left-hand patio door. Pulled the barefoot girl through with him. Still carrying the bag.

'Run!' he yelled.

Dragging her to the bottom of the garden was hard work, with Degsy behind them. Past a cherry tree they sprinted. The trunk exploded, as a shotgun cartridge found its home, disintegrating in the wood. The sound of footsteps thundering down the lawn behind them.

'You're dead, Bell!' Degsy shouted.

'Faster!' Lev urged Irina.

But suddenly, he was aware of a moment's peace. Daring to glance backwards, he saw Degsy holding the shotgun over his arm. Reloading.

'We can do it,' he said, pointing to the fence at the bottom of the garden. Knowing that beyond it was an alley for the bins. If they could only scale the fence, they stood a chance.

Another glance back at Degsy. Reloaded now and marching smugly towards them, his yellow Adidas tracksuit splattered with the gore of the house's occupants.

'Not so fucking cocky now, are you, pal?' he said. Mean words from his wizened junkie face.

'Climb!' Lev ordered Irina.

She hoisted herself up, pressing her foot into his cupped hands. One leg over. Her gown caught on a nail. A delay of too many seconds. A series of ominous clicks said Degsy had two cartridges ready to fire. He took aim.

Chapter 19

Irina

Running, running, panting so she could hardly breathe any more. A stitch in her gut. Lactic acid searing her muscles. Too aware of the incessant ache in her unsupported breasts as they pounded up and down so violently, it was as if they wanted to shake themselves free of her. But the acute burning in the soles of her bare feet was the worst. Stinging where the glass from the litter-strewn cobbles had cut her or bedded into the skin. *Push it out of your mind*, she counselled herself.

A shotgun cartridge ripped into the red-brick garden wall that loomed above them to her right. She yelped. Close. Too close. No time to think about dying. Not now.

Behind her, the gun-toting mad man picked up his pace yet again. Gaining on them, every time she turned her ankle on a dislodged cobble. She prayed for smooth asphalt. Within sight, now.

All those years, sitting in the onion-domed Slovakian church, sandwiched between Mama and Babička, who wore a black shawl and smelled too strongly of mothballs. Praying to the golden icons of Jesus and the Virgin Maria. Behaving as a good, obedient daughter should . . . until the accident. Falling for the wrong man. *This* was now Irina's fate: to be dragged down a back alley by a gangster who was neither black nor white, whom she had seen only once or twice before. Being shot at by a rival criminal. Another few paces and she would be dead, she was certain of it. And her baby would die with her. Her baby's life would be over before it had even begun. Both of them, punished for her sins. Babička had been right.

'Faster!' the man shouted, grabbing her hand so hard that it hurt.

Just a second allowed her a glimpse of his wide eyes and agonised expression. The vein, protruding in his forehead. The sinews in his neck, taut and shining with sweat as he ran.

Irina had nothing left. She was ready to stop. What was the point anyway? Die here, swiftly, in this alleyway, or die slowly in agony, having to share her body with strange men, late into her pregnancy. Pretend to like it or take a beating. Get through it by drinking the wine they plied you with or the pills they made you take. Perhaps she would be sold to another refugee as a bride. Perhaps they would just take her baby away and sell that.

Decision made.

She slowed her pace.

'What are you doing?' the man shouted. 'Come on!'

She shook her head. Unable to speak. Sank to her knees on those old, uneven cobbles, despite there being a busy road just in sight. In her own tongue, she shouted, 'Enough!' Gathered her yellow robe to her. She started to weep, still looking up at the man to see what he would do.

Footsteps getting louder said the assailant with the gun was almost upon them, now. Irina didn't see the point in looking round to face her executioner.

The man breathed heavily through his nostrils. Glaring

at her, he screamed, 'Get up, for Christ's sake!' He yanked at her hand. 'Please!'

But her strength had evaporated. Ashamed, she looked at her belly. *Sorry, baby. Sorry I wasn't strong enough for us both.*

She expected the man to run away; to save his own skin. Why wasn't he running?

Almost entirely lost in her own fear, guilt and misery, she was dimly aware of her companion thumping the wall. Just about able to see through her veil of tears how his expression changed from dismay to one of apocalyptic thunder. Noticed how he ran in the opposite direction to the road. Back towards the gangster with the gun.

Empty metallic clicks.

'Aw, shit!'

More clicking.

'Not so brave now you're out of ammo, are you, you big, lanky turd?' she heard her companion shout.

'Come on then, hard man,' the gangster with the gun shouted.

Her heart fluttered. The baby in her stomach kicked, and with it, her body was infused with a sudden lightness. Buoyed enough to allow her to look round.

Their attacker was tall but skinny and sallow, like a plant that had grown too long and thin in the dark. The hollows in his face put her in mind of the old folk back home, whose teeth had long rotted and been yanked. Her companion, by comparison, was muscular. Looked healthy, like a prize bull.

Covering her belly, she scrambled to her feet. Leaned against the wall as her companion grabbed his opponent's hand that held the shotgun and nutted him squarely in the forehead.

The thin gangster staggered back. Stunned. Shook his head, clearly dazed, as her companion tried to prise the gun free. But he wouldn't let go.

'Gimme the gun, Degsy. Give it me, or I'm gonna lay you out.'

'Cock off, Bell!'

A clumsy tussle between the men. Pulling at each other's jackets. Trying to kick at each other's legs. The gunman took a swing at her companion's face. Caught him on the temple with the metal twin barrels. A gash in his skin started to pour with blood immediately. Her companion wasn't fazed. He responded with a right hook, the likes of which she'd never seen before. Gunman fell against the wall with such force that the crack of his head against the brickwork made Irina wince. His eyes crossed, the junkie's half-light in them already fading. He stood but started to totter backwards and forwards like a drunk.

Irina took careful steps towards the road. Slowly. Deciding that perhaps today was not the day she and the baby would die. When her companion finally wrenched the shotgun from his opponent's hand and started to beat his face repeatedly with the wooden butt, pushing him to the ground as he rained down blow after blow, she resolved not just to survive this ordeal but to escape. Somehow. She closed her eyes as the gunman's face started to turn red and pulpy like tenderised meat.

Don't let the baby see this. Get away from here. Just run to a shop and ask for help. You can do it.

Walking briskly backwards, she was just about to turn and sprint to freedom, when her companion grabbed her arm.

'Where you going?' he asked, frowning quizzically. His face was spattered with the gunman's blood. His head-wound oozed onto his neck and shoulder.

Irina yelled, 'Let me free!' in English. Annoyed by the hot tears that leaked onto her cheeks. Drowning, sinking, sucked deep into a quagmire of disappointment that she had blown her chance of escape. 'Bastard! You let me free!'

'Shut your trap and walk,' he said, taking off his blood-stained jacket and wrapping it around her shoulders. Ushering her towards the road. 'Don't look at anyone. Just walk. Quickly.'

'Where you are taking me?' she shouted, stumbling ever on with stinging feet.

'Shush, will you?' he said, glaring at her. Looking over his shoulder. 'Walk quicker. There's more of them out here. They'll be looking for us.'

He marched her briskly along several backstreets, always moving uphill, until they reached a bustling main road. Buses queued along it. Taxis, flashy cars, beat-up old people-carriers, weaving in and out of the lanes to beat the traffic lights. The smell of diesel was heavy in the air. Burning charcoal and spice, coming from a nearby kebab shop. Nobody looked twice at her as they went about their business. Women in full burka, carrying shopping bags with tiny chattering children following in their wake; Hassidic Jews, behind the wheels of the people-carriers – the stolid women in their austere black clothing and wigs, hastening somewhere, pushing baby strollers; Africans in colourful dress; Asian women in glittering, brightly coloured fabric and old bearded men, wearing tunics and trousers with overcoats on top. They were choosing exotic vegetables, that looked nothing like the humdrum root crops and cabbage Irina was familiar with, from the display outside groceries, where the signs were written partly in a strange, scrolling script. Girls, roughly her own age, wearing school uniform, gossiping and shovelling chips into their mouths with wooden forks from white paper wraps. What was this place? Normally, she wasn't allowed to go anywhere beyond the brothel except to the factory to give the fat white boss a blow-job. She certainly hadn't been here before.

'Where we?' she asked. 'Who you call, gangster?'

Her companion was staring down at his phone. Scrolling, scrolling. Peering furtively around, but always dragging her forwards.

'Cheetham Hill. Look, my name's Lev. Call us Lev, right? And I'm not ringing no one. I'm looking for somewhere. Just walk, will you? You talk too much.'

'Lev.' She tried his name out for size. It was easy to pronounce, at least.

He pulled her into a brightly lit clothes shop, where browsing women were bellowing strings of nasal words at one another in tobacco-hoarse voices; guffaws of dirty laughter; their sentences, punctuated with 'fuck' and 'right'.

Never letting go of her arm, Lev looked her up and down. Pulled a pair of black leggings, a baggy black top and a pair of cheap trainers from the various carousels, overloaded with polyester offerings. Took them to the till and paid a narrow-eyed manageress whose pursed, prune mouth denoted that she didn't relish the look of semi-naked Irina. But she was more than happy to accept cash from the bloodstained Lev.

'Put them on,' he said, pointing to a solitary cubicle at the very back of the store.

Wondering what lay in store for her, she did as she was told. Surprised that he turned his back on her when she disrobed. He wiped himself clean with spit on her discarded yellow robe.

'That'll do for now,' he said, tossing the bloodstained robe onto the floor. 'Come on.'

142

Once she was dressed, he led her back out, along the uneven pavement, taking what seemed to be a shortcut past a school, surrounded by razor wire, and an MOT centre that reeked of car oil and fumes.

'We go back to boss?' she asked. 'Please, I don't—'

'No.'

'Don't take me back to boss. I don't like.'

'I said, no.'

He sounded impatient. Was he going to imprison her in his own home? Would she have to give him sex too? All she wanted to do was be left alone to look after the baby in her belly. Why couldn't she be like one of those carefree schoolgirls? Why had her life disintegrated into fear and sex-slavery? Why did God hate her this much?

She stopped dead. Wrapped the regret around her like a comfort blanket. It was all she had. Allowed the tears to come. 'Please. I can't do this any more,' she said in her own tongue.

Lev lifted his hand to her. She flinched, expecting him to slap her hard like the others. But he didn't. He put his arm around her shoulders. Ushered her onwards and pointed to a shopfront way up ahead. The sign painted onto the window in gold said something in that scrolling foreign script. Stuck with Blu-tack to the inside of the window was a giant poster of a jumbo jet with 'PIA' written in green on the side.

'You buy ticket?' she asked, hopeful. Then, disappointment as she remembered that the boss had taken her passport on her arrival in the UK.

'No. Look up!' he said, gesturing to a hoarding above the travel agency where the acronym 'ARAS' was painted in blue and white. She had no idea what that meant. 'We're going there.'

Through a separate glazed door, they found a narrow, steep staircase that led up to a scruffy office, stuffed with too many dented brown filing cabinets. A black woman sat behind a desk. She wore glasses and a suit. Looked efficient. By the window was an old, threadbare sofa. Lev motioned that Irina should sit. He spoke quickly to the woman, jabbing his thumb towards Irina. Would Irina be deported? Was this woman friend or foe? Folding her arms tightly across her painfully swollen chest, she was, at least, relieved that it was a woman in front of her rather than another man.

To the left of the desk was a door with mirrored glass, beyond which Irina could not see. The black woman made a call and within a few minutes a middle-aged Asian woman emerged. She was smartly dressed, with her black hair in a chignon. Advancing towards Irina briskly, she held out her hand.

'I'm Anjum Khan,' she said, speaking slowly and clearly. 'I'm the director of Asylum-seeker and Refugee Advocacy Service. ARAS for short. Welcome.'

Irina forced a smile and nodded. Didn't really understand what was happening. Felt bilious and light-headed. A sudden prickling in her extremities and icy shiver in her core warned her that her consciousness was ebbing away ...

But Anjum Khan didn't notice. She was looking askance at Lev. Frowning.

'Don't I know you?' she asked him.

'No,' he said. He took his wallet out of his jeans pocket and pulled out five twenty-pound notes. Pushed them into Irina's hand. 'Just look after her, right?'

He was edging towards the door. Irina sat back down, feeling light-headed and barely there.

'Don't you work for my Tariq?'

'Good luck,' Lev said to Irina.

He was turning away; leaving. But wait! She didn't want him to go. He was all she knew in this place.

She stretched out towards him but felt herself slipping, slipping.

'Hey! Come back here!' Anjum Khan shouted after Lev. 'I *have* seen you before! Oi!'

But the door slammed shut and Lev was gone.

Chapter 20

Lev

'Tommo and Kai are dead,' Lev told Tariq. 'All the girls are dead, from what I could see. It was a slaughter.' Only now that he was sitting in the boss' office did Lev realise what a prick he had been. His gallantry over Irina meant he had some explaining to do. He hoped Tariq couldn't see the sweat breaking out above his top lip.

Nodding slowly, Tariq sat in silence behind his stately desk. He was studying Lev's face intently. Drumming his immaculately manicured fingers on the keys in his jeans pocket, the paisley of precise henna tattoos spiralling its way up his hands and the insides of his forearms into the crisp, fitted lumberjack shirt that he wore.

'You're alive,' he said.

Think fast. Come on. Lev tried to conjure a justifiable reason for running. His thoughts were sluggish. But then, he remembered the rucksack at his feet.

'I had the money with me, didn't I? I had to make a choice to stay and fight or leg it with the cash. I reckoned you'd want the cash and at least one of your men staying alive to tell the tale.'

Closing his eyes, it seemed that Tariq was weighing up

his excuse. He laced his fingers together and brought them to the short, immaculately-shaped beard that covered his chin. Exhaling through his nostrils. The Fish Man was standing outside, waiting for the verdict. Lev knew he could be filleted, dressed with cucumber slices and served up in a dumpster by the time the sun went down.

'Clever boy,' Tariq finally said, opening his eyes.

He smiled, though the smile seemed measured. Clearly, some calculation was still going on behind it. Tariq was no fool, Lev knew. He hadn't co-built a criminal empire in the UK's second city by being a pushover, despite the quiet, laid-back façade. What was it Smolensky had told him? That Tariq had a law degree from some posh place like Oxford? Nothing like the chumps he had working on the factory floor, gabbling away in Punjabi all day long, packaging shit into shitty packaging for re-sale. Oh, Tariq loved to make out he was just another family guy, trying to make a living in his little tight-knit community, but Lev knew better.

Just act cool, man. Be calm. You go looking for trouble, it'll find you.

Lev placed the bag on the polished surface of the immaculately tidy desk, praying that Tariq's wife Anjum would forget that a familiar-looking mixed-race man with a distinctive pattern cut into his crop had come into her Asylum-seeker and Refugee Advocacy Service with a pregnant, teenaged, trafficked sex-worker on his arm. Jesus. Was there any end to this angst?

'It's all there. And on the bright side, I managed to put that skinny junkie Degsy down with my own bare hands. Left him for dead in the alley behind the house.' He grinned at Tariq, willing his boss to approve. 'Took a nasty knock off the butt of his sawn-off shotgun, though.' He pointed to the crust that had formed on the side of his head. 'I've got a clanging headache, man.'

'Weren't you packing?' Tariq asked, raising an eyebrow archly.

Shit. Shit, shit, shit. 'Didn't think I'd need it, to be honest.' Lev rearranged his blood-encrusted features into that of an unwitting, devoted underling. It felt like walking through customs at the airport with a big bag of Dutch E sewn into the lining of his case. 'It's not like I don't know and trust the lads, is it? Honour among Boddlingtons and all that.'

Breathing in sharply, Tariq arranged his collection of pens into a succession of parallel lines. Fat, black and shiny with a white flower on the end. Gold trim. They had cost more than the yearly rent on Lev's poxy flat, no doubt.

'Never leave home on Boddlington business without your piece,' Tariq said. His voice was barely audible. 'Unless you plan to be taken into custody by the police or you're going to be searched. Aren't those the rules? Aren't those the rules we instigated for your protection, Leviticus?'

His voice was so calm; the volume so low. But he was blinking repeatedly behind his glasses. His phone pinged on the desk; he ignored it, so intent was his focus on Lev.

Lev looked down at his filthy hands and swallowed hard. There was no point trying to appear cool. This guy could see right through him.

'Sorry, Tariq. I really am. I forgot. My son's very poorly. Like, proper poorly. I wasn't concentrating.' Damage limitation. That's what the apology was. Not a show of weakness, which would be unacceptable for a brother like him. Just tactics. Fall out with your boss in the normal world or piss off the twat that interviewed you at the Job Centre and all you got was a rap on the knuckles, at best; booted out, at worst. Piss off Tariq Khan and the consequences would be deadly. *Please, God. Don't let Anjum mention me to him.*

Pursing his lips, Tariq stared at the wound on Lev's head until Lev touched the scab self-consciously.

'Never, ever let me hear—' he began, leaning forward; slamming his hand onto the luxury pens, sending them spinning across the desk top.

But he was interrupted by Jonny barging into the office with such gusto that the door crashed against the wall. Smolensky followed in his wake – a long, black shadow.

'Is it true what I hear?' Jonny said, looking from Tariq to Lev and back to his business partner. Unbuttoning his coat and wiping his sweaty brow with the handkerchief from his top pocket. 'I take my Mia to a doctor's appointment and while I'm gone, O'Brien's taken out our men? The girls?' His jowls wobbled with indignation. The inflection in his voice climbed steeply with disbelief.

'Afraid so,' Tariq said. 'Lev here managed to get away with the cash. Tommo and Kai are apparently toast. I've sent the cleaners in. Best we don't go near. Once our little friend Ellis James gets wind it's an O'Brien/Boddlington scuffle, the place will be crawling with cops.' Finally, Tariq lifted his smartphone from the desk and thumbed the screen into life. His thick black eyebrows bunching together in apparent consternation.

'You had a call or a text off Paddy?' Jonny turned from Tariq to Smolensky. 'Have *you* heard anything from Conky McFadden? Maybe his men have gone rogue.'

Smolensky shook his head. Fiddled with his white tassels. Shot an accusatory glance at Lev. 'There's something fishy going on and it's not just me for once.'

'This is what Paddy has to say for himself.' Tariq held his phone up. Lev leaned forward to get a better view but was pinioned back in his seat by a hand on his shoulder. Fingers of steel digging painfully into the muscle. Smolensky, of course, putting him in his place.

Jonny took the phone from Tariq. 'You want war, you've got war. Deal's off,' he read aloud. Dropped the phone back onto the desk with a clatter. 'Bastard.' An anxious flicker of a glance at Smolensky.

'Typical!' Tariq said. 'I should have known it wouldn't last. He's got a mill of our cash as well.'

As the colour drained from Jonny Margulies' flushed face, and Tariq thumped the desk in temper, Lev said a silent prayer, begging an indifferent God that nobody in the room would notice that he could barely suppress a satisfied smirk.

Standing outside the warehouse in the dark, Lev was gripped by fear and nausea. He breathed heavily through his nostrils, realising he hadn't eaten all day long. Flicked his tongue over the roof of his mouth. It felt like chinchilla. If he vomited now, it would be bile coming up. Luckily, the dark kept his secret from the others; he didn't want them to know that he was feeling dizzy. Swaying slightly, he wondered if it was delayed shock kicking in or some sort of karmic punishment for not having gone to A&E to get his head-wound checked out.

Smolensky was leading the charge, of course, carrying a Bren gun that looked too heavy to aim reliably at anything. But Smolensky was military. A crack shot. He had assembled a small unit of dealers – mainly muscle from Lower Boddlington and a couple of Salford lads, who were toting handguns. Sitting in Jonny's Maserati, parked some hundred yards down the street, Jonny and Tariq were watching them make their preparations, no doubt with the engine running and in air-conditioned comfort. Lev knew that the moment there was a whiff of trouble, the bosses would be gone, leaving only exhaust fumes and a dim memory of something powerful and beautiful having been in an area of town where the disenfranchised and the ugly lived.

'We go in. We kill everything. We get out,' Smolensky whispered, holding the weapon across his long torso. He looked at the pocket watch concealed in his waistcoat. 'No longer than ten minutes. No stealing the weed or meth. If I find any O'Brien drugs on anyone when we get back to T&J for debrief, I'll kill you myself.'

The other men nodded and all murmured their agreement.

'In and out. That's your mission. Okay?' Smolensky's eyes reflected the yellow streetlight, putting Lev in mind of a sleek black panther on a night-time hunting trip. 'Watch out for Degsy's number two, Maggie. She's a lethal bitch. Put her down a.s.a.p.'

Bitch, pronounced 'beach' in Smolensky's Israeli accent. Made Lev think of Gloria. Thick-skinned old Gloria, hiding from her frailty and maternal guilt behind a Wailing Wall of her own construction. And Tiffany. There was a lousy beach. Full of love and promise when her tide was high. Now, all washed up, leaving only a trail of shit and broken dreams. The women in his life he could do without. Then came a thought of poor pregnant Irina. He hoped she would be tucked up somewhere in a women's refuge, safe from harm and strange men's cocks, dreaming of a better future for her baby than the one Jonny Margulies and Tariq Khan had planned for her. A moment of silence passed in which Lev considered he might die in the next few minutes inside this O'Brien cannabis factory. And finally, he thought of little Jay and of the money that would be in his account any day now . . . Hope. Yes, there was still hope.

Live through this, Lev. For the boy.

'Stand back,' Smolensky said, sticking a small square package to the lock on the thick, steel door. Retreating some ten metres to where the group was huddled. He pressed a detonator that he produced from his coat pocket.

With a boom that made Lev's ears ring and a billowing puff of smoke, the lock was blown. A military-grade battering ram, wielded by the biggest of the Salford lads, made short shrift of the door.

Following the others, Lev quick-marched through the smoke, gun drawn. Safety off. The sharp smell of cordite was quickly replaced by a damp, organic fug. Intoxicating and cloying, the smell of high-grade marijuana leaped up Lev's nostrils and lodged itself between his eyes. He started to weave down the straight path. Steadied himself. Difficult when he had to check left, check right to see if anyone was coming at him through the pungent leafy growth of the O'Brien cannabis crop. His focus was waning. Was it merely psychosomatic or was he really beginning to feel spaced out? But there was no time to contemplate just how high he could get off the fumes alone. Smolensky was already a way ahead. The rat-a-tat of the Bren gun made the concrete floor shake beneath him. Screaming from every direction. High-pitched voices of the trafficked Chinese and Vietnamese kids that the O'Briens used to farm the weed. Brap, brap of Boddlington handguns and the coarse shouting of his compatriots, as they silenced one squeak after another.

Not the kids, you arseholes.

It was Maggie that he was after. That shitty ponytailed little witch with her shell suit and scabby mouth and rabid, fuck-ugly Staffordshire bull terrier that she called Shep, like the brainless half-wit she was. She would be hiding out here. Somewhere. Lurking like a coward, waiting to pick them off one by one. With lush green plants growing tall as far as the eye could see under huge UV lamps suspended from the ceiling in the hot, clammy warehouse, Lev felt like he was a GI hunting the Viet Cong in the jungle.

'Come out, come out, wherever you are!' he said under his breath, giggling inappropriately.

Chapter 21

Sheila

'Come on! Come on! Get inside before anyone sees us,' Sheila said to Amy and Dahlia.

Looking over her shoulder, she ushered her daughters from the busy south Manchester roadside, beyond the 1930s façade of a long-dead cinema and into the lofty sanctuary of the local bingo hall. Drank in the nostalgic smell of cheap carpet, Babycham and old ladies' talc, feeling a rush of adrenalin at the thought of what she was attempting. Her heart thumped inside her chest like an over-zealous boxer pummelling a speedball. No sign of Paddy or anyone who worked for him. Good.

'In, I said!' She let the door slam behind her and exhaled heavily. Focused on what lay ahead.

'Where is she?' Amy said, barely concealing the excitement in her voice, like a kid awaiting Santa Claus. Undoubtedly, Amy was the obvious carrier of unadulterated O'Brien genes with the strawberry blonde hair and freckled skin but her exuberance reminded Sheila of herself as a young woman. Before Paddy.

Dahlia, on the other hand, who had the dark looks of her maternal grandfather, looked solemn and unimpressed by the ex-cinema full of grandmas with their brassy-blonde-dyed helmet-hair and support stockings. 'I'd sooner go home and mourn our Jack. I am in mourning, you know. Can I go and mourn? Really, Mum, I was happier being miserable.'

Sheila rounded on her daughter. Lowered her voice to a whisper, lest she draw the gathered bingo aficionados' attention away from the announcements of the bingo caller to their trio's subterfuge.

'Stop moaning. She's not seen you since you were four! This is special.' She clasped her eldest in a bear hug, pinioning her arms to her sides. Willing her to be more enthusiastic. 'I thought it would take your mind off Jack. And your dad's busy with some emergency, so . . . I thought we'd make hay.'

Dahlia fixed her with hard, accusatory eyes. A lawyer's stare.

'Please, love. Do this for me.'

The preoccupied pensioners, scrunched up in their seats like decaying foetuses, did not look up from their bingo score cards, which they marked with fat pink pens, or tablets that they poked methodically with arthritic fingers, their brows furrowed with concentration and wishful thinking.

'All the sevens; seventy-seven. On its own; number four.'

The monotonous voice of the bingo caller droning on through the PA whisked Sheila back to her childhood, when she used to slip into the bingo on the sly with her mam and Auntie Fionnula. She smiled.

'There she is!' she said, grabbing Amy's arm. Trying her damnedest to stem the threatening, roiling tsunami of emotions from sweeping her away. Regret, anticipation, love, guilt . . .

The elderly woman sitting in the orange seat, wriggling

the toes on the end of swollen feet which she'd shoved shoeless into the aisle, looked up.

'By Christ,' she said. 'Sheila.'

'Mam,' Sheila said, holding her hand out. She sat down in the seat next to the woman that had given birth to her. Put her arms around her, pulling her into an awkward hug. The old lady smelled of chips and hairspray. A familiar smell, instantly triggering memories of a blissful childhood.

Her mother looked up at her with eyes that were substantially more crepey than she remembered. Spidery lashes, coated in cheap, claggy mascara. Watery blue irises that had none of the youthful vividity of Sheila's, as though the colour had leached out over time. A reflection of how Sheila might look at seventy, should she lead a different life without the cash and the Botox and the spa treatments.

'I didn't think you'd come,' her mother said.

The sound of the bingo caller continued in the background. 'Two little ducks.'

'Quack quack,' her mother shouted in response along with her rapt compatriots.

'Twenty-two.'

Her mother's eyes were back down to the score card. Scanning her lines for a match. She hadn't even registered the presence of the girls.

'Mam. I've brought Amy and Dahlia.'

'Never been kissed; number sixteen.'

'House!' somebody shouted several rows down on the left.

Finally, her mother looked up at Sheila, scowling. 'That's Elsie Shufflebottom,' she said. 'Jammy old bastard won fifty quid last week.' She folded her arms, the pruning deepening around her lips, as Elsie jumped up and down in her seat, pumping her swollen red hand in the air and high-fiving what appeared to be her daughter in a matching lilac fleece with a matching giant arse.

'Jesus,' Sheila said. 'I remember her from when I was a kid. Is that Julie, her youngest?'

'Yes.'

'She's . . . quite a unit.'

Her mother wheezed with laughter and winked. 'Good to see that ferrety little arsehole you married hasn't sucked all of the fun out of you, our Sheila.'

Finally the old lady turned to Amy and Dahlia. Looked them up and down. Her face crumpled and tears started to leak from those wrinkled, tired eyes. 'Come here, you beauties.' She held her arms wide, encompassing her grown granddaughters in the sort of hug only a grandmother could give.

'Oh, Mam,' Sheila said, stroking her mother's shoulder. Enjoying the warmth that emanated from this long overdue girls' reunion. 'Thanks for agreeing to this. I've missed you *so* much. I can't tell you . . .' She swallowed the threat of tears, not wanting her own daughters to see her pain and judge her for inflicting that same anguish on her own mother. *Keep dignified, She. Hold it together.*

Her mother dabbed at her eyes with the napkin from her half-eaten chicken-in-a-basket and fries. 'I couldn't believe it when I got that email. Your dad only got me online last Christmas, so I could speak to your Auntie Fi in Queensland. She's in Queensland, now, you know?'

Clasping her mother's nicotine-stained hand inside hers, Sheila drank in the sound of her voice, rendered rough and deep by too many Lambert & Butler, or whatever it was she smoked nowadays. She committed to memory the details of her face. Tried to see herself in the bone structure. Wondered how she had looked in the years they had lost.

'Did you tell Dad I'd be here?' she asked.

Looking down at her giant pink marker, her mother shrugged. 'He didn't want to come. I asked him. He's not up to another run-in with Paddy.'

'It's been twenty years, for Christ's sake! Couldn't he have put the past behind him? Especially after I'd been so brave, getting in touch.' Sheila slammed her hand down onto the table but the sound was drowned out by the crowd singing 'Happy Birthday' to somebody's great-nana, who had just turned eighty-six. 'It wasn't easy you know. All that sneaking around.' She visualised the antique Ottoman flintlock rifles in their case, and Paddy's overwhelming disinterest in them as a peace offering. 'You've no idea what it cost me.'

Her mother looked up. Met Sheila's inquisitive gaze. The softness around her eyes had been replaced by something colder and less forgiving. 'And do you think we haven't had to pay a heavy price all these years?' She looked at Amy and Dahlia with accusatory eyes. 'Not seeing these lovely girls grow up. Our grandchildren. Not being able to speak to our own daughter.'

Sheila looked down at her diamond eternity ring. 'I'm sorry. I'm so—'

'Your dad's not well.'

Sheila held her breath. Felt her pulse pounding in her neck. Fingered her charm bracelet nervously. 'Not well? How do you mean?'

With closed eyes, her mother spoke so quietly that Sheila had to strain to hear her above the chatter and hubbub of the bingo hall, between games. 'It's the aggro. He's had a stroke. Lost all the movement in the left side of his body. He gets very frustrated. His speech isn't . . .'

'Shit. You're joking.' Sheila clasped her hands to her mouth.

Her mother's lips thinned to a hard, straight line. Her voice growing in power and acerbity. 'No, Sheila. I'm not joking. And you can blame that scumbag you're married to for banning you from seeing us. He's poisoned your mind, She. Poisoned!' Her mother took out a new score card. Waved it at her daughter. 'I run the gauntlet every time I come to bingo. I have to leave your dad propped in front of an old VHS of *Falcon Crest*. The sight of Jane Wyman is the only thing that calms him down.' Disengaging suddenly, as if her long-lost family wasn't sitting there, Sheila's mother shoved four cold chips into her mouth and started to study her numbers, chewing ferociously.

'Mam!' Feeling frustration mounting at her mother's manner and the news that she had not been there for her father when he had needed her most, Sheila wished she could have done things differently. But there was no opportunity to undo the past. She shook her mother's forearm. 'Mam! I didn't risk lumber off our Paddy to watch you play frigging bingo.'

Her old lady looked up. Glanced over Sheila's shoulder and tutted. 'Oh, here we go. Nothing bloody changes, does it?' She raised an eyebrow at a tall, smartly dressed figure who trod a sure path across the gaudy blue carpet towards them. 'There's a blast from the past. What was his name? Beaky? Always hung around you like a bad smell.'

Sheila rose from her seat and approached the interloper. 'Conky. What's the matter? How the hell did you find me?'

Conky took her arm. His demeanour was stiff; tension and urgency emanating from his every pore. 'Two things,' he said. 'First, Paddy knows you're here and he's on his way.'

Open-mouthed, Sheila frowned. She felt the blood drain from her lips. Her heartbeat quickened. 'But how?' She looked around the bingo hall, expecting to see her husband running towards her with a thunderous expression on his red face and his fist raised in readiness for retribution. Her very own god of hell-fire.

'He's got a GPS tracker on your car, She. I should have told you before.' Staring down at his feet, Conky took his glasses off and treated her to an apologetic shrug. 'There's nothing Paddy doesn't know about your movements. And he's had some kid hack into your email since he found out you were in touch with your mother and you changed your password.'

'Mum! Are you okay?' Amy asked, putting a hand on Sheila's shoulder.

Feeling her legs give way beneath her, Sheila steadied herself on a chair.

'I'll be back in a second, love. Talk to your nan.' She nodded unconvincingly and smiled at her youngest. 'Go!'

The hubbub in the room fell silent. 'Eyes down!' The bingo caller proclaimed the start of the next game. Sheila pulled Conky past the rows of concentrating gamers, into the foyer, where the air was cooler and their conversation would go unheard.

'Why isn't he with you?' Sheila asked, searching Conky's bulging eyes for the truth. She dabbed at her top lip with a tissue. The bead of sweat that tracked its way from her shoulder blades to her bra strap tickled.

'He's with the firm's "cleaners", trying to sort a shit-storm out. There's been a raid on one of our factories. The Boddlingtons sent a death squad in and killed a load of our cannabis farmers.' His voice was almost a whisper. Conky looked up to the ceiling and closed his eyes, as if trying to un-see carnage. 'That's why I'm here, She. I gave him some cock and bull about having a bad reaction to

160

my medication. I knew I had to get to you before he downed tools and came here, looking for you.' He reached out as if to grab her hand but seemed to think better of it. Clasped his together formally over his gut.

'Well, thanks,' she said, glancing at her watch. 'I'll get the girls.' She turned to go back into the bingo hall. They could be out of there and on their way home inside two minutes flat. She could do this! She would foil that suffocating, spying arsehole she was married to.

Conky's large hand fell gently on her shoulder. 'Wait! That's not exactly why I came.'

She turned around to see the big henchman wearing an uncertain expression on his craggy face.

'Sheila, I've got a favour to ask. You're the only one I thought could help.'

He led her outside to a white transit van, parked in a quiet spot in front of a closed down travel agent's. Opened the door to reveal a young girl and a man, both sitting cross-legged in the centre of the loading area. Gagged with their hands tied. They both looked Chinese, Sheila assessed. The man, dressed in cords and a tank top like a maths teacher, was in his thirties, by the looks. But the girl couldn't have been more than thirteen or fourteen. The utilitarian overalls that she wore were covered in what appeared to be soil and blood. Sheila could smell the familiar botanical tang of cannabis on both of them and something sulphurous and chemical beneath that.

'What the fuck is this?' she said, staring from the wide-eyed girl to the silently weeping man. 'I don't want anything to do with Paddy's unsavoury shit. I know what he does for a living but I don't need it ramming down my throat.'

Conky held his hand out in front of the two. Spoke in a placatory tone. 'Wait there. It's going to be okay.'

161

He slid the van door shut, concealing the couple inside.

'What's going to be fucking okay, Conky?' Sheila asked, pulling her cashmere cardigan closed against the stiff summer breeze. 'You've got a Chinese feller and some trafficked girl in a van, covered in blood. For Christ's sake!'

'Can you take her? For your cleaning company, I mean? Her name's Mae Ling. She's a good worker. These two were the only survivors. The bastard Boddlingtons slaughtered the rest like sacrificial lambs. It was like an act of genocide in Cambodia or bloody Rwanda. I've never seen anything like it.' Conky looked away and blinked hard behind those Ray-Bans.

'I'm surprised our Paddy hasn't put the kid on the game. Does he know you've got one of his girls in a van?'

'Please, She. He told me to put a bullet in her because she's too ugly to work in one of the brothels. I just couldn't do it.'

Sheila looked down at the chewing-gum-spattered pavement and sighed heavily. 'Paddy's made me close the cleaning company down,' she said. Shook her head. 'What about the bloke?'

'He's our pharmacist, Colin Chang. Got a chemist's in town but supervises all our meth production. He's into Paddy for quarter of a mill. Bad gambling debt. I like the eejit. Couldn't bring myself to shoot him, you know? He's not like one of the little shites who deals for us. Fate's foisted a bad hand on him. Sure, he's just got caught up in unfortunate circumstances.'

'Paddy's going to end you if he finds out you're rescuing his bloody workforce. Are you *mental*?'

'Maybe it's a midlife crisis, She. Maybe I'm just losing my touch.'

Checking her watch again, Sheila bit her lip. Felt the

weight of this conundrum pressing down on her already overburdened shoulders.

'Jesus. Why did you have to dump all this crap on me?' Looking up at Conky, she felt the sudden urge either to kiss him or slap him. 'I turn a blind eye and get on with my own business. That's how I sleep at night. Now I'm involved!'

Conky touched his elaborate hair arrangement awkwardly. The gusting wind blew his comb-over awry, revealing clips, hair-piece and the naked scalp beneath. He looked suddenly fallible and far from the usual super-human persona of the Loss Adjuster. 'I'm sorry. I didn't know who else to ask.'

Sheila tutted. 'Just threaten them and let them go, for God's sake. And don't let Paddy ever find out about this.'

Chapter 22

Lev

'Let us in!' Lev shouted through the letterbox. 'Gloria. Please! Mam!'

He peered over his shoulder to check nobody was watching from the bedroom windows on the opposite side of the leafy road. But this was Chorlton. Home to long-standing local residents, well aware of who came and went on these streets. Home to upwardly mobile trendies, with their wooden shutters, who were always on the lookout for suspicious types who had wandered with thieving intentions into the hip enclave from Whalley Range or Withington. Of course they'd be watching, even if he couldn't see them.

'I know you're in there. Open the door, for God's sake.'

Eyeing the Mazda on the drive, he wondered briefly if she had walked to the shops with Jay in the trolley. But Gloria was an exhibitionist, despite the church elder meek-inheriting-the-earth bullshit. She wouldn't have gone more than 100 yards without those gleaming wheels.

Stepping back, he surveyed the windows of the neat semi with its honeysuckle growing around the arch of the 1930s porch. A middle-class, aspirational world away from the dump across town where she had dragged him up. And then he saw what he needed. A twitching curtain in the third bedroom, where Jay was staying.

'Gloria, open the fucking door!' he yelled, knowing that by causing a scene, she was more likely to usher him inside. All about the appearances, was his mother. She always had been.

The door was wrenched open. There she was, wrapped up in a kimono with her feet stuffed into bejewelled flip-flops. Painted toenails. A towel on her head. Her attractive features were contorted into a thunderous glare. 'Get in here now or I'm calling the police!' she said between gritted teeth, jerking her head backwards. 'And keep your voice down. I've just got your son to sleep.'

The house was warm from the morning sunshine that streamed in through the side window in the hall. It smelled of clean washing, beeswax and nail varnish remover. Lev remembered the comforting scents from childhood but defiantly pushed any nostalgia to the back of his over-wrought mind.

'Is Jay alright?' he asked, wishing he could bound upstairs and whisk the boy to a different life and a better future. He noticed a food stain down the front of Gloria's kimono. A faint whiff of Sudocrem about her.

'He's fine. Thanks to his nan coming to the rescue at no notice whatsoever! Certainly no thanks to you and that junkie harlot, Tiffany. I take it she's still in hospital.'

A mental image popped unbidden into Lev's mind. Tiff in the stifling, packed side-ward, harnessed to a web of tubing and machines that bleeped. The nurses, treating her as though she were some kind of suicide risk. Screw her.

'She'll live. But I'm in trouble,' he said. 'Big trouble. I need a place to stay. Lay low, like.' He stood, propping himself on the highly polished sideboard in the hall that showed photos of Gloria with the pastor. Gloria with her church cronies. Gloria with Sheila O'Brien, holding up some gaudy golden award in the shape of a yard brush saying, 'Scrubbers of the Year 2014'. Frame after ornate brass frame, set out in neat rows on doilies. Nothing showing him. Naturally.

'I'm going to a funeral, Leviticus,' inglorious Gloria said, arms folded across her chest. 'Jack O'Brien's funeral. They've finally released the body. It's time the poor boy was laid to rest.'

'That prick?' Lev said. Immediately wishing he hadn't. He needed Gloria. Now was not the time to wind her up. Too late.

'Hey,' she said, poking him in the chest with an electric blue fingernail at the end of a work-worn finger. 'Show the dead some respect! That's my business partner's nephew. I knew Jack from birth. I changed his nappies when I babysat for his dad. I hoovered his bedroom and wiped down his cot when I was still mopping Frank and Paddy O'Brien's floors to feed you, you ungrateful boy!'

'Spare us the lecture,' Lev said. 'Look, can I stay here for a couple of days or not? I'm due the money for Jay's oper-ation any day now. I just wanna book the tickets and go. The specialist reckons he can book in the surgery at short notice.'

Gloria snapped her fingers, indicating that Lev should follow her into the kitchen. She filled the kettle and switched it on. Spooned instant coffee into two china mugs.

'What's going on with you?' A shapely raised eyebrow. 'What in the Lord's name are you up to now, Leviticus?'

Lev bit his lip. 'I've got Asaf Smolensky watching me every time I fart. I told you it was him that OD'd Tiff the other day. The guy's a wanker. Nearly kills my babymother off just so he can warn us he's got his eye on me. He's found out me and you are speaking and he reckons I've got something to do with Jack's murder.'

Gloria flung the teaspoon into her shining sink. Said nothing. But he could tell she was mulling it over.

'So, you know the deal's off between my lot and your lot,' Lev said.

Gloria hooked her hand onto her hip, eyes flashing like a lights on a level crossing.

'I don't know what you mean, "your lot". I'm a respectable businesswoman and God-fearing church-goer. Don't lump me in with a bunch of murdering ne'er-do-wells.'

Lev felt resentment and anger effervesce inside him. Why did she have to be such a bitch? Making him feel like worthless scum. He needed her help but the temptation to treat her to an angry retort was so strong that he had to bite down hard on his tongue. He succumbed.

'Yeah. Whatever. Well you should know that it was me who stabbed Paddy O'Brien and put him in hospital a few weeks ago. Yes. Me.' Raised an eyebrow, matched with a calculated smirk. *Take that, Gloria.*

Gloria's coffee cup stalled in its ascent towards her open mouth. 'You did what?'

'I was in the club. I got fingered as a Boddlington. It's a long story. I knifed him. He had the heart attack because of it, I heard.'

Slamming the cup down on the worktop, Gloria's full lips compressed into a hard line.

'Are you telling me that you're behind Paddy's decision to move to Thailand? Is it down to you that my livelihood and a lifeline for all my employees is going out of the window?'

Lev was certain that if she removed the towel from her

head, her wet hair would have bristled into braided spikes. He shoved one hand deep into his jogging bottom pocket. Drank awkwardly from the blistering hot coffee, risking a scalding rather than letting her read his guilty expression.

'Oh and I battered the living daylights out of Degsy, one of Conky McFadden's best, so I'm gonna have him on my case any minute.' Lev sat the coffee cup down carefully. Rubbed the hot skin of his face. Wishing he could somehow erase the creeping embarrassment. Dispel the fatigue that had set into his bones. 'Last night was the worst, though. I fucked up—'

'Language!'

'I cocked up a raid. Passed out in one of the O'Brien's cannabis farms, when I was meant to take Maggie out. I was under strict orders from the Fish Man. And I just fainted. I was so tired. One minute, I'm on my feet with a gun in my hand. Next minute, I'm on my back, staring at these UV lights. When I came to, there was bodies everywhere. Kids dead. Some of their people dead. Couple of our lads with holes in them like sieves. And the others had gone. They left me. Maybe they just couldn't find me. But when they do, I'm dead meat. And if I'm dead meat, our Jay's toast.'

Gloria drummed her fingernails on the worktop, staring into his eyes, as though she was some lesser holy woman, trying to divine for the soul in him. 'Look after your son while I'm at the funeral,' she said. 'But if you so much as touch a single thing in my house, you're out. If you let anyone know you're here, I'll call the police. Do you understand? And I want you to find somewhere else to go by tomorrow night. I can do without the likes of the Fish Man turning up on my doorstep. And I certainly don't want any truck with Conky McFadden. Keep a low profile. You hear me?'

When Gloria pulled out of the driveway in her Mazda with the top down and her funeral hat in a box on the seat beside her, Lev exhaled heavily. Crept upstairs to watch his sleeping son.

'Hello, love,' he whispered, peering into the travel cot that Gloria had erected in the box room. Expecting to see a peaceful cherubic face. Except Jay's face was anything but. His eyes were screwed tightly shut and his small mouth was set into a grimace. As if sensing his father was close by, Jay started to whimper in his sleep. Within seconds, he was wide awake and screaming.

Lev picked him out of the travel cot. Panicking. Reached for a dummy, lying on the base of the cot. Jay spat it out. Offered him a teddy bear. Jay threw it angrily to the other side of the room. 'Shush, shush, shush, little man,' he said, his useless voice smothered beneath the blanket of agonising noise.

He felt his phone vibrating in his pocket. Repositioning his distraught child on his hip, he tried to pull the device from his jogging bottoms. Withdrew his gun by accident. Placed it hastily on top of Jay's changing bag. Finally retrieved his phone, managing to get the message up from Asaf Smolensky.

You ballsed up. There will be consequences. I'm coming for you.

Shit. Lev swallowed hard and moved to the window. Peered through the net curtain down the street to see if Smolensky's people carrier was within sight. He would surely track him down to Gloria's. He couldn't stay there, not right now.

'Come on, little man. We need to get you somewhere

169

safe,' he said, kissing his son's head. Clambering down to the hall, holding his phone in his mouth, his gun in his pocket, Jay in one arm and the changing bag in the other. Lev found a slightly melted KitKat on the radiator cover and gave it to the boy in a bid to placate him. 'We're going on a little trip, son. Daddy can't stay here.'

He tried to keep his voice calm and low. Inside, he was a tangle of fear, guilt and confusion. Where exactly could he go? Home wasn't safe. The O'Briens had eyes in Sweeney Hall and those eyes would now be trained on him. That irresponsible twat Tiff was laid up and out of commission.

As he strapped the wailing Jay into the pushchair, his phone went. Swallowing down a lump of ice, he expected Jonny or Tariq, demanding to know why he had gone AWOL. But the number was unfamiliar. Maybe it was his benefactor. Hope surged within him at the thought of £150,000 landing in his account.

'Hello,' he said.

'Mr Bell? This is social services. We'd like a word with you about your son's living arrangements.'

No, no, no! This was getting worse by the minute.

'He's with me. I'm his dad. He's fine.'

'But we'd like to come and inspect your abode, because...'

He zoned out from the woman's monotonous voice. Wondering how he could stave off a visit to a flat that was anything but fit; a flat he dare not go back to. How could he take the boy and get on a plane to the US with social services breathing down his sodding neck?

'You're breaking up, love,' he said, and cut the call short.

There was only one place he could go but it would involve a biblical trek across town.

*   *   *

Cigarette smoke rose in acrid roiling funnels above the smokers standing by the Outpatients entrance of North Manchester General Hospital. Their pallor and crumpled faces told Lev all he needed to know – these were the scum stuck to the sole of society's shoe. The kind of fleece-clad, super-strength-lager-drinking no-hopers he would have been one of, if he hadn't been recruited into the Boddlingtons. It had seemed so glamorous when he was in his mid-teens. Flogging wraps of gear to desperate junkies and wearing a gun stuffed inside the waistband of his jeans, pretending he was a real player – going somewhere in style. The girls had fallen for it every time, as though he himself had addictive, narcotic qualities. Now, he knew better. He had seen things he wished he could un-see and done things he would spend his entire life repenting for privately. The worst kind of role model for his infant son, he knew. But at least he had Tariq and Jonny's money on top of his dole, and a semi-structured, Russian Roulette of a career path to follow. You took your chances. He'd always known that much. Take a right turn, he'd be scaling the broken bodies of those who'd gambled and lost to take his place at the top of the enlightened heap. Take a wrong turn, and the unrighteous path would lead him straight into the dark of an early shallow grave with a bad-man's bindi between the eyes. One thing he mused was for certain, as he walked past the rotten, stinking flesh of smokers who were trying on their corpses for size, if he hadn't chosen to pick up a gun and a fistful of baggies instead of a pint and a betting slip, he'd be dead by thirty anyway.

Pushing Jay's pram along the squeaky lino of the corridors, he passed a sea of washed-out, harried faces. Nurses on their break. Hurrying, scurrying doctors, clutching at their stethoscopes as though they were magnetised, drawing them inexorably to some trauma elsewhere. Relatives, looking like they'd rather be anywhere than in this city that never slept. Past the chapel on his left, the snack stop on his right. Praying that nobody would spot him. Delving into his pocket, he took out the piece of paper with her ward number on it. F3. Or was it E3? Squinting, he couldn't clearly read the number, smudged as it was by blood from God knew where. Maybe Tommo or Kai's blood? Maybe Irina's or Degsy's?

With Jay screaming and arching his back in the pushchair, Lev entered a ward, peering at the beds in the hope of finding her. The smell of medicinal alcohol made him feel woozy. He was expecting women in fluffy dressing gowns with lank hair plastered to their heads. Wrong place. It was all men – mainly old guys with yellow complexions and oxygen cannulas strapped to their faces. Worried wives by their bedsides, looking like they'd still managed to get their hair done for the occasion.

'Can I help you, love?' a tubby auxiliary asked. Her greasy locks were scraped tightly into a bun on the top of her head. Her lilac uniform and pink glasses made her look like a nursery nurse.

'I'm looking for Tiffany White,' he said, shuddering at the strange feeling that one of the men in one of the beds was watching him intently. A quick scan of the ward revealed nothing untoward, but his senses burned on red alert.

'Upstairs,' the smiling woman said. Cooing at a grizzling Jay who screamed blithely at her sudden attention. She looked less chirpy, then.

Finally, he entered the ward where Tiffany was being kept under observation. It was brightly lit and swelteringly hot. At first, the stout staff nurse had been reluctant to let him in during lunchtime, but Jay was his green card.

'He needs his mam,' he said simply, looking beyond the heavily fringed woman in the dark blue uniform.

Ensconced in a side room, sitting on top of her bed in a onesie covered in black pup's paw prints, Tiffany was flicking through *Heat* magazine. When she caught sight of Lev and her son, she threw the magazine aside and treated them both to a doleful stare.

'Fucking nice of yous to come,' she said, sarcasm dripping thickly from her grey lips. She tried to fold her arms but became tangled in the drips that fed into a cannula in the crook of her arm and the back of her hand.

'I brought Jay to see you,' Lev said, popping the fasteners and lifting the boy carefully out of the pushchair.

With his hands clamped to his temples, Jay began to scream. Lev had half-hoped that Tiffany would hold out her arms to embrace him, offering a mother's comfort. But she merely looked away despondently, folding her arms even tighter to her chest.

'I need you to look after him for a couple of days,' Lev said. 'My mam's had him since you OD'd. But she's buggered off to a funeral, so she's no use. No change there. And I'm in a spot of bother.'

Suddenly, her eyes were on him; an accusatory glare that could have stripped the flaking drab paint from the hospital walls.

'Aw, don't be like that, Tiff. It's not safe for him to be around us. You seen what happened to you.'

His babymother leaned forward, her jaw set hard so that he could see the nicotine stains on the underside of her bottom teeth. Dark circles beneath her eyes. Hair plastered to her head. Not so foxy now.

'Yes, I bleeding saw what happened to me! And why did I end up in here, Leviticus? Was it because some nutcase

Jew in a cowboy hat shot me up with a load of heroin as a warning because of some shit you've been up to?'

'I'm sorry. I swear on my baby's life, it's all for him. Everything I'm doing is to get the money for his op.'

'Bullshit,' she shouted above her son's intermittent wailing, settling back on her pillow and looking studiously at her heart monitor. Anywhere, but at Lev or Jay. 'This is all about you. It always was. But nobody gives a shit about me, having to cope with that noise all day long.'

Lev stood, feeling a dull ache in his gut as she referred to his precious, vulnerable son's crying as 'that noise'. What a lousy mother she was and what a lousy father he was for having chosen her.

Buckling under the weight of the guilt, he embraced his son tightly and prepared to strap him back into the push-chair. He didn't want to leave him but felt certain this was the safest place. The nurses would help Tiff to take care of him. It was only for a couple of days.

The shuffling figure peering through the glass window of the ward door didn't really register with Lev, so racked was he with anguish and fear. All fingers and thumbs, fiddling with the pram straps. Neither did he notice when that figure entered the ward behind a porter, wheeling a cage full of clean bedding. It didn't occur to him that there was something odd about a man, wearing pyjamas, a dressing gown and red carpet slippers, advancing down a women's ward, his head bandaged up with a large pad strapped to his cheekbone. And by the time the unwanted visitor entered Tiffany's side room, drawing a scalpel from his dressing gown pocket, it was too late.

'Now it's your turn, you bastard!' Degsy said, slashing at Lev with the blade.

174

Chapter 23

Sheila

'What do you mean, stop packing?' Standing in her underwear with rollers pinned uncomfortably in her hair, Sheila placed Paddy's neatly folded T-shirts into the third largest suitcase. The other two were already full; their open lids propped against the sofa at the foot of their bed. She'd tripped over them twice that morning already, laddering her favourite tights. 'We're going to Thailand next week, Paddy. Bloody Thailand. For good! It's not round the corner and we're going to need something to wear.'

Grabbing her painfully by the wrist, Paddy swung her around so that she had no option but to stop and look at him. He was naked but for the towel around his waist. Sweat from the hot shower was still glistening on his florid bald scalp and the fluffy tops of his shoulders.

'It's Jack's funeral today,' he said. 'Your nephew. For God's sake, show some respect, woman.'

Sheila shook her wrist free, willing the tears that threatened at the backs of her already made-up eyes to stay put. Defensively, she took a step backwards, rubbing the place where he'd grabbed her.

'Like I don't know. Do you think I'm not hurting?'

Paddy glared at her. Pulled off his towel to reveal his flaccid manhood and a paunch that spoke of decadence – rich dinners and too much booze. Sheila prayed he wasn't going to start demanding sex when the girls were in their rooms, getting ready. She turned away. Started to brush down the little black dress hanging on one of the mirrored doors of the fitted wardrobes.

'Today's not about your feelings, you selfish cow,' he said, following her across the room. 'Just remember that. Today's about our Frank and the family's loss.' He slapped a hot hand on her shoulder. Made her flinch; her body tensing for what might come. Dug his nails in, then seemed to think better of it. His voice softened. 'We're on show today, She. The whole of Manchester will be watching. I want you to look right. I want you to act right. Do you think you can do that much? Do you think you can shove your selfish, empty-headed shit on a back burner long enough to make people think there's more to you than clothes and a spray tan?'

Not wanting to turn around lest he see the hurt etched into her face, Sheila carried on brushing down the dress.

'Do I ever let you down, Paddy?'

Silently, she prayed the storm would pass. He'd been so easy to rile of late. He surely wouldn't start properly on her. Not while the girls were down the landing. She needed to make sure for their sake. Turning to face him, she was all sympathetic smiles, placing comforting manicured fingers on his freckled chest. 'My poor Paddy. This must be so hard for you, losing our Jack.' She screwed her face up into something resembling empathy. 'I know he's Frank's son – was Frank's son – but I know Jack always looked up to *you* as his father figure.'

Watching his chest rise and his overall demeanour switch

from one of morose threat to puffed-up pride, she held her breath. This could go one of two ways . . . She looked down at his penis, already at half-mast and swelling fast. The glint in his eye revealed his intentions. Paddy wanted to spray his territory. Shit.

Nimbly, she side-stepped beyond his reach, scurrying in her stockinged feet into the bathroom, where she could lock the door until his ardour had waned. Not quick enough, though. He thumped across the room after her. She braced herself to feel his unrelenting arms encircle her small waist from behind.

'Not now, Paddy.' She tried to wriggle free. Felt suffocated by his insistent bulk. 'The car will be here in twenty. The girls . . .'

'Balls to them. They can all wait. Come here. Paddy needs some love.' He started to kiss her neck, biting the soft flesh beneath her ear.

'Don't bite me. I don't want to have to wear a scarf.'

But he had already sunk his teeth into her and was sucking, pressing his erection into her bottom. 'I'm going to take you up the arse, She. You know you like it like that.' He shuffled her into the en suite and bent her over the bidet.

'No, Paddy!' She tried to push him off, wishing she could shout for help. 'Give over! We're going to be late.'

The harder he pressed himself against her, the more she instinctively shrank away from him. Squeezing her eyes shut, she knew it would hurt. There wasn't even any lube in the bathroom. This was the last thing she wanted on the morning of her nephew's funeral.

'Paddy, love. I've just showered and my piles are playing up. Let me give you a hand job.'

He was already rutting against her inner thigh, sticking

his finger inside her silk knickers. She felt the gossamer fabric of the tights give way. Another pair destined for the bin. Behind her, crushing her arms into the rim of the bidet, she felt him part her cheeks with his clammy hands. Groaning with anticipation. Enough.

Bucking him hard with gym-honed glutes, she pushed him backwards enough to catch him off balance. Spun around, kneeing him in the erection.

'Whoops. Sorry, darling. We're going to be late.' She studiously stared down at her Cartier watch. Tapped its diamond-encrusted face. 'Have you seen the time?'

But her husband wasn't interested in the time. His purple-red erection made his intentions abundantly clear. Glowering at her, he lunged for her breast with his teeth bared. She ducked away from the feral bite and slapped him hard across the side of his head. Immediately realised her blunder and ran back into the bedroom, wondering what the hell she could do next to fend off this attack before it got serious. He was escalating quickly today. It was easier when he went nightly to M1 House and had his voracious needs met by one of the bandeau-dress-clad slags that were ferried by promoters to the VIP area. Mainly little scrubbers from Trafford and Stretford – that lot were anybody's for free vodka and the promise of a rich sugar-daddy from Bramshott. As long as Paddy didn't shit on his own doorstep, as he had with Tracy Wheelan, she could rationalise his philandering. Sheila knew the game and she was glad of it, because it gave her breathing space. Not today, though. Not since Frank had gone into mourning.

'Bitch!' Paddy shouted, haring after her.

With the large bed barring her way, he tackled her and flung her on top. Thumped her hard in the stomach with a fist full of venom. Watched her reaction momentarily like a predator fascinated by his struggling prey before going in for the kill. Thumped her again.

The air left Sheila's lungs, replaced with a void that her desperate, futile shallow gasps failed to fill. The vice-like pain in her gut was intense. She clawed at the bedding. Felt her eyes bulging and her face flushing red. Finally she managed to yelp, curling up in a foetal position. Allowing the oxygen back in in agonising, miserly spurts. She was careful to hold her hands above her head. Willing herself not to cry for the sake of her mascara. Paddy drew his fist back yet again. Jesus. He hadn't been like this in a long while. Certainly not since before the heart attack. The optimist in her had hoped he'd turned over a new leaf. The cynic that had devoted an entire adult lifetime to Patrick O'Brien knew better. 200,000 hours of knowing better in fact, her therapist had said. Her disappointment and apprehension manifested itself as a ball of bile erupting into her throat. She swallowed it down. Started to choke and cough, which made her tender stomach throb.

'Go on then, you arsehole,' she spluttered. 'Hit me!'

A knock at the door stayed his hand.

'Mum? Dad!' It was Dahlia, by the sound of it. 'Everything alright in there?'

'Yes, love,' Paddy said, kneeling above her, fist still held high in readiness.

'We'll be out in a minute,' Sheila shouted brightly, not wanting her daughter to hear any fear in her voice. She was a time-served craftsman in the art of concealment. What the girls didn't know about their parents' marriage wouldn't harm them. So it had always been and so it would remain, as long as she breathed.

There was a pause. Sheila sensed Dahlia was merely

listening behind the door. The handle was depressed on the other side. Then released.

'Anyway, the car's here,' Dahlia said at last. 'Me and Amy will wait for you downstairs, okay?' Her footfalls were audible as she walked away.

The fire seemed to subside in Paddy's eyes. He dropped his fist, finally. 'I'm sorry, She,' he said, quietly. 'I'm really sorry, I—' His face crumpled in contrition.

Jekyll and Hyde bastard, Sheila thought.

'Forget it. Get dressed. Frank needs you.'

Clasping her hand to her stomach, she pushed her husband off.

With the girls in the car, it was essential to remain upbeat, Sheila decided. Sandwiched between them, she clasped their hands to her mouth and kissed them.

'It is so lovely to have you both home. I just wish it wasn't under such dreadful circumstances.'

'Will they find who did it? Who did this to Jack?' Amy asked, her red-rimmed eyes blinking too fast. She looked so like her dad, but thankfully hadn't inherited his incendiary nature.

'Jack played with fire,' Dahlia said, rubbing the dark fabric of her conservative lawyer's suit between her fingers. 'He should have known better.'

Sheila could see Paddy's lips thin. She willed Dahlia to say nothing more. Thankfully the peace was maintained until the car pulled up at Jack's place – a smart Victorian terrace in Didsbury. Conky McFadden had beaten them to it and was already standing by the front door, holding leather-gloved hands clasped before him, wearing a grim reaper's expression.

'Sorry again for your loss, boss,' he said. 'Everyone's

inside, waiting for you. I've checked there are no unwelcome faces.'

Inside, the sparsely furnished contemporary living room was already packed with sober-faced friends, family and ushers, all looking as though they had put on their best and only suits. Women's stilettos digging into Jack's beautiful parquet floor. Jack had always made people take their shoes off. Sheila felt it as an affront on his behalf. Gaudy floral tributes dressed with purple ribbon were perched on every surface. The scent of lilies was overpowering. Paddy had had her order a giant 'JACK', studded with white carnations. That would take pride of place in the hearse window at his behest, of course, only marginally upstaged by the blinging coffin.

As she crossed the room behind Paddy, the animated chatter calmed almost instantly to a low, mournful thrum. Everybody took a respectful step back to let the great King Patrick advance to his rightful place next to Frank, who was standing by the white and gold coffin – its lid mercifully closed now that the Vigil had taken place. Sheila had been amazed that her nephew had been made to look like he was just sleeping off a good night in Ibiza. Appearing rather worse for wear than his dead son, however, Frank now looked like he had spent the night at the bottom of a bottle of vodka. Paddy slapped him across the back and cleared his throat, his eyes darting across the room, as though he didn't know how to react to a man who unashamedly displayed the visible pain of the bereaved.

'Sheila,' Frank said, his chin dimpling up and the corners of his mouth turning downwards. He embraced her warmly, leaking hot tears onto her neck. Poor bastard.

'We're here for you, Frank,' she said, beckoning her girls close so that they should also show their uncle moral support. Casting an eye over the scores of O'Brien cousins, uncles, aunties, dressed to impress. 'Your family's all here.'

He shook his head too energetically. Wiped his eyes on the cuff of his jacket.

'*Jack* was my fucking family,' he said, hammering his chest with a nicotine-stained index finger. 'I lost everything when I lost my boy.'

He directed a bitter stare towards Paddy.

Frank staggered out behind the coffin towards the waiting cortege that lined the leafy side-street. The gleaming black funeral limousine and hearse stood out among vehicles of relatives and pimped-up rides of Jack's inner circle and O'Brien firm lackeys.

People thronged the street, as if it were a state burial – the men nodding respectfully and the women offering sympathetic smiles to Frank. Dressed in a fine black suit and slim tie, he looked the part, but Sheila could see from the pitch and roll of his walk and his bowed posture that he was drowning on the inside. A ship threatening to capsize. She linked arms with him, pleased to swap Paddy – who was too preoccupied with shaking the hands of his acolytes to be feeling anything but pride – for a thin-skinned man who was flooded with the full spectrum of emotions.

With the reassuring presence of Conky McFadden travelling behind them and the flower-filled hearse in front, they journeyed through the red-brick streets of south Manchester, bustling with back-packed students hurrying to their lectures, to the Holy Name church on Oxford Road. Focusing on the black peaked cap and creased, red neck of the driver, Sheila was careful to avoid the gaze of Paddy. He was sitting, legs akimbo, like he was en-route to a party, holding a monologue that nobody listened to about the O'Brien dynasty and feudal nature of respect. She made damned sure that he couldn't see her wincing with pain from the bruising caused by his punches.

Finally, as the car pulled up behind the hearse, Sheila understood the enormity of an O'Brien being murdered. Jack O'Brien, of all people. The pavement outside the large, sandstone Catholic almost-cathedral churned with people. Gaggles of young girls decked out in hotpants and vests as though they were heading off to the Trafford Centre for a day's shopping, taking macabre selfies with the hearse in the background. Paparazzi, snapping nattily dressed black guys whom Sheila recognised as rappers, with their arms slung nonchalantly around the shoulders of singers she had seen on the music channels that played continually on the gym's TVs. All fluttering false eyelashes and backcombed 1950s hair. Actors, recognisable from soap operas. The region's glitterati and gritterati had come out in force. Jack clearly hadn't belonged to the O'Briens. He had belonged to the world. Sheila wondered how Paddy felt now, knowing he was a zero next to his dead nephew. The thought made her smile.

As the pall-bearers shuffled forwards, bearing the coffin on their shoulders, Paddy pushed his way between Sheila and the beleaguered Frank. Placed his arm territorially around Frank's shoulder.

'Back off, She,' he said, glancing in her direction but not meeting her disgruntled glare. As he turned to face forwards, she was sure he winked at some groupie onlooker who was dabbing artfully at observant, dry eyes. 'This is brotherly business.'

Feeling her cheeks flush hot, Sheila bit her lip and looked down at her shoes. Acknowledged the pain where Paddy had hit her but pushed it aside, hooking her arm inside Dahlia's. Swallowed hard as her brother-in-law started to sob like a small boy with a skinned knee. From behind, she watched his shoulders heaving, but there was nothing she could do to comfort Frank. She walked three steps behind. Always a cheap afterthought in expensive clothing. At her side, Conky McFadden lifted his glasses and fixed her with his bulging thyroid eyes. Behind the disconcerting frog-like stare, she saw sympathy. Even Conky could see the hurt she thought she was hiding so well.

Inside, the organ played a solemn hymn that echoed around the lofty vaulted ceiling. She had loved coming here as a little girl, on the way back into town from school. Alighting from the bus at the university students' union, she would sit in silence on one of the pews, marvelling that the tiny golden crucifix, hanging above the altar, was such a modest focal-point in such a famous and otherwise ornate church. The Smiths had sung about it. Even Elsie Tanner from *Coronation Street* had had her funeral mass here.

Towards the front, she spotted Gloria, looking prim but proud beneath a fascinator that had Debenhams written all over it. She gave her a fleeting smile that would remind her she was not family. Noticed Maureen Kaplan and her posse of bent accountants on the same row, all deferentially nodding at Frank and Paddy. All except for the man that wasn't one of Kaplan's sons. What was his name, again? Goodman. David Goodman. He looked like he was about to vomit. And, perhaps most interestingly, she noticed that Goodman was staring intently over at a small dishevelled-looking man with a buzz cut and glasses, sitting next to a frump of a woman with hair that resembled a brown helmet.

The detective and the tax inspector. The gruesome twosome. Ellis James and Ruth Darley.

Chapter 24

Gloria

Watching the coffin as it was lowered into the ground in Southern Cemetery, Gloria mused on how sombre Catholic funerals were. Turgid hymns. A dour priest talking about original sin. Very little in the way of passionate outpourings of sorrow. They were all so darned stoic, she observed. Almost Presbyterian compared to her lot. Only Frank, the poor soul, stood sobbing his childish heart out as he shovelled some soil onto the coffin. But Paddy was transfixed by something else – something to her left. Gloria peered around, pushing some feathers from her fascinator out of her eyes to see what was so blasted interesting.

A girl in a short skirt. Typical Paddy.

At his side, Sheila dabbed her eyes, flanked by her over-privileged daughters who showed none of the chavvy, poor-girl-done-good bling of their mother. Admittedly, the passing of a young man was always something to mourn, but Gloria could harness little in the way of sympathy for anyone in that family but Frank. A lost soul, if ever there was one.

Sheila looked in her direction. Their eyes met but there was no response to Gloria's smile. Very frosty of late since the nonsense about going to Thailand and closing the business. But then, Gloria knew the score. She was still just the black cleaner in Sheila O'Brien's eyes. Their sisterly alliance did not run beneath the skin.

Blood's thicker than water.

Delving into her clutch bag, peering at her phone surreptitiously, Gloria wondered that she had heard nothing from Leviticus. She had left him alone with his son in her house, apparently with half of north Manchester's worst after him. Silly boy. He had too much of his father in him. Impetuous and weak-willed. Easily swayed by flattery, keeping company with the wrong kind. You lie with dogs, you get fleas. Hadn't she always told him that?

Looking up to the grey heavens, she prayed silently to Jesus that things would all pan out right; that she'd be the salvation her own grandson was so badly in need of; that she'd continue to set a good example to the women in church of how poverty needn't stand in the way of success or bagging a fine man like the pastor.

So engrossed was she in her prayer and in giving the other women's hats marks out of ten, that Gloria barely noticed the blue flashing lights in her peripheral vision. Beyond the iron railings and low wall that separated the sprawling cemetery from the fast traffic of the main road, bright lights were blinking in a row as though a host of angels had descended to mourn the passing of Jack O'Brien.

Except Gloria was no fool. Surreptitiously, as her mind began to focus, she could see the tall sides of riot vans, their black mesh shields still up. Now, black-clad figures, bulked out with stab-vests and dressed for a day's crowd control, filed briskly into the cemetery's entrance. Shields, helmets, the lot. She recognised the Tactical Aid Unit of the Greater Manchester Police – hadn't she seen them in action often enough on those occasions, when Leviticus and his ungodly little friends had got themselves worked into a tizz and had started a set-to with some rival two-bit gang from Burnage? Oh yes. Gloria Bell knew hell-fire on earth when she saw it – two giant German shepherd police dogs leading this arrow of justice straight to the evil heart of the O'Brien clan.

Stepping away from the graveside and the other oblivious funeral-goers, Gloria was suddenly aware of the whirr and hum of a helicopter. Stepping back, retreating further at speed. She had clocked a crowd of black mourners less than two hundred yards away, burying Moss Side's dead. Keep walking backwards to the brothers and sisters of some wholesome church where people actually read the good book and knew how to praise Jesus properly. Black umbrellas, carried by the women, would provide additional cover.

By the time the police descended on the O'Briens, Gloria had an excellent vantage point from which to watch the action unfold.

'Paddy O'Brien, you have the right to remain silent . . .' As the stony-faced copper read a shocked-looking Paddy his rights, more and more police flooded onto the cemetery.

She could hear Frank wailing, 'No! Not like this. Have a heart. It's my boy's funeral, for God's sake. Are you mental, man?' Trying to shake the strong arm of the law off as though those policemen were merely clubbers on a packed dancefloor, encroaching on his space. He allowed himself to be patted down and cuffed while the young women by the graveside took photos of the fray with their mobile phones.

Dogs, straining at the leash as Paddy O'Brien offered his hands, wearing a supercilious smile that Gloria knew was as fake as his tan. He would be dying inside, she was certain. Exchanging knowing looks with Sheila, who tugged at the sleeve of a detective with a close crop of dirty blond hair, glasses and a shabby, grubby raincoat. She was certain he had been sitting amongst the grieving family and friends in the church, this Judas. Hadn't he been staring at one of Maureen Kaplan's cronies?

Ignoring the askance glances she was getting from the funeral party she had just joined, Gloria monitored who among the O'Briens' gathering was being rounded up and read their rights. She could hear Maureen Kaplan shouting.

'Get your filthy hands off me. I'm a pillar of the Manchester business community. I'm going to have you for wrongful arrest and police brutality!' Her bleached hair was just visible beneath the widest-brimmed hat Gloria had ever seen. A power hat. Typical Maureen, trying to use accessories to make amends for her absence of a penis and God in her life.

Not so powerful now.

The policeman knocked the hat into the mound of soil at the side of the grave in an attempt to wrench Maureen's flailing hands together for the cuffs. Gloria chuckled at the sight of the expensive-looking cream raffia confection becoming dirtied. Felt a little warmth inside her in that windy cemetery at the apparent divine justice she was witnessing.

'Getting stuck in the eye of a needle,' she said, taking a further step away from the scene of mayhem. Something soft beneath the heel of her shoe. A foot.

'Hey. Why don't you watch where you're putting your big flippers, Grandma!' the woman at her side said.

Hardly a woman. A girl.

At a glance, Gloria ascertained she couldn't have been

more than twenty, wearing a dress that was inappropriately short for the solemn occasion of a funeral. The girl's hair consisted of glossy extensions that looked cheaply sewn into a receding hairline. Too much cleavage on show and clear signs of a poorly executed tattoo peeping out of the neckline just above the girl's left breast.

Sucking her teeth, Gloria rifled through her mental Rolodex of known contacts to work out who this impertinent upstart was.

'Shereen Turner,' Gloria said. 'Just you mind what you say to a church elder! Show some respect, girl.'

Gloria looked to the other women for moral support but found none forthcoming. She smiled winningly at familiar faces she recognised from the butcher's and the hairdresser's.

'Sorry for your loss, Flora,' she said to the woman she recognised as the dead boy's mother. Puffy, bloodshot eyes and a snotty nose beneath a terrible beret that only scored four out of ten. She was small and tubby like her son. A Kingstonian who ate too much of her own soul food than was good for her. It was all coming back to her now. 'I heard about your lad, Wesley.'

'My son's called Thomas.'

'I know. Yes, you're right. He *was* called Thomas. Terrible waste. Thought I'd come to say goodbye in person, me being big in the community and all. Help you celebrate the life of poor Wesley with some of my fine singing.'

She wrung her hands in a way she was sure would take the heat out of the situation. Patted her fascinator regally.

But Flora wasn't happy. She blew her nose on a blue-white handkerchief, held her hand up to the preacher, demanding a pause in proceedings and stepped awkwardly across a corner of the grave to reach Gloria.

'I know you, Gloria Bell,' Flora said, staring up at her

with woe etched into her haggard face. 'You stuck-up cow.' She poked Gloria in the chest. 'You lived two doors down from my auntie in Sweeney Hall, didn't you? But that doesn't give you the green light to gate-crash your way into my son's send-off. Nobody here invited you. Certainly not me.' She glanced over towards the scrum of semi-celebrities, dogs and riot police that the O'Brien burial had become. 'I know you're with them lot. Everyone here is respectable, right? Proper respectable. My lad just got caught up with the wrong kind. Your kind!'

'I beg your pardon,' Gloria said, feeling the blood drain away from her cheeks, leaving her shivering suddenly in her Sunday best. 'What kind is my kind?'

'The kind that wants locking up,' Flora said. She placed her fingers in her mouth and wolf whistled with such gusto that the police dogs immediately pricked up their ears and started to bark in Gloria's general direction. 'Over here, officers!' Flora shouted, waving her handkerchief as though it were a white flag. 'I've got a criminal for you.'

Shrinking further into the hostile bulk of congregated relatives and friends of dearly departed Wesley or Thomas or whatever his blessed name was, Gloria stumbled and turned her ankle. Started to fall, realising she had staggered back into the grave itself.

'Jesus!' she shouted.

The only thing that came between Gloria Bell and a broken neck that morning was a pincer-like grip on her arm as the ground fell away beneath her. Hoisted up painfully by a riot policeman who must have been at least six feet four, by the looks of it. He blocked out a diffident sun that had dared to shine through the ominous thick clouds. *A bit late for flaming divine intervention, Lord*, Gloria thought.

'Is this woman bothering you, madam?' the copper asked Flora.

'She's a thief! A dirty rotten thieving harlot,' Flora screamed. 'And my son isn't called Wesley, you cowbag!'

Light-headed and feeling like she might bring up her breakfast at any minute, Gloria wished desperately she could get to her phone to call Leviticus. That boy was a liability but he was her only hope. He was the only person she could whisper her secrets to. The others were all in cuffs alongside her.

'There's no need to be so rough!' she shouted, as her police escort marched her to the van, already mostly full of O'Briens. 'Don't put me in with them. They're common criminals! I'm a God-fearing woman.'

She took her place alongside the others. The doors closed with a finality behind her. She was put in mind of young Wesley in his coffin or Jack O'Brien, covered in forgetful earth. Gloria imagined the pastor there, comforting her, fighting her corner with rousing, convincing words.

'Glo!'

He might put his arm around her and she would weep onto his chest.

'Gloria!'

Gloria looked up as the woman called her name again. Diagonally opposite, Sheila O'Brien was sitting next to a dumpy woman she had never seen before. Perhaps one of Paddy's lot, judging by the doughy face. The familiar sight of Sheila was surprisingly welcome.

'Why have we been arrested?' she asked Sheila.

'I don't know. Something to do with tax, the detective said. I noticed Darley with him in the church, the sly bitch. HMRC has been after our Pad for years.' Her once perfectly made-up face was streaked with black mascara, giving her the look of a dishevelled Pierrot. 'Look, I don't think *we're* in any bother. I think we've both got caught up in the same net just because . . .' She raised her heavily pencilled eyebrows. 'But it's obvious somebody's been grassing if the plod has got enough to make arrests.' She leaned in further, giving her a conspiratorial air. 'So, listen, right! When we get out of here, do some digging. Ask around.' She winked, though Gloria could guess Sheila's true emotional state by the goosebumps on her orange tanned knees and the way her breath came short as she spoke.

Not daring to respond lest she betrayed her own distress, she merely nodded. Wanted to knock that Flora whatsher-face into her son's grave for dobbing her in. Was suddenly fearful that her sisterly-but-not-quite bond with Sheila might not extend to good legal representation being paid for by the O'Briens' coffers, which were presumably now frozen, pending investigation.

I'm going to have to stump for this myself, Lord help me, she thought. *Like I've not got enough to worry about with baby Jay.*

When the van arrived at the police headquarters, feeling at once nauseous and exhausted, Gloria was escorted to the bustling area by the booking-in desk. There was a sea of disgruntled faces of the arrested; world-weary expressions worn by the police officers. And there amongst the ungodly masses who had been brought in for burglary and drunk and disorderly and whatever other temptations Satan had thrown in their way, Gloria spotted the last man she had expected to see. Cuffed, battered, bruised and bleeding from a head-wound.

'Leviticus?!'

Chapter 25

Lev

'How come you got out?' Lev asked his mother.

Gloria tapped the side of her nose. 'Friends in high places, and that includes the good sweet Jesus Christ, my saviour.' She looked up to heaven. Smiled that smug smile that she knew wound him the hell up. *'Believe in the Lord Jesus and you will be saved, you and your household. Acts 16:31.'*

Under normal circumstances, Lev might have fantasised about getting up and walking away from her. Maybe coming out with a smart-arsed retort. But his heart was pounding too hard; his overtaxed mind running too quickly to allow flights of fancy. Not to mention the fact that there was no escaping the visitors' room within the police station. Not for him, at any rate.

'Look, spare me the bullshit,' he said. 'I've got Degsy in a holding cell next door, wants to rip my head off. In fact, he nearly did right in front of Tiff in the hospital. And I'm telling you now, when they cart us off to prison on remand, I know how this will play out. I'll end up bunking up with the arsehole and that'll be the end of me.'

'Whoever walks with the wise, becomes wise, but the companion of fools will suffer harm,' she said, folding her

arms and pursing her glossed lips. 'Proverbs 13:20.' She nodded and raised an eyebrow.

'Fucking hell,' Lev said. 'Who wound you up this morning? You're like a walking bloody bible.'

'I'm a believer and a law-abiding citizen, Leviticus. I was wrongfully arrested. You, on the other hand . . . I notice they've applied for an extension on your detention. You and those other hoodlums.'

'Spare me, yeah?' He looked over her diamante-studded shoulder to the copper that was watching them both intently. Lowered his voice. 'Look. I got special permission for this visit, so don't waste time. What's going on with Jay?'

She sat back in her hard plastic chair and shrugged. 'You tell me. You were the one who wanted to dump him at the hospital, hoping that slattern, your ex and those do-gooding social workers would absolve you of your paternal responsibility.'

He threw his hands in the air. 'See? This is why I wanted him away from you. You don't give a shit, do you? Never did.'

Gloria leaned back in and sucked her teeth. 'If you must know, your son's with *her*. I've been popping in to check she's doing her job properly when I can. Social services are keeping an eye on her too. You know, even with his illness, that child of yours is preferable to both his parents. *You* were a very unlovable boy, Leviticus. I wanted better for us both when that beast, your father, walked out on me. But no. All my efforts at pulling us up, you threw back in my face by hanging out with those scumbags. You were a disappointment then, and you're a disappointment now.'

'Stop trying to bait me for once,' he said, slapping his hands on his knees. 'Focus, for Christ's sake!'

194

'Blasphemy!' A sharp intake of breath from St Gloria. She rose, clutching her handbag to her belly. 'I'm off, if you're going to be so unpleasant.'

Between gritted teeth, Lev apologised. Lowered his voice. 'Look. I need your help. You've got Sheila O'Brien fighting your corner with her posh solicitors. But I've got no one looking out for me. I can't get nothing but crappy legal aid because my bosses have been banged up. This place is bursting at the seams with every player in Manchester. Somebody somewhere has grassed on a grand scale and it's possible I'm gonna go down for a stretch. But that's the least of my worries. Every minute I spend in here, my son's dying. *Your grandson.* He's not going to last more than a couple more weeks with that damned thing in his head. We need to get out the country, Mam. And I can't do that till I've got my hands on cash I'm owed.'

He had coughed up the word 'Mam' with difficulty, like a piece of gristle, lodged painfully in his throat.

In answer, Gloria merely closed her eyes, as though he and Jay were not really her problem. 'I have nothing to do with this unholy mess.' Her eyelids opened fractionally to reveal calculating eyes. 'But who do you think the grass is?' she asked. 'Anyone on your side?' Wide-eyed then. 'It's not you, is it?' Feigned horror.

'Very funny. I need a solicitor. A decent one. And I need to get Jay back off Tiff. She's an accident waiting to happen. A bloody car crash of a mother and my boy deserves better. I wasn't thinking straight when I took him to the hospital. I was just worried Smolensky was coming after me. But the Fish Man is banged up in here too, apparently, so now's the time for me to make a break for Baltimore.' He ended the sentence in nothing more than a whisper, suddenly remembering that the copper would be earwigging every single word. Tried to conceal by staring at Gloria's earring that he had a theory about who had done the grassing.

'Out with it, Leviticus. Who grassed? Tell me, or I won't help you.'

Shit. She had always been so much sharper than him. His dad's brains had always been dangling between his legs. Lev had definitely inherited those, he realised, else he wouldn't be the one with the laces missing from his trainers.

The copper suddenly stepped forwards. 'That's your lot, son,' he said, looking at the clock on the wall of the dismal room.

'Tell me, or no solicitor,' Gloria said, glancing at her watch. Pulling her coat from the back of her chair.

Lev felt the blood draining from his cheeks. A cold sweat breaking out between his shoulder blades. No freedom. No Jay. Gloria couldn't be relied on to step up and save the day or her own grandson because there was nothing in it for her. Knowing what the consequences would be if he opened his mouth, he realised he didn't really have a choice.

'Dunno.' Lev shrugged. 'My money would be on one of Kaplan's crew. The one that's not blood. It might not be him, though.' Even the thought of grassing manifested itself as physical pain somewhere in Lev's chest. 'But if that was me and I was forced into doing illegal shit and wanted to get the likes of Paddy O'Brien off my back, I might go to the coppers too.'

His mother nodded. 'Thank you for your honesty, Leviticus. See? You can do it when you try.'

'You getting me a fancy solicitor, then?'

She waved the policeman aside, as though he were an inconvenience. Turned back to Lev. '*And you will know the truth, and the truth will set you free.* John 8:32.'

196

Chapter 26

Conky

'Get me the hell out of here, you big Irish bastard!' Paddy said, thumping the wall of his holding cell. 'I've got flights booked for Thailand and a demanding bitch of a wife that'll go with or without me, if I know our Sheila. She'll leave me in here to rot!'

He rounded on Conky, who was sitting stiffly on the edge of the bunk, gripping the thin mattress. Packed and ready to go. Desperate to get out of this claustrophobic hole with its smell of second-hand urine, stale alcohol and the desperation of the belatedly repentant. Being cooped up at Her Majesty's leisure with Paddy for company the once had been enough. He had been a younger man then and he had been earning his stripes as a hard man. But this? At his time of life? His calf muscles started to twinge. His thyroid was out of whack.

'Sheila's on with it, boss,' he said, pushing his glasses up his nose. 'When I'm out of here—'

'It's alright for you!' Paddy strode over to the tiny barred window. His shirt tails hung over his trousers, which were set lower on his hips than usual. The slim black tie had been removed, as had his belt, of course. For a man who was perpetually puffed up with a fighter's spirit and an ego to match, Conky thought his boss suddenly looked as though somebody had punctured him to let the air out. He was just a paunchy ageing man. 'They've got nothing they can hold *you* on. You're just paid muscle, aren't you?'

Conky looked down at his unlaced shoes. Still muddy from the cemetery. It didn't matter that he was in here without his thyroxine and felt like a wreck. He was just the 'paid muscle'. And poor, loyal Sheila was apparently a heartless bitch, if Paddy were to be believed. He opted to say nothing in response.

'It's me they're after, Conks. I'm the King. They're gonna throw the book at me. I'll go down. You might have to take the fall for me somehow, mate, because I've got kids, haven't I?' He adjusted his genitals through his trouser pocket. 'And what would happen to our Frank? He needs me.'

The jangle and scrape of keys in the lock came as a relief. Conky looked at the heavy metal door hopefully, willing himself not to answer. With a squeak, it was pushed open by the staff sergeant.

'McFadden. Time to say ta-ra to your girlfriend,' he said. 'I'll give you your shoelaces back as long as you promise not to leave the country.' The sergeant winked at Paddy. 'And you can just think of it as an extension on a spa break. Good for the waistline.'

'Fuck you!' Paddy railed at the policeman, hurling himself too late at the door as it clanged shut.

Outside, Sheila was waiting in the black and white Bugatti. The diminutive million-pound car snarled as she revved the engine. Sleek, low, totally out of place outside the corporate glazed cube that was Greater Manchester Police Headquarters.

Failing to suppress a relieved smile, Conky opened the

passenger side door, withstanding the ache of his stiff knees and sore calf muscles to compress his bulk into the low-slung seat. The tan leather that cocooned them smelled like a million. And above it, a whiff of Sheila's perfume. He breathed the intoxicating smell in. Exhaled slowly and covered his mouth as he grinned.

'Paddy would have your guts for garters if he knew you'd picked me up in his baby, Sheila,' he said. Touched his unreliably attached quiff, praying the hair-piece's glue would hold. Suddenly wondering if he looked acceptable after two nights with no opportunity for personal grooming. He was just a decaying old fart after all and had no right to be sitting next to a beautiful woman in a car like this!

Sheila smiled at him, showing two rows of pearly white teeth. A glint in her eye like the promise of diamonds in a rock face – the perfect antidote to the time he'd spent locked up with her husband.

'I won't tell if you won't, Conks.' A wink. A pat on the knee. 'Our treat. We've earned it.'

We. Our. Conky swiftly turned his attention to the drab surrounds of flat grass, roundabouts and identikit HQ buildings. Prayed she wouldn't see any pink in his sallow cheeks.

She laughed at his side. A gale of mirth that put him in mind of a songbird. The car pulled away from the kerb and howled towards the motorway, following the signs for the North.

'What's the plan?' he asked. 'Are we not going back to yours to chew over who might be behind this?'

Sheila shook her head. 'No need,' she said. 'Turns out Gloria's quite the detective. I've got a little loss that needs adjusting, Loss Adjuster. Are you feeling judicious?'

'Aye. It's my job and I always take pride in my work.'

'You're a professional, Conks. I admire that in you.' She gestured with her head towards the glove compartment. 'Everything you need is in there.'

Inside was a Beretta semi-automatic and a silencer, which he attached as they headed along the M60.

'Who's my target?' he asked.

'You'll see. Turns out, we need to keep our enemies close and our friends much, much closer.'

Chapter 27

Sheila

'You took your time getting me out,' Maureen Kaplan said. Her throaty smoker's voice, full of the usual bluff and confidence, echoed around the disused mill. But her appearance gave away her true state of mind. In the bright moonlight that shone through the giant windows, long since smashed into jagged apertures by vandals, she looked pasty-faced and dishevelled. Smaller than usual, as though being held in a cell had washed the inflated ego out of her, causing her to shrink to normal size. Still wearing the same clothes she had worn to the funeral, minus the hat. That much was visible in the semi-dark. 'What was so urgent you couldn't let me go home and shower?' She shone a feeble torch into the thick blanket of darkness.

'You're out, aren't you?' Sheila said, her heart thumping loud enough for the others to hear, surely. 'I think "thanks" is the word you're looking for.'

Satisfied that Maureen had not been followed, Sheila stepped out of the shadows, pulling Frank with her.

'Hiya, Mo,' Frank said, waving meekly.

'And why's *he* here?' Maureen asked. Disdain in her voice that she certainly didn't use when she spoke to Paddy.

At her side, Frank's shoulders drooped. Poor bastard. Sheila squeezed his arm in an empty gesture of solidarity.

'Because he's family. I wanted him to see what family does to keep strong when the shit hits the fan. While Paddy's inside, he's said I'm his representative, right? Frank's here as my witness.' She turned to the giant loom – the sole relic of a bygone era – that had been left to rot in the vast expanse of the mill floor. The long shadows cast by it almost obscured the figure of a tall wall of a man who leaned against it.

'Come out, Conky,' Sheila said, beckoning him into the light.

Maureen flicked the torch's beam onto Conky's face. In that space, her intake of breath was audible. 'Didn't recognise you without your glasses on,' she said, faking a ha-ha chuckle that everybody present knew masked fear.

'Hello Maureen,' Conky said. 'I took my glasses off so I can see your regret and humility more clearly in this charming moonlight.' His deadpan Northern Irish delivery somehow made the air stiff and brittle. 'Except, I'm not seeing regret or humility. I'm seeing a trembling woman, taken down a peg or two, who still displays an overinflated version of herself.'

'I-I don't know what you mean,' Maureen said, switching the torch on, off, on, off. A substitute for a facial tic, perhaps. 'Why should I be humble? What the hell is this? You take forty-eight hours to get your faithful accountant out of clink and summon me to some condemned shithole in the wilds of Oldham. This isn't even your turf! It's Boddlington turf.'

Conky advanced fully into the moonlight, cutting an eerie figure. Scratching his temple with ominously leather-glove-clad hands. Seemed fitting that the Loss Adjuster should wear the skin of another over his own skin, Sheila mused.

'The Boddlingtons are still indisposed, along with most of our lot. Anyway, I'd say, given you've brought the wrath of HMRC down on everyone's heads, you owe Sheila one big bloody thank you, not a load of attitude.'

'Me? I've saved you millions of pounds over the years. Not to mention kept you all out of prison!' Maureen clasped her coat shut with her free hand. Switched off the torch and slid it into her pocket.

'That's true,' Frank said, rocking back and forth on his heels. Hands shoved into his anorak pockets. 'She's been nothing but a star for keeping the M1 House books straight, has Mo.'

'Shut it, Frank,' Sheila said. 'Let Conky speak.'

Maureen took several swift steps forward so that she was close enough to enable Sheila to smell her beneath the clothes. Unwashed. Dehydrated.

'Why don't *you* speak, Sheila O'Brien? You dragged me here. You tell me why I'm responsible for what's happened? Eh? All these years I've kept my gob shut.'

Sheila took a step forward to square up to her. Towered above her in her Louboutins. 'All these years, you've lined your pockets, Maureen, so don't give me that holier than thou bullshit.'

Unafraid to meet her gaze, whatever trepidation Maureen had shown on arrival was dissipating fast.

'Kiss my arse, you brainless Barbie Doll bitch. I answer to Paddy, not you!' Her mouth was downturned, her eyes narrowed – angry crow's feet etched into her cheekbones, telling the story of a long-harboured animosity towards Sheila. The moonlight and sharp shadows gave her a ghoulish appearance as she spoke.

'Hey. Back up, Maureen. Show some respect,' Conky said. Steel in his voice. He reached inside his overcoat and pulled the Beretta out of his breast pocket. It glinted in the light of the moon. Beautiful and deadly like a piece of poisoned treasure. He screwed on the silencer with practised fingers. 'Sheila is in charge while the boss is in absentia. Those are the terms. Sheila is doing the boss' bidding. So, you treat her with the same deference as you show your King. Is that understood?'

Maureen eyed the handgun and retreated. Shot a nervous glance towards Conky. A pleading look at Frank, whose arms were folded tightly across his chest like a chastened little boy. 'You going to put a bullet in me?' The tremor in her voice had returned. She looked back to Sheila. 'Is that how you treat your loyal business partners?'

'Pack it in, She,' Frank said. 'Let's go home and have a nice brew.'

'Button it, Frank!' Sheila said, never taking her eyes from the accountant. 'There's no such thing as loyalty between business partners in the criminal underworld, Maureen.' She folded her arms, stifling the inclination to slap the mighty Maureen Kaplan to the floor now that she had finally revealed frailty. 'You know that better than anyone – kissing Jonny Margulies' and Tariq Khan's arses and then my Paddy's without so much as cleaning your teeth in between time. If there was honour amongst thieves, Mo dearest . . .' Sheila stalked towards her captive, enjoying the way her eyes darted furtively around the expanse of the mill. Maureen was clearly seeking an escape route, feeling certain she was just another loss about to be 'adjusted'.

'. . . If there was any honour, Mo, Frank's Jack would still be here, and me and Paddy would be jetting off to Thailand, leaving this shifty, shithole city of violence and rain behind.

None of this crap would have gone down.' She halted in a blissful shaft of pure moonlight, the broken glass casting jagged patterns on the old splintered wood flooring. 'But you know and I know that a gangster's word is not his bond. This isn't some sticky-handshake, legalese Mason bullshit that you professional arseholes do. This is Manchester's bad-boys playing the game. Paddy said he'd never shagged you, and I know he lied. The Boddlingtons said they were buying us out, and I know they lied. Your lot said our accounts were safe from HMRC, and now, I know you lied.' She stuck out her chin in defiance. Flicked her hair over her shoulder triumphantly. Savouring the contrition in Maureen's haggard face. In that cold light, the show-stopping platinum blonde of the accountant's hair had dulled almost to grey.

'I had nothing to do with this raid,' Maureen said. Not tearing her gaze from the gun. 'My conscience is clear. I've devoted my entire career to being discreet. Even my boys have been roped into serving the O'Briens faithfully. A dynasty of loyal Kaplans. You talk about the loyalty of blood. There's loyalty for you.'

'Leave her be, Sheila, love,' Frank said. 'I trust Mo. I've known her for years, haven't I?' He shuffled towards the cornered Maureen, arm extended, as though he could somehow shield her from this deadly confrontation.

'Step aside, Francis,' Conky said, waving the gun dismissively as though he were an indulgent parent herding wayward children. Frank nodded silently, sidling back towards Sheila with an apologetic shrug. 'And ladies, let's allow for a little sober reflection here.' He pointed the gun directly at Maureen once again. 'The fact remains that all the wrong files have apparently fallen into two wrong sets of hands – namely, Ruth Darley's and Ellis James'. And we know that information could only have come from someone playing on your team, Maureen.'

'Who?! I trust my boys with—!'

'Although that person has demonstrated a woeful lack of gumption and commitment,' he continued, ignoring her protest. 'And, whether through the overdeveloped conscience of a born hypocrite or some misguided notion of self-preservation, was easily swayed into handing sensitive information to the authorities. Which means you have a conundrum on your hands, Maureen. Sheila here wants you to make a choice. She's going to give you two options. You take the bullet. Or you order the loss-adjustment to be visited on the guilty party.'

Maureen sank to her knees. Clasped her hands to her mouth. Wide-eyed now in that eerie light.

'What? You want me to sanction a hit on one of my sons? What kind of person do you think I am?'

'Did Abraham not prepare to sacrifice baby Isaac at the behest of a vengeful Jewish God?' Conky asked. 'Was that not the ultimate test of fidelity?'

Shaking her head, Maureen started to sob. 'Which silly bastard is it? Not my Zac! Surely not Steven. Or Louis. None of them! None of them! I'll take the bullet.'

'Ah, eh, Mo,' Frank said. He turned to Sheila. 'Stop it, Sheila. This is bollocks, man.' He pointed towards Maureen. 'She doesn't deserve this. Shit happens, man. The coppers and the tax and government are all in cahoots. I bet they broke in and stole a load of files. You don't know who's tapping your phone or listening in on your frigging emails nowadays. We're in a surveillance society, man.'

There were tears standing in his eyes. Her chest ached at the thought that Frank had to bear witness to this unpleasantness. Sensitive Frank, who had already suffered enough. The younger brother whom Paddy so often shielded from the tougher side to the business. But tonight, she needed Frank to see, so that Paddy would hear how she had done her husband's bidding, meting out the proper punishment on their firm's behalf as though she too had O'Brien blood running through her veins. She sighed, unexpectedly bowed beneath the weight of her responsibility as the dutiful wife of a bastard.

'Back off, Frank. Come on, Maureen. Let's stop pissing around. What do you choose?' She turned to Conky. 'Bring him out.'

Kneeling with her hands raised in supplication, Maureen watched agog as Conky retreated to the far side of the old loom. There was a scraping noise. The sound of wood on wood, as something heavy was dragged across the floor. Superseded by the muffled groaning of a man who had been silenced by duct tape.

With a racing heart, Sheila watched the two blurry figures sharpen as the moon spotlit the scene. Conky, stooped over his quarry – a man strapped to a chair, hands tied at the back. Wearing a pair of pyjamas, since they had pulled him from his north Manchester bed. The sound of his wife and children screaming, still ringing in her ears.

'David!' Maureen said. She gasped. Her crocodile tears subsided abruptly. Dry eyed, she appraised her son-in-law with the keen gaze of a nocturnal bird of prey, scoping out a mouse in the long grass. 'You went to the police? Why? How could you, when you knew how high the stakes were? We'll all go to prison.'

In his seat, David Goodman struggled. Tried to yell. Tears ran down the sides of his bright red face. The veins in his neck stood proud like green cord. Anger as well as fear in those bloodshot blue eyes. Sheila was sure she could sense a little loathing for his mother-in-law too. A cheering thought.

Scrambling to her feet, Maureen advanced rapidly towards the chair and planted a right hook on Goodman's left cheekbone with such force that his head flicked to the side with an unpleasant cracking sound. She retreated, nursing her knuckles.

'You idiot!' she said. Disgust in her voice, a good octave lower. 'You've ruined it for the whole family. Everything I built up over the years . . . I'll do time. We'll all go down. And your wife – my daughter – will have to live with the shame.' Pointing, pointing as though with every stab of her index finger, she hammered the blame home deeper. 'All the money will go. Your kids' futures are ruined. And it's your fault, you weak, loose-lipped shmuck.'

He shook his head vehemently. Eyebrows arched in apparent regret.

Maureen turned to Sheila. Wearing the grim face yet again – a mask lost, then found.

'Well?' Sheila asked.

'What have the police and HMRC got precisely?'

'Our brief says they're relying on his testimony at the moment as principal witness. The warrant to search your Spinningfields offices still hadn't come through this evening. That's why they tried to detain us all for as long as possible. But they've also applied for permission to search above a butcher's in Cheetham, apparently. Is that your "other" office, where you keep all our dirt?'

Maureen closed her eyes and smiled. Exhaled heavily. 'Yes. But that's okay, because everything was moved two days ago by my Zac, and this almighty grassing gobshite didn't know anything about it. I move the files to a new location every three months to be on the safe side. Short-term lets for cash in obscure places. No questions asked.'

'Well, if they can't get their hands on the documentation, all they've got is him.' Sheila slapped her hand on Goodman's sweaty shoulder. 'And they haven't even got him, because he's here with us. So, what do you want us to do with him?'

Maureen turned to her son-in-law, her eyes devoid of any warmth. 'Kill him.'

Chapter 28

Lev

Where's my money? You owe me. Time's running
out. I want paying now.

Lev thumbed the text deftly into his phone and sent it off.
Stiff from sleeping the night on a friend's sofa in one of
the Salford high-rises, as he pulled his hood up and wove
his way through the grey-faced crowds of Cross Lane market
he wondered briefly if his benefactor had tried to make the
drop while he'd been detained. Maybe there was an unde-
livered bag of cash with Leviticus Bell written on it, lying
on a desk somewhere. Who knew? Deep down, though, he
felt certain that he was being given the run-around, if not
duped entirely.

Kicking aside the muddy leaves of rotten cabbage that
had fallen from the vegetable stalls, he wondered what
his next move should be. Three texts had come in from
Tariq Khan since he had been released from police
custody, demanding that he show for work and explain
himself.

Walking briskly towards the bus stop, he glanced down
at them.

You owe me some answers. Come into the office.

What happened to Irina?

Smolensky's out of action. Report to me or Jonny immediately.

The Fish Man was out of action. This was the best thing he had heard since the coppers had told him he was free to go. But what did it mean? Did it mean he was merely staying out of mischief but was still on the prowl? Or had the police found one of his machetes or boning knives on him and kept him in the cells?

As he swung himself into a seat on the top deck of the bus into Manchester city centre, Lev watched the ugliness of Salford whizz by. The bizarre mid-century totems of the university stood tall on his left; to his right, the ungainly orange, brown and white tower of Spruce Court where he had bedded down. Last night, he had lain awake, contemplating if it might be easier merely to hurl himself from the fifteenth floor like so many tenants had apparently done over time – body at the bottom, wallet in the road, the wry NHS grin of false teeth some quarter of a mile away as the only farewell bid by the jumpers. But then he had remembered his son needed him. And now, he was travelling through this swirling mess of dual carriageways that marked the emergency exits for Salford residents, lest they should try to escape their miserable Pendleton prison for somewhere only nominally better with good shoplifting prospects, like Salford Quays' Lowry Centre or Ordsall's TK Maxx.

No answer to his text. And he was still studiously avoiding responding to Tariq's repeated prompts.

Trying to work out what his next move should be, he

called Tiffany. She answered on the sixth ring, just when he'd been prepared for voicemail to kick in.

'What do you want?' she asked. Ominous quiet in the background. 'I'm painting my toenails.'

'How's Jay?' he asked.

'Look, Lev. I feel rough. He was doing my head in, crying all the time. I couldn't get hold of you.'

'Liar. My phone's been on. What's happened to Jay?'

'Are you starting something? Shall I put the phone down on you, Leviticus, because I haven't got the energy for this.'

Lev bit his lip, feeling certain that she'd ring off at any moment if he didn't keep his cool. He could hear post-OD fatigue in her voice and a general impatience. He really didn't have the energy for *her* bullshit. Why was it his fate to get embroiled in the sorry lives of women who always demanded to be centre of attention, even if they could only claim that by acting up? Tiffany. Gloria. They both knew exactly which buttons to push to get a reaction from Lev. And he was left with the sinking feeling that if Jay did somehow reach adulthood, he would grow up to be a slave to their egos, just like him. 'I just wanted to know how he was doing.'

'He's not here. He's with your mother.'

She hung up before Lev could express his deep misgivings that Gloria should have the boy in anything but an emergency. Bollocks to it. Faced with the prospect of being interrogated by a suspicious Tariq if he ventured up to T&J Trading, Lev decided he had better check on his son, even if it did mean speaking to Gloria.

He dialled his mother, wishing his life had not taken this turn for the terminally disappointing.

'What do you want, Leviticus?' Gloria sounded agitated as she answered his call. 'The charges were dropped, weren't

212

they? You got what you wanted.' The noise of tinkling lift-music in the background and the chatter of African women standing close by, talking animatedly about who knew what? Jay, screaming near the mouthpiece. He'd know that sound anywhere. He felt a visceral ache inside him. Tears pricked at the backs of his eyes.

'I want my son.'

'I'm busy with him.'

'What do you mean, you're *busy with him*?'

'A new business enterprise for my ladies.'

Shit. What the hell did that mean? 'Where are you?'

'Primani. Sleepwear section. You can come and help if you like.'

He ended the call and groaned. Wiped the treacherous tears from his eyes. *You're a brother. Pull yourself together and stop whingeing like a kid. Jay needs you.* Looked at his phone screen; a text from Mia Margulies showing her tits, but still no answer from his duplicitous benefactor.

Praying he wouldn't spot one of the O'Brien crew, he jumped off the bus and made his way across the bridge that spanned the grey-brown roiling mass of the River Irwell. He briefly considered throwing himself in but merely spat into the inky water. Past the Ramada Hotel and over Deansgate to the fancy shops of St Anne's Square and New Cathedral Street. Hadn't he hoped to buy Tiffany real Uggs with his drug money when they were first dating? Fortuitously, the riots had intervened, offering the luxurious elephantine boots for free instead. Better that he didn't have to blow £200 on making her look like a tree trunk. He smiled at the memory. That was a time before she had been ensnared on a daily basis by the lure of narcotic amnesia as an antidote to the grind of bringing up a sick child.

Lev headed up a chewing-gum-spattered Market Street, past the chuggers, trying to sell him a rosy glow, past the hawkers, trying to sell him broken lighters, past the preachers, trying to sell him eternal life, praise-Jesus-Hallelujah, towards a windy, pigeon-shit-festooned Piccadilly. He was sick of Manchester and all its empty promises. He was sick of his small, brutish life. All thanks to his mother. The Lord giveth and Gloria taketh away.

In Primark, he spotted her immediately. She had a formation going with her cleaners that would have put Alex Ferguson to shame. All working their way through the pyjamas section, pushing prams.

'Why's Jay in his pram?' he asked, pulling the hood of the pram back so that he could inspect his son's face for signs of maltreatment. There were none, fortunately. 'He's way too big for that. He should be in his pushchair, to get stimulation and that. What the hell you up to?'

His mother looked round furtively. 'You want some jimmy-jammies?' she asked. 'You look peaky.'

He watched with idle fascination as she snatched a pair of men's pyjamas from a carousel. Placed them on the counterpane of Jay's pram. Pushed them inside with the boy. Lightning quick hands for a woman showing the early signs of arthritis.

Jay squealed with delight perhaps for the first time in months.

Hardly believing what he had seen, Lev glanced over to the other women. One was studying a shopping list. Another hastily pushed a negligee into her buggy.

'You nicking to order?' he asked, a half-smile tugging at his lips.

'These are my ladies,' Gloria said. 'They're illegals. If I don't get them work now Sheila has closed the business, they'll starve. They'll end up on the game. I'm saving them from a life of immorality.'

'By getting them to shoplift? From Primark of all places? Jesus. Can't you do better than that? Even M&S would be better than here.'

'No blaspheming! They're training, Leviticus. Practice makes perfect.' Gloria winked.

'Where did you get all these babies?' He glanced around at the prams, though with the rain hoods up and the covers on, it was impossible to see if there actually were any babies inside at all.

'Babies? Oh, yes.' Deftly, Gloria held a tomato-red plush-pile dressing gown up to her body, then flung it into the carry-basket beneath the pram. 'I've also started running a little baby-minding service on the side.' She smiled primly. A vision of respectability in her polyester flower-print dress and court shoes. 'I'm helping all the single mums in the area get back to work! Isn't that tremendous? The pastor's delighted with my charitable nous!'

Lev sucked his teeth and shook his head. 'You're the limit. Do you know that? You always were the biggest hypocrite I ever met. Is it any wonder I turned out the way I did?'

His mother's expression was suddenly sour. 'You ruined your life all on your own, Leviticus. You've got too much of your father in you. And now all you've got to show for your tender years is a criminal record and a son with a tangerine for a brain.'

Had he heard her correctly? 'I beg your fucking pardon.'

'Stop swearing. It's ungodly. And the Lord is listening.' Gloria scowled at him. Looked up towards the lighting, as though Jesus were perched there, judging all that came to pass in the fleshpot of consumerism that was Manchester's Primark.

Lev grabbed the pram, pulled the stolen goods from their various hiding places and threw them at his mother. 'You haven't got a clue, have you?' he asked. 'There's a word for people like you. Socialpath or something. That's you, that is. Well, I've had enough.'

'Give me that pram back! I'm using it.' She tried to tug the handle from his reach.

Jay started to scream, his angry face just visible beyond the counterpane and rain hood. Lev noticed the tomato-coloured dressing gown in the basket beneath the main carry cot. Pulled it out and flung it onto a startled Gloria's head. 'And you can take your shitty dressing gown and all. You cow! Calling my son a tangerine. You're tapped! That's what you are.' He hammered on the side of his head with his index finger. 'Completely frigging tapped.'

Not knowing where he would go or what he would do, Lev hastened towards the lift, shushing the bellowing Jay as he ran through the various possible scenarios in his head.

'Come back!' Gloria shouted.

He ignored her. Stepped into the lift with a young couple who were arguing in an Eastern European language. They looked askance at Jay and immediately fell silent.

Take Jay back to Tiff's, eat humble pie and go after this money I'm owed.

Or, take Jay to T&J Trading, face the music over Irina and hope Tariq and Jonny don't think I grassed and got them all locked up.

Or, stay and get the old cowbag to help.

As if she could read his thoughts, Gloria stood before the open door of the lift with her arms folded across her chest. Stern-looking, like a deliverer of fire-and-brim-stone sermons and bullet-hard cakes at a church fair. 'If you turn your back on me now, Leviticus, don't expect me to come running and help you with that boy ever again.'

Lev offered her his middle finger. He knew he had only moments in which to mull over his options. Then, the doors would close and his options would dwindle to two.

'*Children, obey your parents in everything, for this pleases the Lord!*' she shouted with wide-eyed fervour. 'Colossians 3:20.'

Nope. Enough craziness. He would let the doors shut and be done with the old nutter.

His phone pinged as the lift started to close. The doors immediately slid open again as the hood of the pram was picked up by the sensor. Closing. Opening. Gloria was still standing there expectantly. But Lev had to read the text.

Truce is being called. Try harder. Then you'll get your money.

Lev felt the blood drain from his body to who knew where. His world felt like it was spinning the wrong way on its axis. His vision blurring like a bad signal on an old TV. He looked down at Jay, who had sat himself bolt upright, partially ripping the rain hood from its anchor. Clutching his temples, shrieking with staring, apoplectic eyes at the open-closing, open-closing doors as though they were shutting repeatedly on his little head.

Sighing, Lev lifted his son out of the pram, gathered him to his chest and stepped out of the lift back towards his mother, pushing the clumsy pram with one unpractised hand.

Gloria beamed at him. Arms wide open in anticipation of an embrace that he did not offer. 'See, Leviticus? *Before I formed you in the womb, I knew you.* Jeremiah—'

'Shut the fuck up, Mam. I'm in trouble. I need your help.'

217

Chapter 29

Paddy

'Thanks for coming, Katrina,' Frank said, embracing his sister. His voice bounced off the stainless steel of the air-con vents, exposed above them in the lofty, industrial-style space that served as the private function area of M1 House.

Paddy sized his older sibling up. She was dressed in a frumpy midnight blue A-line skirt and a baggy navy jumper, marked out as a nun by her navy veil. She always had been a plain Jane, he thought. A world away from a proper woman – a fuckable woman.

Katrina returned Frank's hug with obvious affection. She swept her veil aside. Her face flushed red, kissing her favourite baby brother on the cheek.

'How could I not come to our Jack's wake? Second time lucky, eh?' She took a step back, holding Frank's emaciated, sleep-deprived face in her mannish, short-nailed hands. Winked. 'You'll give him the send-off he was always meant to have, love. It's an absolute disgrace that the police wouldn't allow the boy a dignified funeral. A scandal of near-biblical proportions. God bless you, Francis. You always had a good soul and a pure heart.'

'Ta,' Frank said, looking at his shoes. 'Help yourself to

butties while me and Pad have this meeting. People should start to trickle in in a bit. You'll be alright, won't you? Auntie Theresa's coming, so you won't be on your own.'

Paddy watched the chummy way in which Frank squeezed Katrina's hand. Irritated by the intimacy, he turned his attention to Sheila, who was standing like a mannequin with Gloria next to some profiteroles and pink wafers on a long buffet-laden table. An elaborate ice sculpture of a man wearing headphones and spinning records on two decks sat alongside the traditional fayre that Frank had insisted upon. The frozen carving was impressive, Paddy decided. His own homage to Jack that he had commissioned while in custody. At least Sheila had got that right. The two women were deep in conversation about some shit or other. Probably nail polish.

'You'll look after our Kat, won't you, She?' Frank said.

Sheila nodded. Treated Katrina to a false smile. Paddy wanted to slap his wife for insubordination. She ought to show a nun more respect. But Sheila had never really found time for Katrina. Sometimes, Paddy wished he had married a more traditional girl. More respectful. He eyed his wife, dressed to kill in a tight beige dress that accentuated her figure and showed the world how amazing those legs were. There was a downside to having a beautiful wife. Paddy wondered if she had been shagging someone while he was being detained. Inadvertently, he clenched his jaw – with such force that his back molars ached with the pressure.

'Right girls, this is man's work.' He pushed up the sleeves of his suit jacket. Legs akimbo, feeling the effect of the two lines of coke he'd just done in the toilets. His overtaxed heart told him that perhaps he should have erred on the side of caution. His overhyped brain told him he was master of the universe. 'You'd better just make sure everything's right for the guests. It's a big night tonight.' Locking eyes with Gloria, he said, 'Can you check the cutlery's shiny, love? Don't want to give the relatives anything to slag us for.'

Katrina left Frank's side and strode over to him. Put her hand on his arm, as though ministering to one of her flock. Lowered her voice so that she was almost inaudible.

'Now, you're lucky to have been released, Patrick,' she said, eyeballing him like she used to when they were kids. Well-meaning and utterly unswerving in her stance. Paddy was transfixed by Jesus, looking more than very hacked-off with his lot on her sizeable crucifix. 'Just you remember those flight tickets that Sheila has been keeping warm in her handbag.' She nodded meaningfully. 'Your daughters are relying on their daddy to do the right thing in this instance, as far as doing the right thing is even possible in your crooked line of work.'

Paddy sniffed hard. In his head, he told her to cock right off. He nodded briskly. Feeling fidgety, as though the last thing he wanted was to be rooted to this spot in his brother's nightclub, being given a lecture by his do-gooding sister. 'Yeah,' he said. 'Thailand.'

'It's for your own good, Patrick. Leave that life behind and repent at your leisure in the sun.' She angled her head so that he had no option but to look into those deep blue eyes that had apparently seen God and that were full of celestial wisdom. Bitch had always been the best O'Brien. 'This is your chance to show you're made of better stuff than Dad.'

Nodding with vigour, he ushered her towards the buffet table, pleased to see that Vernon, their cousin, had arrived from the wilds of Stretford. Someone to keep the old God-botherer out of mischief.

'I'll catch you later. It's sorted, alright? Everything's bob on.' He sniffed hard and wiped his nose.

When he returned to the VIP area, Jonny and Tariq were seated, awaiting the audience. Paddy inhaled deeply. Felt the rush. Lit a contraband cigarette, just to make the fellers wait. He contemplated how best to open this awkward meet. Magnanimously, Sheila had recommended. He didn't even know for the life of him what magnanimous meant, but she'd opened her arms when she'd counselled him, so now he did the same.

'Gentlemen,' he said. 'Welcome.'

Jonny Margulies looked like he might vomit into the complimentary peanuts at any given moment. He sipped from a margarita that the barmaid had prepared especially for him. Best to make these twats feel wanted. Tariq, not a wrinkle on his face, as usual, was sipping from a Diet Coke.

'Paddy,' Jonny said, grinning like a piranha. Lounging on the leather sofa, with his arm across the back as though he owned this place. Cheeky, presumptuous fat bastard. 'I'm glad we can finally parlay again.'

Standing at his side, Paddy felt Frank stiffen. 'You killed my son,' he said in a strangled voice. Twitching like he had St Vitus' Dance, as per usual, but emitting a dangerous vibe, as though for once in his life as a shag-sack of a Beta male, he might actually make a beeline for Margulies and plant one on him.

'Can it, our kid. This is not the time nor the place.'

When the omnipresent Conky placed a large hand on his bony shoulder, Frank fell back, taking a seat on a sofa next to some Boddlington muscle that Paddy didn't recognise. Paddy seated himself regally in the special armchair that had been put out for him. Deliberately positioned at the head of the gathering.

'We've come here to discuss terms,' Tariq said. Sober. His kind always was. All business. He crossed his right foot over his left knee. Confident, the sort of educated, arrogant ponce that Paddy couldn't abide. 'We don't want to intrude on your brother's grief for any longer than is necessary.' He nodded respectfully to Frank, who folded his arms tightly and scowled, though the dimpling in his chin suggested sorrow lurked just beneath the façade.

Paddy poured himself a whisky from the bottle of single malt waiting for him on the coffee table. Took his time deliberately, cigarette hanging artfully out of the side of his mouth.

'Look.' He leaned forward, legs splayed wide. 'We've had a near miss with Maureen's man cocking up. We're all having to take steps.' He focused on Jonny. Paused until Jonny nodded. Turned to Tariq, who grabbed a handful of nuts from the bowl on the table top – inspecting them carefully, before popping them into his mouth, one by one.

'They're still holding Smolensky,' Tariq said, wiping his salty hand on a napkin. Raking his fingers through his black-and-steel-coloured thatch. 'When he gets out, *if* he gets out, he's going to have to dress a lot of actual salmon for a long while.'

At his side, Frank fidgeted with the sleeves of his best shirt. Erupted suddenly. 'You killed my fucking son,' he said, pointing at Jonny with his cigarette. 'All of this shit . . .' he pointed at everyone in the circle '. . . put my Jack in a box. My innocent boy.'

Quietly, Jonny exhaled a breath he had clearly been holding for a while. 'Shall I save us all the embarrassment of discussing the rape of my young daughter?'

With Katrina standing over in the function area, just on the periphery of his vision, watching his every move like God's emissary on earth, Paddy opted to say nothing. But

Frank stood abruptly, kicking out at the table. Swallowing what sounded like a sob, he stormed off towards the far side of the club. Turning back to face Paddy and shouting to make himself heard in the echoing space. 'You make your entrée cordial or whatever the bleeding hell this is.' He poked himself in the chest. 'Count me out, man. I've got a wake to sort for my dead thirty-one-year-old son.'

'Look, there's no need for us to prolong the agony, here,' Tariq said, meeting Paddy's gaze with those unfathomable, almost black eyes. 'We're all taking heat since the raid. It's not going to do any of us any good. Bodies stacking up. Fights in the street between our people and yours. Tit for tat. You've suffered losses. We've suffered losses. And I personally can't afford to lose my family and my liberty and my reputation.' He threw a peanut high into the air. Caught it squarely in his mouth. Bumped fists with Jonny. A weird hybrid of a man who dressed and at times behaved like a posing prick of a youth but who abruptly switched back to demonstrating the gravitas and savvy of the man in his mid-forties that he was.

Paddy couldn't work the arsehole out. 'So, you'll agree to a truce?' he asked. 'Deal's back on?'

Jonny folded his hands on top of his belly and smiled broadly, though Paddy was sure there was animosity behind the show of teeth. If his own daughter had been raped, he would have executed every last one of the mongrel Boddlington morons.

'If you can guarantee the behaviour of your crew, we'll keep a tight rein on ours,' Jonny said. 'Ten mill. As agreed. No more bullshit and you're on that plane to Thailand. You've already had the deposit, which we broke our backs to deliver in good faith. We want the transfer of all assets inside a week.'

Paddy nodded. Swigged from his whisky tumbler. 'What seemed like a shit-storm was lady luck stepping in to deal us better cards, gentlemen. I personally had the leak plugged quickly. We've chatted here today like the businessmen we are.' He held out his hand, which Tariq and Jonny duly shook.

'Our gain is Ellis James' and the tax bitch's loss,' Tariq said.

As Conky ushered the guests towards the exit, Paddy swaggered back across the club to Sheila and Gloria. With every step, he contemplated those agonising few days he had spent behind bars. Sheila at the helm, running things smoothly. Had she missed him? Had she needed him? Had Frank been glad that his older brother had been out of the loop?

'What you looking at, She?' he said, grabbing her and sucking on her neck. Feeling disconcertingly less than triumphant.

'Just wondering how it went, Paddy. Are we good to go, then? Is it Thailand, here we come?' Though she was smiling, he could feel the rigidity in her body.

'Couldn't have left you and our kid running the day-to-day, could I?' He laughed too heartily. 'Pair of spastics like you. Even with me giving orders from inside . . . You're a woman and he's a limp dick. It would have been the end of the O'Briens. Much better this way.' He jammed a fat Cuban cigar into his mouth. Pretending to be Hannibal out of the A-Team. Where was Conky with another bottle of whisky? He had a thirst on, as could be expected from any King who had just saved his court from collapse. 'I love it when a plan comes together.'

Chapter 30

Frank

Sitting in the armchair that had been brought for him to the buffet area by a barman, Frank breathed deeply into a paper bag. In. Out. Almost in time to the thumping music that had started up in the club, signifying the beginning of a long night of mourning, O'Brien-style.

'That's right, Francis,' Katrina said, rubbing his back. 'You breathe steadily and you'll soon be back to normal.' She held his plate of mini-muffins (with surprise filling), sausage rolls and egg sandwiches on her lap. 'You should eat. Mam always said life's trials are easier to conquer on a full stomach.'

'Mam's dead,' Frank muttered inside his damp paper bag. 'Like Jack.'

He took the bag from his mouth, studying his sister's well-meaning face. Smooth and wrinkle-free despite her advanced years. A woman who slept nights and who wouldn't know one bite of a super-skunk hash cake from another. Hers had been a sheltered life.

'You're not daft, you,' he said, snaffling his fourth narcotic chocolate muffin. Talking while he chewed, praying the fear would soon be transplanted by the giggles. How he wished

225

he'd done some whizz instead. He wedged a sausage roll into his mouth. Starving now. 'Getting out of all this crap. Getting away from Paddy before he got his meat hooks into you.'

Katrina stood. Her swollen knees cracked audibly as she straightened up. 'Now, now, Francis. I still believe in loyalty to the family name. Patrick is a fallible man, but he's your brother. Try to forgive him his trespasses and weaknesses. Turn the other cheek.' She scanned the densely packed function area hived off for the wake. 'And don't let Auntie Theresa and Sheila hear you bad-mouthing him.'

Amid all those people at this hastily rearranged send-off, Frank had never felt so alone and misunderstood. It was hard to tell if it was the gange or stress or the acute stinging pain of grief, but pinned to that seat with the music in the main area pounding like his overburdened heart and with those O'Brien faces reminding him that he had been born into a family of violence and perpetual struggle, Frank felt the world collapsing in on him. Biting angrily on an egg sandwich, he allowed hot tears to well in his eyes, spilling onto his cheeks. Wished at that moment that he could climb into that white and gold coffin beside his son and enjoy perpetual sleep. How could he unmake himself?

'Cheer up, Frank,' Auntie Theresa said, patting him on the head as she'd always done when they were children. Just like Mam in looks, but much older now. In her seventies. A good two stone heavier, too. 'Our Jack's with Jesus, now.'

'Cheer up? Cheer up? Is that the best advice you've got to offer? You walking fucking bunion. Why are you still alive when my son's pushing up daisies in Southern Cemetery?' A surge of anger galvanised Frank suddenly.

Launching himself out of the armchair, his plate crashed to the floor, scattering food everywhere. He shrugged

Theresa off and barged through the phalanx of distant relatives to the buffet table. Grabbed hold of Paddy's tie. Paddy, who was standing in the centre of things, holding court as usual. 'Our Paddy's got the gift of the gab,' Dad had said proudly, when he wasn't pulverising the living daylights out of both of them. 'Our Paddy's a chip off the old block.' Now, Frank's golden older brother was chugging at one of those stinking cigars. Hand on the arse of one of their nieces, several places removed on Mum's side. He looked surprised when Frank yanked him nose down to the decks that formed the base of the ice sculpture.

'Is this how you pay tribute to my Jack?' he shouted, pointing to the ghastly, semi-melted mess. He pulled Paddy back up, fixing him with the eyes of a desperate man so he might see the suffering his bullying ways had caused. 'Doesn't matter that the kid is dead, because you paid some arsehole to carve this crap. Well, I can't hug a lump of ice, Paddy. I can't leave my club to some melted water.' Frank tugged the tribute forward with his free hand; the sculpture smashed to the ground, scattering the floor with a soggy veil of ice cubes on the melt. He could feel bitter, festering words trying to force their way out of his mouth. Words that had been proving inside him like hot dough for decades. Rising, rising and now, fully baked. 'I wish you were dead. You're a bastard and I wish you'd died when you had your heart attack and then we'd all be free.'

Paddy was wide-eyed. Face reddening. Trembling. He gripped the table edge in silence, white knuckles testifying to the rage that was blossoming within.

'That's enough, Frank,' Conky said, pulling him back by his upper arms. Holding his hand up to Paddy, like a traffic cop heading off rush-hour disaster. 'You're upset. We're all upset and tired and had a bit too much to drink. Why don't you go for a dance?'

'Tyrant!' Frank screamed, feeling deliciously high on his own daring and energised by his fury. 'You're a fucking tyrant! A violent dictator like Stalin or Hitler. I've always done what you said. I always trudged along in your shadow because you told me I couldn't do nothing without you. Well, shove it up your arse, Paddy. I wish you'd let Dad kill me when I was a kid and he used to batter ten shades of shit out of us, because you didn't do me no favours by saving me. And I wish he'd beaten you to death too, because then, none of this would have happened and a shit load of people would still be alive. And my Jack would never have been born, so he'd never have died alone and in pain and I'd not be stood here, wishing that God would strike me down just so's I didn't feel nothing no more.'

Aware that the entire gathering of close relatives and trusted friends had fallen silent to witness this dissension, Frank took a final swipe at his brother.

'Bastard!' he shouted.

But his aim was cannabis clumsy. Paddy took a step back, giving Conky the opportunity to sweep Frank off his feet – a man mountain and a broken, shuffling figure not much larger than a youth, caught in some strange semblance of choreography like a pair of fucked-up figure skaters.

Stepping forward to confront him, Paddy grabbed Frank by the throat with a sweaty hand. The feel of his hot clammy skin brought the memories of those arguments in their little shared bedroom flooding back. Once they were older and Paddy had realised he could unleash his frustrations at their father on his physically weaker brother.

'Easy, boss,' Conky said, setting Frank down.

'Leave him, Paddy!' Sheila cried.

Frank could smell the sour whisky on his brother's breath. Could see the loathing and naked fury in his eyes. So reminiscent of Dad. A bond for life forged in equal measure with love and hate.

'Come on then, Pad,' Frank wheezed. 'Finish it.'

Paddy released him. Smoothed his collar down. Grabbed the back of his neck, yanked him towards his mouth and kissed him hard on the forehead. 'Twat.'

The high tide of guests started to ebb away into the main body of the club after that; the older people heading home, offering words of condolence to Frank and curt smiles to Paddy. Even Auntie Theresa, who was often the last to leave gatherings where there was single malt on offer, swiped a plate full of sandwiches into her handbag and left with a mild look of disgust on her face. Finally, with only Paddy, Frank, Katrina, Conky, Sheila and Gloria left, they retired to the office at the back. Frank's uncharacteristic rage had long since subsided – unavoidably so, given the number of relatives he'd had to put on a brave face for.

'I brought something for you, Frank,' Sheila said, pulling several heavy-looking packages from a plastic bag she had stowed beneath the desk.

Gloria looked on silently, opening a bottle of wine and pouring the contents into six glasses. 'What have you got there, Sheila?'

'Photos,' Sheila said, smiling. She offered the pile of albums to Frank.

'Photos of what?' Frank asked, his heart rate loping placidly along once more, calmed even further by Sheila's kindly attentions.

'Just look.'

Pulling the five chairs in the office into a circle, Frank felt calm envelop him once more. The fire had subsided in

Paddy. Perhaps it had been just another scuffle between brothers, after all. In any case, he was so stoned, drunk and melancholy that he no longer had the energy to rail against the life that Paddy had ordained he should lead.

'Are these pictures of little Jack?' Katrina asked, sitting down on the last vacant chair, leaving Gloria standing with full glasses of Merlot in her hands and only the edge of the desk to perch on.

'Aw, these are gorgeous, She!' Frank said, poring over page after page of beautifully mounted mementoes of Jack's childhood.

Sheila leaned sideways to examine her handiwork. 'I thought you'd like them.'

'What a lovely boy he was,' Katrina said. 'So much like his mother in looks. So much like the O'Briens in his go-getting spirit.' She clasped her hands together and chuckled. 'You know, Frank. Nobody can take your precious memories away from you.'

Frank nodded thoughtfully, running his fingers over the pages of photos with a certain reverence. Jack as a baby, cradled in his mother's arms at the time when she was at her most beautiful because she'd been clean throughout her pregnancy. Jack growing into a toddler, holding Mum and Dad's hands. Frank smiled at the photo of himself as a young man. All sinew and shiny, healthy skin, with an optimistic sparkle in his eyes, clutching Jack's chubby hand on the beach in Ibiza. So vivid was the memory, now that he was looking at the photo, he could almost feel the burn of the hot sand on the soles of his feet and smell the suncream on the boy. Jack with Paddy's girls, his poor mother six feet under, by then. Jack as a handsome teen – all arms and legs at that stage. By the third album, the photos included shots of Jack DJing in the club, interspersed with clippings from music magazines.

'My lad made something of himself,' Frank said, smiling sadly, allowing a heady mixture of pride and regret to rinse through him. He shook his head. 'By Christ, he was something else. I wanted all the things for him that I never had. And he was everything I'd hoped to be as a nipper, except I never had half of the drive and talent in me that that boy did. What a waste.'

Conky placed a heavy hand on his shoulder. Removed his glasses ceremoniously and scanned the images. 'These are terrific, Sheila. You've given Frank a very special aide-memoire, here. That's very thoughtful of you.'

Everybody except for Paddy murmured their agreement. Frank noticed Sheila blushing and smiling coyly out of the corner of his eye. He glanced back down at the pictures, his attention snagged by a series of photos taken in the winter – at the New Year's Eve party in M1 House, in fact. He felt Gloria's eyes on the photos as well. Unsurprising, because when Frank scrutinised the faces in the background of the photos taken of Jack with his arms around various promotions girls, he noticed a scenario that was distinctly off. And he wasn't the only one to spot it, because Conky spoke up before Frank had even had a chance to open his mouth.

'Fancy that, eh? Mia Margulies in the background, there,' he said to Paddy.

'Well, I still don't believe that he raped her,' Paddy said. 'I remember she was all over him like a rash on a cheap prozzy. I thought they were going out.'

Conky nodded in agreement. 'Except there Mia is, smooching with another lad. In not one, but in five of these photos.'

Behind him, Frank was aware of Gloria craning her neck to examine the familiar face in the frame with Mia.

Paddy looked up at her. 'Did you know about this, Gloria? Did you know your Lev was poking Jonny Margulies' daughter? Because it sodding well looks that way in these photos.'

Standing, straightening her skirt, Gloria glanced nonchalantly at the albums. 'How in the good Lord's name would I know what that morally bankrupt little twerp was up to?' she asked. 'I haven't seen that boy in five years or more. And I say, good riddance to bad rubbish.' Gloria grabbed her clutch bag and poked at her elaborate hair. 'Anyway, it's getting late so I'm going to take my leave from you fine people.' She smiled expansively at Sheila, though Frank was certain the smile never made it to her eyes.

When she had left the Green Room, Paddy and Conky exchanged a knowing look, focusing anew on the photographs of Mia and Lev. Pages in, and there were photographs of them together, months later. Caught kissing on the dancefloor with the long-lens Nikon of the club's official photographer.

'Looks like little Mia couldn't make up her mind if she liked mince-meat or fillet steak,' Paddy said, raising an eyebrow.

'So, she went for both,' Conky said. 'In some kind of erotic Mancunian club sandwich. Aye. Fishier than the Fish Man himself.'

'And then, she's screaming rape the minute Jack gives her the brush-off, just at the point when I've done a deal with her father.' Paddy caught the fist of his right hand in the palm of his left with an ominous smack.

'I think young Mia is not as innocent as she likes to make out,' Conky said, pushing his sunglasses back up his nose in ceremonious fashion. 'What do you want to do?'

'Kill the bitch!' Frank said, slurring; draining his second

glass of wine. 'Actually no. Don't kill her. That makes us as bad as them. Teach the slag a lesson, though.'

'No,' Paddy said, locking eyes with Katrina. 'The deal's on. I'm getting out of this shit. We're going to Thailand. No more bullshit tit for tat.'

Chapter 31

Tariq

'We got any branflakes left?' Tariq asked, staring into the larder unit at box after box of cereal. Mildly irritated that his children had put them back in wrong size order.

'No. We've got cornflakes. If you want branflakes, get them yourself before you take your dad to the mosque,' Anjum said, slamming her handbag and car keys onto the kitchen island. She thumbed her password into her phone. 'Some of us have got serious jobs to hold down.'

There was a sharpness to her tone that made Tariq shiver. She had been like this since that evening she had returned from work, quizzing him about the Slovakian girl, Irina. Of all the places the silly pregnant bitch could have sought help, she had to go to Anjum's place. And of all the days when Anjum was out, lobbying this, that and the other and pressing the flesh with dignitaries and the council and various embassies, she had to pick a day when the big Dr Do-Gooder boss-lady was actually in for once.

'Okay. Not a problem, my love,' Tariq said, selecting muesli and making a failed attempt at kissing his wife on her freshly made-up cheek.

Anjum had swiftly turned to their children, Shazia and Zahid. Tariq watched her fussing over them, wiping their faces in readiness for the school run. Telling them in Urdu to brush their teeth and stop dawdling. She threw her pink silk dupatta over her shoulder repeatedly. Bangles jangling. No power-suit today. She liked to wear her traditional salwar kameez on a Friday, and she always tied back her thick black hair. Everything was seemingly normal for a Friday morning at the start of a school day, except her movements were jerky and stiff. Her shoulders were hunched, her posture unrelentingly ramrod straight. More to the point, she was avoiding making eye contact with him, he was certain.

He held out his hand to her. 'Are you going to cheer up and tell me what's bugging you?'

'Don't be puerile,' she said, packing some samosas into a Tupperware container and stuffing the container into her handbag with unequivocal hostility. 'You know exactly what's the matter because I've tried to have this conversation with you already. Several times! I recognised him, Tariq. The boy with the pattern shaved into his hair. A zig-zag. I know he works for you. I've seen him in the factory when I've dropped stuff off for you. And she described you, the Slovakian girl. To a T! You and Jonny. She even said where you worked.' She lowered her voice so that it was audible only to the two of them, with the noise of the children arguing over who had the better snack in their lunch packs, providing a useful diversion to allow for this interrogation. 'And then, you disappear for three days. Come home, wearing the same clothes you went out in. What am I meant to think? I think you're up to no good. That's what I think.'

'What is this? Guantanamo Bay?' Tariq asked, pouring

milk on his muesli. 'I've told you. That Eastern European girl – it was mistaken identity. How many brown men do you know who run businesses at the back of Strangeways, for God's sake? There must be hundreds.' He tutted loudly. Trying to arrange his features into a semblance of hurt sensibilities and innocence. All these long years he was certain she hadn't suspected a thing, and now, Leviticus arsehole Bell and that girl had had to let the cat out of the bag.

'But there aren't hundreds with Jewish business partners, Tariq!' Anjum said, pouring the curry she had prepared after dawn prayers ready for the evening meal into an old margarine tub. Shoving it into the fridge. Even washing her hands seemed to be an act of passive aggression. 'Think it through! She didn't know your name but she knew Jonny's.' Turning to the children, she snapped her fingers abruptly. 'I told you two to get upstairs or we'll be late. Come on!'

Tariq forced a smile as Shazia and Zahid bustled out of the kitchen, disappearing upstairs in a tornado of energy, limbs and gleeful giggling. 'Did you have to bring this rubbish up with them in the room?' Alone with his suspicious wife, without the buffer of his father or the children, Tariq felt fear manifest itself as a heavy sensation, weighing down his head so he could barely look up from his muesli. Was this it? Was this The Big Confrontation? The point at which he would lose everything that really mattered to him just when he had won a long-fought war?

'I love you, my darling,' he said. 'I thought we were a team. I thought we trusted each other.' He reached out to grab her hand but closed his fingers around nothing but negatively charged air.

Anjum pulled a small mirror out of her handbag. Started to apply deep rose-coloured lipstick to her shapely mouth.

She rubbed her lips together and regarded her image. Sniffed and returned the mirror to its place. 'I am utterly trustworthy, Tariq,' she said, collecting her paraphernalia for work – her pad, her pen, her phone. 'You on the other hand . . .' She treated him to an accusatory stare. Those large, dark eyes suddenly seemed devoid of warmth. 'I thought I knew you. But running brothels staffed by trafficked girls? She said you'd tried to sell her as a sham-bride to some dirty old Afghani. Is that where you were when you didn't come home? Sampling your product?' Her dupatta slid free. She tossed it over her shoulder once again. 'You make me *sick*.'

Holding his head in his hands, Tariq wondered if there was any way back from this. Was she toying with him, like some cat playing with a spider? Pulling his legs off one by one. Anjum was the brightest woman he had ever met. Being economical with the truth for the past fifteen years was one thing. She'd always been too busy with the kids and her own career to probe him, and he, after all, was the master of subterfuge. But lying to her . . . ? That would be folly. Nevertheless, what option did he have but to try? There had been nothing but a wall of ice between them for days. He was sick of sleeping on the sofa.

'It's mistaken identity, love. And coincidence. That's all. Just coincidence.' He examined his perfectly clean nails, looking for a blemish that wasn't there. 'Some girl comes in your office, banging on about an Asian bad man who made her do terrible things. What's the likelihood that she's racist or an Islamophobe? They all think we look the same for a start.'

'It's the description of Jonny that was telling! And she wasn't complimentary.'

'Maybe she hates Jews.' He forced himself to look her

237

directly in the eyes. Fronting it out for all he was worth. 'Maybe she's disturbed. Some of these Eastern European girls have very traumatic childhoods at the hands of the Russian Mafia, Anj.'

'Now who's succumbing to racial stereotypes?' she said, zipping up the children's school bags. She looked down dolefully at the Star Wars and Adidas rucksacks. Blinked hard as if checking her next words on some production line of thought for quality and consistence. 'I've worked with refugees and asylum-seekers for over ten years, Tariq.' She narrowed her eyes. 'Before that, I represented the ones who were threatened with deportation in court. I've met murderers, gangsters, dealers, rapists, suspected terrorists. I told you I got your dad's pharmacist in my place the other week with a Chinese girl, didn't I? He left sharpish when he saw me, but it was definitely him. Everyone's at it. This city's got too many dirty secrets. Nothing surprises me. I've seen it all!' She spoke each word with conviction. Sounded each vowel and consonant with a richness she normally reserved for public speaking. 'And I've met victims. Thousands of victims from all corners of the world. I know a liar from someone telling the truth no matter what bloody language they speak.' She strode over to a pile of cookbooks stacked against the worktop. Took a small lozenge-shaped case from the top and removed her glasses: no-nonsense black-framed Prada glasses with four diamante studs along the arm.

Tariq balked. Anjum meant business when she put those on. He could feel the end of his marriage drawing near. Would she dare divorce him if she found out the truth? Surely not! 'I'm telling you, love. I had to go to London unexpectedly on business. I couldn't ring you because I lost my phone. And the pregnant girl – it's all a big mix-up. How can you put two and two together and make seventeen?'

'Who told you she was pregnant? I certainly didn't.' Her face twitched with deadly fury.

The sound of uneven footsteps on the stairs heralded his father's imminent arrival at the breakfast table. They both fell silent. Suddenly, it was as if the clouds had parted and the sun had come out.

'Morning, Youssuf,' Anjum said, beaming at her father-in-law. 'Sleep well? I'll do you some toast before I go out.'

She turned her back to the dishevelled-looking elderly man, still wearing his baggy pyjamas over his painfully thin frame with an old sweater on top. She switched the smile for a scowl, directed at Tariq. Pointed to both of her eyes with her index and middle finger. Pointed to him.

Tariq swallowed hard, counting the minutes until his wife left the house with the kids. When they were gone, he closed the front door, stroking his beard and exhaling slowly. Realising that his back was pouring with sweat. He would need another shower before he left for work.

'Tariq! Son! Are you coming in?' Youssuf called from the kitchen.

Sighing deeply and wishing he could somehow wake from this terrible dream, Tariq dragged himself back to the reality of Friday mornings. Sitting at the island with a hunched back, panting, though he had done nothing of note apart from walk down the stairs, his father looked even more unwell than usual.

'You been taking your meds, Dad?' he asked, putting his arm around the old man.

Youssuf looked up at him with milky cataract-eyes. Breathless and open-mouthed. 'Ya-allah, that's what I wanted to talk to you about,' he said. 'My pharmacist. He's a nice boy. I get my repeat prescriptions from him when Anjum takes me into town. Sometimes he drops them off, here. But he's gone.'

'What do you mean, he's gone, Dad?'

'Disappeared. The shop's locked up. It's not like him. He normally leaves a girl if he goes away. Sometimes he goes to Hong Kong, apparently.'

'Well, maybe he's there now. There are other pharmacists, Dad. Loads of Asian ones.'

'But I like this one. He's a Chinese. They're very respectful.'

Escorting his father into the downstairs bathroom, Tariq wondered if his father's favourite missing pharmacist and the O'Briens' loose cannon of a Chinese chemist were one and the same man. Perhaps he'd absconded after the cannabis factory raid and blown the whistle. Perhaps the O'Briens had caught up with him and neutralised the threat. In this business, there were always too many loose threads, threatening to unravel at all times.

He said nothing. Helped the old man to shower and then dressed his bedsores. Carefully assisted him as he donned the thermal underwear and thick socks that would keep his frail frame warm. Slid his tunic and pants over the ensemble in readiness for the mosque. Trimmed the moustache above his upper lip and neatened his white beard. Nagged him to eat the toast that Anjum had made. Wondered who the hell would look after him if Anjum went to the police. Would she accompany him to hospital appointments or leave him to travel alone in an ambulance with strangers, forced to starve or eat a haram sandwich from the café?

'You look preoccupied,' Youssuf said, touching Tariq's cheek tenderly. 'You're in trouble.'

Tariq shook his head and sighed. 'You've no idea. Just

240

when I thought I'd imposed some order on the madness . . .'

Even beyond the opacity of the cataracts, he detected disappointment in his father's eyes. 'She's found out, hasn't she?' He encircled Tariq's hand inside his own. 'A boy like you could have done anything. Why did you choose this path?'

'Nobody chooses to become a career criminal, Dad. I just slid into it. You know that. We needed the money. One thing led to another.'

'Nonsense. With your education you—'

'Okay!' Tariq shouted, withdrawing his hand from the old man's bony grip. 'Okay! I didn't want to be dirt poor like you and Mum were when you first came over. I was frightened.'

'You're a law graduate from Oxford.'

'*You'd* been an architect in Lahore but you ended up breaking your back for tuppence a week in a crappy factory off Bury New Road, sewing up cheap duffle coats till all hours! Even when you opened the shop, we were always scrabbling around for cash. And I hated it. I hated that estate, with all those fat white kids jeering "Paki" at me. Having to run the gauntlet every day, just to get to the bloody bus stop to get to school.'

'Come on! What were the odds of you having to live on a council estate in Sweeney Hall? You could have been a hot-shot solicitor, working in London. Didn't one of those big city law firms offer you a job? *You* could have been Mayor of London! I worked my fingers to the bone and sent you to a good school so that you wouldn't end up some two-bit gangster, running with the Mirpur wide-boys, talking Desi-English.' His father bit into a piece of cold toast from the plate in front of him and chewed defiantly.

Smug in the knowledge that he was absolutely right and that anything Tariq said was a poor excuse.

'I couldn't go to London. Mum got ill, then I had to look after you. So Sadiq Khan can kiss my Mancunian—'

'Watch your mouth!'

'I was bored with the law. I like the thrill of what I do. I get to be around for you and Anjum and the kids, don't I? You'd never see me if I was a hot-shot in the city. I couldn't bunk off and take you to the Masjid every week, could I? And I thought, if I could just balance it all up by doing the charitable stuff and encouraging Anjum in her work . . .'

His father snorted. 'You embarrass me. If Anjum does go to the police, maybe she'd be doing us all a favour.'

Enough. He had had enough. Ignoring the cold, clammy sweat that clung to his skin like shame, Tariq padded calmly to the hall, adjusted a family portrait on the wall, put on his sneakers.

'I'll pick you up later, Dad,' he shouted. 'How about you have a little think about what it might be like when the money's gone and they put you in a filthy NHS nursing home in Cheetham Hill?'

Slamming the door, he inhaled and exhaled deeply, relishing the fresh Boddlington Park air that was so much easier to breathe than the Sweeney Hall stink of his youth, heavy with poverty and desperation. Here, it was heavy with the aroma of newly mown grass. Summer blooms. Affluent perfection, disturbed only by the incessant noise of leaf blowers in winter and hedge-trimmers in summer. Tariq climbed into his gleaming car, savouring the sense of wealth that manifested itself in the hand-stitched leather. His heart rate slowed as he watched the impressive wrought iron gates swing open with a press of his fob. He edged forwards out of the drive, noticing as he passed Jonny's house on the cul-de-sac of mansions that an unfamiliar car was parked outside the Margulies' pile. Peering into the driver's side window, he was certain he saw two unlikely visitors – one of them almost certainly unwelcome.

Chapter 32

Gloria

'Was that Tariq Khan?' Gloria asked, craning her neck to see out of the hire car's rear window, watching the Mercedes CLS as it glided slowly past. She was sure their eyes had met for a split second. And those were definitely Tariq Khan's heavy black eyebrows knotted together. Had he placed her?

Lev dropped his head into her lap, clamping his eyes shut. 'Oh, shit. If he knows we're here, we're stuffed. We might as well go back to yours now and cut our wrists.'

Gloria slapped him repeatedly on his head. 'Get off, you silly boy. Nobody said you could put your bowling ball of a head on my lap. You're not five any more. Lord have mercy!'

Sliding back up in the driver's seat and gripping the wheel, Lev mumbled, 'Sorry.'

In the rear of the car, Jay was finally sleeping in his car seat, his head lolling onto his shoulder with spittle spooling slowly out of his mouth. His golden curls were plastered to his honey-brown forehead with sweat. Gloria could smell the testosterone on the boy. Reminded her of Lev when he had been sleeping as a baby. He had always sweated like a horse too. She stifled a smile.

'Run through the plan again,' she said.

'I feel sick. I want to turn back.'

Lev's pallor bore testament to him having lost his nerve. Under the circumstances, she had no time for his cowardice. She said a silent prayer to Jesus for forgiveness, mindful of the fact that what they were about to do could not be rationalised as an act of kindness.

'There's no turning back, Leviticus. Not unless you want that boy to die. Now, run through the blasted plan.'

'I can't do it!' Lev shouted. 'Tariq's seen us. He's on my case anyway. I'm dead meat.'

'Not if you get your money and get on a flight to Baltimore, you're not. Grow a pair, son. If Tariq Khan suspects you of anything, he's hardly likely to go to the police, is he?' She studied his face. He had always been beautiful. Had always had a certain femininity to his bone structure. So much of her in him. But that weakness was all his father's. 'We do it here or we wait for her to come out and do it somewhere else. It's your choice. But this is the only way. The piper calls the tune.'

Switching on the engine, Lev shook his head abruptly. 'No. This is wrong.' He drove up to the cul-de-sac's turning circle.

'Where you going?'

'Home.'

'To watch your son die? Back to your squalid little flat on the estate? Because you're not coming to *my* house, young man. How about you toddle off to Tiffany's to watch her doping herself up to the eyeballs? She could leave your boy in dirty nappies like usual, because I don't think I've seen nappy rash that bad in my life. It's a wonder Jay has any skin left.' She faked a smile, all wide-eyed surprise and blistering sarcasm. 'Hey, maybe Asaf Smolensky will bring you over a nice piece of halibut. Or Degsy might turn up, wanting to get even for you battering his face to a more interesting pulp. You've got options, Leviticus. Not many can say that.'

Lev stalled the car. Turned to her with tears in his eyes. Lips pressed so firmly together that the colour had drained from them almost entirely. The flinching muscles in his cheeks told her all she needed to know. Her own son hated her. 'I can't do it. I'm not a murderer.'

She gasped. 'You carry a gun around with you and shove it in people's mouths if they don't pay up. You said yourself, you stabbed Paddy O'Brien!'

'That's not me! It's all for show. I backed myself down this blind alley when I was too young to understand what the hell I was doing, what I'd end up having to do just to keep my head above water and keep my nose clean with the likes of Tariq and Jonny. But I don't think I can do this.' With a shaking hand, he wiped his eyes. 'Me and Mia . . .' His chin started to dimple as it had done when he was a little boy. His mouth turned downwards. 'But if I don't . . .' Checked Jay's reflection in the rear view mirror. Mercifully still sleeping. 'There must be another way.'

'How else are you going to kick-start war when everyone else wants to uphold peace? Where else are you going to get a hundred and fifty K? Beggars cannot be choosers, Leviticus.' She turned around to look at the sleeping child she had not met until a few weeks earlier. A child she had planned to have no feelings for whatsoever. Gloria's plan had only been to look out for number one and to serve the Lord Almighty, once her son had started down the unrighteous path. She had been doing just fine until . . .

'Give me the gun,' she said, holding her hand out.

Knowing that she would face eternal damnation for this. But didn't Timothy 5:8 say, *But if anyone does not provide for his relatives, and especially for members of his household, he has denied faith and is worse than an unbeliever*? She was sure of it. In which case, her actions could still be interpreted as those of a Christian. Wasn't Mia the whore's daughter of a heartless gangster? Vain and self-interested? Spoiled and profligate in her consumption and waste. 'Now!' Opening and closing her fingers. 'Gimme!'

Lev handed her the weapon slowly, as though he couldn't quite believe what he was tacitly agreeing to. Withdrew it. 'No. No way. I can't let you do it.'

But she prised the heavy gun from his hand. Held it against his temple with the safety off.

'What the bloody hell?!'

'Drive me to the gate. Do it! I can't have the neighbours seeing more than they already have. And take off your hoody. I need it.'

One last look at the cherubic boy on the back seat was enough to strengthen her determination. Hood up for the entrance. Once she was standing outside the front door, pressing the bell, she pulled the hood off, knowing most women would open the door to someone who looked as respectable as she did.

A dumpy girl with a mass of long dark hair came into view, padding barefoot to the door on the other side of the frosted glass. Soulful but tuneless humming, audible even from outside. The door opened a fraction. Mia looked first at the black skin of Gloria's chest, then at her face. No flicker of recognition, thankfully.

'I'm sorry. We're Jewish,' she said.

'I'm not a Jehovah's Witness.'

The girl's impassive face was almost dayglo with tan

makeup. False eyelashes batted up and down, giving her the look of a fat plastic dolly from the 1970s.

'Oh, we don't need a cleaner, thanks,' she said.

Gloria lifted the gun, enjoying the feel of it in her hand and the God-like power it suddenly bestowed on her. 'Inside, harlot! Make a sound and I'll kill you.'

Mia lifted her smooth, pudgy hand to her mouth. Nodding. Backing inside, allowing Gloria over the threshold. Gloria slammed the door behind her.

'Take whatever you want,' Mia said. 'It's all insured. Just don't hurt me.'

'Further in!' Gloria shouted. 'And don't speak. Hands above your head where I can see them.'

The girl started to weep, her hotpant-clad legs clearly buckling. This wasn't going to be as easy as anticipated, Gloria mused. Employing trafficked labour was one thing. Those women enjoyed a fresh start in a better, safer country, thanks to her. But to kill in cold blood?

'Where do you want me to go?' Mia asked, glancing behind. Mascara and eyeliner streamed down her tan cheeks in rivulets.

Gloria knew that the longer she idled, waving the gun in the girl's face, the less likely she would be to do it. Silently, and as quickly as she could, she said the Lord's Prayer. Knowing she was about to cross a line from which there would be no return. Realising that this was war and that killing in war was honourable, especially when the salvation of her family was at stake. It was almost self-defence. Wasn't it?

'Kneel down,' she said. 'Hands on your head.'

'I don't know what you want, you mad black junkie bitch, but just take it and get out!' And there it was. A flash of haughty defiance. The confidence of a rich man's daughter who had been over-indulged for every year of her young life. The assumptions of a racist.

'*They shall be like mighty men in battle . . .*' Gloria said, taking aim at the girl's head. ' *. . . Trampling the foe in the mud of the streets; they shall fight because the Lord is with them, and they shall put to shame the riders on horses.* Zachariah 10:5.'

Mia grimaced. 'What? I don't like horses. They smell of shit.'

Two bullets were all it took. Brap, brap, like some small-time gangster cartoon killer. The Lord had steadied her hand, allowing her to make the girl's death instant and painless. Gloria staggered backwards from the recoil, feeling pain shoot up her ageing arthritic wrists. On the ground, Mia lay with the top of her head and the majority of her brains redistributed all over the cream carpet in dazzling shades of red, grey and salmon.

That was surely enough to guarantee the money.

Chapter 33

Jonny

Kneeling by Mia's body, Jonny Margulies felt like a hand had closed tightly around his neck. He reached out to touch her but his fingertips were numb. Shivering. Shuddering on that fine summer's day, in the grip of his own personal wintry blast.

Barely able to keep his finger steady, he punched 999 into his phone. Felt the sob trying to push its way out of his constricted throat as he asked for an ambulance and the police. When quizzed as to what the problem was, he replied, 'Somebody killed my princess.'

Beyond that, Jonny didn't know what to do. Still clutching the phone, his left hand clasped to his mouth, he just knelt on the ground, transfixed by the impossible sight of his daughter's corpse. Had he fallen and hit his head? He had left the office in a hurry to nip home, pick up the golfing gift for a big customer that he had left on the side in the kitchen, get back before the meeting. Perhaps he had been driving recklessly. Been involved in a car crash and knocked out. Anything but the reality of this.

'This can't be happening,' he said aloud. He slapped himself in the face. 'Come on, Jonny. Wake up, you silly fat turd.' But the reflection in the mirror of an overweight man kneeling over a dead girl corroborated his worst fear. This was no bad dream.

'Ring Sandra,' he said softly. But hadn't she gone off to the spa, telling him that under no circumstances must she be disturbed on her girls' weekend? This would surely count as an allowable exception. But Jonny's overloaded brain was sputtering. He could not bring himself to dial her number. Had the sudden urge to text Tariq, but it didn't seem appropriate. He looked up at the spotlights sunken into the ceiling. 'What should I do, God?'

No answer was forthcoming. The only sound came from his own chattering teeth. The sight of his lifeless daughter made him certain that God had never been further away than at this moment in Jonny Margulies' cursed life.

'Wake up, bubbele,' he said, realising the utter pointlessness of the request.

Mia's half-open eyes were dull and unseeing. Her skin was pale yellow. How long had she been there? Gingerly, he reached out to touch her arm. Cold. Not daring to look at the coagulating mess of blood, bone and brain matter above her head, he felt her neck. Still warm. Funny that. All the executions that had been carried out at his behest and yet he knew so little about the dead. He hadn't expected them to stay warm. Was her spirit still within her or had it already gone to heaven, if there was such a place for the daughter of a flagrant sinner? Why was she so yellow? Had Jack O'Brien looked like this when he was found?

Jack O'Brien. Was this a revenge killing sanctioned by Frank? No. Not Frank. He didn't have it in him. 'Paddy.' With sirens wailing in the distance, getting nearer now, Jonny realised who lay behind this travesty of biblical proportions. 'Paddy O'Brien. You ruthless, lying monster.'

It was as if he had suddenly woken from a medicated, troubled sleep. He shook his head, dispelling the urge to weep. Dialled Tariq, who answered on the third ring.

'I need your help. Mia's dead,' he said. 'Some bastard shot my baby in the head in my own house. I don't care how much heat we're getting off the cops. Tell Smolensky to get in touch.'

Chapter 34

Asaf

'A nice piece of hake, please, Asaf. My Monty loves a bit of hake. And I'll have some fish mix, but make sure you give me good weight. Last time, the baitzke served me . . .' Mrs Bamberger shot Asaf's non-Jewish assistant with a disparaging glance '. . . and I only got eight pletzels out of mix for ten. You want to keep an eye on her.'

Asaf Smolensky looked down at the tiny bent-double figure of his oldest customer, trying to suppress the urge to yawn. In her Germanic, clipped accent, she started to talk about the merits of fried plaice, touching her wig with the gnarled fingers and the ridged horn-like nails of the very elderly. Tattooed numbers just visible on her forearm. He wondered what she would look like if he filleted her. Would a nonagenarian bleed less than a young person? Would they fight for life the same as someone sixty years their junior or receive death with a certain dignity and resignation? Possibly even gratitude. She'd survived worse by decades. He pushed the thought out of his mind, realising that it was disrespectful. He had boundaries, after all.

Slapping a heavy, slippery fish onto the scales, he relayed the weight and price to Mrs Bamberger.

'This is a good fish,' he said. 'Fresh as a daisy from Fleetwood this morning.'

'Make sure you bone and skin it, won't you?' she said. 'I can't stand bones. They stick in my throat and choke me. My Monty gets them under his false teeth.'

'Yes.' He slid the sharpest of knives beneath the fish flesh, removing the silvery grey skin with ease and plucked out the stubborn bones with pliers. He placed the hake inside some brown paper and showed it to his discerning customer. 'Well?'

'You're an artist!' she declared.

'It's a mitzvah to do my job properly.'

'Gott sei dank. The whole of Boddlington Park fresses the best, thanks to you.'

When his phone rang and he saw that it was Tariq's number, he discarded the fish on the counter. Disappeared into the back, ignoring the bewildered complaints of Mrs Bamberger.

'What is it?' he asked, relishing his accelerated heartbeat.

'You've got a job.'

Adrenalin coursed through his body, dispelling that horrible feeling that he was being sucked down and down into quicksand. He visualised himself wriggling free. 'The solicitor told me to keep a low profile. He said they'd lock me up without hesitation if I was caught with so much as a potato peeler on my person outside the shop.'

'That's for us to worry about,' Tariq said. 'Do this job and we'll guarantee your safety. Haven't we always? Do this for Jonny.'

Ending the call, Asaf savoured the feeling of his brain clicking into manoeuvre-mode. Just like old times. Receiving the mission. Planning the campaign. Stealth attack in enemy territory. Perfect execution and home, to celebrate discreetly.

Dishonourable discharge may have torn the stripes from Asaf's uniform but it would never strip out the prize fighter in him, he realised with a grin.

As he packed up his knives in the back, leaving his assistant to deal with the now irate Mrs Bamberger, he probed the inner workings of his mind to see how he felt about the news of the apparent hit on Mia Margulies. Realised sympathy should lurk there for Jonny, a man who always put family first, no matter how morally dubious his methods were. But there was no sensation in Asaf's body or brain other than the sheer thrill and anticipation of what was to come.

Chapter 35

Frank

'I want everything perfect,' Frank told the lighting manager. He looked up at the giant rig over the dancefloor – a geometric mass of criss-cross scaffolding containing projectors, spots and laser units that would transform the place into a visual feast. His homage to the Haçienda. His tribute to his son. 'Make sure the lasers spell "Jack". No cock-ups, right?' He forced a half-hearted smile as he visualised the display. 'And it's got to be in blue, 'cos our Jack loved the blues.'

'Twelve-bar blues?' the man asked, removing a small screwdriver from his mouth. A southerner, by the sounds.

'Ha ha. Very fucking funny. This is Manchester, mate.'

Frank cajoled himself into doing a tour of inspection around the club, checking and double-checking every element. Behind the main bar, bottles in jewel shades gleamed in the row of brightly lit fridges. Optics lined up like loaded guns. Shelf after shelf of exotic and esoteric spirits, rising up in tiers. The barrels of draught beers had all been changed, the smell of fresh lager reminding Frank of music festival heydays and better times spent outdoors on blankets in the sun. The toilets, slightly shabby from overuse and due renovation, were at least clean and fully functioning. In the men's he saw scrawled in silver pen on the back of one of the cubicle doors the words:

'In the beginning there was Jack

And Jack had a groove.

Jack is the one that can bring nations and nations of all Jackers together under one house.'

He ran his finger tenderly across the long string of words, penned in his son's handwriting. Determined to have some sort of art made around those words and have it hanging prominently in one of the bar areas. The dancefloor area where Jack's blood had seeped into the parquet, staining the wood from golden to a harrowing shade of rust, had been sanded and refinished. He bumped fists with the incoming DJs as they arrived, nodding enthusiastically at their playlists, though he wasn't really listening or looking at the contents of their DJ boxes. He sat behind the enormous mixing console during the sound check. The show must go on. What Jack had started, he would finish. Frank swallowed down the lump in his throat and retired to the back office to be alone with his crippling emptiness and a baggie of whizz.

When he emerged, everything seemed to be travelling at the speed of light. Young revellers were streaming into the cavernous club, hanging out by the bar to spot the scantily clad or beefed-up talent, depending on their gender. Some were already throwing shapes on the dancefloor as if nobody was watching. But the place was still only half full. Imagining positive energy emanating from the fore-running clubbers like heatwaves rising above a desert road, Frank breathed in their youthful scent of warm air, perfume, sickly booze and hairspray. The smell of fine times. A midsummer's Saturday night. Finally reopened after the club had been forced to close its doors, following Jack's death – tonight would be M1

House's biggest night of the year, stretching the club to the outer limits of its 4,000-strong capacity, streaming the live performances to millions all over the world via social media. Frank saw his son's handsome face in every lad that turned his way. Even the whizz wasn't enough to dull that ache.

Summer evening sunlight poured through the corrugated Perspex skylights in the roof of the warehouse, filling the dancefloor with early evening optimism and hope. It was empty enough for there still to be an echo as the music thump-thumped out of the giant sound system. Frank was lost in his own Large Hadron Collider of good memories, racing to embrace the bad in a head-on collision inside his arrhythmic heart and mashed-up head.

Muscles have memories too. Almost as a reflex action he found himself waving maniacally from the sparsely populated dancefloor.

'Paddy!' he shouted enthusiastically at his brother, who marched in, flanked by Conky and a bandaged, black-eyed Degsy.

Then, he remembered that he hated Paddy. With the amphetamine buzz coursing through his bloodstream, the toxic mix of love and hate enmeshed his heart. Suddenly, he was sweating and breathing too hard. He staggered off the dancefloor, counselling himself to keep a lid on the combustible vitriol.

'We did it, Frank,' Paddy said, putting a territorial hand on his shoulder. 'We got the club back open for Jack.'

'*We?*' Frank said, inhaling sharply through his nostrils and smelling the £200 a bottle aftershave on his brother. 'Did *we?*'

Paddy laughed and clasped Frank to him with an affectionate hand on the back of his head. Any tacit rejection had been lost on him.

As they grabbed their drinks in the VIP area, Frank's initial high had been replaced by a racing heartbeat. Panting like a thirsty dog. Every thud of a bass drum seemed suddenly too loud and aggressive, ramming against his cranium as if to force entry to the delicate matter inside.

'What's up with you?' Paddy asked, sipping Cristal from a cheap flute. A long-legged girl who could have been no more than twenty was already sitting astride his knee, kissing his sunburnt wrinkled neck.

'I've got a funny feeling,' Frank said, tugging at the hem of his T-shirt.

Suddenly, the hedonistic air of freedom felt oppressive. The sight of Paddy groping the bottom of the young girl looked wrong. Frank wanted out.

He pushed through the burgeoning, thronging mass of dancers towards the emergency exit. Flung open the doors. The throbbing music was so loud, he knew nobody would notice the weedy alarm going off. Cool summer evening air blasted inside the stiflingly hot club. Night had fallen now, transforming the glorious red and teal sunset sky into deepest navy. Brighter inside than out with all the flashing lights, he could just about make out the giant wheelie bins and bottle banks. His senses were sharpened out here in the fresh air. Wanting to become invisible just for a moment, he pushed the exit doors almost closed behind him and slid into the deep shadows of a bin to light a cigarette.

'I'll never see him again,' he whispered to the unforgiving white disc of the full moon.

As loss began to envelop him once more, he stared out into the black of the service area. His eyes became accustomed to the barely there shapes. And presently, amid the now-dulled thunk, thunk, thunk of the music coming from inside, he was aware of a car pulling up on the other side of the high brick wall that separated the club's land from the street. Doors slamming shut in unison. The sound of men, whispering, just audible above the beat and the bass. A scrabbling noise against the wall. Frank held his breath. Stubbed the glow of his cigarette out and watched as six men clambered over the wall, dropping down into the service area below. Each one of them carried a weapon – be it a handgun or a rifle. In that darkness, it was hard to pick out details. But there was one figure, silhouetted against the moonlight and the backdrop of an imperfect midsummer night's evening, whom Frank recognised immediately. Tall, slender, wearing a large-brimmed hat. He brought with him his own distinctive scent of death.

Chapter 36

Asaf

Dropping over the wall of M1 club, Asaf felt only the blissful anticipation of what was to come. Giddy with adrenalin, he carried the Bren gun across his body like a sleeping hound, just waiting to be roused. He had gone beyond the point where he was concerned that he might be arrested and sent to jail for a long stretch. He was all about the mission, now.

The music came out to meet him. The repetitive thud-thudding reminiscent of the beat of helicopter wings in the Negev. He was at one with his weapon and the men he had assembled for the mission. Get in. Wreak havoc. Get out. Message sent. Those had been his instructions.

In an arrow formation, he led the six inside. Like the waves of the Red Sea, the crowd parted almost instinctively to allow their safe passage to the centre of the club. If some girls started to scream, Asaf could barely hear them. He was two thousand miles away on an exercise in the Golan Heights, looking out over the Sea of Galilee and the verdant irrigated pastures. The drone of his psychiatrist during those psychotherapy sessions for post-traumatic stress disorder only a dim memory operating as a soundtrack.

'Look out for Paddy O'Brien,' he shouted to his companions. 'If you see him, kill him.'

When he reached the middle of the dancefloor, he was in hostile territory. Every party-goer was the face of the enemy. *Open fire*, a voice inside him said. *Kill or be killed.* Obeying, he roused the sleeping Bren gun, mowing down those who stood before him. The sight of blood made him feverish with excitement, batting away the instruction that Paddy O'Brien was to be his main target. Focus was becoming increasingly difficult of late. But the drive to end life and render himself invulnerable was stronger than ever. A continual re-enactment of what had happened on manoeuvres, in that hot dusty village on another continent, in a different time in his life; somehow hoping he'd get it right, this time. That he'd save his unit. That it would be the enemy who would be in the ground by sundown.

'Please, no!' A young man screamed, taking slow steps backwards with his hands held high. The only boy left where others had fled or fallen.

Asaf let the Bren gun hang loose on its strap against his body. Pulled a machete out of the specially sewn knife-holder inside his coat. As he was about to bring the blade down on his fresh-faced foe, bullets struck the ground by his feet – inaudible beneath the towering wall of sound coming from the speakers all around. He looked up to locate the source of the enemy fire. Spotted Conky McFadden and Degsy advancing with murder in their eyes. Saw the flash of further shots being fired his way. Felt a bullet brush his sleeve. Was faced with a decision. Advance and engage in hand-to-hand combat – or retreat?

Too slow. Asaf yelled as one of McFadden's bullets plunged into his shoulder.

'Retreat! Retreat!' he shouted, grabbing at the agonising wound.

But his soldiers had already fled. He was alone. Surrounded by the enemy with McFadden and the sunken-faced Degsy almost upon him.

Chapter 37

Conky

'Get him out of here!' Conky shouted to one of the M1 House bar staff, wielding a tray full of empties. He put a protective arm around his King, feeling his own shock being kicked brutally to the back of his mind by the adrenalin of battle.

'Bollocks to that, Conks. I'll stay,' Paddy said, shrugging him off and pulling a gun from his waistband with a flourish. He snapped a full cartridge of bullets into place. Taking aim at the dancefloor, fixing his sights on the bar area, moving the barrel towards the DJ booth, then back again. 'It's a bloody scrum. I can just about hear them, but I can't see the bastards. We need that music off, now!' Squinting, he lowered the gun uncertainly.

Glancing over at the empty DJ booth, it was immediately clear to Conky that it was unmanned. Unsurprisingly. Defending the O'Briens in a fire-fight was not in the contract or included in the DJ's fifty-grand fee.

'Shall I go and switch it off, Conky?' Degsy asked, shifting from his left foot to his right like a coked-up, jaundiced Rocky Balboa preparing for the big fight. His right eye was still bandaged where Gloria's arsehole of a son had beaten him to a pulp.

'No way. I need you here. How's your depth perception?'

'What?'

'Can you fucking see to shoot, Derek?'

Degsy shrugged. Held his gun across his chest like some bad ass hip-hop type, except Degsy was milky white trailer trash from Parson's Croft. Prick.

Conky gave him a withering glance. 'Don't shoot the dancing children, for Christ's sake, or I'll knack you in the bollocks myself. Okay?'

The girls in the VIP area had already fled, screaming and clattering off in their high heels. With only the three of them remaining plus the hyperventilating barman who was still holding a tray of glasses, Conky stood on a sofa. Scanned the club, processing images of the scattering crowds like a super-computer, determining who was reveller and who belonged with the Fish Man. 'Six of them,' he said under his breath. *Three of us against six Boddlingtons. No sign of the bouncers. Shite odds.*

'Paddy, you have to go,' he said. 'I insist. If they don't get you first, this place will be crawling with coppers any minute. Best you're not here.'

Paddy paused, looked towards the fray where Asaf Smolensky was spraying bullets at every kid in his path with a monster of a machine gun.

Conky grabbed the tray from the ashen-faced barman. Thrust Paddy's car key into his hand. 'Get Mr O'Brien out through the back to the car, now! And find your boss. Frank is missing.'

Advancing towards Smolensky, Conky tried to keep his breathing steady.

Now, he had a clear view of Smolensky. Drunk on death. That much was obvious, though he still couldn't fathom why any of this was happening after the truce had been agreed. Writhing, wounded or dying bodies at his feet, the Fish Man had cornered some young lad. He drew a machete from inside his coat. It glinted lethally under the club lighting. The word 'JACK' strobed against the back wall in blue lasers. Conky felt loyalty and anger surge inside him. Pushed his sunglasses onto his forehead and aimed carefully. He loosed a bullet.

Smolensky grabbed at his shoulder, grimacing in pain. 'Gotcha, you bastard!'

The others had already started to run. Someone had switched the sound system off at last. Sirens were audible. Not far away, now. Conky kept marching forwards towards the Fish Man, but the lanky fiend about-turned and ran through the side exit. And boy, could he move. Struggling to follow, Conky chided himself for having been made sluggish by age with the aching legs of a man who had forgotten to take his thyroxine that morning.

'Shite!' he said, gasping and clutching his knees.

The Fish Man swam away upstream against the flow of scurrying, petrified clubbers, darting hither and thither like confused minnows out of the path of a giant leaping salmon.

As uniforms flooded the dancefloor, the only souvenir of the Fish Man's visit was his hat and a pile of bodies.

Gun concealed about his person from the cops' prying eyes, Conky bent to retrieve the hat, fingering the brim thoughtfully. Contemplated the broken bodies of young-sters at the very dawn of their adult lives. 'This place has had it,' he said.

'You're telling me,' said a voice just by his ear. He jumped.

Turning around with his fists balled and ready to strike, Conky exhaled heavily when he realised who it was. 'Jesus, man. You're lucky I didn't flatten you then.' He stared at the dishevelled-looking Frank, who visibly seemed to have shrunk by several inches in the course of the past twenty minutes. His glazed eyes were darting everywhere. Even with his hands jammed deep in his jeans pockets, Conky could see he was quaking.

'Are you hurt?' he asked, placing a hand on Frank's shoulder.

With a shake of his head, Frank merely looked up at the giant blue 'JACK', still shining in laser stripes from the front of the club onto the back wall.

It was hard to tell whether he was in shock or whether something else was afoot. A nagging sensation pulled at Conky's innards, a voice in his head asking, 'Where were you, Frank, while this shit was going down?' Except, it wasn't in his head at all. He had said it out loud without realising. Definitely low on the old thyroxine.

Frank shrugged. Still wouldn't meet Conky's astute, if bulging-eyed gaze. 'Behind the bins. I went out for a smoke. I-I was just frigging paralysed when I saw them hoofing it over the wall. I tried to come in, you know . . . to raise the alarm and whatnot.' He looked at his finger-nails but his hand shook so much that he pushed it back into his pocket. 'But then I heard the guns going off and I just couldn't, Conk. I just sat there behind the bin, wishing it was all a bad dream and praying they wouldn't find us.'

Conky felt the reassuring outline of his gun, concealed in the lining of his coat. He was mulling over Frank's explanation and body language, feeling as though something didn't quite add up. Just as he was about to quiz him further, the unwelcome and annoyingly familiar figure of Ellis James entered his peripheral vision.

'Oh, shit. I've got to go, Frank. I'm sorry. My priority is

to get Paddy away from here safely. I've got to drive him home.'

Frank finally met his gaze with wide, desperate eyes. 'No. Don't leave me to sort this mess on my own, Conks.'

'I'm packing, Francis.'

James was only metres away now, being debriefed by one of his uniforms. Conky imagined he saw the glimmer of a grin on the detective's face. A little schadenfreude perhaps. Now he was speaking to a bouncer, but he had one eye on Conky. If the little shabby-arsed bastard arrested him, he would have some explaining to do once he was strip searched. He felt the throb of his accelerated pulse in his neck.

'Well, well, well,' Ellis James said, coming towards them, scratching his buzz cut with a chewed-up biro. Dog-eared notebook in hand. He was wearing the same soiled beige raincoat he always wore. The same worn-down, scuffed shoes that always made Conky feel slightly itchy. The collar of his shirt was frayed. And yet, he sensed a certain buoyancy in the detective at the sight of the blood and the mayhem. 'It seems like my dance card has been filled by you entrepreneurial sons of Manchester of late. First I get a call that Jonny Margulies' daughter has been topped. Then I get a—'

'You *what*?' Conky asked. 'Mia Margulies is dead?'

Frank blanched visibly and clasped his hand to his mouth. 'Get out of town!'

Ellis James smirked. 'Oh come on, boys. There's no need to be coy with me. Your rival's daughter is found with two bullets in her and the top of her head all over the shag pile. I think I can put two and two together and make—'

'No disrespect, detective,' Conky said, careful to gauge Frank's reaction from behind his sunglasses. 'But I don't think you should put two and two together to make anything. That sounds rather like hearsay and slander, never mind circumstantial evidence. Why don't you check your facts before you point the finger in our direction? The O'Briens run a respectable builders' merchants and a night-club. Any judge who thought he could convict them of the organised crime and murder that you seem intent on sullying their reputation with would have to be wired to the moon with a faulty fucking plug.'

'Spare me, McFadden.' The smile was gone from Ellis James' thin lips. 'Mia Margulies is executed in the morning in her own home by a pro, and before I even get time to get into my jim-jams for bed, I get a call telling me that there's been a slaughter at Frank O'Brien's grand reopening. It's already all over YouTube and Twitter thanks to a couple of little twats who tried to get a bit of shaky footage on their phones. That's before they real-ised they were about to be filled with more holes than a colander. Imagine my surprise, gentlemen, when I saw a blurry clip of a big lanky Orthodox Jew who looks suspi-ciously like Asaf Smolensky, aka the Fish Man, toting a machine gun. Fancy that, eh?' He stroked his chin archly. 'The police aren't dicks, Mr McFadden. We know what's going on when the hashtag *NorthVSouth* starts trending on Twitter.'

He smiled widely and rocked back and forth on his heels, waiting for a reaction from Conky McFadden that never came. Because Conky's mind was preoccupied only with questions: Who had ordered a hit on Mia Margulies? Why had Frank not been inside the club when Asaf Smolensky and his Boddlington foot soldiers had been spraying the place with bullets? Where in God's name had the bouncers been while all this was going on?

From behind the tinted lenses of his glasses, Conky McFadden appraised the shivering, unassuming figure of Francis O'Brien with newfound suspicion and respect.

Chapter 38

Jonny

'I wish you a long life,' the girl said, kissing him on the cheek.

Jonny felt the warmth and wet of her tears on his skin. Tried to place her and realised, in the bewildering semi-fugue state that bereavement ushered in, that Mia had been at school with her some years ago. Not so different from his daughter, with her long dark hair and almost childishly over-made-up face. Even the tunic and miniskirt that she wore were reminiscent of Mia. By the time he remembered her name was Jodie, she had moved on to wish Sandra a long life and Jonny was faced with shaking the hand of one of the guys he had played football with, many years earlier, when his life had been that of a nice, ordinary Boddlington Park boy.

'I wish you a long life, Jonny,' the man said, not making eye contact. Immediately supplanted by another acquaintance waiting in the queue to offer condolences.

The living room was stiflingly hot. Jonny opened the top button of his shirt, lifted his yarmulke and wiped his bald pate with a handkerchief. Dabbed at his top lip, wishing everybody would just piss off out of his house, leaving them to their private suffering. Praying that Sandra would start to eat something and speak to the boys. Looking beyond his wife, down the line of low stools at his gangling teenaged sons, wearing their best suits with their hair spiked as though they were heading off to a party – utterly at odds with their red-rimmed eyes and hunched postures. Jonny was suddenly overwhelmed by shame.

Where was Tariq? He scanned the packed room, glimpsing him chatting to another of the neighbours by the entrance to the orangery. Only Tariq would understand the crippling sense of having failed his family and his God.

'I'm sorry,' Jonny said, launching himself from his low mourner's stool. He turned to Sandra. 'I feel funny. I've got to get some air.'

But he might as well have said nothing. Sandra was just sitting with her knees pressed primly together, looking like an elaborate carving of a grieving mother. All the agony still locked inside her emaciated body. How much of that pain had she already been carrying before Mia's murder? It hardly mattered. He had caused all of it.

Craving fresh air that wasn't heavy with feverish sorrow and the nervous sweat of do-gooding well-wishers, he pushed his way into the orangery, pulling Tariq with him en-route. Ignoring the disapproving glances from the Rabbi and the old men from the synagogue. Fierce faces from Sandra's visibly broken parents.

'What's wrong, mate?' Tariq asked, clasping Jonny's forearm. 'Is it all getting too much?'

Unable to speak, Jonny kept walking, pulling his partner along past the lush palms to the door, as though he were on the brink of drowning in a sea of stifling expectations unless he could break the surface and breathe.

Outside, dappled in the shadows of a half-dusk, the large

garden was strung about with fairy lights but blissfully empty of people. An early evening fragrance of mock orange provided a welcome exchange for the gut-wrenching smell of pity and loss inside. Jonny peeled off his clammy suit jacket, savouring the cool air on his skin.

'I can't bear it,' he told Tariq, pulling a packet of cigarettes from his trouser pocket and lighting up. Coughing as the stinging cocktail of noxious chemicals hit the back of his throat. Feeling the nicotine rush wrap greedy tobacco tendrils around his sluggish brain and pull tight.

'Since when did you smoke?' Tariq batted the blue cloud away, wrinkling his nose.

Jonny tossed his spent match into a stone urn full of cascading white petunias. 'We're to blame, Tariq,' he said, searching his partner's eyes for sympathy or at least, honest corroboration. 'How did we end up like this?'

Tariq took a seat on the garden bench, leaned forwards and rubbed his face. 'I don't know what to say, Jon. You've paid the ultimate price. I'm sorry. It's a travesty.'

Jonny lowered himself down onto the bench beside him, dragging awkwardly on the alien-feeling cigarette that didn't sit right between his lips. He stubbed it out on the ground when Tariq started to bat the smoke away dramatically. 'If only we'd never been tempted by that first dodgy deal,' he said, throwing the dog-end into the urn. 'Just fencing some stolen goods. A few moody PCs and a job lot of power tools from a ram-raid on Currys and B&Q. Do you remember? That's all it was. We should have left it at a one-off.'

'It's never that simple, though, is it?' Tariq said, leaning back and staring blankly into the lilac-grey memory of a fiery sunset. 'You make good money, but you've sold your soul to whatever shaitan pays you. And without realising,

273

you enter into a binding confidentiality agreement that ties you in in perpetuity.' Exhaling heavily, he tutted and shook his head. 'There was no getting out for us, once we were in.' He clapped a hand on Jonny's shoulder. 'Maybe it was destiny. Or maybe we were just two unlikely childhood mates, thrown together as adults by fortune. Both stuck in Manchester because of family. You needed a business partner with a head for contracts and figures. I needed to be around someone with a wild-west spirit and a bit of entrepreneurial flair.'

'A marriage made in heaven,' Jonny said, half-smiling. Feeling a bittersweet pang of regret in his heart. Remembering his younger self. Slim, with a full head of hair and a mind crammed with dreams of success.

Tariq sighed. 'Do you remember how we used to stay late in that old warehouse, eating kebabs and talking about cars and agonising how to manage the cash flow before the bailiffs turned up on the doorstep?'

Jonny chuckled and nodded. Wistful for those innocent times, which had seemed so frightening back then. Didn't dare speak lest his emotions overwhelm him.

'I suppose we were tested and we failed,' Tariq said, examining his immaculate fingernails. 'We were wet behind the ears and greedy. It's a terrible combination. I realise that now.'

They sat in silence as the sky turned a little darker still, the shadows lengthening.

Jonny pictured Mia, lying in the hallway. Her life's blood emptied out onto the floor –whatever memories, thoughts and sensations she had had that made her the girl she was, fragmented and destroyed by two bullets. That strange rubbery yellow of her skin. The still-warm neck. All he wanted to do was visualise her as a chubby little girl or even as a beautiful young woman, only months before her death. Always singing and dancing. Always wanting to entertain and delight. Anything but the ugly finality of a violent death.

'Jesus!' he said, pinching the tears from his eyes with his finger and thumb. Shaking his head to dispel the image. 'We both knew the personal risks to *us*. We accepted them like grown men. But I never thought for a minute my family might be in danger. How could I have been so naïve?' He turned to face the aquiline profile of Tariq, a man who still had a complete set of living children and who was deep in thoughts that almost certainly didn't feature a mental snap-shot of a dead girl. Jonny swallowed the envy down, knowing it was poison that was best left buried deep. 'It's like something's clicked, and all of sudden, my perspective has changed. I can see my life in all its shitty true colours instead of through rose-tinted glasses. All the money, all the power, all the whores . . .'

'We've been kidding ourselves,' Tariq said, swallowing hard. Still looking straight ahead. 'I thought I could hide it from Anjum forever behind a bullshit façade. All the bad things we've done. But now, she knows.' He turned to Jonny. 'She hates me, Jon. And my dad's ashamed of me. He won't walk near me when we go to the mosque. He looks at his feet and shakes his head when I bung some of the fellers a few quid – you know. The ones who are really struggling to make ends meet. I know Dad loves me, but he doesn't bloody like me.' He clenched his hand into a fist. 'Everything we did, we did for our loved ones, didn't we? And yet, we've screwed it all up. Screwed them all up.'

'This is all down to Paddy and Frank O'Brien,' Jonny said. 'As much as I blame myself for Mia, that family of evil scumbags . . . They're not like us.'

'No, they're not,' Tariq said. 'Paddy's the old guard. He thinks he rules by divine right. It's all about the bloodline to him. The O'Brien family name. We're a republic. We're loads better, man.' He offered a fist-bump to Jonny, which he returned without any real enthusiasm.

Jonny took the packet of cigarettes out of his pocket and ran a finger over the logo. Sighed heavily. 'Why couldn't Smolensky have taken the bastard out last night? The idiot kills a pile of innocent kids but misses both O'Briens entirely. Now, I've got other people's children on my conscience as well as my own!' Rising from the bench, Jonny kicked out at the petunia-filled urn. Grinding his molars until they ached with utter frustration at his own impotence.

'I think Lev Bell's mixed up in this,' Tariq said.

'Lev?' Jonny turned back to the bench. Wafted away a fluttering moth.

Tariq rose and started to walk the length of the garden, giving Jonny no option but to follow. 'Smolensky had got all Mossad on him. You know what the Fish Man's like. Obsessive and weird at the best of times. Anyway, turns out he'd stalked Lev all the way to Gloria Bell's front door.'

'His mother? She's one of them!' Jonny said, trying to second-guess how this puzzle slotted together. 'Works with Sheila O'Brien, doesn't she? But the lad swore blind he never had contact with his mother. They've not spoken for donkey's years.'

Tariq clasped his hands behind him. Came to a standstill. 'I saw Lev in a car with his mother outside your house on the morning of Mia's murder.'

Jonny grabbed him by the collar. Pulled him close. 'Why didn't you say something?'

Tariq levered himself deftly from Jonny's grip. Smoothed

his collar down. 'Chill your boots, for God's sake! I needed to know more, right? You can't jump to conclusions, Jonny. It could have been a coincidence. You know Lev was having an affair with your daughter, don't you?'

Visualising the young gangster who reeked of poverty and had a softness in his eyes at odds with his tough posturing and the Sweeney Hall drug-dealer's haircut, Jonny held his breath. Counted to five slowly. Exhaled. 'We bring him in, then. Smolensky can torture the worm until he gives us answers.'

'Well, I told the Fish Man to pick Lev up and bring him to the office after the M1 House job. But Fish Man ballsed that up so royally that I've had to put him on a retainer. The guy's lost it, Jon. He's unreliable. I don't know where we'll get a good replacement. Nasim's nowhere near ready yet.'

'But I still don't understand. Lev's one of our best men,' Jonny said, screwing his eyes up as he concentrated hard. 'Do you think he's defected? Maybe Frank or Paddy have bunged him some cash to do my Mia over.'

'All I know is the little turd has ruined my marriage. After Tommo and Kai's brothel got stung by the O'Briens, Lev shows up at Anjum's asylum-seeker place with that pregnant Slovakian girl. You know? The one we couldn't sell on as a bride. Well, she's blown the bloody whistle on us, hasn't she? All thanks to Leviticus sodding Bell and his big conscience.'

Jonny put his arm around Tariq. Slapped him on the back. Glad of physical contact with someone who wasn't wishing him a long life and looking at him with eyes full of told-you-so judgement. 'You'll get through this,' he said. 'You're not a bad person. You're just human. Anjum will understand that. As for me . . .'

'Same goes for you, bro,' Tariq said. 'You're flesh and blood. Not God. You've got to forgive yourself.'

Shaking his head, Jonny looked up at the band of midnight blue that had appeared in the sky above them. Remembered Mia learning her Shakespeare at school. A brave o'er hanging firmament that was now nothing more than a foul and pestilent congregation of vapours.

'If Leviticus Bell killed my girl,' he said, 'he's a dead man. And if Smolensky doesn't end Paddy O'Brien after all this, I'll take one of his boning knives and do it myself.'

Chapter 39

Sheila

'The panic room has to be completely secure,' Conky told the man from the security installations company. Towering above the tradesman, looking like the grim reaper in his Loss Adjuster's uniform of black with those shades on, the Irishman cut an impressive figure for an older man, even with the stupid dyed hair. 'And I mean, completely. There needs to be a console in there to operate the CCTV around the house. You'll have to make sure it functions in a damp environment.'

He pointed to the main family bathroom. Despite its slick slate floor-to-ceiling tiling, it had been deemed to be the most logical place to camp out in the event of an emergency situation, though Paddy had wanted the guest bedroom. Stupid bastard.

'There has to be a phone line and broadband that's entirely separate from the system in the rest of the house,' Conky said. 'This rig-up must be unimpeachable. Do you know what that means? Like Fort fucking Knox. Do I make myself clear?' He poked the man in the shoulder. Took his glasses off for emphasis.

Sheila watched with interest and a degree of satisfaction as the security guy blanched. Took a step backwards.

'Yeah. Okay, mate. You gave us the brief already.' He spat slightly when he spoke. Touched his lips self-consciously. 'We're here to install it, now. Take it easy. We're professionals.'

Conky grabbed the straps of the guy's white workman's dungarees and hoisted him off the ground by several inches. Read his name, embroidered onto his company polo shirt. 'Do you know who you're working for, Gary?'

The man swallowed hard. Nodded. 'Mr O'Brien. And my name's Steve.'

'Your name is whatever I say it is. Capiche, Gary?' Setting him back down, Conky smiled and put his shades back on with a flourish. 'Excellent. Here's a cup of tea from the wondrous Mrs O'Brien.'

Sheila suppressed the urge to grin. Proffered the tray to the workman, who was frowning as though he couldn't work out if he was more frightened of or affronted by Conky. 'Biccy?' she said.

'Don't get comfy, Gary,' Conky said, grabbing the workman's cup of tea and slurping it himself. Snatching the Jaffa Cake from his hand. 'You're here to do a job, not engage in existential pondering with a cup of tea in another man's luxury bathroom.' He turned to Sheila and winked. Laughter in his bulging eyes. 'Let's walk and talk. I want you to take Mrs O'Brien here and explain to her everything that's being done to keep her safe from the nasty, dangerous people out there.'

Above the incessant, bone-shaking drilling and hammering, Gary or Steve or whatever he was called led Sheila from room to room, explaining what was being installed by the team of builders and electricians.

'So, your ordinary doors are being replaced by ones that have been reinforced with steel,' he said, pointing to the mess that had been made of Sheila's beautiful contemporary plaster architraves. 'We're putting in remote-controlled deadlocks that close at the touch of a button. They're fire, bullet and bomb proof too. So you can seal any part of the house off at any time.'

Sheila could see the enthusiasm in his face. She guessed that though the company had had this kit in its brochure for years, they were almost certainly the first people ever to shell out for it.

'How do you arm it?' she asked, watching an electrician, who was standing on a stool, insert some cabling into the newly created cavity. His hairy belly was on show as he stretched. Tongue lolling out of his mouth. An average man, grafting in an average job. If she'd married a man like him, would she still see her mum and dad?

'There's a keypad being installed in the hall, but it can be overridden by the kit we're putting into the panic room. You can alarm any part of the house at any time of the day. There are laser sensors that will pick up the slightest movement anywhere.'

'Like on the films?'

'Exactly. *Mission Impossible* has got nothing on this, Mrs O. There are fibre-optic cameras installed in every room too, feeding into the panic room. So, if you ever had an intruder, you'd have hi-res footage from anywhere in the house without ruining your lovely decor.'

'And disabling it?'

'If you know the master code, you can kill the system at any time. From your mobile phone too. I assume Mr O'Brien will want to do all that.'

Sheila smiled warmly. Rearranged her features into her best concerned wife face. 'Oh, my poor Paddy is very rough with a migraine today. You can tell me everything, Steve.

How about that? And I'll teach him when he's better.' She nodded and beamed at him. Fluttered her eyelashes.

'Of course. Whatever you think is best.' Steve blushed and looked at the blue plastic overshoes on his dusty work boots.

They moved through to the kitchen, where Frank was sitting on the leather sofa, regaling a man holding a drill with tales of his appearance at Glastonbury in 1989 – tales Sheila recognised as having been told so frequently and honed with each re-telling, that if the stories were stones, they would have been polished to gleaming opals.

Smirking, she offered Steve a secondary cup of tea. But her offer of hospitality was cut short by Paddy yelling from the bedroom. 'Sheila! Get up here!' Audible even above all the industrial noise ringing throughout the house. A heavy sensation dragged at her shoulders. Tension, burning in the muscles.

Tutting as an outwards show of rebellion, gulping and sighing as an inward revelation of her true desperation, she thrust the empty cup into the workman's hands and made haste up to the master suite.

'Where the fuck have you been?' Paddy wailed, barely visible beneath the duvet. 'Flirting with the bastard builders instead of looking after your own husband? I'm dying here. Get me some painkillers! And tell those arseholes to keep the noise down!'

Sheila pondered his angry red face peeking out at her. He had those shadows beneath his eyes and that slightly green tinge to the skin around his mouth. Tell-tale signs of a humdinger. Once, she had thought him sweet when he had one of his migraines. Vulnerable. Once upon a long, long time ago.

'I'll get your tablets. But Pad, there's nothing the builders can do about the noise. It's that, or risk a break-in from whatever psycho case the Boddlingtons send after you next. You asked for an "impenetrable fortress". That's what you're getting. And I'm glad, because I don't fancy joining our Jack in the cemetery, thanks very much. You were just lucky in the club.'

'*You were just lucky!*' Paddy repeated her words in an unflattering, nagging pitch. His features screwed into a freckled, shrewish ball as he threw the duvet back defiantly to reveal his body, naked but for his pants. 'I pay people to guard me with their lives. It wasn't luck, She. Them kids that got killed . . .' He poked himself in the chest, only millimetres from a love bite that Sheila certainly hadn't given him. '. . . They died to save me. Our Katrina said that's God's fucking will, that is.'

Sheila filled a glass of water from the tap in the en suite. Recognised the tautness in her face as she spoke, reflected in the mirror. 'Those kids were murdered for sod all in cold blood by a nutcase, paid by your business rivals to go on a killing spree. Because you're a gangster, Paddy! Not a postman, not a plasterer and certainly not a saint.' She walked back into the bedroom. Thrust the glass of water and the packet of Migraleve into his hands. 'You want to play Mr Bigshot, you've got to own that guilt. The blood of them kids is on your hands, whichever way you look at it.' She felt she could risk a little antagonism while he was laid up. Hadn't he been at his most sanguine and bearable while he was in hospital after his heart attack? 'And you wouldn't have to install all this expensive shit if we'd just got on that plane to Thailand.' She pointed to the half-packed suitcases, now shoved against the wall with the lids closed to stop dust from gathering.

Grabbing her wrist painfully, he pulled her close. Baring

his teeth like an agitated lion. 'We're not going. I told you. I'm staying here now until I've squashed those Boddlington bastards beneath my iron fist.'

She tried to wriggle free. 'Ow. Let me go!' Annoyed with herself for misinterpreting his mood. She'd have to be careful. 'You're hurting me, Patrick!'

'Good. Might teach you a bit of gratitude. Anyway, I'm doing you a favour, aren't I? You were the one who didn't want to go to Thailand. I thought you were all for staying here to run the Shit Shovellers' Union with that silly cow, Gloria.'

Despite her best efforts to bite her tongue, Sheila found confrontational words escaping her lips.

'Does it matter what I think?' she shouted, wrenching her hand away. 'Does it matter what anyone thinks apart from you? You say, "jump" and we all say, "how high?" It's always been the same. It's all about you. You're only getting this security cobblers because you're worried about yourself. Not me. Not our daughters. Not Frank. You!'

Throwing the full glass of water and the tablets at her head, soaking her through, Paddy bounded out of bed, grabbing her by her throat. He flung her onto the chaise longue at the foot of the bed, squeezing tightly.

'Everything I've done to bring this family out on top and that's how you speak to me, is it? When was the last time you did a proper day's graft or had to worry about paying a bill? Do you have to dye your own hair and buy your clothes on the cheap, like the old Wythenshawe slags? Do you?'

Lights exploded in Sheila's peripheral vision; her eyes felt like they might burst from her sockets. If only she could shout for Conky, who was standing only a matter of metres away in the bathroom, lecturing Steve anew, by the sounds.

If only she could drum on the floor with her heels, she might alert Frank, who was sitting in the kitchen, directly beneath them, telling his tall tales. She tugged uselessly at Paddy's fingers, the weight of him on top of her rendering any attempt at escape fruitless.

'You were nowt when I met you, Sheila.' A fine film of spittle wet her face. Though her consciousness was ebbing away, she could see the angry vein bulging in his forehead. Sensed the rage of a wounded predator. 'You were nothing but a two-bit model wearing cheap rags in a nightclub. And now, look at you. You're my Queen.' He loosened his grip on her neck. Caressed her cheek. Started kissing her collarbone.

As the blood rushed back to her head, her vision returning, Sheila's only thought was to get out of the room before he could force his horrible angry cock into her.

'Not while there's so many people in the house, Paddy,' she said. 'Later, eh?' Her voice was hoarse, her throat painful. No doubt there would be bruising, which she would have to cover up with a scarf for a good week. *Stay calm*, she counselled herself. *Just ride the tantrum out. You're strong. You can do it.*

But Paddy had grabbed something. Something she had observed him perusing earlier in silence, mouth opening and closing as he struggled to read the words that accompanied a photograph. His colour had drained rapidly at the time. It was the local newspaper. Now he pushed it into her face so that she was breathing newsprint. 'Is that why you're tormenting me?' he shouted. 'You think I did this?'

Snatching the paper from him, she scanned the headline beneath a formal, posed picture of Mia Margulies with a classic muddy-brown photographer's backdrop, presumably taken when she had been in sixth form at school.

Her dark hair had been piled high like a low-alcohol Winehouse.

Daughter of local businessman found murdered.

'Is that why you're being a bitch?' he said.

'*Did* you do it?' she asked, raising an eyebrow. 'I thought that was the whole reason the Boddlingtons came after you and Frank.'

He shook his head, as she wiped the stink of ink from her face with a tissue from the box by the bed.

'By rights, I should have had her done,' he said, puffing his chest out. 'An eye for an eye and all that. But I didn't want my girls losing me to another heart attack. You lot would be lost without me to look after you. See how I think about you all the time?' He reached out and caressed her hair using the same hand he had just strangled her with. 'That's the whole reason why I'm sticking to the truce, even after what happened with our Jack. And if I say the deal's back on, I mean it. I'm a man of honour, me. That silly little Margulies tart obviously had enemies of her own. Or who knows?' He grinned. 'Maybe our Frank grew a pair of balls and had her popped. But I didn't order the hit, babe. I swear on my mam's memory.'

Sheila laid a placatory hand carefully on his arm, praying he would calm down and get back into bed.

'I'm sorry,' she said. 'I should have known it wasn't you.'

'You just don't trust me.' He folded his arms and pressed his lips together. An upwards tilt of his chin. 'I'm insulted. You're so hurtful when you want to be. Always belittling me.'

'I'm so, so sorry, Pad. Forgive me?'

The fight had gone out of him, she could tell. She ushered

him under the duvet, popping two Migraleve into his hand. Picked up the empty glass from the carpet and refilled it. Stroked his forehead.

'Get some sleep, love,' she said.

He took her hand into his and kissed it. 'I love you, She. I always have. I loved you twice as hard when your mam and dad disowned you, because I wanted to make up for what shite-hawks they were. They thought you were a useless little slapper, but I know you deserved better, and I wanted to give you the world. You don't need anyone else. You've got me, babe. And I'm always going to be here for you. Always.'

The tightness in her stomach made Sheila feel nauseous. She forced a wide smile and retrieved the glass. Swallowed hard. Tried to pull away but he wouldn't let go of her hand.

'As long as you stay in the house and don't go out, you'll be safe,' he said. 'Promise me you'll not leave the house. Promise me, She.' Fixing her with a gaze that was pleading on the surface but threatening immediately beneath, like a shark circling the bottom of a shallow reef.

'Course, my love.' She pulled her hand free.

'Oh, and She,' he said.

She had reached the threshold. Her escape still precious inches away. Turning around, wearing a smile. But she didn't need to see his face to know that there would be more than love, regret and gratitude etched into it. The tone of his voice sounded more than just heavy with migraine medication. It had a dangerous edge to it.

'While I'm in bed, I'm going to have a good think about how everything's gone tits up,' he said, folding his hands over the top of the duvet contemplatively. 'Because someone's put a dirty big hole in my ship just as I was about to set sail. And the ship's taking on water fast. But, do you know what? I'm damned if I'm going to let some scheming bastard sink it. I'm gonna work out where the leak's coming from and I'm going to plug it with the severed head of whoever it is.'

'That's nice, Pad,' Sheila said, gripping the architrave to steady herself.

'Oh, and tell Conky, I think I just did a metaphor. He'll be dead proud.'

As Paddy laughed out loud to himself, Sheila ran to a guest bathroom and vomited.

Chapter 40

Lev

'Look, how much longer are we gonna have to wait?' Lev asked the paediatric nurse. He reached over to Jay, who lay on the gurney, and stroked his curls with a shaking hand. Felt anxiety pushing his throat closed; pulling his heart apart. Unable to placate the screaming boy even by identifying the Disney characters in the mural on the brightly coloured wall of the A&E side room. Jay was red in the face and clutching at his head. He had been inconsolable for hours, now, with none of the usual signs of let-up.

'The doctor will be with you as soon as he can,' she said, eyeing the lightning bolt in his hair and surreptitiously judging his dealer's attire – Lev could tell.

'He's made himself puke four times with screaming,' Lev said, pressing the back of his hand gently to the boy's scorching hot chest. He turned back to the nurse, willing her to show a little sympathy. 'He won't drink sod all. His nappies are dry as a bone.'

'Don't worry about that. We won't let him dehydrate. I'm going to hook him up to a drip in a minute. We're waiting for his blood test results,' the nurse said. 'The doctor can't do anything until those come back.'

'He needs a fucking brain scan, not blood tests!' Lev shouted. 'That thing in his head is getting bigger.'

'No need for language like that.' She raised an eyebrow. 'And your son has a temperature, so there's some kind of an infection going on. The bloods will tell the doctor more. We can't rule out meningitis at this stage. We might have to do a lumbar puncture test.'

'What the fuck's that?'

'Language, *please!*'

Lev grabbed the sleeve of her blue V-necked top. Released her when he saw fearful indignation in her eyes. 'I'm sorry. I'm just bricking it. I told you, didn't I? He's got an advanced inoperable brain tumour. Please! I'm dead scared. He's definitely loads worse than what he was. I think he's dying.'

Her fear seemed to subside. The nurse smiled kindly at an oblivious Jay and felt his pulse. Checked her watch. Frowned. 'His heart rate's accelerated. Someone will be along to do an ECG in a minute.'

'In a minute? Why not right now? Can't you do it?'

The nurse looked apologetic. 'Try not to panic. It's kicking-out time at the pubs. We're mad busy. The doctor is on his way, I promise!' She looked him up and down again, narrowing her eyes when she spied the tattoo on his neck. 'Where's his mum?'

'Stoned off her box somewhere. I'm his dad. I'm looking after him now.'

'Oh.' She gave him a tight smile that didn't reach her eyes. 'Do you have a social worker?'

'Are you taking the piss? I see how you're looking at me. But I didn't come here to be judged by strangers. I came here because I think my baby son's on his last legs.'

'I'll get the drip.' Looking visibly punctured, the nurse left the room.

Lev thumbed a text to Gloria.

In A&E. J gettin worse.

He wasn't entirely sure what he expected from his mother by way of support. He had asked her to come to the hospital with him, but she had insisted she couldn't possibly miss her elders' meeting at the church. Swanning around with a grin on her face as though she hadn't just topped a young girl in cold blood. Deranged, heartless witch.

Lev looked nervously through the window at the night sky, wondering if somebody was watching him from outside. The feeling that he was being observed was persistent and crippling.

'Come on, come on, come on!' he muttered under his breath. Inhaling sharply with anticipation every time somebody in a green or blue scrub suit passed by the door to the side room. Feeling the weight of parental responsibility and the sight of his shrieking son dragging him down, down, down.

The minutes trudged by. Still no sign of the drip. Jay started to cough, scream and choke. Lev knew what was coming next. The boy doubled up. Lev snatched a cardboard bowl and held it under his chin, catching a violent expulsion of bile and mucus.

'Help!' Lev shouted, not tearing his gaze from his son. Where was the damn call button? Distracted, he tried to seek it out, whilst at the same time holding the bowl to Jay's face. Towels. He needed paper towels and some water to clean him up. Where was that po-faced nurse? 'Hello! Is anyone there?' he yelled.

'Ah, Leviticus,' a familiar voice said. 'You called.'

Feeling the blood slow in his veins as if somebody had

291

pumped him full of liquid nitrogen, turning everything crystalline-frosty and brittle, Lev turned round to see the intimidatingly large figure of Jonny Margulies.

'Jonny,' Lev said, gulping. 'I . . .'

His boss was wearing a raincoat on a hot, dry summer's evening. One hand in a pocket that bulged. Lev didn't like the odds.

Jonny swiftly withdrew a handgun. 'Pick up the boy, arsehole. You're coming with me.'

Lev stared at the weapon in disbelief. He followed the line of sight along the barrel pointed at his chest to Jonny's shovel-like hand, up his arm to his grimacing, sweating face. The skin beneath his eyes was puffy. His colour was high. But his eyes were shining with fervour. This was not good, Lev assessed. But Jay's condition was potentially worse.

'Nope. I can't leave. Sorry. Shoot me if you like, but I'm not moving from this hospital while my little boy's like this. That's why I've not been around to see yous. Because he's . . . he's . . . dying. I'm sorry. I should have—'

'Don't lecture me about dying children, you murdering little twat,' Jonny said. He aimed the gun at Jay's head. 'You come now, or I'll shoot him. Save the NHS a few bob.'

Lev felt his extremities start to prickle. His mouth was suddenly dry.

'Pick him up and walk out of here with me,' Jonny said. 'We've got talking to do.'

A snap decision to be made. The barrel of the gun and the resolute expression on Jonny's face ruled out any option of staying. Lev recognised the desperation of a grieving father in his boss' eyes. Saw himself reflected in them.

'Don't harm my boy,' he said, lifting Jay from the gurney. Realising they might both never make it back to the hospital alive if they left. The choice was dying now or dying later.

'Move!' Jonny said, pocketing the hand that held the gun, now pointed at Lev's kidneys.

'Can't I take his stroller?'

'Move it!'

Wrapping his arms around the writhing, yelling Jay, Lev walked briskly past the front desk of paediatric A&E. Wishing he could shout for help. Wishing it were just him being held at gunpoint, so he could take his chances and try to disarm or disable Jonny by force. The doctor sitting behind the counter staring at the flickering screen of a PC didn't even look up. If only she had. If only Lev could somehow have communicated to her his fear.

In the car park, a van was waiting.

'Get in the back,' Jonny said, sliding the door aside.

'My boy's going to die tonight if I don't take him back.' Lev was pleading now. 'He needs a drip and antibiotics. Please, man.' Tears rolled hot and full of woe onto his cheeks. He felt foolish. 'Let me get him sorted and then I'll come with you. How about that?' Stalling, in the hope that Jonny would somehow change his mind. The hundred and fifty thousand and the flight to Baltimore now constituted merely a container ship out at sea, fleetingly within reach of the shipwrecked man but moving further and further away; hope drowning as it dwindled to nothing more than a speck on the horizon. The life-saving operation had been just another empty promise he had whispered to his son on a rainy night when he wasn't dealing. They would drown together, now, their raft broken up by Jonny Margulies and a manipulative bastard who refused to honour a promise.

'Give me your phone,' Jonny said.

With bitter reluctance, he handed it over, silently saying

goodbye to his emergency beacon. 'Will I get it back? It's got all my photos of Jay on.'

Jonny pocketed it. 'Shut it and get in.'

Lev sat on a wheel arch, struggling to sit a rigid Jay on his knee. The door slammed shut, leaving them in total darkness but for the sparks of panic going off like fireworks behind Lev's eyes. The change in lighting didn't jolt Jay out of his apoplexy. Even the engine starting up had no effect on the boy. Lev dug deep for optimism, praying to his mother's God that somehow this would end well. Perhaps Tariq would just be waiting at the other end to grill him and then let him go. Jay was a convincing excuse for his radio silence. But Lev was a non-believer, these days. Once upon a time, when his mother had kicked him out because it was easier to turn her back on her truanting, wayward teenager than to face his trials and tribulations with him, he had been sustained by his well of youthful optimism. Now that well had all but dried up.

The van did not have to travel far down through Crumpsall onto Cheetham Hill Road and through the potholed streets of run-down warehouses behind Strangeways. Even without the ability to see, Lev knew by the very turns to the left or the right and by the sounds outside that they were scudding past Asian groceries, slum housing, abandoned churches and The Fort with its temples to consumerism in B&Q and TK Maxx. Onto Derby Street and the roads that branched off it – a no-man's land for anyone but dealers and prostitutes after dark.

When the door opened, flickering streetlight streamed into the rear of the van, making Lev blink. As his eyes grew accustomed to the glare, Lev realised they were not at T&J Trading's premises but had come to the other factory. The secret sweatshop. Shit. He knew exactly what went on there at night.

Jonny loomed before him, flicking the gun in the direction of the heavy door.

'Get moving,' he said.

Chapter 41

Lev

Lev's heart pounded so violently and unrelentingly, he wondered that it didn't simply give out. Sweat poured down his back. The muscles in his arms twinged painfully with the effort of holding Jay as still as possible. 'Please, Jonny. You're making a big mistake, man. I had nothing to do with Mia's death. Honest.'

The factory was in total darkness, meaning Tariq probably had no idea of this abduction. Lev swallowed hard, walking towards that door, realising he was at the mercy of a vengeful father acting as a lone wolf – closer to the truth of what had happened than he knew. Once inside, he felt the barrel of the gun press into his spine. Jonny patted along the wall and switched a solitary light on. The glow was barely enough to navigate the path through the boxes of semi-assembled merchandise and motionless conveyor belt to the back, where dissenters were taken.

'Don't put me in the hole,' Lev said. 'For God's sake, Jonny. You're not like this! This is the Fish Man's work.'

'And who do you think pays the Fish Man, you bloody fool?' Jonny asked, kicking him in the back of his right knee so that his legs, already trembling and barely able to carry his weight, gave way. 'I didn't get to the top of this game by being a pushover.'

Lev stumbled against a large cardboard box with Chinese script on the side. It tipped to a forty-five-degree angle, spilling what appeared to be deflated blow-up sex dolls onto the floor. Jay thumped him in the face with an angry little balled fist, as if reminding him he needed to be strong for the both of them.

'Can't you get him to shut up?' Jonny snapped.

Lev didn't answer. He merely turned around and treated his boss to a look of pure disgust.

'Don't moralise at me, boy,' Jonny said, urging him towards the hole. There was that lethal hard edge to his voice that Lev had heard before, when one of the workers had been caught stealing or one of his colleagues had been 'punished' for having sticky fingers. 'You're nothing but a two-bit pusher, Leviticus. Doling out my coke and smack to the underbelly of Sweeney Hall. You collect my immoral earnings from my brothels, staffed by illegal, underaged girls. I don't see you turning down your wages. You normally carry a gun, paid for by me, which you wave in people's faces when they don't do my bidding. You are every bit as tainted as me, you hypocrite.'

'I'm just earning a wage,' Lev said, feeling resentment gnaw away at him on the inside.

'Alright, smart arse. You keep telling yourself that.'

The door to the hole was open already. A foetid, airtight room once the security door was shut. Soundproof. No windows. Only a hard chair to sit on, a bare bulb hanging from the ceiling and the bloodstains on the floor – a macabre visitors' book of sorts, signed by those who had been guests in the hole before – as the only form of distraction from thoughts of dying.

'Sit,' Jonny said.

Lev turned to him, holding a purple-faced Jay. 'How can you do this? Years of loyal service I've given you. I'm a Boddlington through and through. How can you do this to my son? He's an innocent baby.'

Jonny raised his hand and brought the gun down hard on Lev's cheekbone, knocking his head back. Fiery stinging told him the skin had split. A tickling sensation as the blood trickled from his jaw bone onto his jeans.

'Don't talk to me about having sympathy for your child,' Jonny said, slamming the door behind him. 'What happened to Mia? Why did you kill her?'

'I didn't! Honest! You've got to believe me.'

'Liar!' Jonny bellowed. 'Tariq said he saw you and that mad bitch your mother, sitting in a car outside my house on the morning of Mia's murder.'

Lev shook his head. Formulating an alibi. 'I dropped round to see her. That's all. I loved Mia. We were going out, but she wanted to keep us a secret. She was scared of what you'd say if you found out she was going with someone like me.'

The fist that flew into his left kidney winded him, but Lev was merely glad he had been spared another pistol-whipping. Jay was curled into foetal position, whimpering now.

'Don't give me that bullshit,' Jonny said. 'You killed her. I don't believe in bloody coincidences. The police said the bullets in her skull matched the sort used in the gun you were given. Hollow point imports from the States.'

'Do me a favour, Jonny. No disrespect, like, but every dealer in town uses the same sort of hardware. Half of us use the same supplier, for God's sake! It's not like there's a bullet shop on every street corner.'

'You're lying! You broke into my house and blew my daughter's head off.'

'No. I swear on my baby's life, I didn't. Ask your missus. She copped me legging it from Mia's room down the fire escape not so long ago. I'm telling you, Jonny. I swung by to see how she was after all the rape business with Jack O'Brien. I hadn't seen her in weeks. I'd been so busy working for you and Tariq on the raid. Our Jay was ill and my ex OD'd. Then we all got banged up, didn't we? Mia asked me to bob round, so I did. I'm heartbroken that she's gone, Jonny. I'd do anything to get her back. But you've got to believe me when I tell you I had nothing to do with it. Wrong place at the wrong time. That's all there was to it. Whoever topped her went in after I left. I could only have been there twenty minutes. My money's on Paddy O'Brien. Maybe even Frank, as revenge for Jack.' He was certain that he could see Jonny's taut facial expression start to relax just a little. Softer around the eyes. 'Think about it. You must think that too, else why did you send the Fish Man to M1 House?'

Scratching his nose with the gun, Jonny's nostrils flared. His eyes narrowed. 'Sandra did mention a boy had been in Mia's room.'

'See?'

'But that doesn't explain why you took the Slovakian girl to Anjum Khan's refuge or whatever cock and balls do-gooding business she's got going there. You should have brought her straight back here. It's not your place to hand my trafficked girls over to the authorities. By rights, I should kill you just for that.'

Stroking Jay's curls, Lev bought himself seconds by inhaling his son's scent deeply and kissing his hot skin. He was burning up. Starting to go limp. That didn't bode well.

And his skin had become blotchy. *Keep strong, Lev. Convince him. Get Jay back to that hospital before it's too late. Don't let the kid down like Gloria let you down.*

'She was pregnant and showing, Jonny. I've got a baby of my own. I couldn't watch it happening, man. Not after Degsy and Maggie gunned down Tommo and Kai. I wanted to get her to safety. I'm sorry if you thought I was over-stepping the mark, but it didn't sit right with me to leave her in the middle of a blood bath. She's only a kid. My bad, right? If you have to kill me for doing what I thought was the right thing, then go ahead. I've got nothing left anyhow, because the woman I love – your daughter – has gone and my boy's not gonna make it. He's got meningitis or some shit and a brain tumour the size of an orange in his little head. Go on, Jonny. Shoot me. But get my boy back to A&E, so I can at least say I tried.' He bit his lip. Locked eyes with his anguished boss. 'Isn't that what every father wants? To die knowing he tried for his kids?'

Jonny clicked the safety off the gun. Took aim at Lev's head. Ragged breaths in-out, in-out through his nostrils. He took a step back, legs astride now. Scowling as though voices were at war inside his head.

'Rot in hell,' he said.

Chapter 42

Frank

'Pass me the gun oil,' Conky said, grinning up at the bright light of the screen, where the action was unfolding. He held his hand out expectantly. Frank reached over to the coffee table and obliged. 'Ah, I love this bit. Wait for it! It's the best. Here we go . . . Ow!'

On screen, Marvin had just taken an accidental bullet to the face in the back of a car, listening to Samuel L. Jackson getting irate at John Travolta about blasphemy and stained upholstery.

Conky roared with laughter, rocking in the home cinema armchair. 'That black bugger cracks me up. I love the way he talks. Don't you?' Turning to Frank with bug-eyes full of mirth, clearly expecting a response. 'And Tarantino's a genius. Am I right? He just nails it! One day, Degsy will pull a stunt like that and shoot some fecker's head off by accident. He's a liability, so he is. You couldn't watch that prick with a bag of fucking eyeballs. But this . . . ? The storyline. The dialogue. The soundtrack. Genius.' Rubbing ferociously at his gun part in some sort of masturbatory exercise, the moves to which only a gangster could truly master. Across his lap, he wore a tea towel to protect his smart trousers from the mess, presumably.

Stiff arse.

'Yeah, mate,' Frank said, wishing he could switch the film off and put on some anodyne music channel. Better some idiot rapper and naked, writhing chicks in hotpants than this aide-memoire to the shittiness of his own life. How he wanted to forget just for a few minutes, while Sheila prepared dinner upstairs, that they were all under siege and that his progeny lay rotting in a casket. 'Me and Jack always reckoned *Pulp Fiction* had the best soundtrack.'

'I wouldn't mind giving that Uma Thurman one. She's got a face like a rubber duck, but what a body. Did you see her in *Kill Bill*?'

Frank had no answer to give. He was all out of light-hearted words. Only mental images of the dead youngsters on his dancefloor and the 'Police line – do not cross' tape that had sealed his beloved club shut to a shocked, bereft public who needed desperately to dance their blues away.

Outside, darkness had fallen. The mood had been sombre once the builders had left. Everything installed to perfection inside one working day, thanks to Paddy's ability to pay four times the going rate, leaving them all incarcerated in splendid isolation. In the film's quieter moments, the tension was palpable.

Conky screwed a brass-bristled brush onto the end of a long, shining rod and rammed it down into the barrel of his shotgun. 'You're not really enjoying this, are you?' he asked.

Frank took a drag from his cigarette and swigged from his beer bottle. 'My mind's elsewhere, if I'm honest.'

Reassembling the shotgun with the deft hands of a skilled

marksman, Conky hoisted the weapon high on his shoulder and aimed it at Frank's head.

'I think you and I need to have a little chat, Francis,' he said, smiling like a hyena sizing up an easy meal.

'Woah, put your gun away, Dirty Harry. I think Sheila's already making your day with chilli con carne,' Frank said, making a poor stab at laughter. He could hear its hollow ring like an alarm-bell, calling time on this poor facsimile of happy bromance chit-chat.

The smile slid from Conky's face. He set the shotgun back onto the coffee table, lifted the towel from his lap and laid it carefully across the arm of his chair. Stood and diligently brushed any cleaning debris from his trousers, before grabbing Frank swiftly by the collar and hoisting him out of his chair.

Frank managed a solitary shocked squeak in response, walking in thin air like a marionette as his body tried to satisfy his flight impulse – only to be thwarted by the crane-like traction of the man-mountain that was Conky McFadden.

'Woah, mate! What are you doing? Put me down!'

'Now I've got your attention,' Conky said, dropping him back into his seat. He turned the sound on the giant TV up, wielding the gun yet again, this time poking the newly cleansed barrel into his Adam's apple.

Realising the volume had been turned up so that Sheila would not be able to overhear this confrontation above the fanciful sound of Hollywood gunfire, Frank felt his bladder beg for release. Willed himself to hang onto the pee, lest Conky see how weak he was. 'You're being uncool, man. Put the bleeding gun down and talk to me like a normal human being. You're not Loss Adjusting tonight. Remember whose brother I am.'

'That's exactly what I'm mindful of, Francis,' Conky said, closing one of his bulbous eyes; staring at Frank with the other. 'You're Paddy O'Brien's brother – my boss. And the boss might be upstairs, sleeping off his migraine, but I'm still on duty, even while I'm watching the lovely Marcellus getting medieval on some hillbilly's arse and John Travolta putting in the only decent performance he's given since he was Tony Manero in *Saturday Night Fever*.'

'I saw that film at the pictures,' Frank said, smiling weakly. 'Paddy bunked off school and took me.'

'Your brother is a challenging character, Francis. It must be trying to play second fiddle all the time to a man who is so driven to succeed at all costs.'

Frank blinked hard. Said nothing.

Conky moved his face closer. His breath smelled of bitter coffee with the medicinal high-notes of throat sweets. 'Which is why I'd understand if you were trying to sabotage him. If my son had died because of my brother's criminal proclivities, I might also light a fire under his enemies in the hope of getting rid of him.' He dug the gun a little further into Frank's neck. 'You can tell me, Frank. We've known each other for decades. There's much about you I like, and I hope that you regard me as a trustworthy servant to the family.'

Nodding with cautious, small movements, Frank whispered, 'Yeah. Very trustworthy.'

'Which is why it's only right that I ask you if you have anything to do with the situation we find ourselves in now. Do you have anything you'd like to tell me, Francis? About Mia Margulies and the general unrest that's come about in the face of an intended cease fire that everyone bought into, with the mighty Maureen Kaplan arbitrating. Because in my experience, if a cease fire fails, it's because someone, somewhere is engaging in acts of sabotage. And now, it seems pretty bloody ironic that one of the Boddlingtons has lost a daughter where you lost a son.'

Though his pulse raced and his breath came short, Frank was transfixed by Conky's protruding eyes and the swelling in his throat. He had the look of a man who was pregnant with other people's secrets. But this wasn't a friend of old talking. War had brought the combatant out in him. Conky, the man, had been bodysnatched by the Loss Adjuster, the machine, and Frank knew better than to let that psycho arsehole anywhere near the contents of his mind.

'It's coincidence, Conks. That's all. Everything's gone tits up, man. It's like the whole of Manchester's got a cactus rammed up its jacksy. Nobody knows if it's safe to sit down. Even Paddy hasn't got any control over any of it and he started this buyout retirement bullshit.' Feeling like the only way to get this crazed Alpha to back down was to reassert his dominance as an O'Brien, Frank grabbed the barrel of the shotgun and pushed it gently but firmly aside. Holding his breath for an agonising split second to see how Conky would react. There were days when he wanted nothing more than to die, but at the hand of his brother's henchman was not the peaceful end he would choose. 'So, when you're poking that gun in my gullet, just remember that I'm not the only one this war is affecting and I'm not the only one who's heartily pissed off with everything. But I *am* the poor bastard who's suffered the worst in all of this. I've lost my child *and* my livelihood. I'm not saying it's my fault or Paddy's fault. I blame the game, me. And I blame those two Boddlington twats and that lanky streak of piss, the Fish Man. So, the last thing I need right now, Conky mate, is a cross-examination from you. Alright?'

Studying his face for at least sixty deeply uncomfortable

seconds – so long that Frank started to see recognisable shapes in the open pores on his prominent nose – Conky presently backed off and put the weapon carefully, reverently onto the coffee table next to the gun oil and cleaning accessories.

'I'm sorry if you felt my line of enquiry was offensive or even slanderous,' Conky said. 'But you must realise you're currently the most likely suspect for having ordered the murder of Mia Margulies! And given that has stoked up a shit-storm for your brother where previously there was calm, you must appreciate that I have to ask you potentially difficult questions. I can't make exceptions for you because you're his brother, Francis. Paddy expects that impartiality from me.' Conky sat back down and turned the volume on the enormous screen to a more comfortable level. He spread the towel over his lap once again. Started to methodically take apart a handgun, placing the parts side by side as though they were shiny offerings to the God of Gang Warfare. 'Christ, I could do with some tortilla chips. Sheila said she'd bring some down, so she did. My stomach's growling like an old man's prostate.'

Frank wiped the sweat from his top lip and swigged the dregs from his beer bottle. Stared at his companion in disbelief. 'You're sorry if I felt . . . *what*? You accuse me of having some girl topped – and I don't care who the hell her dad is – and all you can say is, "You're sorry if I felt . . ." You're not even apologising, are you? Jesus, Conks. You're nothing but an oversized Action Man and our Paddy's yanking your string.' He pointed to his eyes with the neck of the beer bottle. 'You've even got the eagle eyes.' Shook his head and tutted. 'I'm sick of it, me. You can all work it up your arses, the lot of yous. If Jonny

Margulies and Tariq Khan want to come and blow my knackers off, let them come. I've had it, me. I'm going home to watch Channel Dave and wait for death in a less stressful environment. The vibes are all wrong in here, man.'

Conky stood abruptly, dropping the towel and the handgun pieces to the plush carpeted floor. 'You can't go. We all have to stay here because of the threat. Paddy's orders. It's a safe house now.'

Frank shrugged. 'I'd be safer in a nest of vipers, mate. Paddy knows where he can stick his orders.'

Pursued by an insistent Conky, as he pulled on his jacket and made his way swiftly to the kitchen. Expected to see Sheila, frying meat at the hob or busy washing some vegetables in the sink. The chandelier over the island burned brightly, but the kitchen was empty and silent, but for the chunner of talk show chatter on the small TV that was recessed into the wall. A pan containing delicious-smelling chilli beef simmered on the hob, but a chopping board containing vegetables and a knife said she hadn't yet finished her preparation and couldn't have gone far.

'Where's She?' Frank asked, turning to Conky with a quizzical frown.

'Toilet, maybe?'

Frank stood in the hall by the downstairs toilet. Shouted, 'I'm going now, Sheila. Ta-ra.'

No answer.

He shrugged. 'Tell her I'm sorry I'm missing dinner. Or maybe I should say, "I'm sorry if she feels I'm missing dinner."'

'No need to be a prick,' Conky said, folding his arms.

'Every bloody need.'

Time to go. Crossing the hallway beneath the chandelier

that hung over the galleried landing, Frank passed the keypad on the wall in the hall. But there, he noticed a light flashing red on the new security system. Stopped dead in his tracks to read the label above it. 'Shit. There's been a breach upstairs.'

Chapter 43

Sheila

'Where's my coffee?' Paddy shouted from the breakfasting area. 'Come on, She. I'm gasping.' He clutched dramatically at his throat.

Sheila's breath came short with adrenalin. Ever since the security breach, she had felt the threat of an unwelcome visitor in the house like a tight hand around her throat. An ominous, foreboding sensation that she had no intention of discussing with Paddy.

'It's on its way, love.' Her hands shook as she poured coffee beans into the Gaggenau coffee machine.

Tutting, Paddy retied his dressing gown with exaggerated movements. Obviously making sure she got an eyeful of his paunch and saggy, naked undercarriage as a veiled threat or some kind of reminder of his supremacy.

'Fuck this for a game of soldiers,' he said. 'Bring it down to me in the spa. I've got a mouth like a mink coat but if I stand here watching you faff and fart around, I'm going to blow a frigging fuse.' His face was flushed with obvious irritation. All signs of his migraine gone, now. Back to normal.

As he padded away, Sheila exhaled heavily, only then

realising that she had been holding her breath. She clutched at the worktop to steady herself. Slowing her breathing to rein in her galloping heartbeat. The hairs on her arms were standing proud in her goose-pimpled flesh.

She glanced nervously over her shoulder, expecting to see somebody standing there. More than a sixth sense that she was not alone and that she was being watched. But scanning the kitchen, the only signs of life were her, the glittering goldfish in the tank and the gurgling coffee machine. How she wished she could hear the house's sounds above the noise of the brewing drink and spitting water.

'Calm down, She. Deep breaths. There's nothing there,' she whispered to the distorted image of herself in the induction hob's gleaming black surface.

She poured the latte into Paddy's favoured tall glass. Tried to check a reflection of the kitchen in the stainless steel of the machine. But the brushed matt finish would reveal nothing. With a pounding heart and a sense that she was definitely not alone, she turned around. Dropped the cup when she saw the tall man, dressed in all black, wearing that trademark wide-brimmed hat.

Chapter 44

Conky

Running down the stone steps, gun drawn, Conky McFadden's breath came short; the four-storey bulk of the Bramshott mansion bearing down on him. Sweat was already rolling down his back on this oppressively warm morning. The usual fine mist of Manchester rain falling, though. Fogging his glasses. Heightening the risk. Damned rain.

'Come on, Conks, you fat shag-sack,' he counselled himself. 'Don't screw this up.'

Heaving open the heavy wood and glass door to the spa, he could now hear Sheila screaming.

'Paddy! Don't leave me! Somebody, help!' Her voice was amplified, as though she was calling from the inside of a cathedral. Wailing. Keening. The sounds of mourning. Not good.

Entering the pool area, Conky drank in the strange scene. There was Sheila, hunched over the body of the boss. The boss, lying in a rich, burgundy puddle of his own blood, which had begun to track along the grout between the tiles, drip-dripping into the turquoise waters of the pool to form a billowing cloud of aubergine. An almost tranquil scene, without the harrowing sounds: spotlit ripples reflecting from the water onto the vaulted ceiling. But Conky spied a tall figure, carrying a holdall – almost too swift to spot, hastening through the door to the boiler room and back stairs on the far side of the complex.

Squeezing the trigger on the gun, now. A deafening bang that ricocheted around the lofty space. Pain spasmed along Conky's arm from the recoil. The bullet missed its target narrowly, splintering the architrave of the door as a lick of black fabric from the hem of the attacker's coat was all that remained in view. Gone. Shit.

Conky heaved himself across the pool area; skidding in a tributary of the boss' blood. Above him, the growl of a car reverberated through the ceiling, shaking the still, damp air. No. More of a howl. It was the Bugatti Veyron. Squealing tyres bemoaning the slippery polished concrete of its garaging.

Two, four, six: Conky bounded up the back stairs, praying he would have time to put a bullet in this bastard before the garage door opened fully. Panting. Feeling the chilli con carne from last night's dinner push acid up into his throat. Clicking knees.

At the far end of the cavernous garage, beyond the lesser supercars that were lined up, buffed to showroom perfection in a state of semi-permanent disuse, he saw the Bugatti. Black and white and diminutive. A million pounds' worth of thrust, quivering like a prized stallion waiting to bolt from its starting gate.

Conky squinted through his rain-spattered, steamed-up glasses, but could not make out the driver's face from that distance. Not that it mattered. A glimpse of that beard and the hat was all he really needed to make an ID.

'Stop, bastard!' he shouted, running along the rows of

slumbering vehicles, pointing his gun towards the Bugatti's tinted rear windows.

He knew the odds were stacked against him. A 200 mph beast with a getaway driver who had everything to lose by being caught. The automated garage door, rising in segments on the track, only inches from being open now. To shoot, or not to shoot? The boss would kill him if he damaged the car. That's supposing the boss lived.

Put a tyre out.

Two bullets whizzed towards the car but struck concrete uselessly. The Bugatti had screamed away, leaving a momentary cloud of gravel and the lasting stench of exhaust in its wake. Lurching, swerving too fast down the drive. Conky followed in overheated pursuit, wondering if the driver would crash.

But the gates were standing open.

No time to think. Conky's heart felt like it would burst. Flickering memories of running from the violence during the Troubles back home. A young soldier, in those days, wearing a balaclava his mammy had bought that always itched his face. Leaving a Molotov calling card as he sprinted in the opposite direction to the police. *Run, Conks. Run! Don't let him get—*

Too late. The car was nothing more than a howling wind and two red orbs in the distance, reducing to pinpricks.

On the brink of vomiting, Conky cursed, gasping for breath and clutching his knees. He slapped himself in the forehead with the barrel of his gun. He had failed even to get a clean shot at the tyres. Thwarted by age, the shaking hands of a man with a thyroid problem and four stones of excess lard he could do without. He was nothing but a dinosaur on the brink of extinction, he conceded silently.

All he could do was cling to the hope that the police

would pick up some arsehole, driving like a drunk in a million-pound car. Sirens in the distance said Sheila had phoned for an ambulance, at least.

But hang on. Why had the damned gates been open? Weren't they in the midst of war? Conky frowned. It was as if the assailant had planned an automotive getaway all along. He glanced up at the CCTV, buzzing from its vantage point, attached to an ornamental garden lamppost. The tapes could wait.

Re-entering the spa area, the tang of blood and the smell of chlorine stung his nostrils.

'They got away,' he said to the forlorn-looking figure, still kneeling beside the boss. 'I'm so, so sorry. I'll find them.'

'He's gonna die!' Sheila cried. She held her hands aloft, coated in a red so vivid, Conky's head hurt. 'My Paddy's dying.' The startling blue of her eyes seemed diluted by tears that streamed over the contours of her cheekbones, falling mournfully onto her collarbone.

Conky felt the boss' neck for a pulse. A weak flicker beneath his fingertips said he still lived, but only just. Carefully wiping his glasses on the hem of his shirt, he assessed the damage.

Paddy O'Brien had been sliced down the middle, fatally, judging by the blood loss. Out cold, of course. He lay carefully positioned on his side by the pool's edge, as though his attacker had clearly intended to display him. Decorated by slices of cucumber, laid in rows along his pyjama-clad flank, reminiscent of a dressed salmon.

'Only one person I know leaves his kills like this,' Conky said, contemplating the delicate artistry of the incongruous green and white slices. He removed his shirt, pressing it hard against the gaping wound. Too little, almost certainly too late. 'Asaf Smolensky.'

Sheila stared at him, wide-eyed at first. Then, fury burning its way through the tears. 'The Fish Man? The Boddlingtons' hit man?'

Conky nodded slowly, blood oozing between his fingers, already saturating the shirt. Trying not to react to the terrible stench coming from the boss' sliced lower intestine. Knowing his efforts were near useless. 'You ever heard of another headcase that does mental shite like this?'

'But this place is supposed to be safe,' Sheila said, grabbing his arm with a blood-slick hand. 'A fortress, you said. You saw to it. *You* put in the new security measures.'

'I did. It is. I don't know how the hell Smolensky got in here. I swear to you.'

There was a flash of green in Conky's peripheral vision. The paramedics had entered the spa. They marched smartly across the pool area, carrying their equipment. One woman. Two men. Flashing blue outside said the police were pulling up too. He manoeuvred Sheila away from Paddy, though she was weeping afresh now.

'Don't hurt my Pad, will you?' she begged the woman. Wrapping her arms around herself, smearing her baby pink gym clothes in second-hand red, she looked suddenly frail and lost. Her face streaked with blood; her blonde hair hanging loose. A runny nose and puffy eyes, as though she was trying on widowhood for size.

But still, Conky thought her beautiful. At that moment, he wanted to embrace her and make it better. Dug the gun, now safely stowed in his trouser pocket, into his upper thigh to remind himself through the pain that he was not there to comfort Sheila and capitalise on Paddy's misfortune. He was a loyal soldier, sworn to serve his King.

'Sure, it'll be fine. I'll get to the bottom of this, Sheila. Don't you worry,' he said.

The police were visible just outside, descending the stone steps. Black uniforms marking them out as interlopers, though chances were they were probably on Paddy's payroll too. Inside, the paramedics were strapping Paddy onto their stretcher. Bearing him away to Wythenshawe hospital and whatever fate awaited him there.

Sheila's thin, steely fingers gripped Conky's naked torso. Fingernails digging into his hairy love-handles. He felt heat creep into his cheeks. Self-loathing. Guilt for worrying what she might think of his unsightly bulk. Like she'd be eyeing him up when her husband had just been felled! *Get a grip on yourself, you foolish, self-indulgent twat.*

She transfixed him with her cobalt blue eyes, sharpening by the second. The lines in her athlete's face deepening. 'I want you to do more than get to the bottom of this, Conk. I want you to find the Fish Man and stick a bullet in his skull. And then I want you to get to Khan and Margulies and finish this.'

'Now, let's not be hasty, because—'

'I said finish it. Finish them.' Hatred in that small face. 'And get that wanker Frank over here. Tell him his brother's been left for dead. And tell him he'd better bring a pair of damned balls.'

The uniforms were approaching. Speaking into hissing radios on their shoulders. She smiled weakly at them. All butter wouldn't melt. Thanking them for responding so quickly.

But when she turned back to Conky, the scorching fires of hell were in those eyes.

'The Boddlingtons set out to end my Paddy. They wanted to kill the King. But I'm not having it. Right? We're O'Briens. We bow to no one. Do you hear me? Take them down, Conky. That's an order.'

316

Chapter 45

Conky

'Describe to me what the attacker looked like,' Ellis James asked him, clicking his biro into life, pad at the ready.

Conky levered himself down onto the end of the teak sun-lounger by the pool, looking up through the high spa window at the scene that was unfolding at ground level. Dumbfounded by the sight of Sheila, covered with a white honeycomb ambulance blanket, clambering into the back of the ambulance. The gurney that conveyed a wan-faced Paddy had already been installed. Blues and twos started up, making Conky jolt.

'Was he tall, short, fat? Come on, McFadden. You know the drill.' The detective's eyes spoke of biting hunger, verging on desperation. He hunkered down beside the sun-lounger – an overly pally air about him as though he were some kind of brother-in-arms.

'I never really saw him,' Conky said, replaying the discovery over and over again in his mind's eye like the sort of irritating GIF Sheila sometimes showed him on her Twitter feed. Asaf Smolensky. There was no doubt about it. 'It was a man. I'm fairly certain of that. But I couldn't tell you anything more.'

Ellis James grunted as he took a seat next to Conky on the lounger, shunting himself uncomfortably close. 'A man.' He wrote in his notebook. 'That's a tonne to go on. Black, white, indigo, violet?'

Removing his sunglasses and rubbing his face, Conky wanted nothing more than to go to his own place, take a shower, make himself a hot toddy and go to bed. The lunacy of the past weeks had worn him thin and baggy, like over-stretched elastic on old man's pants. 'I told you. I don't know.'

'But you saw enough of him to let a couple of shots off, didn't you?' Ellis James said, winking. 'I've seen those bullet holes in the doorframe over there. I've got a ballistics guy on his way.' He checked his shitty cheap watch. A Rolex wannabe from some Arndale Centre jewellers that sold carriage and cuckoo clocks. 'Any minute now, he'll be here. And I bet if I asked him to take samples from your hand, he'd find cordite on your skin.' He nudged Conky's knee with his own like a schoolboy enjoying a smutty joke with a co-conspirator. 'Come on, McFadden. Show us your big gun.'

'With all due respect, I think you should piss off, detective.' Conky rose and walked over towards the forensics team, who were dusting for prints. Praying that they didn't apply for a warrant to search the place. The home cinema alone held an arsenal behind secret panels inset into the walls that would make the Queen's guard green with envy.

'I'm watching you, girls and boys,' he told the team in their jumpsuits and overshoes, scouring the spa area for evidence. Parasites. If they found anything incriminating, Paddy would be reliant on the retainers he had paid bent cops over the years to ensure nothing ever made it to court.

'Just let them do what they need to do,' Sheila had whispered to him as the ambulance men had carefully ministered to the prone form of her husband. 'If we get shirty with them, they'll start asking too many questions. We deal with this our own way, right? Remember what I said, Conks. The Fish Man and the Boddlingtons . . .' She had drawn a line with her index finger across her neck.

But that was before that shambolic prick Ellis James had turned up, sniffing like a bloodhound for any trace of weakness or fault in the O'Briens' wall of secrecy. Greedy eyes all over the place; unsurprising given it was the first time he had ever made it through the door to Paddy's Bramshott stronghold.

'Stop following me like a wet fart,' Conky said, turning around to find Ellis James only two paces behind. Clutching that damned notepad. 'Go and find that Bugatti! That's a million right there. Can't be many of those to the pound even in a place like Bramshott. Find the car and you'll find whoever did this.'

'Had the O'Briens had any kind of threatening letter or phone call that you know of before this attack?' the detective asked, unperturbed by the stinging rejection.

Coming to a standstill, Conky looked down at James. Noticed the grubby cuffs on his raincoat and wondered what the chump spent his salary on. It certainly wasn't dry cleaning. 'There was an incident last night, actually,' he said. 'There's a new alarm system in the house. Mr O'Brien was in bed upstairs, sick with a migraine. I thought maybe he'd got out of bed and triggered it by accident, but when I investigated, there was nobody there. It was as though the system had malfunctioned. It had only been installed that day. Teething problems, I guess.'

'Was the alarm triggered when the attacker struck this morning? Were you on site?'

'I was here, alright, but not in the house. I'd just walked down the drive to fetch the post for Mrs O. I never heard the alarm going off. Only thing I heard was Sheila – I mean, Mrs O – screaming her head off. That's when I ran back inside and saw the attacker making his getaway.'

Ellis James frowned. 'I thought you're meant to be a simple office bod at the builders' merchants, McFadden. How come you're so indispensable to the family that Sheila O'Brien has got you checking faults on her alarm system and fetching her post?' The frown gave way to a faux-perplexed smile that was underscored by pure, undiluted smugness.

'I'm *very* handy,' Conky simply said.

'Stay in town where I can find you, please.' James grabbed his right hand suddenly and sniffed the skin. 'Soapy?' He pursed his lips. 'Been washing your hands in a hurry? Maybe getting rid of a little evidence?'

Conky snatched his hand back. 'A: that's assault and B: I take hand hygiene extremely seriously.'

When the police had packed up their sneaking suspicions and investigative tools, Conky stood in reverential silence by the puddle of Paddy's blood. Coagulating now, it was almost the shade of uncooked black pudding. He took out his phone and re-read the text from Sheila, saying Paddy was in a critical condition with no improvement. Once again, he dialled Frank. Straight to voicemail. Subjected to the irritating recording of Frank speaking over the song he was once famous for half a lifetime ago. Duplicitous little dipshit. Conky thumbed his name on the phone's screen, pondering where he could have absconded to and whether he was somehow in bed with the Boddlingtons. It was the only feasible theory. And the science of being a Loss Adjuster demanded that Conky was methodical and thorough in testing any theory.

Grabbing the keys to Paddy's Jaguar, Conky floored his car past Stockport on the M60, following the motorway round past east Manchester. On his right, the undulating green Peaks gave way to the brutal rain-soaked foothills of the Pennines – both encapsulating Manchester in a permanently damp basin where precipitation was always likely. Presently, the great phallic spire of Heaton Park loomed into view, with all its satellite dishes clinging to the top like bristles on a gun-cleaning brush. Unfamiliar territory for him, though he located the neighbourhood of Higher Boddlington easily enough.

Here were street after street of red-brick semis, all extended in improbable and often unsightly ways. Housing that harked back to a bygone era. The people carriers and Volvo estates that were double parked on the scruffy streets a testament to each household boasting many, many children. This was the place, Conky knew, where God's chosen people dwelled in near-total separatism that would have some of the folk back in the Northern Ireland of his youth crippled with jealousy.

A row of shops punctuated the scene. The kosher butcher, the baker, the candlestick maker. Incongruously opposite the Polski Sklep that sold Tyskie beer and kielbasa. Outside, women wearing ugly wigs and black clothing pushed double buggies along the pavement. Men dressed in black suits and big hats like the Fish Man, hastening to the synagogue or Talmudic college with prayer books and bags containing their prayer shawls tucked under their arms.

Conky scanned the locale, remembering the address

that had come up on Google. Sure enough, there, at the end of the row, was what he sought. 'Smolensky's Fresh Fish' in scrolling black Perspex on a white sign above the picture window. Nothing in the window apart from an empty display counter and some green AstroTurf. This was a utilitarian place for serious fish connoisseurs. No sign of the Fish Man from outside. Conky parked up, checked his gun was loaded and approached the busy shop.

Inside, it was bustling with locals, bellowing their orders enthusiastically at the serving girl. The fridges were stacked with wholesale polystyrene trays of fish from the market. The smell of the sea stung the back of Conky's nostrils as he walked in, almost forcing him to retreat. A smell from his childhood, conjuring the memory of oysters, tipped from their pearlescent shells down his daddy's throat, washed down with Guinness. His father had allowed his wee man to sample those delights on birthdays, as long as he didn't tell his mammy about the Guinness. Now, he held his nose. Tried to push to the front, understanding that his was surely a commanding presence among these people who were largely short of stature.

'Hey, there's a queue you know!' one of the customers shouted in a shrill voice. A tiny speck of an elderly woman, pulling a tartan shopping trolley. She wore a scarf on her head, tied tightly under her olive-skinned chin. 'You wait your turn.'

Conky spoke over her head to the assistant. 'I want to speak to Asaf Smolensky,' he said.

Studiously ignoring him, or perhaps she simply couldn't hear him over the din, the assistant continued to weigh and package the wares for the clientele.

His hand itched. Almost tempted to reach into his

pocket and draw the gun. It made everything so easy. But then, these women didn't deserve that kind of treatment. They were ordinary folk, blissfully unaware that the proprietor of their favourite fishmonger's was an ex-Mossad hit man.

'Asaf Smolensky!' He raised his voice so that the women turned to him, askance. The shop was suddenly silent. 'Where is Asaf Smolensky? I demand to speak to him.'

Finally the assistant looked up at him with an exasperated expression on her face. Wiped her hands on her apron and picked up a boning knife – the kind he had seen the Fish Man wield on the odd occasion they had clashed on the battlefield.

'He's in Israel,' she answered, simply.

'You're lying,' he said.

She pointed to the door with the blade of the knife. 'Listen,' she said, fixing him with the dead eyes of a cod. 'You want fish mix? Get to the back of the queue. You wanna insult me in the workplace? There's the door! I told you. Smolensky's in Israel. He went three days ago. He's not due back for a fortnight. And if you don't believe me, ask Bracha here, because he's gone to her nephew's best friend's Barmitzvah in Tel Aviv.'

Bracha, an attractive middle-aged woman in an expensive-looking black wig, nodded. 'It's true. The Barmitzvah boy said his piece perfectly, Baruch Hashem,' she told her companions, smiling skywards. 'I saw the photos on Facebook. Mr Smolensky was there.' She gave a diffident shrug.

'Are you sure? When was this?' Conky asked.

'Yes, I'm sure. It was this morning.' She took out her mobile phone. Scrolled through some notifications. Showed him a photo of the Fish Man, surrounded by other Hassidic men – all smiling at a beaming boy in an oversized prayer shawl. The photo was indisputably tagged and dated around the time when Paddy O'Brien had been filleted by his swimming pool.

'It wasn't him,' Conky said under his breath.

Chapter 46

Sheila

'It's been days now. Will he make it?' Sheila asked, clutching Paddy's hand. She looked up at the staff nurse who was wrapping a blood pressure cuff around her husband's deathly pale arm. Flinching at the grinding noise of the inflating cuff. No response from the unconscious Paddy whose face was obscured by the tubing and mask of a ventilator. The incessant, not quite syncopated bleep-bleeping of the oxygen and heart monitor set her teeth on edge. She had a perverse desire to unplug everything. 'He looks . . .' Wiping at her eyes, she swallowed painfully. 'He still looks on death's door.'

'Sorry, love,' the nurse said, frowning as she wrote the blood pressure reading onto the clipboard at the end of the bed. She reached over and patted Sheila's arm gingerly. 'He is *very* poorly. They put him into this induced coma to give him a chance to recover, so they must hold out some hope.' The nurse adjusted the flow of the drips that hung from a stand by the bed. 'His colour's improved a bit now he's had the blood transfusion, but the collapsed lung . . .' She grimaced, contemplating her prone patient who had been reduced to a mass of tubes and wires. Turned back to Sheila with a sympathetic smile. 'Nab the consultant when he does his rounds later. He can tell you more than me. In the meantime, why don't you grab yourself a coffee, lovey?' She gesticulated towards the bed with her pen. 'Your hubby won't know if you slip out for half an hour. You look like you could use it.'

Clutching her cardigan around her, Sheila slipped out of Intensive Care, away from the hiss and bleep of the machinery. In a daze, she hastened down the corridor to the café, considering all that had gone on. Days, now, and her life had already become a dull carousel of questioning by that little arsehole Ellis James, regular reports from Conky, who was getting precisely nowhere with his own investigation, and maintaining this arse-numbing bedside vigil, waiting for Paddy to die. Punctuated only by once-daily visits from the girls, who seemed more intent on catching up with their old friends while they were home than spending time with their father in what could be his final hours.

You reap what you sow, Gloria had told her. Paddy had sown a lifetime of avoidant dismissive attachment and dysfunction into the hearts of his family. Her therapy sessions had told her that much.

'Sheila! Sheila!' A woman's voice called out after her. Sheila turned around to find Katrina padding along the corridor towards her, plod-plodding in those ugly ortho-paedic shoes that nuns wore.

'Oh, God give me strength,' Sheila muttered under her breath. 'Here we go.'

'Wait for me! I wanted to speak to you.'

Her nun's veil flapping as she walked, Katrina approached, linking Sheila by the arm. Sheila's viscera knotted into a tight ball, feeling as though she had been annexed by one of God's emissaries who spoke not only with the conviction of the holy but also with the bombast of an O'Brien.

'I've just spoken to the consultant,' Katrina said, lowering her voice to a conspiratorial pitch that had a whiff of the confessional about it. Rubbing her fingers together as if there were beads between them. Maybe she was saying a rosary in her head.

'Oh yeah?' Sheila said, shaking her arm loose. 'How come you got to speak to the consultant and I didn't?' The lack of sleep was making barbed wire out of her silken tongue. *Try harder, Sheila. Make an enemy of Sister big bollocks Benedicta at this stage, and you're just swapping one thorn in your side for a whole crown of them.* 'Sorry. I mean, what did he say?'

Her sister-in-law scrutinised her face, presumably seeking a shred of sincerity that had long since vanished. She toyed with her crucifix and dropped her inquisitive gaze to her highly polished shoes. 'Well, he said that it's likely Paddy's going to be in a coma for a long while. He possibly might never wake up. The collapsed lung and internal damage don't bode well for a man who already has heart problems.'

Sheila breathed in deeply through her nose and closed her eyes. Processed the news, though she would have preferred to hear it for herself from the consultant's own lips. 'He's not going to make it, is he?' She felt certain that some platitude about the Lord working in mysterious ways was just about to trip off Katrina's tongue. But it wasn't.

'I think we should bring him to my nursing home to die,' Katrina said. It felt more of an order than a suggestion. She fixed Sheila with hard, clear eyes, devoid of emotion that spoke to a familiarity with death. 'He shouldn't be in this highly medicalised environment. It's no place for a man at the end. He needs his family around him and his creature comforts.'

Numbed by everything that had come to pass, Sheila arranged her face into an approximation of sorrowful surprise. 'So, he *is* dying. Is that what they told you?'

Katrina started to walk towards the café. Sheila grabbed her by the sleeve and pulled her backwards. The nun looked disdainfully down at Sheila's manicured hand, clutching at the rough fabric of her ecclesiastically appropriate cardigan.

Peeling her hand away, Katrina said, 'I manage a clean, homely nursing home with a large staff of experienced nurses and care workers. We specialise in palliative care, as well as meeting the spiritual needs of the terminally ill. I can't think of a more suitable place for my own brother. Can you? Or would you rather leave him with strangers in here?'

'I'll give it some thought,' Sheila said, rubbing her eyes as though tears were brewing. Using the gesture as a foil for rapidly calculating the pros and cons of Katrina's suggestion. In hospital, they would try their damnedest to save Paddy. With Frank and Katrina breathing down her neck, she had had no choice but to refuse the Do Not Resuscitate option. 'What's your security like?'

'As good as we make it,' Katrina said. 'Sometimes the protection of the Lord Jesus is not enough, and our Patrick has led a somewhat unusual life that has made him enemies.'

Sheila chuckled. 'You're telling me!'

Katrina leaned into her and whispered in her ear. 'Shame you didn't look after him better, then, isn't it, you selfish, narcissistic woman? A good wife would have talked him out of leading a life of crime. And Patrick wouldn't be hooked up to that life-support machine.'

Leaving Sheila open-mouthed, Katrina padded off into

the café, smiling benignly at the harried-looking clientele, who sat staring mournfully at their gnat's piss tea or shrink-wrapped ham subs.

Cheeky bitch, Sheila thought, unsure whether to run after her and take her to task over the criticism or whether to let it go. There was too much of Paddy in Katrina. She hadn't reckoned on swapping one O'Brien despot for another.

Chapter 47

Frank, then Katrina

'You need to be aware, Sister Benedicta, that there's a strong possibility that your brother won't make the journey to your nursing home, even if he's transported in a specialist ambulance,' the consultant said, glancing at Sheila for signs of approval. He started to roll up the sleeves of his shirt, revealing the sort of muscled forearms that had been developed in the gym. 'Mrs O'Brien, is this what you want? He doesn't have to go. I recommend that he stays under our care in the ICU.'

Frank deliberately turned away from the consultant's forearms that reminded him so painfully of his son. Observed Sheila instead as she sat by Paddy's bedside with a faraway look in her eyes. She was pale. Appeared fragile. Beaten down by the experience. They all were. Apart from Katrina, who seemed visibly invigorated and a good ten years younger than she had before she'd had the opportunity to feast on everyone's misery like a locust, Frank mused. No different when she'd been a kid.

Sheila's gaze flicked absently towards the consultant. 'Yes. Let him go.'

'That's decided then,' Katrina said, smiling. 'Paddy's

coming with me.' She held her unconscious brother's hand territorially and said a prayer under her breath.

Frank watched her taking charge. The words of protest welled up inside him. He willed them to come out loud, clear and authoritative instead of his usual garbled mutterings.

'You're fucking loving this, aren't you?' he said to his sister.

'Whatever do you mean, Francis?' Katrina appraised him through hooded eyes, running her little finger over her crucifix.

The consultant blinked repeatedly and flushed red. 'Er. Listen, I'll erm, prepare the discharge documentation and leave you to it. In fact, really, only Mrs O'Brien should be here, so if you can take your discussions outside . . .'

Katrina stood and smiled sweetly at the doctor. 'Of course. How selfish of us. Please excuse my younger brother's language.' She gathered the fabric of Frank's hoody in her fist and dragged him out of his seat. 'Get up, Francis,' she said in a soft voice that was marbled with a streak of pure titanium.

Outside in the corridor, the three stood together in a triangle that was far from equilateral. Frank put his arm around Sheila, feeling that, even combined, their strength was no match for the mighty Sister Benedicta who positively shone with religious conviction and an ego the size of a good Glastonbury turnout.

'We don't see you for years,' he said, cleaving his sister-in-law to his shoulder. Pointing at Katrina with an index finger so rigid with resentment and frustration that his whole arm ached. 'And the minute it all starts to go tits up, you're all over Paddy's downfall like flies on dog-shit.'

The beatified smile on Katrina's ageing face slid abruptly,

like a loose-fitting mask. Clearly bristling with indignation. Her bosom heaved beneath its humble outer wrappings.

'Think about what you say before you speak, Francis. You're embarrassing poor Sheila. She's suffering enough.'

'Sod that, Kat.' He knew she hated any abbreviation of names. 'I'm speaking out for She as well as me. You're shoving your neb in where it's not wanted. It's not down to you where Paddy gets treated. Whether he lives or dies. That's all down to Sheila. His wife!'

'I'm the eldest!' Katrina shouted, making several passers-by look askance at her. 'I get a say. Sheila's in shock! And we can't expect her to make these big decisions.' She treated Sheila to a harsh stare. 'Can we Sheila?'

But Sheila remained silent. Frank found it impossible to intuit what was going on behind those bright blue eyes, now bloodshot and unadorned with makeup after sleepless nights. He turned back to his sister.

'You're tapped. It's like you're getting a kick out of all what's gone on with me and Pad. Know what I think?' He swallowed hard, knowing this constituted a sucker punch that he couldn't come back from. 'I think you're *glad* Paddy had his heart attack and you've loved every minute of my Jack dying.' He took a step closer. Tempted to poke her in the shoulder but resisting . . . just. 'And Pad's plans to escape to Thailand were ruined. Bet you loved that too, especially now he's on his deathbed. I think you're lapping it up because us tainted sinners are all getting our comeuppance, and that makes you right, at last.'

Katrina shook her head. Tutted loudly, clasping her hands behind her back. 'I thought there was hope for you, Francis, but I can see how the years have ground away at your spirit, leaching the goodness and leaving only a bitter and twisted runt of the litter. I'm sorry for you. I really am.'

Frank stared at her open-mouthed. Felt tears stab at the backs of his eyes, realising that blood may be thicker than water, but he'd take water any day of the week.

*

Sister Benedicta stood on the steps of the nursing home the following morning, awaiting the arrival of her brother in the special ICU ambulance. Having rained overnight, it was a damp, cool morning. The kind she liked, where the aroma of recently mown grass in the adjacent fields suffused everything with a blissful freshness. Like the world was washed clean of sin, if only superficially.

The odd visiting relative came and went, during that wait. She spoke kindly to them and cracked the odd joke. Providing comforting words to those whose relatives were near to the end. But she did not leave the steps.

After forty-two minutes, the white and fluorescent green bulk of the ambulance appeared at the end of the drive. He was here. Now it could all begin. She had planned everything. She was ready.

Chapter 48

Conky

Conky sipped thoughtfully from his whisky glass, occasionally writing words in his pad that meant something to him. Names, mainly.

> Frank
> Boddlingtons double-cross
> Smolensky – he had since drawn a line through the Fish Man's name
> Maureen
> What was in the bag?

He cast his mind back to those moments where Paddy had been sprawled on the poolside floor, bleeding out and dressed like a salmon with cucumber. Someone had been at pains to make it look like one of the Fish Man's distinctive hits. Someone was trying to deflect attention from their own subterfuge by implicating Jonny Margulies and Tariq Khan.

Conky pressed the ball of his biro into the line, 'Maureen'. Had she sabotaged her client because of some long-standing grudge? Perhaps Maureen wanted out of the business and considered bringing Paddy down the only way out. God knows, the boss tied people in for life, whether they wanted that level of commitment or not.

No. 'No,' he said out loud in the empty back office at M1 House.

What about Colin Chang? The Chinese pharmacist who had got away – wriggly little bastard. Could he conceivably have hired someone to take down the crime lord who had kept him as little more than an indebted slave for years?

'That would take some balls,' Conky said, scribbling down Chang's name and then immediately striking it out. 'And if Hong Kong Colin had any of those, he'd have told Paddy where to go quite some time ago.'

With the club still closed after the slaughter, the silence echoed ominously around him. No music. No hubbub of workers preparing for the night's revellers. Only Frank, out there, somewhere, wandering around his little fiefdom, wondering what the hell had gone wrong. Or was he? Perhaps everything that had come to pass was part of his master plan.

Conky drew a line under Frank's name. Whispered, 'Francis O'Brien' to the four walls. It was almost a trope in literature that one lesser brother should seek to undo another. Genghis Khan – the plucky boy, Temüjin, who systematically did away with his siblings to gain dominance – sprang to mind. Good old Genghis. And here was docile, passive Frank, who had played second fiddle all these years to his over-bearing narcissist of a sibling. A man who had lost his wife *and* his son because of the narcotic, violent life that Paddy had foisted on his kid brother, poisoning everything that had once been good. Conky knew the two men well enough to understand how their iniquity had come about and how volatile a brew festering resentment could be.

He couldn't articulate why, but he was suddenly drawn to the shelves that contained album after album of photo archives from the club. Conky took down the collection that he had pored over at Jack's wake. 'Something in here,' he said, tapping the spine of the album. 'I'll bet my first edition of *Finnegan's Wake* on it.'

Draining his whisky and pouring himself another, he lit a cigarette, sat back and reflected on the photographs from the winter. Flipping through page after page, he arrived at a collection of action shots. Jack, DJing, clasping those trademark cans to his ears with a muscled arm. Ravers in the background. Some minor local celebrities, hanging out in the VIP area. Flip forwards, and the photos depicted the spring. Repetition, as Conky scrutinised snaps of Frank with his arm around various punters. A starlet from *Coronation Street*. A footballer from Manchester City. There was Paddy, clutching a bottle of champagne in one hand and a cigar in another. But wait. Here were photos of the VIP area, showing Jack and Frank, arm in arm. The same photos he, Frank and Paddy had reminisced over at the wake. Once again, Conky studied the revealing sight of Leviticus Bell in a clinch with Mia Margulies. Mia Margulies glaring at Jack O'Brien. It was telling. Two out of three of those youngsters were now dead. At a time when peace had been declared, this whole war had escalated because of Mia's rape claims.

Conky wrote Love triangle? in his pad.

Remembering the tall figure that had sprinted out of the spa area and practically sprung up the back steps, decked out in a long coat and wide-brimmed hat with the beard and sidelocks, Conky reasoned that the Fish Man's impersonator had displayed the agility of a much younger man. Dark, olive skinned, like Smolensky at a glance. But better built than Smolensky, now he came to think about it. Broader in the shoulders.

'Lev Bell,' he said, writing the name in his pad and underlining it several times. 'It was you, wasn't it, you little bastard? What was in the bag you were carrying?' He visualised the heavy-looking holdall. Heavy enough to slow him down. What might a man with murderous intentions risk being slowed down and potentially captured by the enemy for? 'Guns? No. Money. Somebody turned the alarm system off so you could get in.' He chewed the end of the biro, savouring the thrill of piecing this jigsaw together. 'No, someone let you in the night before when the alarm went off. They hid you, didn't they?'

Contemplating all those workmen who had been crawling all over the boss' Bramshott mansion, Conky pondered how likely it was that any of them had been involved. But they had all left, one by one, at 4pm. Conky had counted them in and out. So, the only theory that held water was that one of the remaining people in the house had let Bell inside. Frank, Paddy himself, one of his daughters, or Sheila.

Suddenly aware he wasn't alone, Conky looked up.

'Alright, Conks,' Frank said, standing on the threshold to the office, staring at the albums that were spread out on the desk.

Conky reached for the handgun tucked into the back of his waistband.

'Francis. Just the man.'

'I hope you understand my need to be thorough and leave no stone unturned,' Conky said, peering at Frank through the rear view mirror of the Jaguar.

On the back seat, Frank squirmed against his bonds. Tried to speak through the makeshift gag that Conky had innovated using a strip of torn office curtain. Muffled protest and clear hurt in his eyes. Or was it fear?

At this time of night, there was little traffic on Wilbraham Road. The leafy Chorlton suburb was devoid of life but for a gaggle of bearded young men, clad in tight jeans, ironically bad jumpers and sneakers. All heading towards the tram station, presumably in search of a good time in the city centre.

Turning into the side-street, Conky counted the houses and pulled up outside the neat semi-detached that belonged to Gloria Bell. A Mazda MX-5 on the drive, shining like an automotive halo under the streetlight.

'Don't try anything stupid,' Conky told the struggling Frank. 'And you mustn't take this personally. I happen to hold you in very high esteem, Francis. I'm just doing my job.'

Locking the Jaguar with his prime suspect inside, Conky approached the front door. Hammered out a short tattoo using the brass lion knocker. Nothing. Peering in through the darkened windows, he could spy no evidence of Gloria being there. Perhaps she was asleep. Glancing up, he realised the bedroom curtains were only half drawn. Crunching on the gravel path round to the back, there were no signs of life there either. He inferred from the washing strung across the back garden that if she wasn't home, she couldn't have gone far. Withdrawing a hammer from his coat pocket, he snatched a tea towel from the line. Wrapped the hammer's head in the cloth and smashed the back door window smartly. A key in the lock on the other side. Gloria of all people should have known better. Had she gone somewhere in a hurry?

His point of entry took him into the kitchen. Daring to switch on the light, he rifled through some papers stacked between cookery books on the worktop. They revealed nothing but utility bills, old birthday cards and recipes for cake. No clues as to her whereabouts. But there, stuck to the stainless steel fridge–freezer beneath a fridge magnet that showed Jesus with his arms held wide, was a sheaf of note paper and scraps containing scrawled telephone numbers. Conky removed them and leafed through. Stopped at the small sheet of lined paper that had been torn from a spiral pad. On it was exactly what he sought. Leviticus Bell's Sweeney Hall address.

Switching off the light and closing the back door, were it not for a yowling cat, Conky would certainly have missed the fact that Gloria Bell had a garage at the end of the garden. Unsure as to what he expected to see, he approached the somewhat ramshackle structure. It wouldn't hurt to have a look. Glancing back at the front drive, he hoped that Frank wouldn't try to break his bonds and escape. Did he have time for this? Yes. Two seconds, just to make sure.

There was a filthy old window set into the pebble-dashed render. With his sunglasses on his head, he peered through the glass as the clouds parted, allowing a glorious bright moon to shine through. It lit up the garage's contents. And there, under the corrugated iron roof, sat one million pounds' worth of stolen Bugatti.

'Got you, you shifty cow!'

Chapter 49

Conky

'You wait here!' Conky said, tearing the duct tape from Frank's mouth. It left an angry red rectangle on the lower half of his thin face.

Frank yelped. 'Shit, man! Like I can go anywhere when you've tied me to a fucking chair, you ranchpot! Seriously, Conks. You've lost the plot,' he shouted, struggling against his bonds. 'I've got naff all to do with any of this. I swear on my Jack's . . .' A shadow passed over his face. His eyes darkened. 'I swear on everything.'

'Do you want me to put the tape back on your mouth, Francis?'

Behind the counter, in the shop of the builders' merchants, Conky looked down at Frank. Wondering what steps he should take next. He looked through the window. The sun was rising on a rainy Sunday morning. It was cold in the Portakabin. The late-night trip to the seedy, damp Sweeney Hall flat had yielded little – certainly not Leviticus Bell.

'Where on God's earth is that cheap two-bit little gangsta arsehole?' Conky asked, perching on the counter and running his fingers over the keys on the till.

'How should I know?' Frank asked, shaking his head. Resignation in his weary voice. 'You've got this all arse about tit, man. Our Paddy's a stone cold wanker and, Christ knows, he's ruined my life. But he's still my brother. I wouldn't touch a hair on his head. You should know that.' He looked up at Conky, tears swimming in his eyes. 'I'm not a murderer. Paddy's that man. You're that man. Not me. I haven't got it in me. You've known me since I was a young lad. If I wanted to pop our Pad, I wouldn't have waited this fucking long, would I?'

Conky folded his arms and crossed his long legs, appraising the bewildered face of Frank. Saw the truth in it. Sighed deeply and started to untie him.

'Don't try anything funny,' he said. 'Remember I'm the one with the gun.'

With his hands sticky from used duct tape, he pulled Frank up out of the chair. Embraced his wiry, insubstantial body and felt an overpowering wave of guilt threaten to drown him. 'I apologise, Francis. It was just that as I said before, your motivation to put a hit on the boss was beyond doubt. You must see that. And my judgement of your character was clouded by the need to solve this dastardly fucking mystery. We have a traitor among us. Until I find Lev Bell and hear from the horse's mouth who paid him to impersonate the Fish Man, I'm totally stumped.'

Frank rubbed his chin and rotated his arms in windmills. 'Don't sweat it, man. No hard feelings. You're a mad bastard but I know you're loyal and that counts for everything.' He waved his hands dismissively. 'Anyway, I'm too knackered to start bitching about a misunderstanding. Too much has gone on. I couldn't give a monkey's any more. Want a drink?' He walked stiffly to the drinks machine, switched it on and pressed the button for black coffee. Hissing and spitting as the scalding liquid spurted into a brown plastic cup. Handed it to Conky.

Conky eyed the back of Frank's head, marvelling that he had subjected the poor wee bastard to a night of torture and yet, here his victim was, making them hot drinks as though they had merely spent the night in a bar, shooting the breeze over a few beers until the sun had come up. Releasing him had been a gamble but, without any evidence whatsoever, he had to assume Frank's innocence. The Loss Adjuster had to remain unimpeachably fair.

'What was Lev's place like?' Frank said, blowing the froth on the top of his coffee. Grimacing as he sipped it.

Visualising the dingy interior of the tiny council flat, Conky remembered the mess of the bedroom in particular. A dusty, stale smell, as though nobody had slept there in a while. The place had felt like an icebox, even though it was the height of summer. He tried to conjure a memory of the bed. Clasped his hand to his forehead.

'There was a rectangular indent in the duvet,' he said.

'A suitcase,' Frank said.

'Aye. And a couple of the drawers in a tall-boy were open, with the contents all messed up. Why didn't I realise it last night? I was looking but not seeing.' He thumped himself in the temple. 'Fecking eejit.'

Frank reached out to touch his arm. Seemingly thought better of it. 'Take it easy, man.'

Striking himself again, Conky felt frustration twist and knot his insides into an uncomfortable tangle. 'He could be anywhere.'

'Well, if Gloria's missing too, maybe they've had some big reunion and both run off.'

Taking out his phone, Conky scrolled through his contacts until he found the name he was looking for. 'Paddy has a guy in customs on the payroll,' he said. 'If the Bells have left the country with what I presume was a bag of cash, he might be able to check flight rosters. And if they've flown the country, there's an outside chance their tickets were paid for by someone else.'

Chapter 50

Sheila

Sheila walked along the corridor of the nursing home, clutching a bunch of white roses. Cheaply framed portraits of religious scenes hanging on the wall registered in her peripheral vision: stations of the cross; Jesus, the centre of attention during the Last Supper; the Virgin Mary clutching her holy infant. Plastic flowers in a cut-glass vase on a half-moon table, part-way up the corridor, trying to make the place look cheery. Marching along with purpose, she made virgin footprints with her stilettos on the well-hoovered utilitarian grey carpet. Trying her hardest not to inhale the smell of incontinence incidents, poorly masked by spray air freshener. Attempting not to listen to the shouts, whoops and wails of some of the residents, who were trapped by their troubled minds inside some alternate reality. Looked into the rooms on either side as she advanced towards Paddy's new home, glimpsing the agonisingly slow onset of death in the faces of the dementia-stricken. There they lay in institutional beds, with the cot-sides up. Mouths open and staring into the abyss.

'Depressing shithole,' Sheila grumbled. 'Why the hell did

he have to come here? I'm gonna give that Katrina what for. Bloody bossy, shit-stirring old bitch.'

'I'm so sorry,' one of the nurses said, hastening to the threshold of the nurses' office to greet her with an apologetic face. Biting her lip.

'Sorry for what?' Sheila asked, gripping the roses tight enough for the thorns to bite.

'Sister Benedicta called you, right?'

Sheila felt her smile freeze along with her heart. The questioning tone and darting eyes of the nurse told her something was more than amiss.

'What's gone on?' she asked. 'Where's Paddy?'

The nurse was wringing her hands. 'Your husband passed this morning.'

Blinking hard, Sheila studied the well-scrubbed face of the nurse. 'You what?'

'Mr O'Brien, I'm afraid he's gone.' She picked up a file and read the notes. 'I'm so sorry. Yes. Says here, registered time of death was seven fifteen am. Sister Benedicta told me at handover. The doctor's been and confirmed the death. I'm to give you the paperwork for the death certification. Like I said, I'm so very sorry for your loss.'

The nurses' room felt suddenly freezing cold. The rose stems inside Sheila's right hand burned her skin. 'Take me to him,' she said. Her voice sounded like it belonged to somebody else.

She followed the nurse along the corridor, feeling her ankles threaten to give way. When the nurse pushed the door open to a cold, dark room, the first thing Sheila saw was Katrina sitting bolt upright in a straight-backed chair, perfectly still at the side of a single bed. Dramatically lit by a solitary Anglepoise lamp. The gaudy blackout curtains were closed, not allowing a shred of daylight in. All the life-saving machinery had been switched off. Beneath a sheet was a long lumpy form, approximately the size and shape of Paddy.

'Ah. Sheila,' Katrina said, rising to meet her, hands outstretched as though she had been plucked from one of her religious portraits. The fine lines in her face seemed deeper with that directional, unforgiving light. 'Poor Paddy. He never made it.'

Sheila moved towards the bed, feeling like she had left normality back in the driver's seat of her car. She was dimly aware of Katrina's hand on her upper arm.

'I don't understand. He was in a coma but I thought he was stable.' She pulled her arm free. 'Why did he suddenly go downhill?'

'There, there,' Katrina said. 'The Lord has saved him from further suffering. But don't worry. I've made all the arrangements to make it easier on you and the girls.'

This wasn't happening to her. It was happening to somebody else. Perhaps she had fallen asleep and this had been an elaborate dream. 'I have to see him,' she said, reaching out to clasp the top of the sheet.

But Katrina manoeuvred her bulk deftly between Sheila and the bed, proprietorially taking the sheet herself and lifting it back with a certain ceremony, as though unveiling a precious religious portrait in a gallery.

Paddy O'Brien, the man Sheila had spent all of her adult life deferring and pandering to, lay slightly open-mouthed with his eyes closed. Gone were those ruddy cheeks and that overwhelming vitality that had always flowed from every pore. Now, Sheila drank in the sight of an ex-man whose face had become merely a ghastly pale death mask with a bluish tinge to the lips. She leaned in closer, narrowing her eyes. Sniffed the still air around him. 'He smells funny. Sweet. Like talc.'

Katrina swiftly covered Paddy's grey face anew with the sheet. She ushered Sheila away from the bed. 'We cleaned him up a little. It's not nice for you, otherwise. Don't distress yourself, dear. He's with God now. It was a peaceful end. I was here with him. You're a strong woman. You'll get through this – for the sake of the girls, you'll have to.'

Backing towards the door, Sheila clasped her hand to her mouth, taking shallow breaths. Trying to absorb the unbelievable, indigestible news. Paddy was dead. After all that had gone on – decades of tyranny, the stabbing, the heart attack, the war, his hopes and dreams being built up and then dashed finally by the attack in the spa – he had been undone. Sheila had been left behind. The grieving Queen. She realised that that was exactly the role she must now play.

In the dim light of the nursing home room, as Katrina faffed anew with the sheet, with her back turned, Sheila allowed herself a broad smile.

Chapter 51

Conky

As he carried the long, gleaming black coffin from the church to the cemetery, Conky marvelled that his boss seemed taller than he remembered him in life and yet had been so light – almost inconsequentially so – at the end. Perhaps the blood loss and rapid slide into death had done that. Perhaps the body stretched and sagged when the life went out of it. Without doubt, though, his was less burdensome to carry than Jack's coffin. Unexpected for a small stocky man, who had enjoyed good food and his fair share of the drink for all of the years that Conky had known his employer. Standing shoulder to shoulder with a stony-faced, red-eyed Frank, as the pall-bearers all shuffled from the church to the hearse, carrying their burden, Conky was left with a hollow feeling. No more Boss. After in excess of twenty years' loyal service, he had lost his employer and a friend, of sorts, though in truth, Conky McFadden was painfully aware that he didn't really have friends. Not proper ones. More than that, though, Conky had lost his raison d'être. It was over.

The King was dead. It was like Genghis, finally succumbing to an arrow of the Western Xia. A noble death for a born warrior like the boss. Fitting.

Southern Cemetery was warm and sunny on the day of Paddy O'Brien's funeral. Hundreds had gathered from all of south Manchester and beyond to pay tribute to one of the city's most infamous sons. At the graveside, as the coffin was lowered into the ground in some mournful episode of O'Brien-family déjà vu, Conky considered his discovery. Recollecting the contents of the revealing email that had come through from Paddy's contact in customs, who had managed to access the flight booking system and trace not only the whereabouts of Leviticus and Gloria Bell but also who had paid for their flights. The information had not been what Conky had been anticipating. The looming spectre of a confrontation was inevitable. But it would have to wait. Now, while Sheila stood weeping openly by her husband's graveside, legs visibly buckling, forcing her to clutch at her ashen-faced daughters for support, was neither the time nor the place.

Turning his focus to Katrina, Conky found it odd that the apparently unassuming old nun who had been absent in the tumultuous lives of the O'Brien family for years, operating only on the fringes as someone who came and went on high days and holy days, had suddenly taken the pole position at the head of the family. There she was, standing next to the priest, staring solemnly into the hole in the ground at her brother's coffin, as he intoned the burial rites.

'In the midst of life we are in death;
From whom can we seek help?
From you alone, O Lord
Who by our sins are justly angered.'

Peering out from behind his sunglasses, he observed Katrina cock her head to the side, clasping her unadorned hands primly before her, her nun's habit flapping in her face on the warm summer breeze. The oldest O'Brien child. Only she and Frank were left, now. Conky wondered how the future would shape up for the family without Paddy at the helm of their dynasty. His had been a mighty presence, his death rending a gaping, seemingly irreparable split in the fabric of their lives.

As they one by one started to cast earth onto the coffin, Conky was taken aback by the hot tears that leaked from his eyes. Relieved that they were, in part, obscured by the glasses. Though he was without a job or an employer now, it would not do for half of Manchester's criminal under-world to see him as anything but the Loss Adjuster. He looked at the faces of the guests from out of town – the Burroughs Brothers from South East London; the Taverner Gang from Liverpool. Most of the country's major firms had turned out to pay their respects to dear departed Paddy – almost certainly hoping to snatch the lucrative territory and business interests while they were being temporarily shepherded by the hapless and bewildered Frank. Even Tariq Khan had shown up – the brass neck of the bastard – hoping to pay his respects and labour the point that Asaf Smolensky had been framed by an unknown saboteur, seeking to slander the Boddlingtons. Conveying his sincerity with a giant wreath of lilies, no doubt whispering to Frank at some opportune moment during the wake that the deal could just as easily still be on the table as off.

As day turned to early evening and the funeral party transferred to the Hilton on Deansgate, for the most part expressing their loss in the guise of raucous laughter and drunken reminiscences, Conky sat at the table sandwiched between Frank and Sheila, morosely sipping on his single malt. Katrina drinking tea laced with whisky on the oppo-site side, offering distant relatives religious platitudes and tales of Paddy as a child, as if she were the only person in the room who had lost someone close to her.

'How am I going to cope without him?' Frank said, pulling something narcotic from a tiny pill box concealed in his suit breast pocket. Dropping it into his pint. 'I'm the man of the family now. That's more than weird. I'm the only one left, Conks.'

Conky turned to him, patting his hair-piece to check it was still present and correct. 'You're free now, Frank. Your future's your own. You can get the club back on track and do your music. Keep your nose clean. Reinvent yourself. Kick the dealers out, if you like.' He clapped an arm around Frank's shoulder. 'But if you want my advice, my advice is not to try to step into your brother's shoes. If ever you craved Paddy's death . . . if ever you had a hand in his undoing—'

'I didn't!' Frank's eyes widened. Sincerity plastered all over his waxy-looking face as the ecstasy tab started to kick in.

'Well, anyway.' Conky patted him on the back and drained his drink. Poured another, rolling the amber liquid around the crystal and watching the jambes cling to the sides in straight lines. 'Whatever shape your youthful sibling jealousies and fantasies of usurping your brother might have taken, leave that all behind now. Let it go. Get yourself some bereavement counselling. Understand what a huge effect your brother had on your life.' He visualised a younger Paddy, sitting on the edge of his bunk in their prison cell all those years ago, rolling a cigarette and talking at speed. A force of nature, full of plans about how he was going to become a master of the universe as soon as he got out. Pull off a bank job. Get some cash to float a drugs operation. Supply the newly opened clubs on Manchester's emerging dance scene with cheap E from the Netherlands. Fill the gap in the market, dealing pharmaceuticals in south Manchester, where the marijuana and smack coming in from North Africa, South East Asia and the Caribbean was not enough to keep the kids happy. He had had a five-year plan. A ten-year plan. Like a business mogul, like Genghis, he had had the future mapped out in his head, complete with cash-flow projections, staffing structures and potential franchises. Now, he was rotting in a box, two clicks down from his nephew. Survived by people he'd always considered his inferiors. 'Your brother became like a red giant. You know what one of those is?' He took out a cigarette and savoured the flavour of the tip. Wishing he could light up. 'It's an old expanding star. A dying sun, if you like. To the naked eye, it looks bright and twinkly and harmless in the night sky. But it's bigger than anything around it for light years. And this bastard engulfs everything that's unfortunate enough to be orbiting it in its hell-fiery inferno. Red giants are tumours of the universe, masquerading as beauty spots.'

'What are you on about, Conks?'

'Your brother was a red giant. He seemed like the most impressive, stylish motherfucker there was, with his flash cars and fancy lifestyle and all those women. But he chewed up and spat out every poor bastard that ever got sucked into his orbit. We're all that's left, Frank.' He took his glasses off and stared wistfully at a dejected-looking Sheila. Turned to Frank and patted his face. 'Being the right-hand man to someone who was reluctant to trust anyone was as near as damn it to being Paddy's friend, and I value the years I had with him. But I'm sure as hell going to try to move on now he's gone. I don't know what I'll do, but I'm going to try my damnedest to stay out of the cemetery. Don't waste your freedom, Francis. Make the most of being alive and kicking . . . if only to honour Jack's memory. And be there for Sheila. She needs you.'

'My ears are burning,' Sheila said, leaning in towards him and putting her hand on top of Conky's. 'What does Sheila need?'

He peered down at her red varnished fingernails, stared at the glittering solitaire rock and diamond-encrusted eternity ring that graced her slender wedding finger. It was difficult to tell if she was drunk or merely tired, but there was definitely a looseness to the way she enunciated. She was on her fifth glass of red, he estimated. Her lips were a deep burgundy, her tongue was blood red and her teeth had turned that unpleasant shade of purple-grey that came from too much Shiraz. Perhaps he should wait until she had sobered up and was on her home turf, but somehow, Conky reasoned that gauging the potentially explosive subject of Leviticus and Gloria Bell was better done in a room full of witnesses.

'Go and dance, Frank,' Conky said, using the tone of voice he used in his role as Loss Adjuster. 'It's time Sheila and I had a little chatette.'

The drunken smile slid from Sheila's stained mouth. Apprehension registered in the tightness of her face. But Frank just sat steadfastly in his seat, fidgeting with a loose thread on his jacket.

'*Now*, Frank!'

Chapter 52

Conky

When the gun had fired, shattering the giant plate-glass window, Conky's main thought was not of the wind, gusting through the hole at altitude, nor of the fact that he was now dangling backwards with his head and shoulders suspended forty-five levels above the ground with only certain death below. It was not even of the fact that his hair-piece had regrettably blown away. His main thought was that it was surprising that Sheila O'Brien owned such a stylish little handgun, complete with its own silencer. Nevertheless, this did not stop him from screaming.

'Jesus, Sheila! Let me go!' His voice was hoarse from too much whisky and the weight of the night sky pressing against his windpipe.

Sheila straddled his lower half, mercifully still inside the Beetham Tower apartment. She dug the gun into his chest. 'What's the matter, Conky? Were you more comfortable when I was just Paddy's little show-pony? Don't you like it when the girls are on top?'

Conky shook his head, the muscles in his neck screaming. Above him, shards of glass hung dangerously like some jagged guillotine, waiting to fall and puncture his vulnerable burgeoning gut. Around him, the Manchester skyline stretched for miles over to the brooding bulk of the Pennines, barely visible in the moonlight. The G-Mex spread out in the foreground, with its curved roof like an invertebrate, supported only by rings of cartilage, shrouded in darkness. Spinningfields to his left, all lit up where the bankers and accountants and lawyers had left the lights burning and had gone home, knowing Manchester's wealthy denizens would foot the bill. The gothic splendour of the Town Hall and the neo-classical rotunda of the Central Library, picked out with tiny beacons of glowing gold. Manchester in its modern heyday. Conky was sure this would be the finest it had ever looked and the last thing he would ever see. Worse still, Sheila now knew he was, in fact, bald.

But he could not bring himself to throw her off, even if his stomach muscles had been up to the job.

'I didn't know he was hitting you, Sheila. Honestly. Let me up. Let's talk. Don't throw your life away on me! Not like this. That bullshit's for men. Women are better than that. You're better than that.'

He craned his head around to see what lay at ground level. People had started to gather. Looking upwards, though from that height, he could only imagine their questioning faces. Presumably they were wondering at the sudden shower of glass and the pair of Ray-Bans that had fallen from the night sky. The sound of a siren in the distance could well be coming for them.

'Don't you mansplain to me, Conky McFadden!' Sheila yelled. 'I'm not throwing my life away. I'm showing the world the stuff I'm made from. I was sick of living in Paddy O'Brien's shadow. Well, now he's dead!' She held the pistol aloft, staring down the sights at Conky's forehead. 'Click,' she said. 'That's all it would take, Conks. One click. And then, it's just me and Gloria.'

'You're out of your mind, Sheila. Stop it! Take a deep breath. It doesn't have to be this way.'

'I admire you. Always have.' She raised an eyebrow. Smiled archly, her hair whipping around her face in the wind. 'Maybe I've always been a bit in love with you.' The smile disappeared. 'And I've always known about the hair-piece, you daft bastard. I don't care about that! But you're with me or you're against me.' Her eyes suddenly lost all focus and clarity. He had never seen such an outwardly controlled woman look so wild or so free. 'Say goodnight, Conky.'

She pulled the trigger. The bullet flew from the barrel, and in that instant, the arc of time slowed in Conky's mind, gradually retracing its trajectory to the point at which Sheila had suggested coming up to the apartment she had rented for the night.

'Why did you pay for flights to the US for Leviticus and Gloria Bell?' he'd asked in the lift, when the other guests had stepped out, leaving them alone.

Sheila had looked down at her shoes. Swaying slightly. Those deadly dark red lips pursed. 'I don't know what you're talking about,' she'd said, eyes slow to blink.

'Oh come on. Can you just drop the pretence? I know. Okay? I *know*! I spoke to Barney, the customs feller at Manchester airport. He's boning the girl on the Atlantic Airways desk. She pulled off the flight roster, the payment details, the lot.' As they had stepped out of the lift on the forty-fifth level, there was a glimmer of mischief in Sheila's expression that had made Conky feel less than comfortable. Even at that juncture, when his future had still been unwritten, he had chided himself for agreeing to leave the safety of the wake with all those pissed relatives and unwitting witnesses. Who knew how a grieving woman, who had apparently been engaging in deadly skulduggery like some latter-day Lady Macbeth, could react to confrontation? But he had not anticipated the bullet. Never the bullet.

'Let me get you a coffee,' he had said, as she had kicked off her stilettos, rubbing her feet.

He had turned his back on her, leaving her staring out of the ceiling-to-floor windows at the Mancunian skyline – a poor man's Manhattan, surrounded by green hills that kept all the damp and secrets inside. Perhaps it had been the whisky clouding his judgement, but though he had known then what Sheila's part in this kitchen sink drama had been, he had not considered her a threat.

As he had rifled through the slick rental's kitchen, looking for instant coffee and a kettle, he had been taken unawares by the cold steel of the gun with its silencer pressed into the back of his neck.

'Put your hands in the air and turn around slowly,' Sheila had said, straining to reach him on her tiptoes.

Hands aloft, he had smiled at the ludicrous situation of the doll-sized widow of his dead boss holding him at gunpoint. 'Oh, Sheila. What are you playing at? Put the gun down, will you? There's no need for this hostility between two old, old friends.'

'Isn't there?' There had been no trace of mirth in her face. Only a flintiness that he had never taken the time to register before but which had always been there. Clearly. 'Move to the window.' Such a small hand to be holding such a powerful weapon.

Backing towards that skyline, he had felt anger surge within him. But not anger at her. It was disdain for himself – that he had ignored all the signs, thinking Frank or even Katrina had been behind Paddy's downfall.

'You did it, didn't you?' He had watched the self-satisfied Shiraz smile dawning on her elfin face. '*You* paid Leviticus Bell to pretend to be Asaf Smolensky and then take Paddy out. For Christ's sake, She. Why? Was it Jack's death? Paddy's heart attack? Did he take his frustrations out on you in some way? Had you just had enough?'

'It began long, long before that,' she had said, the pure white summer moon reflecting in her eyes. 'I've been Paddy's punch-bag for donkey's years. Whenever he felt like his sagging ego needed a top-up of air, he got it by knocking the stuffing out of me.' She unfurled the silk scarf around her neck and revealed the green ghost of bruising.

'Shit, Sheila. I had no idea.' He wished he could reach over and caress her injuries away.

'And you think I didn't know about the little slappers he had on the side?' The scarf drifted to the floor like a silken butterfly. 'I knew all about them! And I didn't dare say a single word because the grand Patrick O'Brien was nothing but a pimple-dicked bully. The final straw came after his heart attack, when he said he wanted to pack it all in and move to Thailand. I didn't want to go, Conks. Me and Gloria's business was booming. I was successful in my own right. I'd been planning on getting enough money together and leaving him inside twelve months. Me and Glo just needed one more cleaning contract and I would have been free. But that sanctimonious bitch Katrina talked him into emigrating. A fresh start on the other side of the world. At that stage, I didn't quite have the money. I was trapped.' She sighed heavily, but the gun was still pointing directly at him.

'Surely you could have filed for divorce and come away a rich woman.' He had wanted to enfold her slender frame in his arms. All those times he could have defended her but had taken his boss' side through some misplaced sense of duty. There were amends to make on his part. He was no kind of erudite gentleman, after all. He was nothing but a balding cad with thyroid eyes, a paunch and a criminal record. A spouter of quotes about Medb of Connacht who had been, all this while, ignoring the plight of a real heroine; a thug for hire, pandering to the whim of Manchester's second-rate answer to Genghis Khan. 'You could have just walked away.'

Sheila had shaken her head and wiped a rogue tear from her eye. 'You think he would have let me? Paddy O'Brien? Ha!' She had thrown her chin back dramatically. 'He controlled the finances through Maureen Kaplan. All I had in my name was the money I made with Gloria. You can't get a mortgage with cash earned from trafficked women! And without that bitch Maureen knowing all my bloody business and running back to him with tales, I couldn't even launder it. I needed every penny and more to buy a nice house for me and the girls outright. Know how much they cost in Cheshire? I couldn't even have afforded a solicitor! Anyway, he'd have killed me before he'd let me humiliate him in front of all his lackeys! Paddy O'Brien would never have tolerated treason. You know that!'

Conky had taken a couple of steps towards her, further into the sleek contemporary space of the living room. Sizing up the gun in her hand. Unsure whether it would be appropriate to strong-arm her into giving her weapon up if it came to it. 'How can you be sure, Sheila? He loved you.'

'Paddy O'Brien only loved himself and the thrill of the game.'

He visualised his boss, sliced open on the poolside. 'So, how did you go from feeling trapped to ordering the hit? You had suitcases packed for Thailand!'

Sheila perched on a Perspex dining chair by the door to the terrace. Ran her stockinged toes through a long-tufted rug. 'I was stringing him along, so he wouldn't suspect. Formulating my plan and watching it come to fruition. Me and Gloria sat up late, night after night while Paddy was in the club, talking through scenarios. We decided we needed him to ditch the Thailand bullshit so I could stay in the country and keep the cleaning thing running. But we reckoned Paddy would only stay if the deal was off with the Boddlingtons and an open declaration of war was made.'

'So, you *didn't* want to kill him?' He took another step towards her.

She ran her slender finger along the glass table top. Licked her lips with that purple tongue, putting Conky in mind of a dangerous viper he had mistaken for a harmless grass snake.

'Gloria told me her grandson was dying. She knew Lev was desperate for cash and would probably do anything to save the boy. So first, I dangled the carrot of a hundred and fifty grand. Money he needed for the kid's operation in the US. I told him I'd pay him if he threw a proper spanner in the works between Paddy and the Boddlingtons. Trouble was, everyone was committed to the bloody truce. They all had love in their hearts and pound signs in their eyes. But Gloria, God bless her, let slip that Lev was shagging Jonny Margulies' daughter who had recently been dumped by Jack. It was her suggestion, the rape thing. She didn't tell Lev to put words into Mia's mouth. But she planted the seeds and let him come up with the idea like it was his own.'

'But Jack's dead,' Conky said, registering a queasiness in his whisky-sodden gut that Sheila was responsible for her own nephew's violent demise. 'You wittingly caused that?'

She shook her head. 'Don't be daft! How was I to know it would escalate to that extent, for God's sake? Mia was easy meat. She had a reputation. I thought Jonny Margulies would get pissed off enough to retaliate at our Paddy and Frank, but I didn't think for a minute that he'd send the Fish Man to fillet my own bloody nephew.'

Conky had slapped his thighs. 'Jesus, Sheila! How can you be so naïve? It's not fucking Monopoly or Cluedo! This is dangerous men playing dangerous games with millions at stake and egos that put Mount Everest in the shade.' Enough of this crap. He had advanced towards the dining table, lunging for the gun. 'Gimme that!' But she had darted out of her seat, pressing it into his stomach with the safety off.

'See? That's the kind of bullshit attitude I don't have to take any more,' she had yelled. 'I killed the King. This naïve woman!' She poked herself in the chest with her thumb so hard that Conky could hear the hollow sound of her ribcage being struck. 'Me and Gloria on top, instead of Paddy and Frank. We may not be joined by blood but we were both pushed together by the need to steal back our freedom, money and respect from thieving men who had no right to take that shit from us in the first place. Now, kneel before your Queen!'

It was at that point that Conky had lost his footing, staggering back towards the windows to get away from the gun; to avoid hurting Sheila and in a reflexive bid to defend himself. Crashing to the floor, he had hit his head against the glass. Momentarily woozy, all he had been able to see was her small face, shrouded in a halo of light, coming from the standard lamp in the seating nook. She had clambered on top of him, pressing the gun into his cheek. Used the barrel to move his glasses onto his forehead so that their eyes met without that ever-present tinted barrier between them.

'I've had enough of playing second fiddle to you bastards,' she had said. 'Even you, Conky. Even you. My terms, now.'

Unexpectedly, she had leaned forwards and pressed her lips to his. The sour taste of stale wine on her warm, wet tongue.

He had looked at her, aghast. Unable to wipe the lingering, cooling spittle from her lips off his mouth. A kiss that he had imagined time after time in the privacy of his own mind but had never anticipated would in reality be so unenjoyable and in such fraught circumstances. No flowers. No romance. No declarations of love. The kiss was an act of violence and domination. That was all.

'Jesus wept, Sheila. I think you need therapy.' He had regretted the words as soon as he had spoken them.

'What you gonna do, Conks? You going to grass me up to the cops? Have me put in the Priory permanently? You think that wasn't on Paddy's mind when he sent me to a psychiatrist and convinced me I was depressed? Hoping he'd get me spaced out on happy pills like he got Frank's missus hooked on smack. Well, as it happens, it was just anxiety from living with that bastard. Turns out, you can't put a good woman down.'

He had shaken his head. 'You're mad! This is all crazy.'

'No, Conky. I'm getting even. I realised once Paddy agreed another truce with those arseholes, Margulies and Khan . . . even with Jack dead, he just wasn't going to give up on the daft plan to retire abroad. Katrina had got inside his head like a worm. And then he tried to choke the life out of me and belt me once too often. I stood at our Jack's graveside with internal bruising from where he'd punched me. Did you know that? No! And I bet you never even thought to ask. So, I decided. He had to go. End of. With him dead, why in God's name couldn't I rule the O'Brien firm? I was the only one with the business acumen and the balls to take over, but Paddy made the mistake of overlooking me just because I was a woman and I wasn't an O'Brien by blood.'

Her hair was coming loose. Conky could see fire in her eyes. Could see her as the power-hungry despot Paddy had driven her to become. Or perhaps a little of him had rubbed off on her after decades of them sharing the same bed.

'No, Sheila. This isn't you. You're going to calm down, go home and sober up.' He had closed his large hand around her small fist, trying to prise her gun free.

It was then that she had shot the glass. Disorientated by the bang to his head, Conky had tried to wriggle away from her, but foolishly moved in the wrong direction, edging himself over the empty window frame into the precarious void of the gusting Mancunian night. Dizzy. Pain throbbing between his eyes.

And then, after some preamble, she had fired those damning words right before the bullet had left the gun.

'Say goodnight, Conky.'

He closed his eyes. There was only darkness.

Chapter 53

Lev

'Don't worry, Mr Bell,' the surgeon said. A tanned white man with his scrubs already on. Mid-forties, Lev assessed, but with a lean face and muscled neck that said he worked out or played tennis or some white, rich man's shit. 'Your son is in the best pair of hands in the US, I assure you.'

Lev took a lingering look at his son, prepped and ready for the operating theatre. Stroked his scalp where they had shaved his beautiful blond curls. Knew it may be the last time he ever saw the boy alive. Realised they had been lucky to get this far. 'They were adamant it was inoperable back home. Size of a tangerine, they said. What makes you so sure you can save him?'

The surgeon patted him on the shoulder. Arranged his thin lips into a sympathetic line. A confident shine to his blue, blue eyes. There was a man who got plenty of stress-free sleep. He smelled of soap and wealth instead of mildew. Lev felt dirty, exhausted and low-rent next to him.

'I'm not one hundred per cent sure I can save him,' the surgeon said, smiling with too many straight, perfectly white teeth in his mouth. 'Nobody can know the future or how a patient will respond to surgery. But this is the United

States, Mr Bell. You pay top dollar, you get the best. Believe me, I've been operating on brain tumours for two decades. I've worked on some doozies in my time. And your son's is a doozy and a half. I'm not going to lie to you. But I know what I'm doing and I haven't lost a patient under the knife yet.'

'You'd better not start a losing streak with my grandson . . .' Gloria said, advancing towards him with arms folded over her ample bosom. Wearing her prim, feminine Sunday best. Sugar and spice and all things nice on the surface. But the confrontational flintiness of her hardened features and narrowed eyes revealed what truly lay beneath moisturised skin that smelled of old-lady lavender. '. . . Or I'm coming after you. *Vengeance is mine and recompense for the time when their foot shall slip; for the day of their calamity is at hand, and their doom comes swiftly. Deuteronomy 32:35.'* She was pointing angrily at the surgeon.

Lev blushed. Scratched at his arms, feeling the itch spread up his neck. Jesus. Had she really just threatened the man in whose hands Jay's life lay? He wished she would sod off to get a coffee. But then felt instantly hammered into his seat by the weight of guilt, since it had been Gloria's machinations that had got them to Baltimore in the first place. Well. Not only her. Sheila O'Brien's money and his mother's appetite for murder may have made it possible. But principally, had it not been for Anjum Khan, both he and Jay would certainly have died together at the hand of a grieving, implacable Jonny Margulies.

He stroked Jay's cool cheek, enjoying how the sunlight streaming through the Baltimore hospital's windows caught the down on his peach-soft skin, making it shimmer like white gold, remembering how the boy had burned like an inferno in that hell-hole of a room in the factory, screaming himself rigid with pain, as the infection had raged away, untreated.

They had been there for hours, strapped to that chair, awaiting either God or Jonny Margulies. With a painfully numb arse and jabbing ache in his bladder, Lev had had no option but to urinate in his trousers. The soles of his trainers sat in a foul puddle, mingled with the dried blood spatters from those who had previously earned themselves the Boddlingtons' own brand of purgatory and punishment.

'Don't leave me,' he had muttered to Jay, stroking the boy's head. He had finally passed out. Freaking the hell out of his father with a series of low moans, interspersed with floppy-bodied unresponsiveness and imperceptible breathing. 'Daddy's sorry. I screwed up, bad style. I let you down. I deserve to die. Not you.'

Kissing Jay's hand one last time, as the Baltimore hospital orderlies came to wheel his bed down to theatre, Lev recalled how he had wept long after his tears had dried, becoming nothing more than salt slicks on his cheeks. Nothing left to give but dry, racking sobs. Waiting for Margulies' bullet to stop their broken hearts.

When he had seen the handle of the door to the torture-hole depressed, he had been ready. Resigned to face his end with dignity and a full admission of guilt for his moral bankruptcy and the easy corruptibility that had been the undoing of his innocent child. Expecting to see the blundering figure of Margulies, overripe with vengeance and murderous intent, he had been shocked when Anjum Khan had walked in. Suited and booted like a human-rights avenger.

'You!' she had said, frowning at him. Focused first on the urban-tribal zig-zag carved into his scalp, then on the prone form of the baby on his lap. 'What the hell is going

on? Why are you strapped to a chair? What is this place?'
She had wrinkled her nose. The smell of piss and Jay's
soiled nappy must have been almost palpable on the air.
Even Lev had still been able to smell it. Advancing briskly,
she had pulled a nail file from her handbag, its blade glinting
beneath the naked bulb that hung from the ceiling.

Lev had opened his mouth to speak but only a gasp and
a sob had emerged. Catching his breath, he had compelled
himself to whimper, 'Please don't hurt us.'

'Don't be daft. I wouldn't touch a hair on your head!'
she had said, filing away at the fibrous duct tape.

'My son needs a hospital. If Tariq and Jonny find out—'
Barely able to get the words out for desperation.

'If Tariq and Jonny find out, we're both dead,' she had
said, peering over her shoulder. She lowered her voice. 'I'm
only here because Irina finally caved and told me about
this place. I wanted to see it for myself. Tariq's secret bloody
operation. He thinks he's some kind of Pakistani Bond
villain. Prick.' She had shaken her head. Checked her watch,
blinking hard. Checked over her shoulder, once again.
Resumed sawing at the tape. 'One minute I'm an advocate
for trafficked and vulnerable people. Next minute, I find
I've been sleeping with the enemy. I'm trapped in some
sort of waking nightmare.'

The duct tape had succumbed to her efforts. Lev had
manoeuvred himself stiffly from the urine-sodden seat,
cradling Jay in his arms. 'Look, he needs a doctor, fast,' he
had said, cradling the back of the boy's head. 'If you're
gonna call the cops, let me get the fuck out of here first.'

'I don't know what I'm going to do yet,' Anjum had said.
'But come on.' Checking her watch yet again. 'It's gone five
am. I have no idea what sort of hours an illegal sweatshop
keeps. Let's go before people start turning up to work. I'll

drive you to the Manchester Children's Hospital. The further away you get from this place, the better. I have a hunch that my husband has got his finger in a few criminal pies in north Manchester.'

'A few? Jesus! You don't even wanna know,' Lev had said, forcing his stiff legs to bear him out of that evil place, praying his broken heart would keep going just long enough to save his son.

He had thought all had been lost, back then. With Margulies on his tail and Jay on the brink of certain death. And yet now, here he was in the comfortable Baltimore hospital room that murder had paid for. Watching Paddy O'Brien bleed out while his getaway-driver mother and Sheila had kept lookout for Conky McFadden had been a small upfront payment to make for this. At least now, Jay had a chance. His baby had gone – wheeled off to have his head fixed under the supervision of America's best brain surgeon. Though, what were the odds of success?

'He's not gonna make it, is he, Mam?' he asked Gloria, who sat primly on a chair by the door, reading a small blue bible.

Gloria looked up. 'Don't talk nonsense, Leviticus.'

'But what we both did. You believe in sinners being punished, don't you? God's going to take him from us.'

Closing her bible, Gloria smiled. 'God helps those who help themselves.'

'That's not in the bloody bible! Even I know that!'

'Well,' she looked down at her floral dress, pinching the fabric into pleats with a work-worn hand. 'It should have been. Sometimes even the Lord gets it wrong.' She winked. '*And God blessed them. And God said to them, "Be fruitful and multiply and fill the earth and subdue it."* Genesis 1:28. See? Paddy O'Brien and that strumpet Mia Margulies were long overdue a spot of subduing, Leviticus.' She turned her gaze to the ceiling, wearing a beatified grin. 'It's all in the interpretation, son. Who's to say what's right and wrong?'

'I wish I had your confidence, Mam.'

Pacing to and fro in the side room in that Baltimore hospital, wondering how Jay's operation was progressing, Lev wished he could fast-forward into the future to see if his son lived. If he did and they returned together to the UK, Lev decided he would be only too happy to do time for Paddy O'Brien's murder. As long as his baby was safe and could thrive. Wringing his hands, he calculated how long he might remain unmolested on US soil before Conky McFadden sent either some gun-toting gangster or the cops after him. If anyone had the investigative powers to finger him as Paddy's murderer, it was the legendary Loss Adjuster. Would McFadden accept Sheila's authority? Never! That old school kind remained true to the bitter end. And McFadden would feel the need to avenge his dead boss out of unshakeable loyalty.

'Cheer up, Leviticus! For heaven's sake,' Gloria said, rummaging absently in her handbag. Pulling out a lipstick and vanity compact, as if she had spent the morning drinking coffee at the church. 'This is a new beginning, served up on a plate.'

He scowled at his mother, hugging himself tightly across the chest. 'I don't think stuff like that happens to men like me. Karma's always gonna get in the way.'

'Karma's for hippies and blasphemers, Leviticus,' his mother said. She closed her eyes. Lifted her face to the strip-lighting on the ceiling. Put a hand on her left bosom, smiling, as though the power of God flowed through her entire body like an electrical charge. '*Remember not the former things, nor consider the things of old. I will make a way in the wilderness and rivers in the desert.* Isaiah 43:18–19.' She opened her soft brown eyes – those same eyes that Lev saw when he looked in the mirror. 'Never stop believing, Leviticus. Even a sinner like you deserves a second chance, son.'

Chapter 54

Tariq

'What do you mean, Jonny's AWOL?' Anjum said, glaring at Tariq across the kitchen with only the breakfast table as a buffer for her malcontent. She packed some official-looking documents into her briefcase with such undisguised aggression that she sent the plate of her uneaten toast scudding along the table top.

Tariq leaned against the doorframe, tugging at his hair. It hadn't been long since he'd showered but his shirt was clinging uncomfortably to his clammy skin. He counted the discrepancies out on his fingers. 'He hasn't been into work. He's not answering calls or texts. I haven't laid eyes on him in days.'

'He's a grown adult and he lives *there*.' She pointed through the window in the general direction of the Margulies house. 'You want to know what he's up to? Go knock on the door! For God's sake, Tariq, I wish you gave the kids as much attention as you do your Jonny bloody Margulies.' Buckling up her case with impatient, fiddling fingers. '*You* do the school run this morning. I've got a meeting with the police and a solicitor.'

He looked at her askance. Wondered, just for a second,

371

if she had a clandestine meeting with Ellis James or was planning a divorce. Every word that tripped spikily from her curt mouth had felt loaded of late. Every smile that didn't reach her eyes potentially ushered in the end of life as he knew it. He shook his head, banishing the thought. 'Dad's being weird. Everyone's gone AWOL. I don't understand it,' he said, scratching at the paintwork with his thumbnail. 'One of my staff has disappeared without trace, too. What the hell is wrong with people?'

'If you must know, Jonny's just in the doldrums,' Anjum said, cleaning her glasses on the pristine linen table cloth. Pushing them up her nose like a disapproving school teacher. 'I spoke to Sandra the other day. She said he won't get out of bed. He refuses to go to the doctor for anti-depressants. Mystery solved. I thought you'd know all this.'

He screwed his face up. Felt stress register in his bowels. Tried to keep some civility in his voice though he felt the urge to punch the door. 'Men don't talk to each other about their feelings!'

The unease grew inside Tariq. He found himself snapping at the kids in the car during the school run. Eventually, he made the decision to turn the car back towards home, rather than the factory. Pulled up outside Jonny's place.

Jonny came to the door, wearing only a bathrobe. Looked like he hadn't slept or washed in days. 'What do you want?'

'Nice. Anjum's very hostile and my dad's being off with me.'

'So? My daughter's dead. What do you want me to do about it?' Jonny's breath smelled sour. His long stubble stuck out from his skin like a forest of angry thorns.

'Let me in. We'll talk.'

'Sandra's not here. She's at the hairdresser's.'

'Eh? Since when did you need your wife as a bouncer?

Stop being a turd. Are you going to let me in? Come on, man.'

Following Jonny into the house, he stepped gingerly over the ghostly stain on the carpet in the hallway. Didn't dare ask why the floor-covering had not yet been replaced.

'Why don't you get a shower and come into the office?' Tariq asked, as Jonny flung his dishevelled bulk onto the leather sofa in the sleek, state-of-the-art kitchen. 'You might feel better. You can't be a recluse like this forever.'

'Easy for you to say,' Jonny said, picking up a photo of Mia from the side table and clasping it to his chest.

Tariq padded to the Gaggia machine and started to grind some beans. 'Listen, man. I'm going to make you a nice coffee because I'm your mate. Then, I want you to get in the damn shower, because you smell like a camel's arsehole. And then, we're going to go into the office together. You're going to ring round and ask about Lev.'

Jonny gathered his robe around him, retying the knot. 'Lev? What about the little shit?' His puffy sleep-encrusted eyes darted from the photo of Mia to the coffee machine and back.

'Well, have you seen him in the last fortnight? I haven't personally clapped eyes on him since we did the raid on the O'Brien cannabis farm. Anjum reckons she's seen him around in Cheetham, but it's not like him to skive work. We need to bring him in. We can't have staff unaccounted for. If we can't plot their movements, we can't trust them. And unless you hadn't noticed, we're a man down, with Smolensky in Israel. Now that O'Brien's six feet under and nobody's running the south side . . . *now* is our time! We need to seize it, *rapidemente*.'

The smell of coffee wafted through the kitchen. Jonny sat up, raising an eyebrow. 'Maybe you're right. Maybe I've just been lying here, festering and feeling sorry for myself, when that would be the ultimate revenge.' He smiled.

Just as Tariq pondered that his business partner hadn't said anything about the missing Leviticus Bell, the doorbell chimed.

'You expecting a visit?' Tariq asked, wondering if his father had returned home, spotted his car outside and come looking for him.

Jonny pulled a gun from a drawer in a sideboard. Tucked it into his pants, beneath his dressing gown. When he returned, he bore a giant wreath of lilies, a blank expression and the pallor of the dead. In his hand, he clutched a gift card.

'I thought Jews didn't send the bereaved flowers,' Tariq said.

Jonny set the arrangement carefully on the leather sofa. His Adam's apple pinged high in his neck.

The hairs on Tariq's arms stood on end. 'What does it say?' he asked, pointing to the card.

Holding the card aloft, Jonny allowed him to read its contents.

RIP, Boddlington scum.
The King is dead. Long live the Queen.

'Who sent it, for God's sake?' Tariq asked, his voice sounding thin and strangled.

A disbelieving sickly smile crawled across Jonny's unkempt face. A questioning tone in his voice. 'Sheila bloody O'Brien?!'

Chapter 55

Sheila

'*You?*' Frank asked, a look of utter disbelief on his face, as Sheila finished telling him the news. He shifted his gaze blankly to the joiners who were busy about the club refit. Drills and saws buzzing as a backdrop to their conversation.

But Sheila knew he'd heard her above their industrious noise.

'Yep,' she said, smiling. Savouring the feeling that she was at last mistress of her own destiny. 'I'm taking over all of it. You can work with me in the club like you did with Paddy. Letting the dealers deal. Turning a blind eye. Taking a cut of the action. Or you can get on with your own thing and forget about me. I'll still give you a generous percentage, if you like.'

Frank blinked hard. Grimaced. Popped a chewing gum into his mouth. Chewed far too hard, judging by the clacking sound, audible even over the builders. He turned to Conky.

'You alright with this?'

Conky shoved his hands deep into his coat pockets and shrugged. Smiled. An expression she had rarely seen the dour and serious-minded henchman wear. 'Aye,' he said.

'Fuck it! It's grand. I swore fealty to the O'Brien family when I came out of prison. Sheila's head of the family now. I recognise that. We had a little . . . debate about it, the night of Paddy's wake. But we're all good now.'

Sniffing hard, Frank inclined his head towards the renovation works. 'As long as I've got my club, I don't give a shit, me.' Abruptly, he grabbed Sheila into a bear hug, holding the back of her head, burying his nose into her long hair. Planted a kiss on her cheek.

'I never wanted what Paddy had, She,' he said. 'If you think you can make a go of it, good luck to you.' He waved his hand in the air, describing the lofty, triple-height ceiling of his industrial, warehouse-sized temple to music and dance. 'I only ever wanted this.' He smiled sadly. 'I'm carrying on for our Jack. It's what he would have wanted.' Stared down at his battered sneakers. 'And Paddy's gone. He can rot in hell for all I care. Now he's gone, I feel like I've been set free.' Faced Sheila with a suddenly sharp and unwavering gaze. 'No disrespect to you or the girls, like.'

Sheila patted his hand. 'None taken, Frank. You're always welcome in my house.'

Sitting in the passenger seat of the car as Conky powered the stately new Rolls-Royce into life, Sheila checked her reflection in the sun visor mirror. Deemed herself attractive enough to be a supreme ruler of a criminal empire. Turned to her newly sworn-in ally. Sticking her chest out, pouting slightly. 'That went better than expected,' she said. Giggling coquettishly. Stroking his hand.

He slid his sunglasses to the top of his head – improved with a new hair-piece that actually looked like hair – and regarded her with those intense, staring eyes. She could see a more sensitive soul beyond the hazel irises, ringed with milky white.

'How do you feel?' he asked.

She took his chin between her thumb and forefinger and pulled his face close to hers. Sexy-ugly. That's what they called his type in magazines. The thrill of having found a new lover – a more thoughtful and giving paramour than Paddy could have ever dreamed of being – registered between her legs. She pressed her lips to his and kissed him, enjoying the taste of a man with whom she was chemically compatible. That much she had discovered on the night she had tried to shoot him, when their tussle had turned into something more erotically charged, sealed with a killer kiss. Conky McFadden loved her. Conky McFadden would never hurt her. Conky McFadden would do whatever she told him to do.

'I feel amazing,' she said, having broken away from his kiss. 'I feel like I've got through the storm and everything's been washed fresh and clean.' Placed his hand on her breast, enjoying the warmth. 'I'm glad you're by my side.'

'Good job you didn't put that bullet in me, then,' he said, chuckling. Sliding his glasses back down over his eyes. Removing his hand from her breast to caress her cheek.

'I never would,' she said. 'I was just testing you.'

'And did I pass?'

She threw her head back and laughed, drinking in the smell of a brand new super-car and Conky's aftershave. Savouring the scent of her newfound wealth and freedom.

Outside, a mist of Mancunian rain fell softly on the grey streets, but a shaft of sunlight brightened the scene. There, at the end of the part-cobbled street that ran along the perimeter of the drab industrial estate, she spied a glorious double-bow rainbow.

'With flying colours,' she said.

Chapter 56

Katrina, then Paddy

'Well, Kenneth Wainwright,' Katrina said, patting the freckled hand as she took a seat by his bedside. 'How's life treating you on this fine Mancunian summer's day?' She grinned. Looked over towards the window where the incessant rain fell against the glass that was visible through the almost-closed curtains.

Her patient reached for the cup of coffee on the table suspended above his adjustable bed. The liquid sloshed in the cup as his hand shook. He brought it to his lips, grimaced as he took a sip. Set it back down, spilling only the smallest quantity on the melamine. 'I've got murderous bedsores, my stitches are itching and I look like shit. Other than that, my dear fragrant Sister . . .' he treated her to a North Cheshire Cat's grin. 'Life is fucking fine and dandy. That's quite a stunt you pulled there.'

Katrina breathed in, closed her eyes and savoured the memory of her finest O'Brien moment . . .

Making the sign of the cross on the dead man's forehead, Katrina had pulled the sheet over him, so that she could no longer see his slack, wizened face and his unfocused eyes. It had been gruelling waiting for him to take his final breath. Hours and hours of mucus-filled rattling, as he had battled to the end, breathing in, breathing out, struggling to shuffle off his mortal coil. At long last, he had slipped away with a few final peaceful breaths.

Taking out her mobile phone, Katrina had dialled the number.

'Yes. It's Sister Benedicta here from the Holy Trinity Nursing Home. I want you to send Doctor Williams. One of our residents has passed.'

Already knowing the response she would be given, thanks to a little background research, Katrina had feigned surprise when the receptionist told her, 'Sorry, Sister. I'm afraid Doctor Williams is on annual leave this week. We'll have to send out the new locum who's standing in. It's a lady doctor. Doctor Hardcastle. She's newly qualified.'

'Really? But I want Doctor Williams. Not some wet-behind-the-ears upstart.'

'Oh, this lady doctor locum is very nice. Very under-standing.'

Katrina had toyed with the hem of her skirt. Pitching her irritation just right. 'I suppose she'll have to do. Well, send her over as soon as you can. A swift burial is appropriate.'

Making the call to the funeral director had been easy. He had already been briefed. Quick pickup. A death by natural causes after a long illness. No embalming. Closed casket. The account had already been settled upfront. Katrina had been at pains to explain that she would be choosing the coffin and that the nursing home would be paying out of its charity coffers. It wouldn't be the first time she had done such a thing when one of the home's less fortunate residents had passed on. Somebody had to care, right?

When the doctor had arrived, Katrina had been pleased to see that she was a young woman with a kindly, unsuspecting face. Pregnant too. Good. Pregnant women were always more sympathetic.

'It's tragic, Doctor,' she had said, tugging at her cardigan sleeves. Rearranging her features into something resembling forlorn. 'He had such a fight towards the end, there.'

Doctor Hardcastle had felt for the dead man's pulse. Checked his extremities and read through the notes handed to her by Katrina.

'He suffered from sclerosis of the liver?' she had said, flicking through the paper on the clipboard. 'And heart disease. Right?'

'Yes. That's right. He'd been ill for some time. The nurses administered end of life care. He died fifty-seven minutes ago precisely. I was with him at the end.'

The doctor had looked appraisingly at the corpse. 'Aged sixty-one?'

'Yes.'

'And his name was Patrick O'Brien.'

'Yes.' Katrina had grimaced and nodded at the locum. 'He had no family. If you give me the paperwork, I'll go to the registry office to get the death certificate myself. Make the arrangements. That's what we normally do for our homeless charity cases.' She had wrung her hands and dabbed at her eyes. 'Poor Patrick. At least he had the staff here for him at the end.'

The doctor had smiled. 'I can't issue the paperwork, I'm afraid. I haven't treated this gentleman so I've no way of confirming his identity.'

'Are you questioning the veracity of what I'm telling you, Doctor Hardcastle? You do realise that I run a nursing home with one of the best CQC reports in the area?'

'Oh, of course! I wasn't meaning to—'

'And that I'm a Sister. Do you know many lying nuns, Doctor? Would you deny this man, who suffered great indignity in life as a vagrant, a little dignity in a swift and simple funeral?'

'No! Fine!' The doctor had blushed, hooking her hair behind her ear. 'So sorry. I didn't mean to offend you.'

'Patrick O'Brien,' Katrina repeated, as the doctor filled out her medical certification. 'That's right. O. Apostrophe. B. R. I. E. N. Yes. Thanks, dear.'

Katrina had waved the locum off merrily, pocketing the evidence she had needed to erase her brother from the system. She had walked back through the nursing home, greeting her enthusiastic staff. Satisfied with her morning's work. With a cursory glance in at the freshly dead body of alcoholic vagrant, Kenneth Wainwright, she had closed the door to his room and continued on to the adjacent room that bore no sign or indication of who its new occupant was.

'It's all done,' she had said to her brother, whose eyes flickered gently open. 'You're officially dead, and the corpse of Kenneth Wainwright – one of my homeless residents whom nobody will miss – will be buried in a closed casket as Patrick O'Brien. But before the funeral director picks up the dead body, you – the *new* Kenneth Wainwright – are going to have to give one last performance as Paddy, because Sheila won't believe you're gone until she sees it with her own eyes.'

She had produced a large wash-bag from a cupboard. 'Preparation is everything,' she had said, unzipping the bag and taking cosmetics out. Laying them carefully on the bed. Pale foundation. Talcum powder to seal it. Bluish eyeshadow.

'Christ. I can't believe it,' he had said, his voice hoarse

and cracked as befitted a man who hadn't spoken for days. 'I'm officially dead? I'm home and dry? You're a fucking genius, our kid.'

'I know, Patrick. You owe me. But less swearing! And definitely no blasphemy.' She had snatched up the bottle of pale foundation and a makeup sponge. 'Now, lie very, very still and look dead.'

'I was right,' the recovering Paddy said. 'You *are* a fucking genius.'

'Language!' Katrina winked. 'You know, you remind me so much of Dad.' She tutted dramatically and rolled her eyes. 'I'll have to keep tabs on you!' She wheezed a whisky-drinker's laugh; a blush spreading through her pale cheeks to match the veins in her nose, which Paddy had not noticed before moving into the home and seeing more of her. There was certainly more to Sister Benedicta than met the eye.

The airflow bed, designed to keep bedsores at bay, was overly hard and uncomfortable that morning. Paddy could smell his ostensibly healing body rotting with disuse. Despite daily bed-baths and being hoisted by the nursing staff into the communal tub once per week, he never felt clean. The abiding smell of his own putrefying skin and stale effluent that caked the lining of the adult diaper around the clock, no matter how frequently they changed him, clung to the inside of his nostrils. His wounds ached incessantly, requiring constant morphine, self-administered with a push button. But inside, in the strata of his body that lay deeper than the superficiality of stitches and scar tissue, Paddy felt rejuvenated and reinvigorated. He grasped his sister's hand, though his grip was still weak. 'I owe you,' he said. 'For what you've done. For giving me this opportunity.'

Katrina pulled her hand away. Stood up, smoothing her

A-line skirt down. She started to pour water from the drinks jug into a parched-looking vase of flowers that the nursing staff had bought for Kenneth, wishing him a speedy recovery.

'And what are you going to do with this brand new beginning, Patrick? A clean sheet. An opportunity to reinvent yourself.' She looked over the top of her bifocal glasses at him, like the well-meaning nun she appeared to be. 'What's it to be, kiddo?'

Paddy raised an eyebrow and stared at his own distorted reflection in the disturbed surface of the cooling coffee. The thinning hair, plastered to his head. The overgrown stubble that made him look like Desperate Dan in dead man's winceyette pyjamas. 'I'm going to get myself well, thanks to you. I'm going to gather my strength. And then, I'm going to ruin them. All of them. Every last one. And they won't even know who's behind their downfall until it's too fucking late. I'm the King, Katrina. Nobody kills the King and gets away with it.'

He's watching her.
She doesn't know it… yet.

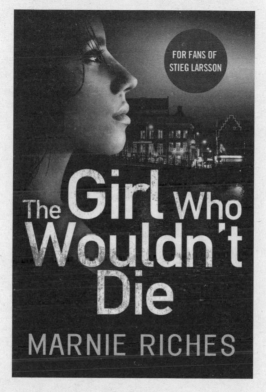

A thrilling race against time with a heroine you'll be
rooting for, this book will keep you up all night!

The second book in the bestselling
George McKenzie series.

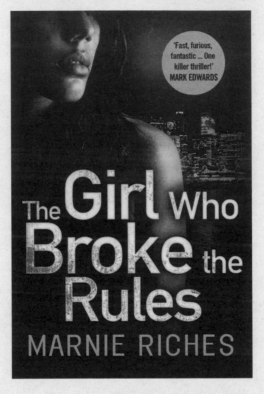

'Fast, furious,
fantastic ... One
killer thriller!'
MARK EDWARDS

The Girl Who
Broke the
Rules

MARNIE RICHES

The pulse-pounding thriller from Marnie Riches.
For anyone who loves Jo Nesbo and Stieg Larsson,
this book is for you!

The third edge-of-your-seat thriller in the
Georgina McKenzie series.

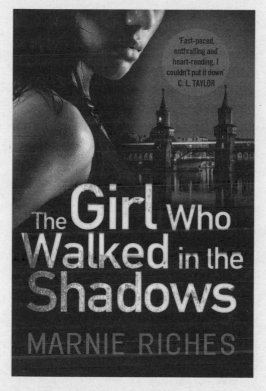

'Fast-paced,
enthralling and
heart-rending, I
couldn't put it down'
C. L. TAYLOR

The Girl Who
Walked in the
Shadows

MARNIE RICHES

Can George outrun death to shed light on two terrible
mysteries? Or has she met her match...?

**The fourth gripping thriller in the
Georgina McKenzie series.**

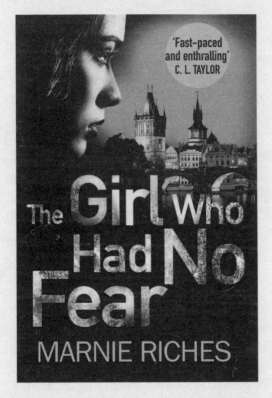

'Fast-paced
and enthralling'
C. L. TAYLOR

**The Girl who
Had No
Fear**

MARNIE RICHES

Four dead bodies have been pulled from
the canals – and that number's rising fast.
Is there a serial killer on the loose?

Acknowledgements

First I'd like to say a huge thanks to the people who are always behind me, every step of the way, and without whom I would struggle to make a go of this writing lark:

Natalie and Adam for their unconditional love, constant cheerleading and patience! Christian, for his child-wrangling skills and invaluable support.

My special agent, Caspian Dennis for his professional guidance and friendship, and all at Abner Stein, particularly Sandy, Felicity, Ben and Laura. You guys are all the best ever.

The hard-working, passionate and committed publishing team at Avon, HarperCollins – in particular Oli, Helen, Phoebe, Helena, Louis, Ellie, Natasha H and Hannah. Also an extra thanks to Sam Missingham for her props on Twitter.

The bloggers who review my books and say such wonderful things, more often than not. You guys are just brilliant and I appreciate every minute you spend reading and reviewing my writing.

The book clubs whose members read my stuff and spread the word. Your passion is invaluable. You are ace.

My other many readers, without whom I would be stuck in a crappy office being curmudgeonly, sweary and unhappy, photocopying shit and filling out funding forms. You've stopped me from turning into Bernard Black entirely.

The cockblankets, for all their moral support, filth and fun.

Next, I'd like to thank those who have helped with some inspiration for this book:

Damian Morgan – very long-standing pal, expert Mancunian and music agent at large; my bonkers family, none of whom are alluded to in this novel but who were part of my upbringing and therefore a major influence for the Mancunianness of this entire series; the people of Manchester, for being among the most inspiring folk in the world; the music scene of Manchester, which remains world class; the criminals of Manchester for being both despicable and sometimes entertaining – none of you are alluded to in this novel, so don't get your knickers in a twist! My criminals are all 100% made-up. Put the shotgun and ego down and go for a pint. Finally, the ethnic communities of Manchester, who have wonderful stories to tell, a fraction of which I've tried to tell here.

That's your lot. Until the next time . . .